Tangled Strands

To Marie,
Happy Reading
Esther Gross

Tangled Strands

Esther Moneysmith Gross

Moneysmith Press
Nashville TN

Moneysmith Press
Nashville TN

Tangled Strands

Copyright © 2017 by Esther Moneysmith Gross

esthergrossts@gmail.com

All Scripture quotations are taken from The Holy Bible, New International Version, Copyright © 1973,1978, 1984 by Biblica US, Inc. ® Used with permission.

Transformed by Ophelia G. Browning and Bentley D. Ackley. Public domain, courtesy of Cyber Hymnal.

Cover by Lynée Ward

ISBN: 978-0-9987011-0-3

All rights reserved. Without the prior permission of the publisher, no part of this publication may be reproduced, stored in a retrieval system, or transmitted in any form or by any means – electronic, mechanical, photocopy, recording, or any other – except for brief quotations in printed reviews.

Printed in the United States of America

To my daughter Lynée
without whom this
dream would never have
made it to a concrete form

To my husband Fred
who has encouraged me
and patiently supported
my yen to write

To my sister Dottie
and all who for long years
believed in this project
and cheered me on

Transformed

Dear Lord, take up the tangled strands
Where we have wrought in vain
That by the skill of Thy dear hands
Some beauty might remain.

    Transformed by grace divine,
    The glory shall be Thine.
    To Thy most holy will, oh Lord,
    We now our all resign.

Take every failure, each mistake
Of our poor human ways,
That, Savior, for Thine own dear sake,
Some beauty might remain.

Note from the Author

I first heard the song "Transformed" in the early **1950s** and liked it so well that the words and music stuck with me. A dozen or so years later in the **1960s,** the main characters of this story were born in my head during a stay at a Michigan lake. In the **1970s** in South America I wrote multiple pages of back story.

In the early **1980s**, I acquired my first computer. Little by little, I transcribed the pages of back story to the computer and began drafting more of the story.

I drafted it in all kinds of places. In the back seat of a car on a cross-country trip, I "wrote" some important elements in my head and scribbled a few notes to remind me when I got home. Many evenings while driving a stretch of Interstate to and from a teaching job, I would compose in my head, then transcribe to the computer when I got home.

In the **1990s**, I puttered with it some more and made first attempts at a sequel. At some point, I considered the story complete. A handful of family and friends read it and said they liked it, but a publisher I approached was not interested.

In the **mid-2000s**, I decided that if I were ever to do anything with it, I needed to get serious about some training. In 2005 I attended my first Christian writers' conference and got my first lessons in fiction in a class by the renowned Christian writer Angela Hunt.

I learned several startling things. I spent the next decade learning how to incorporate those style elements into a number of rewrites of the story. I hope you enjoy it. If you have feedback, you can write me at esthergrossts@gmail.com.

Prologue

The thunderstorm that rocked the evening was abating when the phone call came. Listening to his wife's end of the conversation, Porter Baldwin could tell that a child, out in the storm and soaking wet, needed shelter. He didn't have to wonder how Agnes would respond.

Moments later, before she could explain, a sharp pounding on the front door cut through the noise of the storm. Startled, their two children glanced up from their game. Agnes motioned Porter toward the door.

When he opened it, he noticed the child first. She stood shivering in a wet, clinging dress of faded green, her dark hair plastered in dripping strands around her anxious face. Behind her loomed a tall, shadowy figure in a plastic rain cape the color of the night. A gravelly voice spoke from the top of the cape.

"I'm sorry, but we're havin' some trouble, and my little girl's wet and cold. I stopped at the church, and the pastor he said maybe you could help us."

He hesitated, but Agnes Baldwin was already drawing the bedraggled child into the house and enfolding her in an afghan. "Of course, of course," she said as she gently wiped the little face and pushed back wet hair. "Larry, get a beach towel from the linen closet. Mollie, move your dolls out of that chair."

Porter offered to help the man with his problem, but he shook his head. "I doubt ya can do nothin'. I been writin' a real estate guy, and he told me 'bout a house I could rent. But we just found the people still in it. They say as how they changed their minds. I gotta talk to the agent. I got his number here somewheres."

He rifled through his pockets and pulled out a dog-eared scrap of paper. Porter helped him make a phone call and, after the agent said he would see him, gave him directions. With a glance at his daughter already playing dolls with Mollie, he nodded and left.

When he returned two hours later, Porter smiled as he opened the door. "Your little girl is fast asleep with Mollie."

Standing on the porch, the man shifted his cap from hand to hand. "There's been a mix-up 'bout the house," he said, "so I gotta go to a motel. Come mornin', I gotta go back to the city."

He offered no more information, and Porter chose to respect his reticence. Agnes drew her sweater closer around her. "Instead of taking your daughter out in the wet and cold again, would you consider leaving her to sleep here and picking her up in the morning?"

With little reluctance, he agreed. The men exchanged names.

All the next morning the two girls played while Porter and Agnes watched for the father. At noon Porter called the only motel in Willow Valley. When he hung up, he stared at his wife. "The guy says the battered moving truck left at 7:30 this morning."

In silent disbelief, Porter and Agnes stared at each other.

1

Sharon Casanetti leaned back from the steering wheel and massaged the back of her neck. What did she think she was doing? How dare she come back? Perhaps Mrs. Baldwin would not hate her too much, but would Mollie even speak to her? As for Larry—

The child within her stirred, and desolation washed over her afresh. Once upon a time, she had assumed any child she ever bore would be Larry's. But no. She could not think about Larry today.

The February blizzard—the biggest storm so far in 1954—had abated by the time she drove into Fernville. If she could find her way to the cottage and take refuge there, maybe she could figure out what to do. She tasted relief when the main street looked familiar but frowned as she searched for the turnoff to the lake.

In all the times through the years that she had been to the Baldwin family's Fern Haven cottage, she had always been with them. What if she couldn't find it by herself today? Peering through lingering snowflakes, she tried to remember the building on the corner where they turned. A drugstore perhaps? Yes, that was it under the blinking red Rexall sign. She maneuvered her little green Rambler into the turn, careful not to skid. Now if she could just find the road that would take her out of town. Ah! There it was.

A mile beyond the edge of town, she spotted the familiar brick farmhouse with its dual chimneys. Good. But how would she recognize the right break in the trees that led down to the lake and the cottage when all the mailboxes sported the same rectangular cap of snow and all the driveways the same bedspread of white?

Something familiar about the next one made her foot ease from the gas. Her heart raced when the name on the mailbox became readable: BALDWIN.

At the sight of it, her courage fled. She punched the accelerator, and her car fishtailed away down the road.

——◆◆◆——

When Agnes Baldwin stepped out of the Wells' Corner Market, the biting wind took her breath away. She gave her scarf an extra toss around her face and was relieved to see her parking meter had not expired. She ducked her head against the wind. Though she loved Willow Valley, the winters of western New York sometimes had her daydreaming about the palm trees and beaches she had once seen in a *Life* magazine.

Her black Studebaker crunched its way home over ragged tracks in the snow. They hadn't seen the surface of the streets since Thanksgiving. Today snowmen birthed from the blizzard gazed stolidly at her, while along Lazy River Road children skidded on slippery surfaces, their voices ricocheting through the crisp air. Teenagers with ice skates over their shoulders headed for Willow Pond.

Ice skating always made her think of Sharon. How that girl had loved to skate. When the others got cold, they had to drag Sharon from the ice. Had the girl clung so tightly to the fun because of reluctance to face what awaited her at home?

Agnes sighed. Where was Sharon now? Could it really be six months since she took off with that Casanetti character in his yellow convertible?

Agnes pulled into her driveway, ready to react if her car started to skid. She collected her bag of groceries and picked her way through the snow to the back door. As she tiptoed across the icy porch, the phone began to ring. She snatched open the unlocked door and reached the phone on its fifth ring.

"Hello?"

Silence. She set the bag on the dining room table.

"Hello? Hello?"

"Mrs. ... Mrs. Baldwin?" The voice broke.

"*Sharon*! ... Sharon?"

"Y-yes ..." A sniff punctuated the whisper.

"Where are you?"

"I ... I'm in the phone booth in Fernville."

"You're *what*? What are you doing there?"

Tangled Strands 5

"I want—I'd like to go the cottage—to Fern Haven. Would you mind ...?"

Agnes hesitated. "I ... guess that would be okay."

"And, Mrs. Baldwin, could you ... could you come there, too, please?"

"What do you mean?"

"I mean, could you come to the cottage?" The girl's voice wavered.

Agnes's mind raced. What was the girl up to now?

"Why ... why, yes, I suppose I could. What's happened? Are you okay?"

"I'll tell you when you get here, but ya, I'm okay. Could you come ... soon?" A lacing of pain in her voice quickened Agnes's heart.

"I'll be there as soon as I can throw a few things in a bag. Do you know how to get into the cottage?"

"Is the key still in the same place?"

"It is."

"Then yes, I do. Be careful on the roads. They're treacherous. And ... and ... Mrs. Baldwin?"

"Yes?"

"Please don't tell anyone, okay?"

2

Sharon hung up the pay phone and leaned against the wall of the booth. Had she really called Agnes Baldwin and asked her to come to her? She could not picture herself doing that ever in the past, despite how kind Mrs. Baldwin had always been to her. But that was before, before she followed her heart and a dream she knew the Baldwin family would never approve.

She pushed open the folding door of the booth, closed it behind her, and went to her car. Now that she had committed herself through the phone call, she could not change her mind about the cottage, but she would stop at Pete's Shop and Save before heading out to Fern Haven again. Mrs. Baldwin always kept coffee and peanut butter in the cupboard, but she would need bread and juice—and maybe cheese for a sandwich.

Thirty minutes later she stood surveying the inverted Styrofoam cones in the rose garden outside Fern Haven's living room window. Now to remember this right. Back row, second bush from the door. The snow was deep enough that she almost couldn't make out the bump on the ground beside the bush, but when she pushed the bump with her boot, the brick slid to one side and revealed part of a key half buried in snow. She managed to pick it up despite gloved fingers, then push some of the snow back in place.

Two feet of drifted snow lay against the front door, and it took her a couple more minutes to kick aside enough so she could shove the door open and step inside. She set her valise down by the door and glanced around, for a moment disconcerted by the ghostly appearance of the room. Then she remembered. The Baldwins covered the furniture with sheets when they wouldn't be there in the winter. The hump closest to her would be the overstuffed chair and the larger one the Hide-a-bed davenport where Larry always slept. She fingered the class ring under her shirt. What had possessed her to dig that out and put it on? She drew it out now, slipped it off over her head, and dropped it into her bag. It would never do for Mrs. Baldwin to find her wearing it after what had happened.

She glanced beyond the small room to the dining nook and grimaced. Those striped curtains still hung at the windows. She remembered as a ten-year-old vowing never to have curtains like that in her home. Two steps toward the tiny kitchen told her Mrs. Baldwin's apple theme still held sway—on the wallpaper, the cabinet knobs, the hot pads. The plates in the cupboard would have apples too. The apples she liked.

She drew her coat closer around her. Of course the heat was off, and she didn't know anything about the heating system. Maybe coming here was a bad idea. What about the fireplace? She pivoted and felt a grin tease the corners of her mouth. Several perfectly arranged pieces of firewood lay on the grate, with kindling tucked around the logs waiting for a match. It had Larry's signature all over it. He always kept the fireplace prepared for the next fire.

Larry's signature used to be all over her heart, too, but that was before Tony Casanetti.

She looked at her watch but couldn't read it in the gathering dusk, so she flipped the switch by the front door. Nothing happened. Of course not. The Baldwins would have turned off the power. As fond as her memories of the cottage were, the thought of being in it alone, in these woods and in total blackness, stirred chills—even with a fireplace.

But wait! Hadn't she watched Mr. Baldwin, long ago when he was still alive, turn the power off before they left? It took her only a few minutes to find the switch box on the wall behind the bathroom door, and she smiled with satisfaction when the lights came on.

Back in the living room, she began yanking sheets off the furniture and tossing them in a heap at the end of the hearth. How long would it take Mrs. Baldwin to get here? She glanced at her watch. Oh, my! She could be here soon. Her gut tightened. *Why had she made that call?* With her beautiful dream in shambles, she really had no desire to face the Baldwins. She shuddered, then drew a deep breath and blinked hard. She did *not* want Mrs. Baldwin to find her crying.

Or Mollie.

How would Mollie react to seeing her again—*if* she went back to Willow Valley? Since deciding to leave Chicago, Sharon had avoided thinking about Mollie. Would having been best friends all their growing-up years count for anything now, despite what Sharon had done?

She glanced at her midsection and groaned. How long would it take Mrs. Baldwin to notice? Not long, for sure, even though she was wearing the loosest skirt she owned and an old flannel shirt with the tails hanging out. She grimaced. She couldn't imagine Mrs. Baldwin understanding the terror in her heart about what lay ahead of her with this ... *thing*. As Larry and Mollie's mother, Mrs. Baldwin had obviously had the same experience, but she had probably enjoyed it. Unimaginable!

With a sigh Sharon closed her eyes. When she opened them, she noticed the teakettle on the stove. Maybe it would help if she had hot water ready for some of the tea Mrs. Baldwin always loved—providing the propane tank wasn't empty.

3

The hour's drive to Fern Lake dragged on, the longest Agnes could remember. Even a new set of BurmaShave ads along the road didn't make her smile. Relentless questions assailed her, yet as eager as she was for answers, she dreaded them. What had Sharon done in the months she had been gone, and what had brought her back in this surreptitious way?

Determined not to panic, she tried to focus on her destination instead of on what might happen when she reached it. Thoughts of Fern Haven, her family's cozy cottage, usually provided pleasant anticipation, but not today. Today she found it hard to keep her mind from wandering to the pain her children had suffered from Sharon's unexplained departure in August.

Early winter darkness enfolded the cottage by the time she drove in under the trees. A yellow rectangle of light glowed from the living room window, and when she opened the car door, the fragrance of wood smoke greeted her. Sharon had started Larry's fire. Footprints led through the snow to the front door, past the five inverted cones standing like stiff sentinels across the front of the cottage.

Taking a deep breath, Agnes made her way through the footprints. Before she could knock, the door opened. Her first impulse was to open her arms, but a second one made her freeze. *In what spirit had the girl come?* Agnes couldn't see her eyes, only faint light reflecting off tear-damp cheeks. Then Sharon's arms moved, Agnes's responded, and they clung to each other for a moment before drawing apart.

Sharon stepped back. "Come in."

Ignoring the strangeness of being invited by another into her own cottage, Agnes focused on an appeal heavenward that she would respond appropriately to whatever was going to happen here.

As she stepped inside, a gust of wind and snow burst in with her, and Sharon rushed to shut the door. Agnes pulled off her gloves and rubbed her hands together. What should she say now?

"I see you started the fire."

"Yes. I didn't know how to turn the heat on, and ... and the fire was ready to start."

Agnes wanted to say "Thanks to Larry," but she did not want to be the first to mention his name.

"Would you like some tea?" Sharon motioned toward the kitchen. "I have water ready on the stove. Are you hungry?"

Agnes responded with a small smile. Minutes later, the two sat on the davenport, absently munching cheese sandwiches, sipping tea, and gazing at the fire. Did Sharon have any idea how much she had hurt her friends? Where was that sneaky charmer now? And what happened to Larry's class ring that Sharon used to wear around her neck?

In front of the fire now, Agnes drained her tea and sighed. Her initial flash of anger at the girl last summer had dissolved into an ache of concern. Sharon had been part of their lives too long, and Agnes's mother-heart had never ceased yearning over her. Yet having her show up like this today was stirring emotions Agnes had worked hard to lay to rest. After giving the girl ample opportunities to start meaningful conversation, Agnes took the initiative.

"So, Sharon, why did you ask me to come?"

Silence.

"I assumed you wanted to talk about what you've been doing the last six months."

"I thought I did, but I don't know where to start."

"You could start from the beginning and tell me about what you did last summer."

Sharon drew a shaky breath. "I suppose everyone is mad at me."

"Don't you think we have reason to be?"

Sharon swung on her. "I knew you wouldn't understand." Just as quickly, she turned back to the fire and swiped a finger across her cheek.

"Why don't you help me understand?"

The girl stared at her hands and shook her head.

"Then talk to me about why you're here now."

Sharon rose and walked to the window. Now Agnes saw her silhouette despite the baggy shirt. Ah. So that was it—both why she was back and probably why tears on her cheeks.

Tangled Strands   13

"Do I gather things haven't worked out well for you with Tony?"

———◆◆◆———

Sharon opened her mouth to speak, then shut it again. This was turning out to be harder than she expected. She couldn't imagine telling the whole story, especially the part about what Rita said. Oh, but she *could* imagine Mrs. Baldwin's reaction if she told her that. She turned slowly, walked to the fireplace, refilled her cup from the pot on the hearth, and turned her back to the fire.

"Is ... Mollie mad at me?"

Mrs. Baldwin hesitated. "I have to admit Mollie's been ... upset with you for the last few months, yes."

"I wrote her a letter!"

"Yes—*after* you were married." Mrs. Baldwin stared at her. "Do you know that Mollie had a surprise birthday party ready for you the day you disappeared?"

"She did?"

A chill of silence sank over the room. Sharon left the fire and dropped into the armchair.

After a long pause, Mrs. Baldwin said, "Did you *plan* to marry him when you left?"

"That's ... that's what I thought he had in mind."

"Well, we knew nothing of about that until your note six weeks later." The silence expanded, grew heavier. "And now ... now you're expecting a baby. Am I right in my guess that Tony wasn't happy about that?"

Sharon squeezed her eyes shut, then whispered, "He threw me out."

"Oh, Sharon!" Mrs. Baldwin set her cup and saucer on the side table. "I'm sorry. I'm glad you called. We've missed—"

Sharon waved her to silence, but Mrs. Baldwin only paused before surging ahead. "Would it help if you came home with me for a—"

Now Sharon slammed her cup onto its saucer and didn't miss the look on Mrs. Baldwin's face. "You don't under*stand!* It's not that simple."

"So explain it to me, Sharon. What's not simple? You're expecting a baby, and Tony's upset. You could stay with me for a while until he gets used to the idea. I'm sure he will."

Sharon pressed a fist against her mouth to steady her voice before she said, "Tony ... Tony's dead."

Mrs. Baldwin gasped. "Oh, Sharon—no! When? How—?"

"Last week. He got in a bad fight. The guy slammed him into a brick wall and smashed his head." Pain and disbelief hit her in a fresh wave. *Oh, Tony, why did it have to end this way?*

"Was Tony hanging around with a rough crowd?"

"He wasn't like that!" She couldn't hold back the tears any longer and was glad when Mrs. Baldwin got up, fetched her a Kleenex, and took her cup from her. She blew her nose, tossed the tissue aside, and pulled out another. "Okay, maybe he did have some rough friends. I found that out after we got to Chicago."

"I don't know what to say, Sharon, except that my heart hurts for you."

Tangled Strands

Again silence, until a loud cracking from the fireplace startled them both and sparks exploded up the chimney.

"Let's go back to Tony's not being happy about the baby …"

Sharon started picking at the red polish on her nails. "He … he wanted me to … to get rid of it." She had known Mrs. Baldwin would be shocked but wasn't prepared for the intensity of the horror on the older woman's face. "But I wouldn't!" she hastened to add, her hands suddenly still in her lap. "I was too scared to even think about it."

"Oh, honey, I'm so glad you didn't do that. That would have been illegal, not to mention dangerous—and wrong."

She didn't want to think about that part. "Tony wasn't worried about all that. He just—" She stopped and went back to picking at the polish.

"So now that you're here, you will come back to Willow Valley with me, won't you? You could have Mollie's room. You know she and Chris got married just before Christmas."

No, she didn't know that, even though Mollie and Chris had been engaged when she left. Memories of all the times she and Mollie had fantasized about their weddings washed over her in a fresh surge of melancholy. She couldn't bear to wonder who Mollie had chosen as maid of honor in her place.

She could feel Mrs. Baldwin's eyes on her. What was she thinking? Sharon's fists tightened at the idea of going to back Willow Valley.

Mrs. Baldwin sat up straighter. "I have an idea. Why don't we go for a walk like we used to?"

"You mean in the dark—and the snow?"

"Just up to the road and back. I can tell you about the wedding. You do have a warm coat, don't you?"

Bundled against the cold, flashlights from the kitchen drawer in hand, they trudged the familiar driveway to the road. Instead of the chorus of night sounds so familiar in summer, only the crunch of their feet on the snow punctuated the winter silence. Sharon listened without comment to the account of Chris and Mollie's wedding. So Mollie had invited her *mother* to be maid of honor? Whoever heard of such a thing?

4

Mollie Thorne banged the receiver back on the phone harder than she intended and returned to the kitchen to stir the chili. Why didn't her mother answer? Where could she be? It wasn't the day for her Bible study, and if she went to the market, she should be home by now.

She hoped the chili tasted as good as it smelled. It was one item in her cooking repertoire that her new husband always raved over. The sound of a key in the apartment door told her he was home from work. She grinned. Surely two months into marriage still qualified her as a honeymooner.

He came up and slipped his arms around her from behind, and she turned into his embrace and lost herself in the pleasure of his kiss. "Why is it when you kiss me I forget everything I'm supposed to be doing?"

"You needn't worry about that, my sweet." He wound one of her stray curls around his finger. "I'm considering taking a vow against kissing, especially you."

She shook her finger in his face. "No, no, no, no, Mr. Thorne! You tried that when we were engaged. I laughed about it then, but I wouldn't laugh now." Yet she couldn't suppress a grin as she turned back to the stove. Knowing him and loving him was sheer pleasure, and most of the time she adored his teasing.

Chris went to the sink to wash his hands. "I haven't been able to get Sharon out of my mind today."

Mollie stopped stirring. A beat of silence hung between them. "She doesn't deserve to be thought about after what she did, going off like that and not staying in touch with us."

Chris dried his hands slowly. "You don't mean that."

"Why shouldn't I? What she did to my brother was inexcusable, not to mention what she did to the rest of us."

"I was hoping that, as her best friend, in time you could wish her some happiness."

"Ha! I know you told us what a charmer Tony was, but there's no way I can believe it's turning out well for her." She tasted the chili again and added a couple dashes of salt.

Chris leaned against the counter and studied her. "I keep remembering what happened to her mother and thinking how that must still affect the way Sharon looks at life—why she does some of the things she does."

"You don't mean what *happened to* her mother but what her mother *did*. Horrible as that was, don't ask me to accept it as an excuse for what Sharon's done." Mollie turned the burner low and went to the refrigerator. "The only good thing about not hearing from her is that Larry's had a chance to get her out of his system."

Tangled Strands

"You think he has? When you love someone, you can't just turn it off."

"Just because he was her rock of stability and friendship all those years doesn't mean he loved her. And whether he did or not, and even if she deserved it then, she doesn't deserve it now. So—" Mollie backed out of the refrigerator and slammed the door. "I do not want to hear any more about Miss Sharon Champlin."

———♦♦♦———

Agnes held the door open for Sharon when they returned from their walk. Inside, the house was chillier than they had left it. Instead of taking off her coat, Agnes buttoned another button.

"Sharon, shall I build up the fire again, or shall I turn the furnace on so we can go to bed and talk more in the morning?"

Sharon hesitated, so Agnes went on. "Is there something else you'd like to say or tell me tonight?"

Now the girl met Agnes's eyes for the first time that evening. "You're right, I haven't told you everything, but I'm not sure I can. Maybe ... maybe tomorrow."

"Would you mind if we prayed together before we go to bed?"

Sharon offered no protest, so Agnes stepped to the davenport and sat down. When she patted the space beside her, Sharon joined her. Agnes reached to put an arm around her and was relieved when Sharon did not resist. Halfway through the prayer, Sharon's head relaxed against Agnes's shoulder.

When the prayer ended, Sharon did not move. In a small voice, she said, "When you pray like that, Mrs. Baldwin, I almost feel like there might be some hope for me—for my life—after all."

Agnes weighed her words carefully. "There's always hope if we trust God about what is happening."

Sharon sat up but said nothing.

"I do have a question tonight. Have you been in touch with your dad and your grandmother?"

"No, but I doubt they've given me much thought."

"Sharon! I wish you wouldn't say things like that. You can't mean that."

Sharon chewed the edge of a finger before responding. "The truth is ... I never told either of them I was going away."

———◆◆◆———

Larry Baldwin slammed the ancient-history textbook shut. He was minimally prepared for the lesson he had to teach tomorrow, but he couldn't corral his mind more than a few minutes at a time. He scowled. Academics had always been his life, and he wasn't used to having difficulty concentrating.

All evening a pair of brown eyes had stalked his thoughts, big eyes gazing at him a thousand ways over the years—from a frightened seven-year-old drenched by a storm, to a child rendered speechless by an unthinkable truth, to a teenager sobbing over the loss of her friend and his father, Porter

Baldwin. Most annoying of all, he could not shed the image of the teasing flirt pretending she didn't want him to kiss her.

In the months since Sharon Champlin had skipped out of their lives, Larry had set his mind not to think about her. How had his friend Chris described the guy she had gone off with? Good-looking, self-assured, the kind who could charm the honey from a mama bear. When Larry groaned, Chris finished off with "How about a classy convertible, flashy clothes, and a fat wallet?"

For days he had swung between shock and resignation. Given Sharon's childhood with a distant father, a fault-finding grandmother, and no mother at all, it was no wonder such a temptation had lured her. On the other hand, what happened to the deep bond he and she had enjoyed for years? That bond had everyone, including him, thinking wedding bells might be chiming when he got out of college.

When it was clear she was really gone, he had assigned his emotions to a back closet of his mind. With each month that passed without word from Sharon, he turned the key a little tighter. He no longer awoke each morning wondering if they would hear from her that day.

So why was the door of that closet rattling today?

5

Agnes's head ached all during the drive back to Willow Valley. Though the morning air remained frigid, sunshine and traffic had turned the ice on the highway to slush. With the little Rambler in her rearview mirror, Agnes kept reliving the last twenty-four hours.

She had needed some of her best persuasion skills to convince Sharon to come with her. It hadn't been enough to remind her that Mollie wasn't at her mother's much now that she was married. Sharon hadn't given in until she heard Larry was still away at college, studying and teaching, and had not moved back to Willow Valley after graduation. Agnes neglected to mention that she expected Larry home during Easter break. She would deal with that closer to the time.

But at least Sharon had finally mentioned Larry's name—mentioned it and in a flash changed the subject.

When they were ready to leave, Sharon appeared in the living room with a small bag and a sheepish expression. "Remember what I said about running out on Tony? Well, I left without taking anything with me but my purse. A few days later when I knew he wasn't home, I went back to get my things, but he had changed the locks on the apartment, so I couldn't get in."

"Oh, Sharon! He was that vindictive, was he? Did you ever get your things?"

"Nope. I hadn't taken much with me from Willow Valley either because Tony told me not to. In Chicago, in the beginning, he loved taking me shopping for new clothes—"

"And he was paying for all those things?"

"Oh, yes. He loved whipping out fifty-dollar bills, especially at Marshall Fields and Carson Pirie Scott. When he sent me shopping on my own, he told me to charge things on his account in those stores."

"So you had a lot of new clothes?"

"Oh, yeah. I had some great sweater sets and matching outfits and a dream of a winter coat it broke my heart to leave behind."

"And after he ... was killed, you didn't try to get them back?"

Sharon shook her head without meeting Agnes's eyes. "I–I doubt he kept them around."

As the miles slipped past, Agnes found her mind ricocheting from one thing to another. One moment she agonized over how she would break this news to her children. The next, her heart slammed the door on those thoughts and challenges.

One moment refused to fade, the one when she asked

Sharon when her baby was due to be born.

"I don't know. Maybe ... June."

"What do you mean you don't know? What did the doctor say?"

Sharon bent down and fiddled with clasps on her bag.

"Sharon? Does this mean you haven't seen a doctor?"

She shook her head. Before Agnes could respond, she stood. "I *hate* doctors—*and* hospitals."

Oh, Lord, what are we in for?

In the car now, the more she struggled for calm, the more her head ached.

When they arrived in Willow Valley, they could see the snowplows had been busy. They had even been down Lazy River Road. The plow had piled two feet of snow along both sides of the street, blocking the end of every driveway. Agnes and Sharon had to park on the street and pick their way cautiously through the snow to the front door.

As they entered the living room, Agnes noticed Sharon glancing around as if expecting ghosts to emerge. She wasn't surprised when they did.

"Remember the stormy night my father and I first showed up at your door?"

Agnes smiled. "How could I forget? You looked so forlorn!"

"I was so cold! It seemed like I had been wet for hours. I still remember how good it felt, snuggling on your lap, getting dry, and later going to sleep with Mollie. Were we really strangers to you?"

"We had never seen you before."

Tangled Strands 25

"So why did we stop at your house? All I remember is the thunder and the rain."

"I'm not surprised since you were just seven. Your dad was moving you and him and your grandmother to Willow Valley, but the people hadn't moved out of the house he thought you were going to rent. He stopped at the church hoping to get you out of the storm, and the pastor directed him to our house."

"What... what did you think when he didn't come back for me the next morning?"

"We didn't know what to think."

"How long was it before he came back?"

"About a month—" At that moment the telephone rang, and Agnes went to answer it.

"Mother!" Mollie's voice cut across the wires. "Where have you been? We've been frantic! You didn't answer your phone last night or all day today."

"Take it easy, Mollie. I'm sorry, but I had to ... take care of something, and I wasn't able to call. I do have some news for you. Could you and Chris stop by when he gets off work?"

Agnes had pondered all morning whether she should tell Chris and Mollie first or let Sharon be a surprise. Under other circumstances, a surprise could have been delightful, but not under these, she concluded now. Not under these.

"I suppose we can, Mother. What's up?"

"Sharon's here."

6

Mollie found a parking space in the Thorne Enterprises lot and turned off the engine of the Chevy Bel Air to wait for her husband. She didn't have to wait long. As he approached, she slid from behind the wheel to the center of the seat. When he bent over to kiss her, she drew back. He raised an eyebrow.

"I'm sorry, Chris, but I'm a little distracted. I have news, and we're going by my mom's before going home."

After she told him, he shook his head. "I can't wrap my mind around this, Mol. Sharon in a family way and Tony dead? I mean, the idea of Sharon as ... a widow? I can't picture it."

"And I can't believe she didn't let someone know she was coming instead of just arriving like that and expecting Mother to meet her at Fern Haven."

"That's what she did? How's your mother taking it?"

"She seems okay, but she wasn't very happy with me ..."

"Oh?"

Tangled Strands

"Well, first I said part of me feels sorry for Sharon ...." She paused. Chris glanced at her.

"And?"

"And then I said the other part of me feels like she got what she deserved."

"Mollie!"

"It's true. By running off with Tony, she asked for trouble, so she shouldn't be surprised she found it. I was only being honest."

"In that case, you deserve for your mother to be upset with you!"

Mollie did not reply, and they drove the rest of the way in silence. When they turned on Lazy River Road, the driveways were still blocked with snow, so Chris pulled his car to a stop behind Sharon's on the street. At the sight of it, Mollie stiffened. She wasn't ready for this. She and Chris, Larry and Sharon had been such an inseparable foursome growing up. But Sharon severed that in August, and Mollie wasn't ready to forgive her. She laid her head on her husband's shoulder, and he put an arm around her.

The backs of his fingers caressed her cheek. "It's tough, isn't it? Do you think you can try and focus on all those years she was your best friend?"

"I don't know. I feel so many things all mixed together—anger for the pain she caused Larry, sadness that what she and I had is gone forever, questions about the future. And I admit a corner of my heart is concerned about what this means for

Sharon. I mean, can you picture her a mother—and a widowed one at that?"

"No, I can't." He reached for her hand, and she felt his head bow. "Heavenly Father, we come to you admitting a huge jumble of emotions. Please help us as we see Sharon. Help us give over to you all the things that have happened, and help us find a way to show her your love."

They got out of the car and approached the house. As they crossed the front porch, the door opened, and Agnes stepped back for them to enter. They found Sharon at the mantel looking at pictures, but she turned immediately. Mollie hesitated, but Chris crossed the room in two long strides and pulled Sharon into a brotherly hug. How like Chris to be the one to break the ice.

He released Sharon and stepped back. Out of the corner of her eye, Mollie caught her mother motion to Chris, and the two of them slipped away to the kitchen. Oh, great.

She supposed she should hug Sharon like Chris had—*if* Sharon would let her. She stepped forward and made a half motion of opening her arms. Sharon did the same, and they came loosely together for only a moment before both backed away.

"So. You're back."

Sharon nodded and returned to the pictures on the mantel.

"So what's Chicago like?"

Of course it was an irrelevant question, but it was the best Mollie could manage with her heart reeling from the sight of Sharon's pregnancy. Memories flooded in—little girls with dolls at the ready, watching their "babies" come down through

Tangled Strands

the sky from "heaven," speechless teens listening as Agnes broadened their education about life, and delicious embarrassment as they giggled in hushed tones about what they were learning. *I was so looking forward to experiencing marriage and babies side by side with you, Sharon! Why did you have to go and spoil it?*

———◆◆◆———

In the kitchen Agnes held out the coffee pot. Chris wagged a finger at it, then bent to whisper, "What about Larry? Does he know yet?"

Agnes shook her head. "My heart fails me at the thought of my son."

Chris came and laid his hands on her shoulders.

"Listen, I've been meaning to visit Larry ever since I got married. I think this is the perfect occasion. The weekend is coming up. Let's keep the lid on this until I can drive up and see him in person, okay?"

"That sounds good, Chris. I can't imagine trying to tell him by phone, and with Sharon here—"

"Say no more. If I'm gone a day or so, it will give Mollie and Sharon a chance to do something together. How do you think it's going to go for them?"

"I have no idea. You're closer to Mollie's feelings these days than I am. I know she's been terribly hurt, and I know she's angry over what Sharon did to Larry. Some of how Mollie deals with it may depend on him and how he takes Sharon's return."

"How is Sharon feeling about Larry, or about any of us, for that matter?"

"She only referred to him once, making sure he wasn't going to be here before she agreed to come to Willow Valley with me. She's nervous, and she's worried about rejection—from all of us. I think she now has some idea of the impact of what she did. And now, with a baby coming—oh, Chris, I don't know!"

7

Hours later Sharon rolled over in bed and sighed. It must be near midnight, and she almost wished she were back in Chicago. She had worried that coming to Willow Valley with Mrs. Baldwin was a bad idea, but at the time the prospect of returning alone to Chicago had sent a shudder through her. The dark memory of Rita's claim had given her little choice.

Despite all the good times she'd had in this house through the years, being in it again under today's circumstances set her nerves on edge. The evening meal had been awkward. Mrs. Baldwin tried to start conversations but finally gave up. Sharon didn't want to hear about Willow Valley, and she didn't want to talk about Chicago. Afterwards the two worked in silence while Sharon washed the dishes and Mrs. Baldwin dried them and cleaned up around the kitchen.

Afterwards, watching an episode of *I Love Lucy* together had helped, but when it was over and Mrs. Baldwin excused herself to go upstairs, Sharon took a breath of relief. Now that relief had evolved into a familiar, suffocating loneliness.

She thought about the room that surrounded her in the darkness. Mollie's room. Mollie had always had such a pretty room—all lavender and ruffles. As a child, Sharon hadn't known enough to envy it, but as a teen, she couldn't help comparing it to the shabby one where she laid her own head each night. The wide brown and white stripes on that wall made her think of jail.

She scowled in the darkness. Everything had always come easy to Mollie Baldwin. A warm, loving family. Colorful, fresh dresses and shoes that never looked old. Almost blond hair with just a touch of curl. A brother to champion and protect her. And now the fair Mollie had married her Prince Charming. Sharon felt her scowl deepen. Seeing Mollie and Chris together, knowing they were married, catching the way he looked at her, even the tender way he put his arm around her shoulders, brought back memories of her exciting early days with Tony. And that memory brought a fresh rush of misery.

Chris's hug had been warm and welcoming, but that pretense of a hug between her and Mollie—what a joke. The look on Mollie's face made it clear she felt it, too. Well, tough. It would do Mollie good to deal with something difficult in her charmed life.

Sharon got out of bed and headed for the bathroom. On her way back, she noticed the door to Larry's room ajar. She stared at it a moment. Rhythmic breathing behind the door across the hall assured her Mrs. Baldwin was asleep, so she stepped to his door and touched it lightly till it swung open. In the glow of the streetlight, the room looked as she remembered it. After a brief hesitation, she turned on the light. She was

Tangled Strands

right. The room had not changed. The blue-and-brown plaid bedspread and curtains, the orderly bookcase, a simple lamp, and the desk with the pencil holder, stapler and blotter exactly in place—all were typical Larry Baldwin.

What else would she expect from someone who never rushed into anything and never seemed to crave more than what he had?

What had attracted her to him in those growing-up years? Despite their different temperaments, the answer was easy. From the beginning Larry had believed in her and cheered her on. He always treated her with the same respect as he treated his sister. No one but Larry had had the patience to help her learn to ride Mollie's two-wheeler and to swim at Fern Lake. Later he taught her to dive off the dock and eventually to drive. School was always a struggle for her, yet watching Larry thrive with his studies had provided her a measure of motivation to apply herself to her own. When an algebra problem frustrated her, Larry could help her work it out without making her feel dumb.

Of course it didn't hurt that Larry Baldwin was a dreamboat. She remembered admiring his dark, wavy hair when she was as young as nine. The thought of his charcoal blue eyes and deep voice still sent a quiver through her.

The night after the funeral of her friend Porter Baldwin had cemented the bond between them—and the bond had carried them through the rest of his high school years. It had given everyone, including her, the idea that there would be even more and better in the future.

Until Tony Casanetti blew into town.

Shaking that thought away, Sharon turned out the light, put Larry's door back the way she found it, and returned to her bed.

8

The next evening Agnes smiled as Sharon got up from the table and began clearing up the dishes.

"I'm on clean-up duty, remember?"

"That's right. Thank you, Sharon."

Though the day had begun awkwardly for the two of them, their discussion about how to share household tasks had been pleasant enough. Sharon was content to let Agnes do the cooking, but she insisted she would take over the clean up and vacuuming. Agnes was reluctant to give up the use of her new toy—the automatic washing machine that had recently replaced her decades-old wringer one, so Sharon offered to take over the ironing as her part.

"Wouldn't it be nice if someday they came up with a way to make clothes so they don't have to be ironed?" Sharon mused.

Of greater concern to Agnes now was Sharon's family, and it took more than one suggestion before Sharon consented to call them late on the third day. Agnes stayed in the kitchen putting away clean dishes, making enough noise to cover the conversation in the next room.

She understood the girl's reluctance. Through the years Agnes's efforts to reach out to the Champlin family had met with mixed results at best. She had not understood Willa's attitude toward her granddaughter, Sharon, until that awful day when they found out what had happened to Sharon's mother. That also explained the cocoon her father had built around himself with his endless over-the-road trucking.

Before all the dishes were put away, Sharon pushed through the swinging door and joined Agnes.

For a moment, she looked whipped. Then the old fight returned to her eyes. "Well, that's my grandmother for you! She almost had a heart attack thinking I might be coming back to live with her. As long as I'm not, well, she may be able to stand my presence in town."

"Sharon! That's not fair. I think your grandmother always loved you, but she was a little overwhelmed by the responsibility—"

"—of a grandchild she never asked to be responsible for!" Sharon grabbed the clean silverware and began tossing it into slots in the drawer.

Oh, what Agnes wouldn't give to change some of the history in Sharon's family.

"Speaking of grandchildren, what did she have to say about the prospect of a great-grandchild?"

"I didn't tell her. She would probably just worry about getting stuck with *it*, too!"

"Sharon!"

Tangled Strands

"You said that already. Look, I know my attitude toward my grandmother is crummy, but I learned most of it from her, so the feeling's mutual. I try to keep it in line. I don't say ugly things to her face. I mostly stay out of her way now, and I'm sure she likes it that way."

With the dish rack empty, Sharon began wiping the oilcloth on the kitchen table where they sat. Agnes sighed. "What about your dad? Did you talk to him?"

"He's not home—as usual. Gram said he would be gone another three weeks."

"Three weeks! But you *are* going to drop over and see your grandmother, aren't you?"

"She didn't invite me," Sharon said, sounding more relieved than disappointed. "I didn't see her for six months before I left. But maybe I will—sometime."

A change of subject seemed in order. "Chris is going to see Larry this weekend." She waited for a reaction but got none. "He's going to take Friday afternoon off from work." She paused again. "He's not sure what to tell him—"

Sharon swung around, eyes flashing. "Look, I guess you want me to say something about Larry—" She bit her lip. "but I can't! I can't … talk about him!"

She turned to flee the room, but Agnes intercepted her. "Sharon, I'm sorry." She put a hand on the girl's arm. "I'm sorry, and I promise I won't press you about Larry again. When—*if*—you want to talk about him, it will be up to you."

Sharon drew away. "Mollie's … angry with me … about Larry, isn't she?"

Tangled Strands

Agnes had to nod, and she wasn't surprised to feel the prick of tears.

"I guess I would be, too," Sharon said, "if I had a brother like Larry."

With a swish of the swinging door, she was gone.

That evening as they laughed together over *The Burns and Allen* show, Agnes brought out her handwork. A few minutes later she noticed Sharon wandering around the room appearing to count something.

"May I ask what you are doing?"

"I'm counting these lacy pieces you have on everything. I especially like the big one on the coffee table. The ones on the end tables match it, don't they?"

"Yes, and so do the ones on the arms of the chairs."

"Did you make them all?"

Agnes smiled. "Yes. I started with the big one and just kept adding the others. I think it was two or three years before I got all the small ones done."

"I remember seeing you do this when I was growing up, but I never paid any attention. I can't imagine how you do it." Sharon came closer and peered at the hook and fine thread in Agnes's hands. "Is this knitting?"

"No, it's called crochet."

Sharon shook her head. "It's weird. To me it looks like that little hook is just tangling up the threads."

Agnes chuckled. "I guess it does, doesn't it? The truth is, it *is* 'tangling up the threads'—if you want to say it that way—but in a carefully planned way."

Tangled Strands

9

Larry Baldwin peered into the oven to check the progress of the chicken. The sizzling sound made him grin, as did the deeper brown color since the last time he looked. He didn't have a large repertoire as a cook, but baked chicken was something he could count on. When he and Chris were growing up, they'd had fun vying for the wishbone.

Ever since Chris called, Larry had been grinning in anticipation of his friend's visit. Aside from the activities surrounding Chris and Mollie's wedding and the couple of times they had been at his mother's over Christmas, Larry had not seen Chris since the summer before. The last time they were together, just the two of them, was the night of Sharon's disappearance when Chris had virtually kidnapped him out of his somber solitude in the library and taken him to the stadium at Valley High.

Inside, on the edge of the field, Chris had turned Larry to face the stands.

"See them steps, Pal? Now start running. I'm racing you to the top."

At the highest row of bleachers, they collapsed, panting. Larry gasped, "You old goat, you! What was that all about? Okay, I know—you figured I needed to let off some steam."

Breathless, Chris grinned and punched Larry on the shoulder.

When he caught his breath, Larry said, "Okay, Chris, what can you tell me about this Casanetti character?"

In the kitchen now, Larry shook his head to drive away the memory. A friend like Chris was a treasure, and Larry considered his blessings double because he now had him as a brother-in-law as well. Though Larry loved his sister dearly, she sometimes needed a strong hand to keep her on an even keel. He marveled at how well and how lovingly Chris accomplished that.

The doorbell rang, and he hurried to answer it. When he opened the door, his grin faltered. Though Chris hurried to produce a smile, Larry sensed something amiss. Or maybe not. He would wait and see what Chris had to say.

"Welcome to my castle—I mean apartment. Come on in. There's room in the closet for your coat and space on the window seat in the bedroom for your bag. Then join me in the kitchen. Supper is about ready."

Larry was tossing a salad when Chris arrived in the kitchen. "Boy, do I miss having you around, Chris! It's not the same old campus without you."

Chris gave him a crooked smile.

As they sat down at the table, Larry said, "You okay? You've hardly said a word since you got here, and that's not like you." He studied his friend. "And hey, I don't see the usual twinkle in your eyes. Something *is* wrong! Here, let me say the blessing, and then we can talk."

After the prayer, they began breaking open baked potatoes and doctoring them with butter, salt and pepper.

"So what's up, Chris? Do you have bad news or something?" A thought hit him. "What is it—news about Sharon?" His gut tightened.

Chris grinned crookedly. "I would never make an actor, would I? Yes, it's about Sharon, but I don't know that it should be called bad news. So why don't we enjoy these delicious victuals before we talk, okay?" That broad grin *looked* good, but Larry read fakeness all over it.

They ate with gusto, sharing news about fellow classmates and graduates. When they finished, they cleared the table and stacked the dishes in the sink.

"We'll have fudge sundaes later, okay? First, you have to tell me about Sharon."

They settled on the davenport, kicked off their shoes, and Larry turned expectantly to Chris. For a fleeting moment he thought Chris might hedge again, but he took a deep breath and met Larry's eyes.

"Sharon's back in Willow Valley. She's expecting a ... a baby—and Tony's dead."

Larry's eyebrows shot up, and his mouth dropped open. After a long moment, he rose, crossed the room to the window, and stared out into the night. Finally, he turned. "I guess you'd better tell me all about it."

They talked far into the night, promised sundaes forgotten. Chris told Larry what he knew, but Larry had far more questions than Chris had answers. No, he didn't know Sharon's plans, or whether she expected to stay around, or get a job, or live with Larry's mother. And no, he had no idea how she felt about Tony at this point. He had seen her only briefly. They agreed the vision of Sharon as a grieving widow struck them as abstract.

Between questions, Larry paced. Once when he turned, he found Chris staring at him.

"What's the matter?"

"Nothing. I've just never seen the unshakable Larry Baldwin quite so agitated. But I don't blame you," Chris hastened to add. "My shoulders would sag too if it happened to me."

"So was Sharon with this guy when he got killed?"

"Oh, no, she had moved out."

Larry turned sharply. "Moved out?"

"Tony wasn't happy about the baby. He wanted her to ... to get rid of it."

Larry gasped. After a long moment, he turned to the apartment door and banged his fists on it. When he stopped, he rested his head against his hands.

Chris was quiet a moment. "I guess the guy had a temper. One day he started throwing things, and Sharon got herself out

Tangled Strands

of there." He hesitated. "When she went back for her clothes a couple days later, he had changed the locks."

Larry's mouth dropped open again. Chris went to him and gave his shoulder a squeeze. "I'm sorry, Lare. I'm sorrier than I can say. Maybe I shouldn't have mentioned that."

Larry straightened slowly. "No, I'm glad you did, and I'm glad you came, Chris." He returned to the davenport. "I'm glad you're the one to tell me. With Mother or Mollie, I would have had to worry about how *they* were feeling. With you, I can just—" The words choked up.

"I guess that's what friendship is about."

"Speaking of Mollie, how is she taking this?"

"Not well. She's pretty angry."

"I suppose it is like last summer all over again."

"Almost, but not quite. I think last summer she was more shocked and hurt than angry like she is now. After we saw Sharon, Mollie refused to say a word, but last night I persisted, and we had a long talk. She's going to invite Sharon to go shopping tomorrow. Your mom says Sharon doesn't have any maternity clothes at all."

Larry grimaced. Of course his mother had no choice but to take her in, but what was it going to mean to all of them to have her back in Willow Valley and staying with his mother? What would he do when spring break rolled around?

Chris spoke again. "I tried to explain to her how important it is for her to give Sharon a chance." He paused. "Maybe I shouldn't say this, but sometimes it seems like not a day goes by that Sharon's shadow doesn't fall somewhere across Mollie's and my marriage."

"I'm sorry to hear that, Chris, but I can understand it."

"I told Mollie I've been praying every day that we will allow God to heal the hurts Sharon inflicted on us." He laced his fingers and stretched his arms over his head. "Mollie listened but said little. In the end, she agreed she would be civil to Sharon when they go shopping. She said she'd even try to act as if everything between them is the same as before."

Larry rubbed the heel of his hand against his forehead. "You know, Chris, I feel like I'm being slammed back and forth between emotions on this thing. One minute I'm swamped with sympathy for Sharon and anger at Tony, and I want to rush to her side. The next minute I remember that *she* turned her back on me and walked out of my life."

Chris opened his mouth to speak, then shook his head and remained silent.

"So what do you think I should do, Chris? Could I help Mother and Mollie if I made a trip to Willow Valley?" A moment later he answered his own question. "But I can't imagine facing Sharon under the present circumstances. What do you think?"

"Your mother will do a good job looking out for Sharon, and I'm doing my best with Mollie ..."

With Chris's encouragement, Larry decided to stay at school, at least for the present. Before settling down for the night, the two spent time in prayer. They asked God for peace, for discernment, for wisdom. They asked for his protection over the thoughts and feelings of each of them as they dealt with Sharon's reentry into their lives.

And they asked God's blessing on Sharon and the baby.

10

Mollie Thorne glanced sideways at Sharon as she pulled her Bel Air away from the curb. Did a childhood friendship really have enough power to heal pain and anger in the present? She doubted it, but she supposed she had to try. What did Sharon think she was doing, waltzing back into their lives after what she did? She should have at least called and asked if she could come—and at least said she was sorry.

For the first half hour, the two went through the motions of old friends on a pleasant shopping trip, perusing store windows the length of Main Street. They chatted about fashions on display, gushed over dainty baby dresses, and exclaimed over prices. Three dollars for a baby dress? What was the world coming to?

But when Sharon began trying on maternity clothes, their cheerful front dissolved in an awkwardness they had never experienced together. Mollie tried to pretend it was ordinary shopping, but she found it impossible. In an attempt to keep angry thoughts at bay, she watched without comment and simply affirmed Sharon's choices.

But even those efforts failed. Their first shopping for one of their babies should have been a delightful time for them. *Sharon, why did you do a thing like that?*

Over lunch at the Choo Choo Diner, she tried to interest Sharon in the lives of their former classmates. A couple of guys were off to college, Sally Stauffer was planning her wedding, and Dooby Sands was running the Avenue Garage. All the while, Sharon focused on her salad, offered monosyllable answers, or let her eyes wander around the room.

Mollie tried a new approach. "Tomorrow night our Sunday school class is getting together at Pastor Hawkins's house. We would love you to come—" but Sharon began shaking her head.

"Well, I suppose you might feel a little awkward at firs—"

"It is not that simple, Mollie." Sharon stabbed her fork into her salad and did not look up.

"What's not simple? You have your new clothes—"

"*No*, Mollie, N-O! Period."

"But you *are* coming to church tomorrow, aren't you?"

Sharon concentrated on picking celery out of her salad. "Probably not." When Mollie started to object, Sharon dropped her fork, grabbed her coat and packages from beside her, and slid out of the booth.

"Sharon! What do you think you're doing?"

"Subject closed!" Sharon flung over her shoulder.

"But *why*, Sharon?" Mollie collected her own purse and coat and dashed after her. "Hey! Somebody's got to pay—and you can't leave without me!" People had turned to stare.

Sharon tossed her head, slowed her steps, and stopped short of the door.

After paying the bill, Mollie followed Sharon out the door with an exasperated sigh. "I have a hat you can borrow, if that's your problem—"

Sharon swung around, eyes flashing. "Mollie Baldwin, stop it! You do not understand, so let it go—"

"Hey, my name's not Baldwin anymore—it's Thorne. And what's not to understand? So it wasn't too smart to run off with—"

Sharon's hand moved so fast that Mollie had no chance to duck the slap. Her mouth dropped open, but when she tried to speak, she could only sputter. She caught her breath, then charged around to the driver's side of her car. It would serve Sharon right if she left her standing on the sidewalk.

But by the time Mollie was in her seat, Sharon was in hers. Both doors slammed in a quick stutter step. Seething, Mollie revved the engine and maneuvered sharply to get out of the parking space. The blast of a horn startled them both as a car on the street veered to avoid being hit.

Mollie could still feel her heart pounding when she swerved into her mother's driveway. Neither had spoken a word on the drive home.

As Sharon opened the car door, Mollie spoke, voice tight and eyes straight ahead. "All I've got to say is this, Sharon

Tangled Strands

Champlin—or whatever your name is now. You had better not cause my brother any more grief!"

———◆◆◆———

Agnes looked up from her cookie dough in surprise as Sharon entered the kitchen. "How did your shopping go? Didn't Mollie come—?"

Sharon shook her head and refused to meet Agnes's eyes. She took a glass from the cupboard, filled it with water, and turned to leave the room.

"Hey! Don't go. Is something wrong?"

Sharon kept walking.

Wiping her hands on her apron, Agnes followed. "Sharon?"

When the girl turned, the distress on her face stopped Agnes's heart.

"Sharon!" She held out her arms, but the girl turned away.

"Leave me alone!" She backed through the swinging door and fled up the stairs.

Agnes's first thought was to retire to her bedroom and pray, but halfway up the stairs she heard the kitchen timer ding. With a sigh as heavy as her heart, she made her way back down. She would do her praying as she so often did—while she worked.

Hours later when the evening meal was ready, she called up the stairs to Sharon. The girl appeared, her eyes red and puffy, her face hollow and drained, and took a seat at the table.

After a brief blessing, Agnes passed her the pasta and tuna casserole.

"What happened, Sharon? I had such high hopes when you and Mollie left this morn—"

"I don't feel like talking about it." Sharon served herself and ate in silence without once looking up. Grimly Agnes followed her example.

When she finished, Sharon pushed her plate away. She met Agnes's eyes for a second, then took a deep breath and stared at the wall beyond her. "If you must know, things went very badly between us."

Agnes waited for her to say more, but Sharon pushed back her chair and started clearing the table.

"Sharon, please? I can understand your not wanting to talk about it, but if you and I are going to live here under the same roof, things could get very tense if we can't be honest with each other. Won't you come back and sit down?"

Sharon set the dishes down hard on the counter and returned slowly. She plopped into her chair and started picking at the red polish on her fingernails. Agnes determined to wait her out. Finally she said, "Mollie and I had a ... a fight, I guess you would call it."

"May I ask what it was about?"

"She tried to get me to say I would go to church tomorrow."

That wasn't good news, but it didn't seem like enough to explain how red Sharon's eyes were. "I'm—I'm sorry to hear that. Is that all?"

"Now don't *you* start on me!" Sharon slammed her hands to the table as if to get up again, then jerked them back and buried her face in them. An unexpected sob escaped.

Agnes sat in stunned silence, praying for wisdom. There had to be something else bothering the girl. Could it relate to Tony?

"Sharon? *Please*. What happened in Chicago that you haven't told me about?"

11

Her face still in her hands, Sharon shook her head again. *I can't tell her! I just can't.* The thought of the disgrace it would bring was more than she could bear. Knowing what it would mean to the baby hadn't bothered her at first, but it was beginning to. The thought of Mollie knowing, especially after today, was beyond bearing.

Mrs. Baldwin's voice broke into her thoughts. "Sharon, I'm sure something must be bothering you more than just having a fi— a disagreement with Mollie today. I wish you would tell me about it."

Sharon sat perfectly still, unable to look up or even move at the thought of telling what she had vowed not to breathe to a soul. And yet, if it were true and she said nothing, then she supposed she would be living a lie, one that could perhaps haunt what was growing inside her a long time in the future. *Do it, Sharon. Just do it.*

"I don't know—I mean, not for sure … but I'm afraid—" Finally, tumbling all over themselves, the words rushed out.

"I'm not sure there ever was a real marriage between Tony and me!"

She understood the shock she read in Mrs. Baldwin's eyes. This might be the worst thing in the world Agnes Baldwin could imagine. Sharon waited for her to explode with surprise or condemnation, but her eyes just widened and she stared for a moment. Then she stood, drew Sharon up out of her seat, and wrapped her arms tightly around her.

All the bottled-up emotions of the last months, and especially the last week, bubbled up and boiled over.

Sharon sobbed.

Mrs. Baldwin's arm tightened around her while her other hand caressed Sharon's hair. "Shhh, dear girl, shhh. It's going to be all right."

"How can you s-say that?"

Of course Mrs. Baldwin had no answer. She only drew back and used her sleeve to wipe some of Sharon's tears. "Please sit back down and tell me about it. Here, let me get you a drink."

Sharon drank thirstily. Finally, she took a deep breath and met the older woman's eyes for the first time. "After Tony... died, one of his friends told me—a least hinted strongly—that he hadn't really married me. She said he faked the whole thing with the help of some of his friends." She squeezed her eyes shut and felt fresh tears escape onto her cheeks.

"Exactly who told you this?"

"A-a friend of Tony's named Rita."

"What do you mean by friend?"

Tangled Strands

"She and Tony used to go together before he came to Willow Valley."

Sharon saw a ray of hope flicker in Mrs. Baldwin's eyes, especially when Sharon told her Rita had shown open hostility during Sharon's time in Chicago.

"And you weren't able to check into the truth of her charge?"

Sharon shook her head. "I was ... I was so upset, I just left without ... without talking to anybody about it."

Mrs. Baldwin grimaced, then thought a moment. "Let me call Chris's dad. As a businessman, I'm sure Alec Thorne has someone who could check the facts for us. If a marriage took place, there's a record of it. It shouldn't take long. Can you try not to fret anymore until we find out?"

Sharon dropped her head to her arms on the table. Her emotions ricocheted between shame over the past and relief that she no longer had to carry this burden alone. She heard Mrs. Baldwin's chair pushing back and saw her heading for the telephone.

Sharon came to life. "What are you gonna do? I don't want anyone to know—especially not Mollie! And if we find out it's true ... ." Frantic tears started afresh.

"I understand, Sharon, and I'll abide by your wishes as far as Mollie's concerned. I'm calling Mr. Thorne."

After the call, Mrs. Baldwin came back and sat beside Sharon. For an hour she gently encouraged Sharon to talk about the painful uncertainty with which she had been living.

"I'm glad you told me, Sharon. We have a real chance to trust God about this. If it is true, then it is bad news, but God

Tangled Strands

will help us find a way to deal with it. Whatever happens, you can count on me to stand by you. With God's help, we *will* find a way through this. Can you believe that?"

"I'll try to." Sharon began gnawing on her thumbnail. After a moment she swiped at her eyes.

"Is something else bothering you?"

Sharon hesitated, then nodded, and her tears became a torrent. Between sobs she admitted the disastrous end of the shopping trip.

"I can't believe I slapped her like that." She wiped her eyes with her sleeve, and Mrs. Baldwin pulled a hankie from her apron pocket and handed it to her.

"I can't even picture you and Mollie acting like that. You were always so close, I can't imagine what you've just described to me. However, what you've told me this evening explains at least some of why you got that upset with Mollie. You do realize, don't you, that she had no way of knowing these things you were upset about?"

Sharon nodded. "And now ... she'll for sure never want to be my friend again."

"Let's not talk about *never*. Let's talk about what it might take to patch things up between you two who were best friends for so long."

All was quiet. Finally Sharon said, "I suppose you think I should apologize."

"What *I* think isn't important. What's important is what you think. I remember when my sister Florence and I were teenagers, I hurt her badly by repeating something she had told me in confidence. When I realized how hurt she was, I felt really bad. I was surprised at how much better *I* felt after I apologized. But you shouldn't do it unless you really mean it."

Again, silence. Finally, "I never meant to hit her like I did, so I guess I would be telling the truth to say I am sorry that ... I did that."

"Then I think you will feel better if you give her a call."

An hour later, with the weight on her heart lighter than it had been in a long time, Sharon prepared for bed. She couldn't believe she had unloaded everything to Mrs. Baldwin the way she did. Would she be sorry later? She didn't know, but for the moment she felt relief. After turning out her light and pulling up the covers, she directed a tentative prayer toward the ceiling.

"Dear God, I know I haven't paid attention to you in a long time, and that's probably bad. If you're really there, I thank you for making Mollie accept my apology without hollering at me and that ... that Mrs. Baldwin doesn't hate me. And if you care about me like she says you do, could you please do something with the mess my life is in? I know *I* don't deserve your help, but this baby, God, it hasn't done anything to deserve being born into this mess, so maybe—for its sake—could you do ... something? Well, to be specific, could you make it turn out that Tony did marry me? Thank you. Amen."

Tangled Strands

12

The next morning Agnes set the coffee pot to perking while she listened for sounds of Sharon coming downstairs. When the girl came into the kitchen, Agnes opened her arms for a hug and once again was relieved when Sharon responded. She wasn't surprised, however, that they were quiet over breakfast. As they lingered with their coffee, Agnes breathed a prayer for wisdom to follow up on what had happened the evening before. An idea had been germinating, but she needed to think about it a bit more before broaching it. It would wait until tomorrow.

"Sharon, you know I'd love you to go to church with me, don't you?"

Sharon took bite of toast and chewed it thoroughly then took a sip of coffee.

"Do I take it you're not interested in joining me?"

Sharon nodded without looking at Agnes.

"You used to go with us quite regularly."

Sharon still did not meet her eyes. "True, but I lost interest in church some time ago."

"May I ask why?"

Sharon finished off her orange juice and wiped her mouth with her napkin. "I just don't figure God has any interest in me, so I don't see any reason for me to have any interest in him."

"I'm sorry to hear that, and I hope one of these days you'll change your mind. Right now I have to finish getting ready. I hope you have a pleasant morning. The roast and potatoes in the oven shouldn't need any attention till I get back." She smiled. "I hope one Sunday soon you'll feel like going with me."

"Maybe."

Monday morning Agnes came to breakfast ready to broach her fresh idea to Sharon. *Thank you, Lord, for the thought. Now please help me make it work.* She waited until they had covered morning greetings and the blessing and settled to eat their toast and cooked oatmeal.

"You know, living alone and not having any grandchildren yet, I never have a reason to bake cookies anymore. Would you feel like helping me stir up a batch?"

Sharon did not look up from her bowl. "I suppose I could."

"What kind do you like?"

"I always liked the peanut butter ones you made."

"I remember making those with you and Mollie a lot. That's because I had you two to roll them out and press them with a fork." She chuckled, and Sharon smiled. "The few times I've made them since then, I've discovered I don't have to do that."

"You don't?"

"No, I just drop them from a spoon like other cookies. But I would love to make some rolled-and-forked ones again." Sharon grinned, and Agnes took courage. "Uh, what would you think if ... if we invited Mollie over to help us ...?"

Lord, please ...?

Concentrating on scraping the sides of her bowl, Sharon hesitated. Finally, "I suppose we could."

"Remember, you can count on me not to say anything about what you told me the other night."

"Do you think Mollie would come?"

"How about if we talk to God before we call her and ask him to make her say yes?"

Sharon shrugged, so Agnes said a quick prayer before going to the phone.

———◆◆◆———

Once Mrs. Baldwin had disappeared through the swinging door, Sharon struck her fist against the table. Now why did she have to go and suggest that? She wasn't ready to face Mollie again, but she hadn't found the nerve to nix the idea. She pressed her fist to her mouth just as Mrs. Baldwin came back in the room.

"She said she could come in about an hour." She met Sharon's eyes. "Having second thoughts?"

Sharon nodded.

"I can understand that, and I don't suppose it will be easy. I don't think it will be easy for Mollie either, but I think it could be an important bridge to build back toward that wonderful friendship you two had. I appreciate your willingness to take a chance. Besides," and now she grinned and winked, "I'll be here to pull you two apart if you start swinging at each other."

Oh, great. Now she was making jokes. But Sharon had to admit that the idea of petite Mrs. Baldwin trying to drag her and Mollie apart brought a smile to her own face.

When the doorbell rang, Sharon was relieved that Mrs. Baldwin went to answer it. She could hear them talking in hushed tones before they reached the kitchen—probably talking about her. She grimaced.

When they walked through the swinging door, Mrs. Baldwin started talking before Sharon and Mollie had a chance to greet each other. "You know what I was thinking about while I was getting dressed this morning? The time you two got lost in the woods at the base of Thorne Hill. Of course we Baldwins were panicked because we weren't sure where to start looking for you."

Sharon groaned inwardly about bringing up the past, but she decided not to object. What did she have to lose besides a friend she was sure she had already lost?

"We didn't mean to wander where you couldn't find us," Mollie said, as she measured flour into a sifter, "but we were chasing that pretty butterfly."

"And then Mollie tripped over that root and scraped her knee," Sharon added as she began packing Crisco into a measuring cup.

"You would have to bring that up! As you know, I still have a scar on that knee. Mother, you'd better put baking powder on your shopping list. By the way, is this Aunt Florence's recipe?"

"Yes, it is." Mrs. Baldwin tore a piece of paper from a pad on the counter and picked up a pencil while Mollie sifted the flour and the dry ingredients into a mixing bowl. "So, Sharon, did you do much baking for Tony?" she asked.

"I made cookies a few times, and once I made a cake with one of those box mixes. How much sugar does this recipe call for?"

Mrs. Baldwin told her as she plugged in the Sunbeam Mixmaster that Sharon remembered had been her husband's last Christmas gift to her before his death.

Minutes later, Mollie turned the mixer off and scraped the sides. "I'm glad we're making these cookies, Sharon, because I haven't had peanut butter cookies in a long time."

"You mean you never make them for Chris?"

"Not this kind. His favorites are oatmeal with raisins. You can turn on the oven, Mother. We're ready to start rolling the balls."

They worked in silence while Sharon shaped the dough into balls and Mollie crisscrossed them with a fork. "So, Sharon, have you made an appointment to see Dr. Scott?"

Sharon rolled two cookies before saying a quiet, "No."

Tangled Strands

"What kind of doctor did you see in Chicago?"

Again Sharon delayed answering, and when she finally spoke, she had trouble keeping her voice steady. "I didn't. I don't *like* doctors—or hospitals."

She saw Mollie swing around toward her mother, her eyebrows shooting up. She saw Mrs. Baldwin shake her head and move closer to Sharon. Mollie shrank back.

Agnes spoke gently. "I know you said you don't like doctors, Sharon, but you do know you're going to have to see one, don't you?"

Sharon snapped flour from her hands and stepped away from the counter. "*Why?* Nobody can make me, can they?"

"I-I don't suppose they can, but can we at least talk about it?"

She swung on Agnes. "I don't see why I have to see a doctor."

She heard Mrs. Baldwin take a deep breath. "Surely you don't mean that. You know your baby has to … has to be born … ."

Sharon pivoted away to the sink. When she said nothing, Mrs. Baldwin went on. "If all continues to go well, before your baby is born it will be even bigger than it is now."

"But I *hated* the hospital when I had my tonsils out." Sharon heard her voice tremble and was mortified when it cracked at the end.

"I remember that," Agnes said. "It was about a year after your dad moved your family here to Willow Valley."

Sharon turned to face her as she again swiped tears from her cheeks. "It was awful. I still remember how scared I was."

Tangled Strands

"Look, let's turn the oven off and put the rest of the dough in the fridge so we can sit down and talk about this."

Sharon scowled in Mollie's direction but said nothing as she followed Agnes to the living room.

13

Sharon plopped in the rocker while Mrs. Baldwin sat on the davenport. Mollie hung back at the door. Good.

"Now, can you tell me why it was so scary for you?"

Wasn't that obvious? Wasn't it scary for everyone? "Because ... because I was alone with all those strangers, and they seemed to think they could do anything they wanted to me." She stuck a knuckle between her teeth and pressed them together until it hurt.

"Didn't your dad go with you?"

She shook her head, hard, and squeezed her eyes shut. "He was out in Indiana or somewhere on a trucking job—as always." How come she never got used to that?

"What about Gram?"

"Are you kidding? Gram made it as far as the door of my room, but when she realized I was the one doing the screaming, she didn't even come in."

"Oh, Sharon, I'm sorry. Was that before or after the surgery?"

"Before of *course!* Afterwards, my throat hurt so bad, I just stared at the ceiling and wouldn't open my mouth for *anybody.*" Her voice had risen, but she couldn't stop it.

She heard Mrs. Baldwin draw a deep breath. "Well, Sharon, I can understand what a harsh experience that was, and I'm sorry it happened like that. But you were what? Eight years old? You're a woman now, and you're facing one of the greatest experiences a woman can have."

"Ha!" Sharon popped up and went to the window, rubbing the teeth marks on her finger.

"True, it is a painful one, but in the end it is so rewarding you forget about the pain."

Sharon swung on her. "I've heard people say that, but I don't believe it for a minute." She turned her back again.

"Will you at least let me tell you about our family's Dr. Scott? He's very nice. I think he might have been your doctor when you had your tonsils out. Do you remember?"

Sharon continued staring out the window. "Maybe, but I try not to remember anything about that—and I don't appreciate you bringing it all up again."

She couldn't believe it when Mrs. Baldwin began telling how Dr. Scott's father had been her doctor for the births of Larry and Mollie. *So what?* She started pacing, studying things on the mantel, moving them around. At the first pause in Mrs. Baldwin's account, she turned.

"I'm going upstairs now. You two can do what you want about the cookies." She knew her words sounded clipped, but she couldn't help it. She *had* to get out of here.

Tangled Strands

Mrs. Baldwin put out a hand to stop her. "Please don't go, Sharon. I'm trying to help, and that includes getting you an appointment to see Dr. Scott."

"Well, I don't *want* your help! Why can't you leave me alone?" With a toss of her head, she spun away and took some of the stairs two at a time.

Up in her room, she closed the Venetian blinds and flopped across her unmade bed. How could she explain to Mrs. Baldwin what had been haunting her for weeks as this ... this *thing* inside her made itself more evident?

Of course she knew it had to come out. She knew it better than anyone, and she was terrified. Her tonsils experience had been a spur-of-the-moment smoke screen to get Mrs. Baldwin to back off. Now, in the silence of her room, those other childhood memories forced themselves on her afresh. In recent weeks, the wails from the neighboring house and sobs of children outside the window of her bedroom had risen from the dust of forgetfulness to haunt her. The larger her body swelled, the more the past taunted her.

I have to make it go away! her mind screamed, but whether she meant the memory or the baby, she was never sure. Maybe she should have gone along with Tony wanting her to get rid of it—but the very thought made her shudder. One thing she did know, she couldn't go on like this. She scrunched Mollie's pillow tightly against her mouth and welcomed the tears she had been holding back.

14

Twenty minutes later, Agnes tiptoed ahead of Mollie up the stairs until they stopped outside Sharon's door. When the sound of muffled sobs first reached them downstairs, she had suggested it might be good to let Sharon unburden some of her distress in the healing release of tears.

When Agnes reached for the doorknob, Mollie whispered, "Could I try?"

Agnes hesitated, then nodded. Mollie knocked. Silence.

Finally, "Come in."

Agnes watched as Mollie approached the bed where Sharon lay on her side with her arm hugging a pillow to her face. Mollie stood still for a moment—doubtlessly wondering why she had volunteered for this task.

"Hi, Sharon."

No response.

"Dr. Scott is really nice. I've never minded going to him, even when I was little."

Still no response. The look of frustration on Mollie's face deepened.

"The hospital here isn't very big. I suspect it just felt big to you because you were a child."

The only sound was a teary sniff.

Agnes nodded to Mollie to try once more.

"I can't wait to go to him when I have a baby."

Sharon bolted upright. "Well, of course you can't! You were always the perfect one who did exactly what you were supposed to." She threw herself back down, buried her face back in the pillow, and let out a wail like a wounded animal.

Mollie pivoted and threw up her hands. Agnes thrust her thumb twice toward the door. Two minutes later, she heard the Bel Air spinning its wheels on the driveway snow and roaring away down the street.

In Sharon's room, Agnes studied the weeping girl and breathed a prayer. What on earth was driving her to such emotion? She found a corner on the edge of the bed and eased herself down. Sharon's crying froze, but her breathing came in tearful gasps. Agnes began caressing her back with gentle strokes. Finally she spoke just above a whisper.

"There has to be something more than just your tonsils experience. I *need* you to talk to me about whatever it is because it isn't going to get any easier."

After a long silence, Sharon rolled slowly onto her back and, with a deep breath and eyes shut, she began talking about the family that lived next door before they moved to Willow Valley.

"They had lots of children and there was always a baby in the family. I played with a couple of the little girls." She fingered the lace on the edge of the pillowcase so long Agnes wondered if she would continue.

"One night before I went to bed, there was a lot of commotion at the house, with people hollering and crying. Later I got woke up by loud screaming. There was lots of crying and noise right outside my window."

"Oh, Sharon ..."

"I pulled my pillow around my ears, but I could still hear everything, so I went and crawled in bed with Gram—Pa was away, as usual."

"I'm glad you had your grandmother."

"Ha! She was asleep and snoring, and I knew better than to wake her up. At least the noise wasn't as bad on that side of the house."

"Sharon, that sounds terrible. Did you find out what all the commotion was about?"

Again Sharon was quiet so long that Agnes wondered if she would respond. Finally she spoke in broken whispers. "The next morning ... there was more wailing, and we found out the baby ... the baby had trouble being born, and it ... it died."

Agnes drew a sharp breath. For a long moment they sat in silence until Agnes said softly, "That must have been terrible for you, Sharon, and you must have been awfully young because you were only seven when your family moved here."

After another pause, Sharon murmured, "I guess I made myself forget about it until this ... this baby—" her hand found her abdomen— "started getting ... big. Now I can't stop thinking about it."

Agnes reached out and drew Sharon into a sitting position in her arms. She opened her mouth to speak, but Sharon's whisper stopped her. "Mrs. Baldwin? Does it really hurt that bad ... for a baby to be ... born?" Her voice trailed into a whimper.

Drawing the girl close, Agnes whispered, "That's one of the reasons we need a doctor for times like that."

15

Mollie Thorne had just wrung out her dishrag and hung it on the edge of the sink when the phone rang. She hurried to dry her hands. When she heard her mother's voice, she braced herself for a reprimand.

"I want to thank you for helping with the cookies yesterday, even though it didn't end the way we hoped it would." Well, that response was a surprise and a relief.

"I'm glad I went. I had no idea how bad things are with Sharon and how many emotions she is struggling with. Did you find out more?"

"Yes, I did, but I don't think you should hear it all from me. That would probably be gossip—"

"I'm sorry. I don't want you to tell me more than you think you should." *So bite your tongue, Mollie.*

"Well, I hope in time you will hear some of it from Sharon herself. I can say this much—as a little girl, she had some traumatic experiences besides what happened to her mother and a lot more than the tonsils episode. She's not making up what she feels."

"Well, I didn't suppose she was, and I'm sorry to hear that. You think she can get over it before the baby comes?" She didn't want to think about the problem they would have if Sharon didn't.

"I hope so, but she's going to need help and understanding from us to make that happen. And I'm counting on Dr. Scott's help. I decided to speak to him in person rather than on the phone. I couldn't take any chances on his not understanding Sharon's complex situation."

"Sounds good, but I feel like I made things worse." She hadn't intended to say that, but after it came out, it felt good that she had.

"None of it was your fault, dear, and I was proud of you for trying."

"But we're dealing with more than we thought, aren't we?"

"Definitely."

"I'm still angry with her for what she did," Mollie went on, "but Chris and I are praying that God will help me forgive her."

"I'm glad to hear that, and I'm praying, too. By the way, Sharon surprised me at breakfast this morning by opening the doctor subject on her own."

"What'd she say?"

"She started out with 'So there was another Dr. Scott before this one?'"

"Sounds like a night's sleep helped calm some emotions?"

"Yes, and I'm thanking the Lord over and over. I've already had a short talk with Dr. Scott."

"You did? Does he remember Sharon?"

"Oh, yes." Agnes chuckled.

"She's probably one he can't forget?"

"Well, almost, but he's willing to take her as a patient. The reason I'm calling you right now is to talk about clothes—Sharon's clothes, or lack of them." Remembering the story about Tony changing the locks on the apartment doors, Mollie couldn't decide whether to laugh or cry. So much for Tony's being a heartthrob and a dreamboat. A creep was more like it.

"Of course what Sharon needs now are maternity clothes, and she's going to need more than the two tops she bought Saturday. I plan to make her at least one and to encourage her to make one for herself. Remember how much you two enjoyed the sewing lessons I gave you when you were teenagers?"

"Yeeesss ...? I can guess where this is going."

"Well, I was hoping you might—"

"Mother, that was *then*. I don't think it would be the same now."

"I know. You have your own feelings to deal with, which I understand, and I don't want to pressure you and make it harder."

Mollie twisted the telephone cord around her finger. "Thank you, Mother. After what happened yesterday, I'm skittish about saying yes. Could I think about it and talk to Chris?"

74 *Tangled Strands*

———✦✦✦———

Sharon finally gritted her teeth and agreed to see the doctor. Since it had to happen eventually, she might as well get it over with. She declined Mrs. Baldwin's offer to go with her on her first visit, and instead of wearing one of her new maternity outfits, she dressed again in the oversize flannel shirt and wraparound khaki skirt. No sense letting this doctor person think she was proud of her pregnancy like other girls seemed to be. And just because he had long been a friend of the Baldwins did not mean she had to consider him *her* friend.

She found his office nothing like her memories of the hospital. The cozy, personal feel of the place surprised her. Cheerful colors reached out to her, and bright paintings on the wall almost made her smile. She liked the friendly soft blue walls of the room where the nurse led her, and she almost wanted to reach out and touch the painting of a cuddly kitten on the wall.

She answered the doctor's general questions with short, minimal answers. She was twenty. She had never been pregnant before, and she wasn't sure of a date to expect this baby. At least he hadn't asked her about the baby's father—but of course that meant Mrs. Baldwin had told him at least something.

"I remember when you had your tonsils out as a little girl. That wasn't a good experience, was it?"

She started to laugh scornfully, but at the last moment she couldn't. Instead she settled for, "That's an understatement if I ever heard one."

Tangled Strands

"Besides the pain following the surgery, what made it so unpleasant for you—besides the fact that you were all alone?"

Now he's going to laugh at me. "It was scary in the hospital."

"Do you remember what you found frightening?"

"Everything was *strange*. People were dressed all weird with strange white clothes. The furniture didn't look like normal furniture ... and ..."

"And what?"

"I didn't know a single person, but they all bossed me around like I ... like I belonged to them or something. I suppose you think that's dumb."

"Not at all, Sharon. I can understand why those things made it difficult. One thing I can assure you, Mrs. Baldwin and I are determined to make this experience better for you than you expect it to be."

If the visit could have ended there, Sharon might have gone home hopeful. Why did he have to do that examination? At least Mrs. Baldwin had forewarned her about what to expect. The doctor explained each action before he did it, and it helped that he talked some about other things as he worked. Yes, he had put her more at ease than she had imagined possible.

Maybe she could endure this Dr. Scott person after all.

16

Larry Baldwin sighed as he closed his classroom door behind him and headed toward the stairs. He drew a white handkerchief from his pocket and wiped his brow. What was he doing sweating in February? Until now, a month into the second semester, he had been managing well the challenges of graduate classes for his master's degree and as teacher of Ancient History 102, the freshman class he had been asked to teach when its professor fell from a ladder.

But now he was struggling, and he wasn't happy about it. A moment before, in his eagerness to leave his classroom, he had slammed the chalkboard eraser onto the tray, stirring up a cloud of chalk dust, some of which went on the floor. A clean-up job—just what he didn't need to calm his frustrations.

He liked to excel at everything he put his hand to, and he had been confident he could accomplish this dual role with style. He cringed at the thought of the assignment he had forgotten to collect from his students and the medieval history exam on which he had scored poorly. This could not continue. Maybe a brief break at the campus Coffee Corner would help.

He was adding cream to his coffee when he heard his name and turned to find Catherine Harrison, the school registrar, behind him in line.

"Good to see you, Larry. Everything okay for you?"

He gave a half-hearted nod as he picked up his tray and searched for a place to sit. He didn't feel like conversation, but Catherine attended the same church he did and had been a good friend in the fall when, a week before classes started, he had been asked to teach. He couldn't brush her off now.

He nodded towards a nearby table. "Join me?"

After they settled and had taken their first sips, they chatted for a moment about their Sunday school class, but Larry's heart wasn't in it. He wasn't surprised Catherine noticed.

"Something bothering you, Larry? You seem to be distracted."

He stared into his coffee cup. Should he talk to her about Sharon? He didn't feel like it, but the pressures of uncertainty had been building inside him. Had God brought this Christian friend to him just now?

He gave her a crooked smile. "There's this girl back home ... Sharon ..." He saw Catherine's eyebrows rise in a teasing fashion, and he winced at how juvenile he sounded. He shook his head and hurried on. "She practically grew up with our family, along with my best friend, Chris Thorne. You remember Chris from when he was here in school?"

Her brow puckered. "Oh, yes, I do remember him. Wasn't he the one who always kept folks laughing?"

"That's Chris all right. Well, the four of us were inseparable growing up, though we came from very different backgrounds. My sister and I are pretty down-the-middle ordinary, but Chris's family is well-to-do and Sharon's is ... at the other end of the spectrum." He took a sip of coffee and was gratified that Catherine was now listening without a hint of jest.

"Sharon's home life left a lot to be desired, so our family took her under our wings. When we were kids, we four did everything as two boys and two girls, but when we got to be teenagers ..." He paused. "That's when we ended up relating as two couples—in fact, Chris and my sister are married now." His eyes wandered around the room. How much did he want to say?

Catherine laid her hand next to his on the table. "Go on. I take it you and Sharon haven't ended up the same way ... ?"

"That's putting it mildly. Just when I got out of college last year and started thinking about firming up our relationship, Sharon began giving me a cold shoulder. In fact, by the end of the summer she wouldn't talk to me."

"Ouch. That must have been hard."

"It wasn't just hard, it was confusing because we'd had such a strong bond for so many years. And then in August ... in August, Sharon skipped town with some guy she met at work—a real charmer, from what I hear."

"Oh, Larry! I'm sorry. What's happened since then? Have you heard from her?"

Tangled Strands

"My sister did. She got a letter on fancy stationery saying Sharon had married the guy."

Catherine opened her mouth to say something, but instead put her hand over it. Larry took a deep breath. "Had enough, or want some more?"

"There's more?"

"Oh, yes. Two weeks ago, she turned up again, widowed and in a family way."

Catherine's eyes grew wide. "Widowed? What happened?"

"The guy got killed in a fight out there in Chicago where he took Sharon."

"Oh, my. So where is she now?"

"She's in Willow Valley staying with my mother."

Catherine let out a low whistle. "I can see why you've been distracted of late. How are you handling it—I mean, how are you feeling right now?"

Larry drained his coffee and stared across the room. "Good question."

"How do you feel about *her*, if I may ask, after all that's happened?"

"I wish I knew. Mostly I think that how *I* feel isn't the important thing now."

"Of course how you feels is important."

"Maybe. But my relationship with her in the past is affecting how I feel now." He glanced at the clock across the room. "Am I keeping you from something?"

She looked at her watch. "No, I still have fifteen minutes. Go ahead."

"It didn't start out as a romance between us. I was just her friend, like Chris and my whole family were her friends but, starting the night of my father's funeral, I ended up with a special relationship with Sharon."

"Intriguing. Go on."

"She used to explode at times, often for no apparent reason, and it turned out I ... I sort of had the best knack of any of us for helping her get back on an even keel." He glanced away.

Catherine laid her hand on his arm. "No need to be embarrassed. I can see how that would affect your perspective now."

"The possibility of a genuine romance apparently died before it was born, but I still feel ... I feel like I should find a way, somehow, to help her now."

"Do you have something in mind?"

"Well, she needs a father for that baby. I keep wondering if the right thing to do wouldn't be to ask her to marry me—"

Catherine's eyebrows rose. "You're kidding. *Aren't you?*"

17

After Sharon's first visit with Dr. Scott, Agnes waited for a voluntary report on how it went, but Sharon never said a word. Finally, Agnes took courage to ask her about it.

"Fine." The girl did not look up from the magazine in her hand.

Agnes glanced up from her crocheting. Was this going to be like the beginning back at Fern Haven? Then she would have to take the initiative again. "May I ask what you talked about?"

"About having a baby!"

Agnes raised her brows at the touch of pique in the girl's voice. Relief followed when Sharon glanced up with a crooked smile. "I'm sorry. He asked me a bunch of questions. I kept hoping he didn't remember how I acted when I was a kid."

"Oh, he does," Agnes acknowledged with a grin, "but he wanted to take you as a patient anyway."

"I suppose I should be grateful for that. I guess you would like to know he said everything is going well. The kid should arrive the third week of June." She came over and peered at the thread and hook in Agnes's hands. "How can you tell how to do that?"

"My pattern book tells me what, where, and how many." She held up a slim booklet.

"I would never be able to do something like that."

"Don't say that. Remember, I've been doing it for years. When I started, I was very awkward and made plenty of mistakes. I still do sometimes."

"How did you learn?"

"My grandmother taught me when I was about twelve."

"Do you think I could learn to do it?"

"I'm sure you could. But you mustn't start with fine thread like this. You need to start with yarn."

"Oh? You think I could make something with yarn?"

"I know you could. In fact, you could make something for your baby, maybe a bonnet. But you'll need to practice on just the stitches at first till you get comfortable with the hook and how to work with it."

"I don't have any yarn."

"Then we'll go to Woolworths and buy you some."

A few days later Dr. Scott called Agnes. "Do you have a few minutes? I would like to go back to our conversation about Sharon's delivery."

"I'm eager to hear what you have to say. Sharon wasn't very talkative about her visit with you."

"That's not surprising, but the truth is, I was hoping to get a better rapport started with her. Is she always like this, and do you have any suggestions?"

Tangled Strands

"Not offhand. I just know she had some traumas as a child, something related to childbirth in addition to her negative hospital experience here."

"And I understand she's had no family support through the years?"

"For sure that has contributed a lot to her perspectives on life."

"That's not surprising. Hmm. In that case, what can we do to provide serious support for her now. What would you think about your being with Sharon during the birth?"

Ten days after Chris's visit to Larry, Agnes had a call from him saying he had an invitation to go home with a friend over the upcoming spring vacation. Her hand went to her mouth. She had been afraid of this, but with Sharon here, what did she expect? She hurried to say something—anything—lest he pick up on how disappointed she was.

"You don't mind, do you, Mother?"

She assured him she didn't, that she was happy for him to visit a friend, even as she asked God to forgive her for not being really honest. At least it was good she hadn't found a way to mention to Sharon that he would be coming. Now she didn't have to break the news that he wouldn't.

Undoubtedly Sharon's being with her had much to do with his decision. As she squelched a flash of resentment, she became aware that her disappointment was tinged with at least a little relief.

18

March had floated in with cold temperatures and uncharacteristic calm, but now the winds picked up and made the chill more penetrating. On the tenth Agnes suggested she and Sharon go shopping for fabric to make her some maternity tops.

"I think Woolworths is the only place in Willow Valley that carries fabric. They don't have a huge selection, but I've usually found something suitable for whatever I needed."

Sharon showed no enthusiasm, but Agnes pretended not to notice. Instead, she eyed the oversized red flannel shirt Sharon was wearing. "Do you still wear mostly browns and greens like you used to?"

Sharon scowled. "Those were the colors Gram always dressed me in—I suppose because of my brown eyes, but I've decided I like reds and blacks much better."

Agnes studied her. "I admit you look fine in red, but I would love to see you in something more feminine than a flannel shirt." She smiled. "What do you think?"

Sharon chuckled. "That's what I figured you'd say. So what do you have in mind?"

"Why don't we see what materials they have, as well as patterns?"

In the car Agnes said, "I'm so glad you came back from Chicago *and* that you've come to Willow Valley with me." The girl glanced at her, then looked away without commenting.

"And I can't begin to tell you how glad I am that you didn't try to ... to get rid of your baby. I'm positive God will reward you for that. One day soon he'll make *you* glad about it, too. You'll see. In no time, you're going to love your baby and be thrilled as you watch it grow."

Sharon waved a protesting hand, but Agnes continued. "Oh, I admit it won't be as much fun without a husband and father, but God gave babies a special way with people's hearts, and yours won't be any different. With God's help—"

Now Sharon did swing on Agnes and break in. "You and your family were always great on God. You talked like you thought he was real and cared about you or something. But—"

"But what?" Agnes slowed in front of Woolworths, searching for a parking space.

"But I was never that sure. When I was little, you used to talk to me about God's love, and I started to believe you until ... until ..." She shook her head and turned away. Finally she whispered, "I'm sure you know what I'm talking about."

Agnes's heart pounded, and she didn't respond as she positioned the Studebaker to parallel park. Finally, "Yes,

Sharon, I think I do know what you are referring to. Let's talk about it when we get home, okay?"

With the parking accomplished and a nickel in the meter, they headed into the store. A half hour later, they were back out with a piece of black gabardine and another of deep red taffeta.

"I think we could make this red one into a nice top to wear on Sundays and any other time you need to dress up, don't you agree?" She understood Sharon's reluctance to attend church—understood but did not intend to let it stay that way.

As they walked in the door of her house, Agnes said, "I know we were drinking tea at Fern Haven, but do you still drink hot cocoa?"

The hint of a smile flitted across the girl's face. "Yes, and I remember you used to make it for Mollie and me when we had something serious to talk about."

Agnes grinned. "Then I think now would be a good time for some, don't you? And I think I'll have some tea."

As she headed for the kitchen, she felt her heart speed up. Of course the "until" to which Sharon referred was the unforgettable day when Larry had found her on their front steps, just ten years old, frozen in a silent and horrified tableau. When he could not rouse her, he called his mother.

"Sharon? What is it?"

Silence. Only huge brown eyes staring into space.

Mollie arrived and was equally unsuccessful.

"Larry, get your father."

Tangled Strands

Dear, gentle Porter. He alone had succeeded in getting through to Sharon. Even then, her words came in short, gasping snatches. "She ... she ... killed ... herself ... ."

"Who killed herself, Sharon?"

Agnes trembled at the memory of that moment when they learned that Sharon's mother had taken her life when Sharon was very small. Porter gathered the child up in his arms, carried her into the house, and sat down with her in the rocker. He held her for an hour as the story came out in disjointed fragments. It wasn't enough that Belinda Champlin had taken her own life. Before she did that, she had killed her son, Danny.

"Where ... where were you, Sharon?"

Her sobs now alternated with hiccups. "Gram ... Gram took me ... to the ... to the store ... with her ... to buy milk."

When Porter asked how old she was when it happened, she didn't know, but after a moment she added, "I just know Danny ... was older'n me. He might have been about six."

The shrill whistle of the teakettle startled Agnes, and she shuddered afresh—especially remembering that no one had ever told the child why her mother and her brother suddenly disappeared from her life.

"No one ever told you?"

She shook her head against Porter's chest.

"How did you find out now?"

They waited a whole week before Sharon brought herself to confide to Mollie that her grandmother had burst out with the story when she was upset with Sharon.

"What else can I expect from someone whose mother killed her own child and then killed herself?"

Pain stung afresh as Agnes stirred the cocoa. No wonder the girl's fledgling trust in God's love had suffered a setback at that point. With a deep breath and a prayer, she picked up the tray with the two cups and carried them to the living room.

———♦♦♦———

Sharon watched as Mrs. Baldwin set the tray with steaming cups on the coffee table. She did not want to have this conversation, but she had a feeling it was inevitable. Mrs. Baldwin wouldn't give up until they did. For sure she wasn't going to be the one to start it, and hopefully before long she could turn the conversation to something else.

After they sipped in silence a few minutes, Mrs. Baldwin finally said, "You were talking about finding out about your mother, weren't you?"

Sharon cringed at hearing the words aloud, but at least Mrs. Baldwin said them gently. She managed a nod but didn't look up.

"I can understand how that would shake your confidence in God's lov—"

"All the memories I had of her ... I can't find them anymore." The words came out without her giving them permission. "I don't know whether it was Pa or Gram who wouldn't let us have pictures of her in the house. I suspect it was Gram."

Tangled Strands

"I'm sorry. I noticed that years ago when I used to visit your grandmother. Have you ever talked to your dad about it?"

"Not really. He and I hardly ever talk to each other about anything."

"Well, could we go back to talking about God's love? Did your confidence ever come bac—"

"Are you kidding?" She supposed she shouldn't interrupt, but she couldn't help it. "I was just beginning to believe it again when ... when ... ." The old anger reared its head, and she heard her voice rising. "...when I found out Mr. Baldwin was going to ... die."

The words hung in the air between them. Finally, Agnes said, "I know you loved my husband very much and you were upset about his ... about the brain tumor."

Sharon set her cup down and walked to the bookcase. An informal picture of Porter smiled at her, and she felt her eyes flood. Oh, rats. This was not the time to give in to feelings. After several moments of struggling, she turned. "I couldn't believe God was going to take him away." Why did her voice have to waver like that?

Mrs. Baldwin set her cup down and came toward her. When she opened her arms, Sharon resisted for a moment, but then her resolve gave way. The arms around her did feel good.

"I had a hard time believing it too."

Sharon drew back. "You were upset with me, weren't you, that I wouldn't come to your house anymore after I ... found out."

Mrs. Baldwin took a deep breath. "I was at first, yes, but my husband insisted we shouldn't be—that different people have different ways of dealing with grief. Won't you come back and sit down with me?"

She didn't feel like it, but maybe it would speed up the end to this conversation.

"I had a hard time understanding your actions because, for me, knowing I was going to lose him made me want to spend as much time with him as possible." She paused, and Sharon knew she was waiting for a response. Well, that was too bad because she wasn't contributing anymore. "But in the midst of it all, I could feel God's love as never—"

Sharon's hands clamped against her ears. When she spoke, her voice sounded almost like a hiss, but she couldn't help it. "How in the world can you believe God loves you or any of us when he took such a good man away from us?"

19

Agnes lay awake long after midnight thinking about Sharon's question and challenge. The rest of the day had been awkward. The prospect of a pleasant day of sewing together had evaporated. Except for meals, which had been painfully devoid of conversation, Sharon had kept to her room. Agnes couldn't imagine what she did up there. Mollie's shelves were full of books, but Sharon had never been a reader. Was there any chance the girl was spending the day thinking over what Agnes had said to her? Agnes spent the day praying that was the case.

In her dark bedroom now, memories of the day and her conversation with Sharon closed in on her. As confident she was in her faith, putting it into words for one who didn't have that faith was harder than she wanted to admit. She had tried to tell Sharon that death had never been God's plan for those he created, but by then the girl was too wrought up to listen.

Oh, how she missed Porter at times like this. No matter how hard she tried to resist them, in the silence of night memories of her husband's final weeks reached out to suck her in. Only twice that summer had Sharon gone to Fern Haven with them. When they invited her to his funeral, she shook her head and covered her ears with her hands. Agnes could still feel their collective shock when Sharon showed up at the church with her grandmother, her hair flattened tight against her scalp and her eyes deeper pools of shadow than they had been in a long time. That night she showed up at their house ... .

A soft buzzing near her ear made her peer at the clock on her bedside table. Six-thirty? How could that be? Last she remembered, she couldn't fall asleep.

After breakfast Agnes again swallowed surprise when Sharon voluntarily returned to the topic of the day before.

"When Tony came into my life," she began as she dried the last of the dishes, "I felt like God was finally showing me his love. What a joke that turned out to be! So I've given up on God, though I'm sure you don't want to hear that."

Agnes indicated the chair beside her at the kitchen table. "I'm sorry if that's true, Sharon, but if it's how you feel, I'm glad you're being honest with me. Nevertheless, my faith in God assures me that he *is* in control and he can make good things come out of ... bad ones." She wanted to say *bad choices* but thought better of it.

"Oh, come now! Nobody could make good out of the mess I've ended up with. All I did was go off to have a little fun, and I end up with a husband who wasn't what I thought

Tangled Strands 93

he was, then a dead husband, and now a baby I never bargained for. Nothing's going to change that!"

Despite Sharon's words and the tone of her voice, Agnes snatched at a ray of hope. She chose her words carefully. "You're right, nothing is going to change those things. They will be part of you the rest of your life. But I promise you God can weave those very things into something beautiful if you will trust him."

The girl was slow in answering. "I find that hard to believe, but I suppose I can think about it."

A memory stirred for Agnes, and her mind scrambled to capture it before it escaped. "I remember a song ... our trio at church sang it last year, something about things getting tangled up...." She jumped up and headed for the living room, calling over her shoulder, "I'm going to look for the music."

She returned empty-handed. "I can't find the songbook right now, Sharon, but I can say at least the first verse for you.

> Dear Lord, take up the tangled strands
> Where we have wrought in vain,
> That by the skill of Thy dear hands
> Some beauty might remain.

"What in the world does *wrought* mean?"

"Oh, it's an old-fashioned word for 'tried,' or 'worked.'"

"Sounds like a pretty old-fashioned song, with the word *Thy* and all."

Agnes grinned. "I suppose it is. It has a chorus and at least one more verse, and I'll keep looking for the songbook. But that's what God, our Heavenly Father, would like to do for you—bring something beautiful out of the 'tangled strands' of life you've ended up with—if you would let him."

The girl looked up but did not meet Agnes's gaze. "I would like to believe it. I wish I could, but I can't. It's just not the same for me." She gnawed at her thumbnail. "That song reminds me a little of the stuff you do with that hook and thread—"

"Oh, you mean my crocheting!" Agnes smiled. "That is an interesting thought, Sharon, and we'll have to talk about it some more. But right now I want to ask you one thing."

"What?"

"God promises to care for his children, Sharon. Can you say for sure that you are one of them?"

This time Sharon's hesitation was brief. "Probably not, at least not the way you mean, but lots of people think *all* people are God's children. I will say one thing, Mrs. Baldwin. If I ever come to … trust in God, as you call it, it will be because you are such a good ambassador for him."

Tangled Strands

20

Sharon was in the backyard filling the bird feeders when she heard Mrs. Baldwin hollering her name. Hollering? Mrs. Baldwin never hollered. Sharon dropped the container of seed on the bench and dashed into the house.

"What's the matter?"

"Chris's father called. Are you ready for this?"

Sharon's knees went weak and she reached for the nearest chair.

"They found it! They found the marriage certificate."

"You mean mine—and Tony's?"

"A genuine marriage between Sharon Marie Champlin and Michael Anthony Casanetti III."

"Really? Are you sure?" Sharon began jumping around, laughing and crying at the same time. A moment later she did a double take when Mrs. Baldwin grabbed her and began jumping with her. Suddenly the older woman stopped, and the joy on her face faded.

"What?"

"There's more. Mr. Thorne wants you and me *and* Chris and Mollie to meet him in his office at two o'clock this afternoon."

Sharon's mouth fell open. "Really?"

"Really."

"But why? Why do you think he wants to see all four of us?"

"I have no idea, Sharon, but I trust Mr. Thorne. Let's make sure we arrive promptly."

Sharon gave Chris a weak smile as he held open the door to his father's office. His return smile was stronger than hers, and he patted her shoulder as she followed Mrs. Baldwin and Mollie in. The world needed more people like Chris Thorne.

Mr. Thorne came around his desk, shook hands with each of them, and motioned to four chairs already arranged. She didn't miss the fact that Mrs. Baldwin and Mollie maneuvered her to a chair between them. Though she tried to smile, she knew it was a feeble effort.

Mr. Thorne returned to the large leather chair behind his desk and shuffled papers before looking up, his expression solemn. "I'm glad we were able to locate proof that there was a bona fide marriage, but I'm sorry to be the one to break this next news to you. We discovered more than just the fact about the marriage."

Mrs. Baldwin reached for Sharon's hand, and she noticed Chris had a grip on Mollie's. The silence was laced with tension that almost hurt.

"My people also learned that Mr. Casanetti was involved in some illegal activities and that his death may have been related to those activities."

Sharon gasped, and she heard Mollie do the same. From the corner of her eye she caught Mrs. Baldwin's fingers pressed to her mouth.

Mr. Thorne went on to explain that evidence was now clear that Tony had been involved in a stolen-cars ring. *What?* So that's what he and his cousins were doing in all those secret meetings when she worked for them at Casanetti Auto last summer. She had walked in on them once with a message and been taken aback at the alarm they showed.

Mr. Thorne was still speaking. "At first my people didn't connect it to his cousins here in Willow Valley, but with the inquiries they were making, they soon did. The Casanetti brothers here were arrested this afternoon. It will be in tomorrow's paper. The authorities in Chicago have arrested the man who assaulted Mr. Casanetti. I'm not sure what the charges will be, possibly murder."

Sharon shuddered. How could this be? Her wonderful Tony who had charmed her and thrilled her and offered her the world in a shimmering bubble—but just as suddenly the bubble had burst, the dream had died, and the Tony who took his place in Chicago had turned surly on her. Maybe she should be glad she escaped with her life.

She forced her attention back to Mr. Thorne, who had paused, elbows on his desk with finger tips tapping together as he looked from one to another. "There is another matter," he began afresh, "a rather distressing one. Mr. Casanetti left behind a good many debts."

His listeners glanced at each other, and the alarm Sharon read in her friends' eyes heightened her own. What was happening here? She turned back to Mr. Thorne, who was talking again. "Were you aware, Sharon, that your ... husband owed a lot of money to major retailers like Marshall Fields and Carson, Pirie, Scott?"

"Uh, I suppose. Those were the places he told me to shop. He wanted me to have new clothes and to buy anything I wanted for our apartment ... ." Her voice trailed off. She had loved those shopping excursions. How come everything that brought her happiness ended up turning to dust?

"Anything else, Sharon?" She startled at the sound of Chris's father voice.

"Just that ... just that I thought he was being nice when he encouraged me to buy from those fancy stores. He set it up so the stuff I bought was put on his accounts—he said he would pay everything later."

"That was nice for you, but unfortunately, paying for them didn't happen. We also learned that in the last four months before his death he lost a lot of money gambling. It looks like that's where his money went instead of to the stores." He paused.

Sharon's chest felt as if an elephant were sitting on it. The compassion she heard in Mr. Thorne's voice helped only a little as he went on. "I've spoken to my lawyer and my accountant. Since you were the one to sign the credit slips at those stores, it falls to you to pay them off."

Tangled Strands

"But—but—I don't have any money!" Panic dried her mouth and took her breath away.

"I understand that." He cleared his throat. "I have instructed one of my assistants to contact the proper parties in each store. He will explain your situation and set up with them a plan for repayment. Chris tells me you aren't employed at this time. Wherever you decide to settle down, I assume you will seek employment?"

Sharon nodded, but her mind spun out. How could she do that if she had a baby? Who would take care of it while she worked?

"Another matter is that Mr. Casanetti owed a large amount on the convertible. That, fortunately, can be sold, and that will cover most of the debt on it. Your name wasn't on the car, so that won't come back on you. Mr. Casanetti did have a few assets, as well as a few smaller debts. After the bank in Chicago has analyzed those assets, they will apply them to the other debts. If anything is left, it will go it to the two big stores and then, Sharon, you will be notified of whatever remains."

The room spun, and Sharon found it hard to breathe.

When the meeting finished and they rose from their seats, Mrs. Baldwin, Mollie and Chris closed protectively around her. How glad she was that Mr. Thorne had invited them all.

She felt Chris and Mrs. Baldwin draw back, but she and Mollie continued clinging to each other, both of them sniffling. Mollie's arms around her felt both familiar and strange. Would it be possible for them to be friends again? How odd to feel both hopeful and skeptical at the same time.

When the girls drew apart, Chris whipped out a crisp handkerchief. Leave it to Chris to always come up with the right thing.

"Allow me, ladies?" With a flourish he began dabbing the tears from their cheeks. By the time he finished, she and Mollie had begun to giggle through their sniffles.

21

On the drive home, Agnes prayed silently in the back seat of Chris's car. What could she do to comfort Sharon, to break the dark cloud of this news, perhaps even lift her spirits? When she noticed Sharon's hands in her lap, her bare fingers tightly gripped, an idea was born.

After Chris and Mollie dropped them off, as Agnes held the door open for Sharon, she asked, "Tell me, did you have a wedding ring?"

Sharon nodded, then grimaced. "Yeah, but when Rita told me what she did, I was so upset, I threw it in the trash!"

Oh, my, what next? "Come upstairs with me."

She drew the girl into her bedroom. After a moment of rummaging in an old jewelry box, she drew out a gold circlet, carved in a delicate vine motif. Without a word, she slipped it on Sharon's left ring finger.

"Look how nicely it fits—a bit loose, but I don't think it could come off. That ring belonged to my husband's mother. I am sure both he and she would be happy for you to wear it, especially under the circumstances. *I* would like you to wear it."

A smile teased the corners of Sharon's eyes, still shining with tears. Unable to speak, she embraced Agnes as she whispered a soft thank you.

The next day when Agnes saw Sharon pick up the newspaper and turn to the employment section, she smiled with relief. Clearly, in a community like Willow Valley, being a legal widow was a far different problem than being an unwed mother. But the widow of a criminal? And under the shadow of paying off his debts? How long would it take Sharon to make that kind of money?

On Saturday morning Agnes was dusting the living room when Sharon came in. "Would it be okay if I go to church with you tomorrow?"

"Of course! I've been looking forward to your joining me."

"I've been thinking about it all week, and I almost changed my mind, but I think I owe it to you."

The next day at church, there were a few stares, but several people spoke kindly to Sharon. After the service, Agnes noticed the pastor in serious conversation with her. She held her breath. Sharon was still fragile and could be unpredictable.

When Sharon joined her at the car, her face beamed. "Pastor Hawkins wanted to know if I might be interested in a part-time job for a couple of months. The church secretary, who works mornings, has a new baby and wants to stay home for a while."

Agnes smiled as she started the car. "What did you tell him?"

"I said I would talk to you. I know I need to get a job, especially with this news about Tony, but—"

"But?"

"But when I think about going out among people again and having them ask questions, I feel like forgetting it all. What ... what if they find out about Tony?"

In the end, following an honest conversation with the pastor and some reassurance from him, Sharon accepted the job. On her first day at work, Agnes found herself restless and tense, wondering how things were going. *Please, God don't let anything upset Sharon's delicate new confidence.*

Agnes breathed a prayer of gratitude when her concerns turned out to be unnecessary.

"I was surprised at how well it went. Hannah—she's the lady whose place I'm taking—is great at explaining things. I don't think I'll have much problem doing the work. She said I could call her with questions if I need to."

On Friday, Sharon was feeling confident enough that she offered to make a trip to the market to pick up a few items Agnes needed. When Agnes realized Sharon had been gone almost an hour, she became concerned. She began wandering to the front window to watch for her. It had been snowing since three o'clock, but snow shouldn't bother Sharon.

A little after five, a strange car stopped in front of the house, and a driver got out. She was surprised to recognize Ethan McCrae, the young photographer who directed the choir at church. He hurried around the car and opened the door for Sharon. By the time they entered the living room, snowflakes flecked his neatly trimmed blond beard.

"My car had a flat, and Ethan happened by on his way home from work—"

"You recognized Sharon?"

"Yes, she was standing out looking at the tire, and I remembered seeing her in church with you."

"He tried to fix it for me—"

"But the spare had no air in it, so her car was still parked along Elm Street. I would offer to go home for my pump and get it going for her, but the lady who takes care of Jamie likes to get home before dark. I could do it on my way to work in the morning, if you can wait that long." He glanced from one woman to the other.

"I don't have to be at work until nine." Sharon turned to Agnes. "Can you drive me to pick it up?"

It was arranged. Over supper Sharon asked, "Who's Jamie?"

"He's Ethan's son. He's about four years old. Ethan's wife was killed in a tragic car accident a couple years ago."

"Around here?"

"No. If I remember right, Ethan has only been here since a little before Thanksgiving. I think he comes from Buffalo. He sings beautifully as well as directing the choir."

When they finished eating, Sharon cleared the table while Agnes put the food away, but then Sharon waved her away. "*I've* got the dishes, now shoo!"

Tangled Strands

"Okay, thanks. I've got to pull out two rows of my crochet project—"

"You gotta *what?*"

"I discovered I made a mistake two rows back, so I have to pull out—"

"You're kidding! You would pull apart something you've done? Why?"

"Because I want the finished product to be correctly done so it can look good, can be something I'm proud of."

"Well, if I ever learn to do that, I … I don't think I could bear to pull out anything I've spent so much time doing."

Agnes smiled knowingly but said nothing.

The next day she took Sharon to the Woolworth store to look at baby yarn. No, she didn't want blue; she didn't want the baby to be a boy. Agnes cautioned against pink because she had no assurance it would be a girl. They settled on a soft baby green.

Agnes was not surprised when Sharon turned out to be a capable learner with deft fingers.

"I can't believe you finished that bonnet in a day and a half."

"Well, those two stitches weren't hard to learn. Can I start on the sweater now?"

22

Sharon hung up the phone and climbed the stairs to Mrs. Baldwin's room, where she found the door ajar. She could feel her heart pounding.

Agnes looked up from her crocheting. "Who was on the phone?"

"My-my pa."

"Your pa! He's back in town? Then you *must* invite him and your grandmother to come for a meal."

"Gram will never come!"

"You don't think your father could get her to come? I can't believe she isn't interested in the prospect of a great-grandbaby—"

"She'll probably just figure ... "

"Figure what, Sharon?"

"Figure I'll be looking to dump the kid on her to take care of it." A deep sigh escaped, and Mrs. Baldwin's open mouth and raised eyebrows made Sharon turn away.

"Oh, Sharon, I'm sorry you feel that way. I guess it's true that sometimes your grandmother felt overwhelmed with the responsibility of raising you, but don't you think you're overreacting a little? I would really like to invite them to come tomorrow evening."

Sharon's voice faltered a little when she extended the invitation, and it trembled even more when her pa accepted. She couldn't decide whether she was delighted or scared to death.

She peeled potatoes and carrots for Mrs. Baldwin to put in the old black skillet with the roast. Her first lesson in making homemade yeast rolls intrigued her, and she was relieved when Mrs. Baldwin agreed the everyday dishes for the table might be more appropriate than the Sunday ones.

But when she opened the front door to them and discovered how shabby Gram looked, she cringed. Had she really not had a new dress in—in what? Fifteen years? When they sat down at the table and Gram tucked her napkin under her chin, Sharon wanted to crawl under the table. Despite catching a comforting wink from Mrs. Baldwin, Sharon couldn't help being mortified.

And her poor pa! His shirt was less shabby than Gram's dress, but he was clearly uncomfortable in someone else's home. She could tell he was trying to respond to Mrs. Baldwin's efforts at conversation, yet they never seemed to keep a real one going. Flashes of childhood crowded in. No wonder she had spent so much time here at the Baldwins' when she was growing up. How might her life have been different if she had been born into this family instead of the one she was? The idea that God did not seem at all fair was not a new thought.

Eager to escape the tension at the table, she stood up and began clearing their plates. With a glance at her pa who was still eating, Mrs. Baldwin motioned for her to stop, then gave her a big smile.

"Now, Sharon, your grandmother and I are going to clean up from dinner while you take your dad out for a walk." Her grandmother's scowl deepened, but no one ventured a protest.

Out on the street, Sharon fell in step beside her pa and wondered what he and she would find to talk about. She could remember few times over the years when he and she had carried on a conversation any better than the one at the table just now. Was that why he drove his truck so much—because he liked not having to talk to people?

She supposed the baby would be a good starting point, but Pa beat her to it.

"I hear tell you're fixin' to make me a gram'pa."

How cute to hear a trace of embarrassment shining through his words. She felt herself grinning. She hadn't realized how much her father's pleasure would mean to her. "That's what they tell me, too, and I guess it's getting pretty obvious by now. I'm–I'm glad you're glad."

"How long you still gotta wait?"

"About three months."

"What you aimin' to name the baby?"

"I still don't have a clue about that. I haven't even started thinking on it. You got any suggestions?"

He thought a moment. "Can't say as I do. All 'at comes to mind is me and your ma talking on names when our first baby was ... on the way."

Oh, please! She didn't feel like hearing talk of her mother and the past—but she supposed she had to be polite. "What did you do?"

"Well, I had me a good buddy when I was ridin' the railroad, 'fore I married your ma. His name was Daniel O'Casey, but ever'body called him Danny. He was a right good guy, an' it was a right good name. That's why I chose it for my son."

His son.

Her brother.

A brother who came to her only in rare and fading flashes of memory. Her breath caught, and she couldn't bring herself to comment. Pa said no more either. So much for a breakthrough in father-daughter communication. But she knew she had found a name for her baby if it was a boy. Maybe she could honor that long-lost brother in this small way.

———♦♦♦———

Agnes chatted cheerfully as she helped Willa gather up the dishes and stack them by the sink, but her mind was on the man who just walked out of her kitchen. Even as she drew hot water, added a squirt of Joy, and turned the washing task over in response to Willa's offer, she couldn't get Frank Champlin's dark eyes out of her mind. Life had offered him so little, and her heart went out to him.

Tangled Strands

And the woman standing at her sink—what had life offered *her*? When Larry and Mollie were children, Agnes had tried to befriend her. If she had done a better job, perhaps they would have found out sooner about Sharon's mother. She still had so many unanswered questions about that tragedy. The counters wiped, she picked up a glass and began to dry it.

"I'm sorry I haven't come to visit you in recent times like I used to, Willa."

She tried to draw Willa into conversation by going back to some of the visits they had shared during Sharon's childhood. She asked what she hoped were friendly, unthreatening questions about Willa's present life and activities.

She found there was precious little worth talking about.

When they were finished with the clean-up, she pulled a chair out from the kitchen table and motioned for Willa to sit across the corner from her. She smiled as warmly as she knew how and then grew serious.

"There's something we talked about years ago, Willa, and I wish we had talked about it more. It's about having peace with God and the difference that makes in our lives. Do you know what I'm talking about?"

Willa was silent a moment, staring at her plump fingers. "I guess I ain't given God much thought for a long time now. My folks, they always sent us to Sunday school, and I always made sure Frank went. In fact, Frank and Belinda used to attend right regular for a while."

"I'm glad to hear that."

"But Belinda couldn't get over that baby 'at died, though I always b'lieved it weren't none o' her fault."

Oh, yes. Memory stirred, something about a baby who died. Did Sharon know about that? Expectantly she looked back at Willa, but her gaze was frozen on her tight, still fingers. When at last she spoke, her voice too was tight.

"After what Belinda done to her and Danny, I decided God weren't doin' too good a job."

23

Aside from her son's brief call about visiting his friend during his vacation, Agnes had not heard from him since Chris's visit. She ached to know how he was feeling, what he was thinking—about Sharon, about her return to Willow Valley, about her pregnancy, and especially about his relationship with her. Was he still in love with her? Agnes had no way to know, and she had to be content with what Chris reported. She had sent Larry a couple of notes, making an effort to sound like she always did, only casually mentioning anything related to Sharon's presence in the house. He had not responded.

She was turning out her light on Friday night of his vacation week when the phone rang. Her heart quickened at the sound of her son's voice. He chatted for several minutes, telling about the time with his friend's family, yet she sensed he had more than that on his mind. Her heart tightened when he grew quiet.

"Would it be okay if I come home for the weekend before I start classes again?" Without waiting for an answer, he added, "I'm going to ask Sharon to marry me."

———♦♦♦———

Late Saturday afternoon, Sharon studied her reflection in the hall mirror, turning this way and that in the red taffeta maternity top Mrs. Baldwin helped her make. She had just finished hemming it so she could wear it for this date with Larry. But a date with Larry? What could that be about? Ever since he asked her on the phone this morning, she had been trying to figure out what she might expect from him and how she should act with him.

Her own feelings puzzled her. The prospect of seeing him again made a thread of excitement hum in her veins. Were his eyes still that charcoal blue that had always intrigued her? Probably. But that was only part of it. He had been a solid friend for years, one who seemed to know what was going on inside her and who could set her heart at ease better than anyone.

But that was before last summer and what she did.

When she thought about that, a tightening in her gut stirred alarm at the thought of facing him. Leaving town with Tony without a word to her friends was bad enough, but shunning Larry like she had the last part of the summer had been unforgiveable. Had Tony with all his charms really cast that much of a spell on her?

Though she remembered every word of the brief conversation with Larry, it didn't help. None of it told her *why* he wanted to see her. Was he going to take her to task for last summer? He had every right to, but that didn't sound like the Larry she had always known.

At that moment, the image in the mirror caught her attention. The red top should be making her smile, but instead, she groaned. Why, oh why, did maternity clothes make you look like the side of a mountain? With a cry of frustration, she stripped the garment off over her head and flung it into the corner.

Glancing at the mirror again, she groaned. *You ninny!* Of course they do! She was beginning to *look* like the side of a mountain. She struck her head with the heel of her hand and slumped against the wall. If only she could take this thing inside her and "park" it somewhere for the evening. Larry was coming to take her out, and she liked that idea well enough—but she couldn't bear for him to see her like this.

She dragged herself to her feet, flopped across her bed, and hugged the pillow to her face. Several minutes later, she heard Mrs. Baldwin come into her room.

"Sharon? Is something wrong?"

She rolled over and wiped the back of her hand across her eyes.

"*Oh, Sharon!* What is it?"

"I can't go on a date with Larry—" Her voice broke off in a squeak. "Not when …when I'm in a … family way!" She bit her lip and turned away.

When Mrs. Baldwin sat down beside her on the bed, Sharon rolled off the other side, fled to the bathroom, and slammed the door.

With the sharp crack of the door, she dropped back to the present with a thud. In less than an hour Larry would be here, and she had no idea what he wanted. Could he simply be in search of a pleasant evening with an old friend? That seemed unlikely, but so did the possibility of his wanting to settle some kind of a score with her.

All she could think of was what she had lost when she allowed herself to be swept away by a whirlwind. She had gotten what she wanted. Now she would give anything to give it back.

———◆◆◆———

Trying to remember that rebuffs from Sharon were not to be taken personally, Agnes picked up the offending garment and hung it back in the closet. All the time she and Sharon had invested in the new garment—gone to waste? No! It was a lovely piece of clothing, and Sharon would need it in the weeks ahead.

She had wondered what Sharon's response would be to Larry's request for a date, and she had been surprised when the girl accepted without discussion or comment. She herself had slept little the night after Larry's call. How could he consider marrying Sharon? True, for several years she had anticipated having Sharon as a daughter-in-law—but *now?* She had certainly never pictured her family including someone who ran off with a criminal and married him.

What kind of marriage started out with the bride carrying another man's child? Okay, so Mary and Joseph did it, but that was different. Very different. A marriage like this would be a challenge even for two people deeply in love, but did love even play into this picture anymore—if it ever had?

She crossed the hall to her room and dropped onto her bed. A conversation she had had with her son the morning after Sharon's disappearance reared up to haunt her. Sitting across the breakfast table from Larry, she had watched him move his spoon in idle circles in his coffee and stare into the depths of the steaming liquid. As his mother, she couldn't imagine the bewilderment he must be experiencing.

"She had come so far over the years, hadn't she, Mother? I mean, she didn't seem to be so much at war with the world as she did a few years ago, you know what I mean?"

"Yes, I would have to agree with you."

"I thought ... I really thought the future was going to take shape for us ... ." He pushed his coffee away and rested his elbows on the table before running his fingers through his thick, wavy hair.

"Son, isn't it true this wasn't exactly sudden, that things haven't been the same for some time now?"

Larry straightened and met his mother's eyes in a way so like his father that the old anguish tugged at her heart. However, she couldn't remember ever seeing such misery in Porter's eyes, not even when he knew he was dying.

She had pushed his coffee back in front of him, and he took a sip. "Larry, what ... what do you think about Sharon's relationship with God?"

He glanced at her, then looked away and did not answer. Was he being torn between what he knew to be truth and what he *wanted* the truth to be?

When he did not speak, she went on. "Do you remember her ever making any kind of commitment of herself or her life to God, ever taking a stand in spiritual things?"

"N-no, I guess not. But she always went to church with us—and to all the church activities we went to. I never gave it a thought but that she believed the same—"

"Son, you've been taught all your life that going to church doesn't make one a child of God—no more than going into a garage makes you a car. After you went away to college, Sharon was never as much involved in church activities as when she was younger."

"So what are you saying, Mother? That she simply went along with us in matters of faith—without making it her own?"

In her room now, Agnes shook her head and scowled. Surely, Larry was not going to ignore all that. Nevertheless, after a night of restlessness and prayer, she knew she had to trust her God and her son and wait to see what happened.

She was quite sure Sharon knew nothing of Larry's intentions. She had told Agnes he said he would be in town that evening and would like to take her to dinner. All day Saturday, she had flitted around the house like a schoolgirl, a faraway look in her eyes—until she went upstairs to get dressed.

Heading back downstairs now, Agnes sighed and tried not to fret.

———✦✦✦———

As excited as a child over what he was about to do, Larry could not resist stopping by his sister's before picking up Sharon. He was unprepared for Chris and Mollie's response to his news.

"You're *what?* Larry, you've got to be kidding!"

He stared at his sister—for years Sharon's best friend. Before he could summon a response, Chris spoke.

"Are you sure you've thought this through, Lare? Have you considered everything involved?"

"Larry, you *can't!* You deserve a whole lot better than Sharon after what she did. She isn't worthy of you anymor—"

"Mollie!" Chris cut in. "Mol, please don't—"

"I don't understand you two." Larry looked from one to the other. "True, Sharon has been on a detour from the direction we expected our lives to take, and I admit it has caused pain. But God can forgive her for that. She's back now, and she's free, and she needs a father for that baby."

When he closed the door behind him, he glanced back to see Chris and Mollie still shaking their heads. As he crossed the parking lot, he was whistling.

24

Agnes studied Sharon as she came down the stairs. She now sported a white blouse under an open, flowery shirt Agnes didn't think came from any maternity department. Her dark hair was pulled into a ponytail and tied with a ribbon. One thing she had to say for the girl, no matter how often emotions sabotaged her, she could come out on top of them when she needed to.

Agnes couldn't even tell she had been crying. A touch of color on her eyelids with a bit of red lipstick combined to give her a gentle look that wasn't typically Sharon. She had replaced the garish red on her nails with a softer shade. Agnes could not remember ever seeing her look so vulnerable except the day of Porter's funeral.

She watched her wander from room to room, closing Venetian blinds against the gathering night, straightening a crooked rug, then getting her coat from the closet and laying it over a chair. A prick of shame niggled Agnes for not feeling up to praying *with* Sharon right now. Instead, she sent a silent prayer heavenward as she gave the girl a quick hug before heading upstairs to spend a valued evening on her current quilting project. She had a feeling she would be praying much of that time, too.

She was at the top of the stairs when the sound of the doorbell stopped her. She heard the door open and her son say, "Hello, Sharon."

Sharon's response was too soft to hear.

──♦♦♦──

Afterwards, Larry could not have told how it happened except that it seemed the most natural thing in the world. When Sharon opened the door, his arms opened of their own accord, and she stepped into their circle. For a moment he held her while she nestled against him. Then he drew back, touched his lips to her forehead, and gazed at her. She gave him a shaky smile before turning to pick up her coat.

"Oh, do you mind if I take my bag up to my room first?"

She shook her head.

Upstairs, he stood still and tried to get a grip on his churning emotions. For one sweet, sustained moment, time had evaporated as he stood with Sharon in his arms. It felt as if she had never been away, as if nothing had ever come between them. And then he realized something *had* come between them, quite literally, as he became aware of an unaccustomed pressure on his mid-section.

Sharon's baby.

Tony Casanetti's baby—but no, he would not think about that. Tony was dead. Sharon was very much alive, and so was that baby who needed a father. With a determined shake of his head, he set his bag down. Hearing his mother call to him from her room, he stuck his head in the door and greeted her before returning downstairs. He found Sharon standing where he had left her.

"Where would you like to go for dinner?"

"That's up to you."

"How about the Spinning Wheel?"

Her mouth dropped open, and that made him grin. Had she been to Willow Valley's attempt at an elegant restaurant other than when he took her for her high school graduation?

"Sharon?"

"That would be nice," she murmured, "but I mustn't eat too much."

His raised his eyebrows, and she grinned sheepishly. "If I'm not careful, I'll gain more weight than I should."

Larry carefully avoided the temptation to glance at her midsection. Instead, he held her coat for her, then offered his arm, and they went out the door.

An awkward silence gripped them on the drive to the restaurant. What would be appropriate to talk about? He had no desire to hear about her time in Chicago and certainly not about that guy she took off with. Asking her about her father and grandmother could generate sparks. If he chatted about his classes for his master's degree in history, she would be bored to tears. Bewilderment over Chris and Mollie's reaction to his plan still lurked uneasily in the back of his mind. As he held the heavy oak door of the restaurant for Sharon, he smiled at her, but her return smile wavered and then faded.

He glanced around. The Spinning Wheel had not changed, and the way it managed to make "rustic" look elegant always amazed him. Yes, the lights hung from huge wheel shapes, but those wheels were solid oak and the lights were crystal chandeliers. The ladder-back chairs were also oak, and the crisp calico tablecloths sported matching cloth napkins.

After the waiter brought their glasses of iced tea and took their orders, Larry studied her. "So how are you? How long have you been back in Willow Valley?"

She answered, and he listened, but his mind kept slipping away to his purpose for the evening. He had a mission, and eagerness to get on with it kept his fingers tapping. Their salads came, and they ate them while he listened to her tell about her job as secretary at the Village Chapel. She surprised him when she shyly mentioned that his mother had taught her to crochet and she was making something for the baby, but he knew he wasn't showing enough interest.

He should wait until their dinners arrived so they wouldn't be interrupted by the waiter, but anticipation kept prodding him. So when Sharon set her fork down after finishing her salad, he reached across the table with both hands. She stared at him, then at his hands, her eyes round with questions. Finally she placed her hands in his. For a fleeting moment it occurred to him to panic over what he was about to do, but he ignored the feeling.

"Sharon, I've come to ask you to marry me. I want you to be my wife, and I want to be a father to your baby."

Her eyes widened, and she tried to withdraw her hands, but he held them fast. "Hey! What's the matter?"

The waiter arrived with their dinners, and he released her hands. When the waiter left, Sharon began fidgeting, arranging her silverware just so, rearranging the napkin in her lap, all without looking at Larry and without starting to eat.

"Sharon? Look to me. That's not such a strange idea, is it?"

"I ... Larry ... it's so unexpected."

"Why do you say that ... after all the years we were such good friends?"

"That's true, but ... I mean, everything is different now. I–I wasn't sure you would even want to see me!"

"I wasn't sure myself how to react when I first heard you were back. I wasn't sure you would want to see *me*. But the more I thought about it—"

"What would your mom and Mollie say?"

"I'm not worried about that. Mollie and Mother have always loved you!"

"Your mother has been more than kind to me, Larry, but that doesn't mean she would like you marrying me *now*."

This conversation was not going well. Apparently Sharon needed time to get used to the idea. He pulled his hands back and picked up his fork.

"Well, we can talk more about it after we get back to the house. For now, just relax and enjoy your dinner." He cut a piece of pork chop but kept it on the end of his fork. "So tell me how you found your way to Fern Haven. Did you remember the right roads and everything?"

As they ate their dinner, conversation wandered back to old times at Fern Lake. That seemed to be safe territory.

"Remember when Chris and I tossed you into the lake fully dressed? How old were you?"

"About ten, I think. What about the time Mollie and I had you and Chris thinking we were drowning?"

"We didn't really think—"

"Then why did you go running to the house for your dad?"

The light camaraderie was pleasant, but as hard as he tried, Larry couldn't keep it going. Underneath ran an invisible tension that he couldn't define. Neither said a word as he paid the bill and they went out to the car.

——♦♦♦——

Sharon huddled on her side of Larry's 1949 Plymouth as he drove back to the house. Her mind raced. What was Larry doing asking her to marry him? In all her concerns about the evening, that possibility had never occurred to her. She had expected a simple evening of dinner and maybe a walk along the river, certainly not a proposal of marriage.

In her lap, her fingers were laced so tightly they hurt. She started to touch her midsection, but stifled the urge. She didn't want to draw Larry's attention to it. What could be his reason for proposing—and so totally without warning? She couldn't

Tangled Strands

imagine his wanting to marry her after the way she had treated him and what she had done. And most certainly not now that she was expecting another man's child!

All too soon, the car pulled into the Baldwins' driveway and Larry was coming around to open the door for her. Help! What was she going to say to him?

25

As Larry mounted the porch steps with Sharon, he said, "I wish it weren't so cold. I like sitting on the porch, especially on the swing. You had a swing at your house, didn't you? Is it still there?"

Sharon murmured what sounded like a yes as he held open the door to the house. Why was she so quiet? And what kind of reaction was that to his proposal? He was eager to get back to the subject and find those answers.

He motioned her to sit beside him on the davenport, but she ignored the gesture and instead sat in the rocking chair. What was going on here? How could he recapture the camaraderie they had enjoyed for at least a while at the Spinning Wheel? He went to the kitchen, found some chocolate-chip cookies in his mother's cookie jar, and brought Sharon one. She took it, murmured thank you without meeting his eyes, but did not take a bite.

"Do you remember the time you and Mollie threw cookies to Chris and me out in the lake—but missed?"

That brought a chuckle from her, but it died quickly. Somehow he had to get her to relax so he could renew the marriage discussion.

The next moment, Sharon's face froze, and one hand went to her midsection.

He jumped up and went to her. "Sharon? What is it?"

She shook her head and refused to meet his eyes. "It's no use, Larry." The coldness in her voice sent a shiver along his neck. "We can't go back or pretend nothing has changed."

He reached down, put his finger under her chin, and made her look at him. "I don't agree with you. What just happened? You looked like you'd seen a ghost."

She pushed him away, stood, and walked to the fireplace, her back to him.

"Hey? What *happened?*"

She swung on him, eyes flashing. "All right, if you must know! The baby. It moved, and it brought me back to reality with a thud. What about that, Larry Baldwin? You can't be saying you want to marry me with a baby three months from being born!"

"But that's just it, Sharon. It's *because* of the baby that I want to marry you. This is no time for a girl to be alone. You need a husband and your baby needs—"

Her face changed sharply. What had he said to upset her? With a decisive toss of her head, Sharon pushed him aside and stormed to the kitchen. Nonplused, he stared after her for a moment before following.

Tangled Strands

"Oh, come on, Sharon! Will you please sit down so we can discuss—?"

She swung on him, and the fire in her eyes stopped him mid-sentence. "Let me get this straight, Larry Baldwin. You want to marry me because I'm having a baby but I don't have a husband? Is that right?"

"Well, yes, but—"

She flung herself at him and beat his chest with her fists. "Then, NO! A thousand times *NO!*"

26

The hint of spring that graced the daylight hours had vanished without a trace as Larry Baldwin paced the streets of Willow Valley. He tugged the zipper higher on his jacket and turned up his collar as his mind replayed yet again the evening's conversation with Sharon.

What a moron he had been!

Of course a girl wanted to be married for herself, not her baby! He credited himself with being an intelligent person, but a five-year-old could have done better. He had rushed into the proposal too quickly, without planning his strategy. He should have found a more romantic approach.

But he had been so pleased with himself and his decision, so sure he was doing what was right, necessary, and honorable, that he had not considered the possibility of Sharon responding negatively. When he tried to apologize, to insist she misunderstood his intentions, she refused to listen and asked him to leave.

Leave? Never mind it was *his* mother's home and he was supposed to sleep there tonight. Yet leaving had been the only thing to do at that moment. Nevertheless, the whole scenario had felt so strange. In the past, he had always been the one who calmed Sharon when she was upset, who found ways to distract her from troubled emotions.

But what could he do when she was angry with *him*? He couldn't remember that ever happening before. He had always been able to steady her, to help her sort out her feelings and get a handle on them. She had depended on him, needed him. He realized now he had relished that dependence.

And now? She was right. Things were different. Her life now held a significant chapter in which he had no part. With a decisive shake of his head, he abandoned that line of thought. That "chapter" was now a closed book, over and done with. The future was what they had to look to, to plan for, and to provide for. And that was why it was right for him to ask her to marry him.

He glanced at his watch by the glow of the streetlight. Would his mother and Sharon have gone to bed by now? His mother must have heard Sharon's outburst and the sound of the door she had slammed behind him. Surely she had come down and talked with Sharon? If anyone could make Sharon think more reasonably, it would be his mother. When Sharon calmed down, he would talk to her again, and he was sure she would listen. But he did not have much time. In less than twenty-four hours he needed to be on his way back to his classes at Groverton.

He wandered back toward the house and noted with satisfaction that the lights were out. His mother had left the door unlocked for him. As he tiptoed up the stairs, no sounds came from the other bedrooms. He drifted off to sleep thinking that Sharon, in Mollie's bed, was on the other side of the wall from him.

———◆◆◆———

Sharon lay awake, staring wide-eyed at the dark ceiling, her mind still reeling from the evening's events. She heard Larry's stealthy footsteps on the stairs and the quiet click of his door as he shut it. She too realized his bed was right on the other side of the wall from where she lay. In a gesture she did not understand, she reached out and laid her hand against the cool wall between them. Wouldn't it be nice if they could close the personal gulf that separated them just as simply?

She kept reliving the moment when she opened the door to Larry. The sight of him before her, his smoothly chiseled features exactly as they had haunted her dreams in Chicago, and the sound of her name on his lips had unnerved her. During that moment in his arms, sweet had danced with bitter.

Not in her wildest daydreaming had it occurred to her that Larry might show up asking her to marry him. She still did not understand. He and she had bantered about marriage when they were teens but not since he went away to college. Why was he suggesting it now? The only answer had to be that he felt sorry for her or felt some mixed-up sense of responsibility for this baby that had turned her life so upside down.

She crammed her knuckles against her teeth to stifle an urge to scream. That was not like Larry! He had always been her tower of strength, her refuge, the one who understood her as she was. How could he have changed so?

Don't forget what a bum rap you dealt him! Frustration and pain flooded in again. And shame. She had run away—with a criminal—and married him! When Mrs. Baldwin came downstairs shortly after Sharon pushed Larry out the door, their conversation had been brief and awkward. Larry's mother must have known about her son's intention, and of course she had heard Sharon's raised voice. All Sharon had to do was give a brief report of what had happened.

The fact that Mrs. Baldwin reacted with a long pause before responding carried its own message. Her intuition had been right that Larry's mother would no longer applaud a marriage. Not that she blamed her, but she could not ignore the stab of disappointment the knowledge brought. In the last month, Mrs. Baldwin had been a staunch and understanding friend. In the moment that her silence enveloped Sharon, Sharon felt as starkly alone as she had when she fled from Tony.

But Mrs. Baldwin had not let it end there. Sitting on the davenport beside Sharon, she had reached out her hand and said quietly, "Sharon, I think the only thing we can do is lay all this in the hands of our Heavenly Father."

She bowed her head, and Sharon did, too. The prayer she offered was simple and direct. She admitted having no idea what God's plan was for Larry and Sharon—or the baby. The part that amazed Sharon most was when she expressed confidence in "the God who runs the universe without missing a beat." Surely it couldn't be true that such a God cared about her and her baby, but Mrs. Baldwin seemed to think so.

As Sharon reflected on the prayer now in the darkness of her room, the sense of aloneness washed over her again. Not that Mrs. Baldwin had said anything wrong, yet Sharon sensed a barrier between them. The emotional support she had drawn from the Baldwins through the years seemed to be slipping away, and now—

A twinge against her ribs interrupted her thoughts. An overwhelming feeling of tenderness flowed in to replace the loneliness.

She was not alone!

Her baby was there, as close as any human being could be to another. Her baby belonged to her, only her. While previously that fact had aroused only regret and apprehension, she now sensed it flowing softly over her with warmth and comfort. Her baby would belong to her—and love her.

And I love you, just as you are.

The thought startled her. Did God really love her, as Mrs. Baldwin claimed? Could he really accept her, forgive her, and want to help her?

She rolled over, got out of bed, and walked to the window. A three-quarter moon posed lazily above the horizon. A rush of memories almost took her breath away. Moonlight and

Larry Baldwin were inseparably woven together in her mind. She and Larry had spent so many—

Suddenly a longing for him flooded her so strongly that she felt suffocated. She could not bear that her last words to him had been angry, rejecting words. Without giving herself time to think, she grabbed her housecoat, pulled it on over her pajamas, slipped into the hall, and tapped softly on his door.

27

In the silence that followed, panic struck and she turned to flee back to her room. But the squeak of the floor behind her immobilized her. She heard the door open softly and his tentative whisper, "Sharon?"

She froze but did not turn around.

In a moment, he was beside her. With an arm around her shoulders, he drew her toward the stairs. Down in the kitchen he turned on a light.

"Would you like some cocoa or something?"

She nodded without looking at him.

While he pulled a bottle of milk from the fridge and cups from a cupboard, she watched him. His dark curls were already tousled, and she yearned to smooth them. When he caught her eyes on him, she felt a blush coming on but resisted the urge to look away. Instead, they gazed at each other several silent seconds until a faint hum began in the pot on the stove.

Neither spoke until he set steaming cups between them and sat down at the table with her. Then he took her hand and waited for her to meet his eyes.

"Sharon? What is it? No! First, I want to tell you how sorry I am for handling this evening badly. It was wrong of me to sound like I wanted to marry you just because of the baby. Can you forgive me?"

She hesitated, then nodded and concentrated on stirring her cocoa.

Larry went on. "That would not be fair to any of us. I guess I got carried away and didn't give as much thought as I should have to ... to things being different than they used to be. That wasn't smart of me."

She looked at him then and said wistfully, "It would be nice, wouldn't it? But besides *things* not being the same, I'm— I'm sure *we're* not the same—at least, I know I'm not, and I doubt there's any way to go back ... ."

When he started to protest, she held up her hand to cut him off. "No, Larry. Don't say anything. I'm going to have to do some thinking. I promise I will."

A smile flickered on his face, but she hurried on. "What happened upstairs was—well, I couldn't bear that I had talked so ratty to you, and I wanted to say I'm sorry. For now, could you just talk to me for a little while? Tell me about your classes, your apartment—anything."

"Okay." He thought a moment. "You heard about the teacher I was asked to cover one class for?" She nodded. "Well, he was more seriously injured in that fall than they realized, and he hasn't been able to return to teaching. So I have continued with the class. At the end of this school year, I will be finished with all my courses for the Masters, and this summer I'm going to throw myself into my thesis."

"You won't be going to camp this summer?"

"No. After being a counselor every summer since I was fifteen, this past summer was my last. This fall I will have to finish up the thesis, but I also hope to have more classes to teach. A professor in the history department is going to retire, and I think I have a chance of being offered some of his courses."

Ten minutes later, he pushed an errant strand of hair off her forehead and suggested they go back to bed. He had cooperated with her request, not asking questions about her months away from Willow Valley, and she knew he was too much a gentleman to ask anything about her condition. She was grateful. She had a feeling he wouldn't want to hear about those things anyway.

Outside her room, he turned her toward him and traced her cheek softly with the back of a finger. "Do you think you can sleep now?"

She nodded, then watched, mesmerized, as he brushed his lips, feather light, across hers. Then he turned her around, pushed her gently through the door, and closed it firmly behind her.

———◆◆◆———

The next morning, Agnes looked up from pouring coffee for Larry to see Sharon appearing cheerily for breakfast as if nothing unusual had happened the night before. Dressed in gray pants and sweatshirt, she fixed a bowl of cereal without looking at either of them. She made small talk about the sunshine and then, with bowl in hand, she backed through the swinging door.

"Oh, by the way," she announced airily, "I won't be going to church this morning. I have ... something I have to do." The door swished closed behind her.

Agnes raised her eyebrows at Larry.

"Well," he began, imitating Sharon's nonchalance, "I know at least one thing she has to do. She promised to think about what I said last night."

"What you said?"

"Yeah. We had a little midnight conversation here in the kitchen, and she said she would think about it." He grinned at his mother, but she did not return the grin.

"Larry ... ." *How could it be so hard to express yourself to your own child?* "Do I gather you're truly considering marrying Sharon even if she doesn't have any interest in a relationship with God?"

He looked up sharply. "What do you mean, Mother? I know what we talked about last summer, but can you be sure about that?"

"I think I can. She's told me since she came back that she doesn't have any faith in God's love."

Larry glanced away. "I don't know what to say. I know that's important, but I can't bear the thought of Sharon being alone for all this—"

"But she's not alone! And that's not enough reason to marry her!"

Tangled Strands

"Mother! After all the years Sharon and I went together, don't tell me you never thought about our getting married."

"Of course I did, but that was before she left you for a guy like Tony!"

"And you're going to keep holding that against her?" He set his coffee cup down hard. "What happened to forgiveness?"

Agnes cringed. In all his twenty-two years, Larry had never spoken to her like that. She could hear her voice rise as she answered him.

"Forgiving her is not the issue, Larry. Of course I've done that. What concerns me now is her relationship with God."

He pushed his chair back and shook his head. "Right now I have asked Sharon to marry me, and there's no way I'm going to renege on that. Besides, I don't want to! I want to love her and take care of her. Hey, the Bible gives clear instructions that we're to love and care for the needy—especially widows and orphans!" With a lift of his chin and a satisfied, "So-there!" glance at his mother, he rose and pushed in his chair. "I've got to shave," and he was gone.

Agnes watched him sadly. Everything in her wanted to protest his reasoning, but she resisted. Challenging him might only drive him to further defensiveness. Larry had never been careless in spiritual matters.

28

After Larry and his mother left for church, Sharon got in her car and drove aimlessly around town. She needed to think, but she couldn't do it at the Baldwins'. The house was too full of memories and of the very presence of the people she needed to think about. After fifteen minutes of aimless driving, she pulled her car up to the curb by River Park.

The park was abandoned on a late winter Sunday morning. Sharon locked her car, zipped her jacket to her chin, plunged her hands in her pockets, and wandered downhill in the direction of the river. Naked strands of willow drooped forlornly, yearning for spring to bring them new life. A lone squirrel looking, she thought, equally impatient with winter, peered cautiously from a hole in a nearby oak. He and Sharon gazed at each other a moment before he disappeared.

She leaned against a tree, its sturdy bark rough against her head, and closed her eyes. How could so many different emotions tumble around inside her at the same time? When she thought of her time with Larry in the wee hours, a warm feeling crept over her, but a moment later visions of her angry response to him charged in. Larry had seen her angry often enough, had even calmed her many times, but never, ever, had her anger been directed at him like it was last night. What made her react like that?

In the kitchen he had been like the Larry she had always known. But before that, he hadn't seemed the same. How could he propose marriage without a word of discussion about the past? By the time he returned from his summer on staff at camp, her world was spinning dizzily in Tony's orbit. When Larry tried to see her, she ignored him. When he pleaded for an explanation, she hung up on him.

A gust of wind off the river chilled her face, and she pulled her coat closer. The chill in her heart felt just as real. How could she have treated Larry like that after all those years when he had been a faithful, unfaltering friend?

The answer came along with another flurry of cold air. Could it have been guilt that made her scorn Larry's efforts to communicate with her—guilt over how she was hurting him? Fear had probably played a part, too—fear that if she saw him, her feelings would betray her and Tony's magic spell over her might be broken.

And her friends, Mollie and Agnes, even Chris—she must have hurt them, too. She had stoutly avoided thinking about that, but she no longer could. The words bounced off the sun's reflection on the river: *After all the Baldwins did for you, how could you have treated them so shabbily?*

Disturbed, she left the tree and sat on the riverbank, where the reflection disappeared. What kind of person would do something like that—and for a *criminal* at that! True, she hadn't known then that he was a criminal, but she had known better than to show him off to Agnes and Mollie for approval.

She would have to think about them another day. Today she needed to think about Larry because she knew he expected some kind of answer before he went back to Groverton.

A new question arose to haunt her. With friends like the Baldwins and especially like Larry, how had she turned so readily to Tony Casanetti? That wasn't hard to understand—or was it? Tony made her feel beautiful and exciting in a whole new way. With him she had found a new ability to enjoy life. Being with Tony gave her a new perspective on the Baldwins. He said they took life too seriously! She hadn't realized how much she chafed under their faith-centered lifestyle.

Tony opened up for her a whole new world and dared her to make it her own. What fun they had! When *he* took her out dining, they didn't just eat. He taught her to dance, and she felt like a child with a new toy. She had never been to a nightclub, and Tony took her two towns away to the most exclusive one in the area. Best of all, sure that it made her the envy of all her peers, she loved being seen around town with the top down on his yellow sports car.

A frown creased her brow. Yes, she and Tony had had fun. And, yes, she had been smitten with the way he showered her with attention and flattered her till her head spun. But it hadn't stayed that way. How could she have known that such a different Tony lay beneath the one who stole her heart? When had she stopped enjoying Tony's high spirits and begun to feel threatened by them?

How had the shimmering soap bubble turned into an ugly gum bubble?

She seized a twig beside her and snapped it in two. Life was not fair the way it got complicated. Sorting it all out was too hard. The only important thing now was that Larry had asked her to marry him, and she had promised to think about it. Why on earth not? If they had a good thing going between them before, why not pick up where they left off?

Doing so would certainly lift a lot of pressure from her and answer a lot of questions, like where she was going to live and how she was going to support herself and her baby. She put her hands into her coat pockets, spread her fingers, and caressed the hardness there. Her baby was becoming more real to her each day, less a vague idea and more a living reality.

She closed her eyes and tried to picture Larry Baldwin as a father, bouncing a baby on his knee or wiping a runny nose. She almost giggled. Then she indulged in a leisurely vision of herself as Larry's wife. She would be a professor's wife! How comical—she who had always put up with education simply as a means of getting away from home.

She drew her hands out of her pockets, locked her fingers around her knees, and gazed across the narrow river. She could picture herself fixing breakfast for Larry, ironing his shirts (she might need more practice there), and greeting him with a kiss when he came home from his day in the classroom.

Then her eyes narrowed and her stomach clenched as the intimate side of marriage came into focus. Her relationship with Larry had always been chaste, comfortable, never primarily physical. Oh, they had enjoyed their share of kisses in later years, pleasant and meaningful ones. But their friendship had not been built on physical attraction. Theirs had been first a bond of the hearts, a knitting of spirits strangely intensified by their different personalities.

Now she had experienced the intimacies of wedlock—but with another man. In the beginning with Tony it had all been so romantic, but later, when he became angry with her, he had been rough and crude, even violent. Though they now knew beyond a doubt that her relationship with Tony Casanetti had been a bona fide marriage, she felt soiled and used. A man like Larry deserved the best—not someone giving birth to a criminal's offspring. Memories of intimacies with Tony, side by side with thoughts of marrying Larry, doubled her fists into knots and made her strike her forehead with them.

She did not hear the car stop in the park above her nor the crunch of footsteps on the dead winter grass until they were quite near. She whirled, alarm freezing a breath halfway.

29

At first she did not recognize the silhouetted form approaching her. When she realized it was Ethan McCrae, her breath escaped in a spasm of relief.

"Sharon? Are you all right?" he called as he hurried down the slope toward her. She scrambled to her feet, and he extended a hand to help her.

"Yeah ... sure. I–I'm okay." Her heart still pounded and she felt her cheeks go warm over the train of thought from which she had been aroused.

"I noticed you weren't with Mrs. Baldwin in church—you know how choir directors have to sit and stare at the congregation?" An apologetic grin played peek-a-boo with his beard. "I saw your car alone here at the park—is everything all right?" The concern in his crystal blue eyes helped steady Sharon as she regained her composure.

"I was just ... I just had some thinking to do." She dusted off the seat of her pants with her hand. "What time is it? Church isn't over yet, is it?"

He chuckled. "Oh, no. But Jamie is getting over the chicken pox, so I got our Aunt Marietta to stay with him while I went and directed the choir. I slipped out afterwards because I want her to be able to go and hear the sermon." He stopped, shifting his weight from one foot to the other.

"Well, uh, thank you, but I'm okay. Really."

"Good. Listen, Sharon. I'm going to pick up Jamie and take him for a hamburger. He's not contagious anymore, but he looks terrible, and church nursery folks get nervous about such things. You haven't met Jamie yet. Why don't you come with us?"

When she hesitated, he hurried on. "You could leave your car at my house and pick it up afterwards, and you could call the Baldwins later if they're expecting you for lunch."

He saw her glance from his suit and tie to her sweatshirt and then scowl, so he hastened to add, "I'm going to change into something more comfortable as soon as I get home. How about it?"

It would be a relief to think about something other than what she had been. Besides, thinking hadn't helped a bit. Not having to face the Baldwins right now would be relief. She smiled at Ethan. "Sure, I'd like that." Besides, she needed a little exposure to children if she was going to be a mother.

They got in their cars and she followed him. When he turned into a gravel driveway, her brows creased. The few times she had seen Ethan McCrae, he looked so sharp. Could this shabby house on the west side of Willow Valley be his home? A sagging picket fence made a brave attempt to hem in patches of scraggly, winter-brown lawn. On one side of the door, dingy gray paint was peeling, but the other side boasted a fresh, smooth white. He nodded towards it as he held the wooden screen door for her.

"Didn't get done with the painting before winter set in, but one of these Saturdays it's going to be warm enough to get at it again. I can't wait to start nurturing this lawn, too, and to spiff up the fence."

As she stepped through the door he held open for her, a small, speckled bulldozer charged past her. "Daddy, Daddy!"

Ethan hoisted the boy to his shoulder, where for the first time he noticed Sharon. The light in his face dimmed, then quickly revived. "Who'zat, Daddy?"

"Don't point, Jamie! This is Sharon, a friend from church." He included the gray-haired lady in his sweeping glance. "Sharon, this is Jamie, my #1 son, and Marietta Baker, God's special gift to us. We wouldn't have made it the last couple of years without her."

Marietta Baker protested but smiled and offered to take Sharon's jacket.

"That's okay," Ethan said. "We're going out again as soon as I change. Jamie, you've got to get your shoes on. Hop to it, big tiger!"

Jamie's stocking feet hit the floor running.

The minute they walked into the Choo Choo diner, Jamie grabbed Sharon's hand and began dragging her to a booth. She caught her breath. Apparently this child knew no strangers. Once seated, he kept up a steady chatter, telling Sharon about

Tangled Strands

his pet rabbit, and his friend Joey, and how he was four years old, and wondering if she had any children, or any rabbits, or any friends, and how old was she?

By the time Ethan came with their food, Sharon's head spun. Were all children like this?

"Is my son wearing you out?" Ethan chuckled as he set down the tray with their food. "I know he has a proclivity for talking people's ears off."

"Pro-proclivity?"

He grinned with embarrassment. "I'm sorry. I've loved big words since I was a kid, and I forget not everyone does. I just mean a *tendency* to talk too much."

"Oh."

"Okay, James Lincoln McCrae, slow it down and direct your attention to this burger. Hey! Take it easy with that drink! Remember last time when you knocked it over and got an unwelcome bath?"

In no time, it seemed to Sharon, Jamie had downed his lunch and begun bouncing and fidgeting. Ethan wiped the squirming boy's mouth with a napkin, then reached into his pocket and drew out a miniature car. Jamie seized it and began maneuvering the car around the tabletop with appropriate noises. Ethan glanced apologetically at Sharon. "I-I have a better idea. Let's walk over to the park across the street."

With Jamie conquering the monkey bars, Ethan and Sharon found seats on a bench. An awkward silence settled over them.

"I'm sorry your husband died."

"Thank you." How did he know about Tony? From Mrs. Baldwin? And how much did he know about the circumstances? Groping for a way to keep the conversation going, she asked him about Marietta Baker.

"She was a great-aunt of Jamie's mother. Her husband died about six months after ... after Jamie's mother did, and she sort of adopted us." *My, his eyes were blue—a crystal blue, not dark blue like Larry's.*

"How old was Jamie then?" *Maybe this would help her find out how long it had been since his wife died.*

"He wasn't quite three, a little young to remember her. But I think I've managed to keep some images alive by talking about her, and of course we have pictures. I'm sorry we don't have any movies of her, but I couldn't afford a camera and projector, and of course I didn't know... what ... what would happen."

He turned on the bench to face her more directly. "Sharon? Is something wrong? Anything you'd like to talk about? I've been told I'm a good listener." He smiled again and held her gaze.

I scarcely know this man! I can't talk to him about anything as personal as—" It's just that Larry Baldwin has asked me to marry him," she heard her voice saying, "and I can't decide what to do." A dry leaf floated down from the tree overhead, and she intercepted it then glanced at Ethan. *How could she be so comfortable talking to someone she scarcely knew?*

"You and Larry used to go together, I take it?"

"Yeah, for years, sort of, though we didn't talk much about the future. He was away at college for four years. Then last summer ... last summer I got involved with a guy from Chicago, and–and I was really rude to Larry." She hesitated. Why should she be telling this to Ethan McCrae?

"I'm listening."

She picked points off the leaf one by one. "Well, I never did Larry the courtesy of breaking up with him, and then I–I went off with Tony."

"What does Larry have to say about that now?"

"Nothing, and that bothers me. He seems to want to forget about Tony and ignore that he has been a part of my life."

Jamie had moved to the slide, where he waved at his father. Ethan waved back. "May I ... may I ask how you feel about Larry now?"

She glanced up, shaking her head. "That's just it. I don't know. We saw each other a little while last night, but it was strange. It felt to me awfully like nothing had changed between us—but that isn't true! Things *have* changed. I went off and got married, and now I'm having a baby—"

"How does Larry feel about *that*?"

"Oh, he said that was the main reason behind his proposal—that I needed a father for my baby."

Suddenly the anger of the night before flooded in again, effectively snuffing out the warm glow she had earlier. Last summer did not matter, and neither did last night. All that mattered was that she certainly did not need or want pity from Larry Baldwin!

Tangled Strands

"That doesn't sit very well with you, does it?" Ethan laid his arm across the back of the bench and lightly touched her shoulder. "That's understandable. Do you know how Larry feels about you now?"

"He said—he said I misunderstood him and it wasn't just because of the baby." She focused on the leaf again and turned it over and over, conscious that Ethan was waiting. When she finally looked up, she had to blink against the sting of tears. "He said I misunderstood, but he never said … he never said he loved me."

30

Outwardly, the evening drive from Willow Valley back to Groverton seemed like a dozen others over the years for Larry Baldwin, but it wasn't. He could see spring sunshine warming the earth on every side, and he imagined dormant plant life soaking it up with joy, but warmth and joy were far away from him.

He tried to manage his life so it did not throw him unexpected curves, but this one had struck him head on, and he found himself faltering in the face of it.

It had never occurred to him that Sharon might reject his proposal. His mind still played over her words just an hour ago. Meeting his eyes unwaveringly, she had said, "I'm sorry I got angry about your proposal, Larry. I do appreciate your concern, but I have to say no. Believe me, I was tempted to think maybe we could forget everything that's happened, but we can't, no matter how much we might like to."

He had argued with her, but to no avail. He was not sure he understood her reasons, and he had a feeling she had not shared them all. When he pressed her about what they had meant to each other in the past, she became flustered. Yes, she admitted, they had enjoyed something special for many years. "But we'll never know if we could have built a marriage on that, and even if we could have then, it doesn't mean we could now because things are simply not the same now, and we're not the same either."

He had protested, also to no avail. On reflection, he realized the thing that had thrown him most off balance was hearing Sharon express such a mature perspective. He was not used to her being the strong one. She was right. Things had changed. *She* had changed. She was almost beginning to sound like his mother!

His mother's words flashed in his mind. Had he been ignoring God's will in proposing to Sharon? He hadn't intended to. During all those years when he and Sharon had been so close, he was sure they had assumed a future together. It never occurred to him that God might have a problem with his marrying Sharon.

The changes had begun when he and Chris went off to college and left Mollie and Sharon, two years younger, in Willow Valley. They had all agreed they should date others during those years ahead. Yet, when their foursome got together on vacations or weekends, they continued to function as if he and Sharon were a couple the same way Chris and Mollie were. No matter how many dates they had with others, they could pick up with each other right where they left off.

Was that what he had assumed he would do with Sharon now? Had he unconsciously thought of Tony Casanetti as just another football date? As the full dimension of Tony's role in Sharon's life slammed into his consciousness, he pushed it away. He had to! He must learn not to think about what was over and passed. Tony was no longer in the picture. Larry wanted to look to the future. He had to admit he had never thought of marrying anyone but Sharon, and in the months since she left, he had not allowed himself to think of marriage at all.

A new question reared its head. Was he sure he and Sharon were right for each other, or had they simply become a habit with one another?

The question brought him up so short that he lost ten miles an hour in speed before he realized it. How did he honestly feel about Sharon? Now. Today. Now that she had spent several months married to another man? Now that she was going to give birth to another man's child? Now that she had rejected him for the second time in less than a year?

The only thing he knew for sure was that he did not have any answers.

31

When it was time for Sharon's next appointment with Dr. Scott, she set out with less reluctance but still far short of enthusiasm. A new thought had stung her in the last few days. Why would any baby want to be stuck in *her* family?

Maybe she should give it up to some other family, someone who really wanted a child. Someone had suggested that to her—but not anyone in the Baldwin family. She could not identify the reason, but something inside her kept pushing that idea aside. Reluctantly she focused her mind on what Dr. Scott was saying.

"Sharon, I've been speaking with our delivery floor supervisor, trying to arrange for Mrs. Baldwin to be in the delivery room with you. However, Mrs. Caldwell is not happy about allowing an outsider into her delivery room."

Trying hard not to pick at the fresh polish on her nails, Sharon said nothing.

"What would you think if we planned for your baby to be born at home—at the Baldwin's house?"

Sharon's head shot up. Have the baby born without going to the hospital? "Is that possible?"

"Yes, of course. Babies were born that way for thousands of years, and my father delivered many babies that way."

She stared at the doctor. He was willing to do something out of the ordinary like that for her?

" So ... so where would I be?"

"I imagine in your own bed at the Baldwins', but your Mrs. Baldwin and I haven't talked about that part of it yet."

"And she would be there?"

"Yes ... if that's okay with you."

She almost smiled—and then the rest of the picture slammed into her mind again. This ballooning thing inside her still had to come out—somehow. Her gut clinched, and she pinched her lips between her teeth. Not being in the hospital would help, but even Mrs. Baldwin's being there couldn't change what had to happen.

Dr. Scott's voice broke into the silence again. "Okay, let's talk about now, today. How's it going?"

She stared at the poster on the wall. "Fine."

"Fine? That doesn't tell me much, Sharon."

She knew he was watching her, and she finally looked at him again. "So ... what do you want to know?"

"Whatever you're willing to tell me. We have to be a team in this, Sharon. I know you understand this baby has to be delivered and that it isn't going to be easy. I want to do whatever I can to help you—but I can't do it *for* you." He cocked his head and winked at her, and she couldn't help cracking a hint of a smile.

Tangled Strands 157

As she drove home, her emotions bounced between relief that she wouldn't be in a hospital and the old terror of giving birth. On the one hand, the idea of Mrs. Baldwin being with her brought a stirring of warmth and comfort, yet at the same time part of her was overwhelmed with embarrassment at the prospect.

That Saturday night Sharon excused herself and went up to bed ahead of Agnes. An hour later she was still awake, eyes wide open, staring at the patterns of light dancing on the ceiling from the streetlight and trees outside the window. These days—or rather nights, thoughts of what lay ahead kept her awake. With the baby making its presence known several times a day now, the fact that she could not escape the pending birth became ever more real—and more frightening.

But that wasn't all that kept her restless in her bed. Her mind swirled over all the things that had happened since returning to Willow Valley. Of course Larry's proposal eclipsed everything else, but each day made her more confident that she had done the right thing in saying no to him. Larry Baldwin deserved better than anything Sharon Casanetti could offer him now. Yet if she tried to explain that to him, he would argue with her. She struggled daily to keep her mind closed on thoughts of what she might have had if she hadn't chased that whirlwind.

The fact that Mrs. Baldwin had taken her in without recriminations still amazed her. She supposed her faith in God had something to do with that. What about all her talk of

God's love and his ability to sort out human muddles? Thinking about that had left her sleepless more than one night trying to make sense of it all. Some things in her life, like the friendship of the Baldwins over the years, suggested a God who did love her, but what about all the other things—like her mother, and Gram, and Tony?

A much more pleasant topic of reflection was Ethan. Finding in him such a kindred spirit both surprised her and pleased her. She had run into him and Jamie at the market one day, and he and she had talked favorite foods. Friday night he had invited her to join them for ice cream. Unwilling to admit how much the friendship pleased her, she kept focusing on how much Jamie seemed to enjoy being with her. She couldn't get enough of Ethan's blue eyes, and despite her best intentions, she sometimes caught herself staring. That would never do. On the other hand, what would it be like to marry Ethan and take on a four-year-old stepson? At this point, the idea offered intriguing possibilities, though it still felt like it belonged more in the field of imagination.

And what about Mollie? Would their relationship recover? They were on speaking terms, but not a whole lot more. The anger Mollie harbored over what Sharon had done to her brother remained a wall between them—not to mention how she had sabotaged the surprise birthday party Mollie had put together. That still hurt to think about. Would their friendship—*could* their friendship—ever return to what it used to be? Right now Sharon could not imagine it.

The weight of guilt she felt sapped more from her every day. She had upset the apple cart of their long friendships—

hardly even realizing she was doing it. It had seemed so right at the time. A simple girl like her being chosen by a charmer like Tony—what a fantasy come to life! The cloud she had floated on was too far above reality to allow her to think about what it would mean to her friends. How could she have been so naïve, first about Tony but also about the pain her actions would cause others?

That conviction had been nibbling at the back of her mind. Conviction? Where had she heard that word? Church, of course. Church with the Baldwins. She had paid little attention to it in the past because it had nothing to do with her. But now she had a feeling it did. She remembered what they used to say in church—conviction was something you needed to act on, needed to do something about.

She knew what that something—that action—was. Would doing it bring her relief from the turmoil plaguing her? Could it—could *anything* begin to heal the friendships she had so miserably trampled last summer? Would she get some peace if she screwed up her courage and tackled it?

Tomorrow, when Chris and Mollie came for Easter dinner, she would take a chance and do what she was sure she needed to do.

32

Before church the next morning, Sharon helped Agnes set the table with the "company dishes," a floral pattern on porcelain that had belonged to Agnes's mother. As Sharon placed tableware beside the plates, her mind went round and round rehearsing what she wanted say to her friends—providing she didn't chicken out.

When the four of them sat down at the table and passed the ham and sweet potatoes, Sharon took some on her plate but found it hard to eat. Her heart raced, and the knot inside her tightened. Around her, Chris chatted about his father's latest business venture and Agnes tried to draw Mollie into conversation about a new baby in the neighborhood, but that was the most Sharon picked up of either conversation.

Mrs. Baldwin pushed back her chair, and Sharon jumped at the sound. No more thinking instead of doing. If she didn't do it now, she might not come this close again.

She took a deep breath.

"Could I ... uh, say something, please?"

Mrs. Baldwin dropped back into her chair and glanced at Chris. His eyes were on Mollie. Mollie's were on her plate.

Sharon's nails dug into her palms, and she took another deep breath. "I've been ... doing a lot of thinking. I suppose you know about Larry asking me to marry him, and you know I said no. I don't know how you feel about that—" Mrs. Baldwin started to speak, but Sharon pressed on— "but I need to say something to all of you."

She reached for her glass and took a sip. "I know I–I hurt all of you badly by ... by ... going away with Tony like I did."

At the sight of Mollie still staring at her plate, Sharon's voice wavered, but a glimpse of the compassion radiating from Chris's eyes gave her fresh courage. "It's taken ... a long time for me to admit to myself how *you* must have felt about what I did—especially the fact that I did it without saying anything to any of you."

She stopped again, staring at the napkin she was twisting in her lap. "I want to—I *need* to tell each of you how bad I feel about it, especially after the way you've let me come back ..." She glanced up now—at everyone but Mollie. "And I ... and I want to ask you to forgive me."

The wave of relief that flooded her almost took her breath away. Though she still stared at the napkin in her lap, she stopped twisting it. The sound of Chris pushing back his chair cut the silence and brought her head up to see him come around the table and draw her to her feet. For a long moment they embraced until she pulled back. Hugging Mollie's husband was no way to win back her friendship. The next moment she was in Mrs. Baldwin's arms, and she had a feeling they were mingling their tears.

When she glanced up, she saw Mollie had not moved. Dared she go and sit in Chris's empty chair beside her? She had to try.

"Mollie? I know you love your brother very much, and I don't blame you for being angry with me ...."

The malevolent look Mollie cast her made her cringe, but she had to try again.

"I know that saying I'm sorry can't undo anything, so maybe saying it doesn't help. Nobody feels worse about that than I do." She sniffed and wiped her hand across her eyes. "I hope you'll be able to forgive me someday, even if you can't now."

By then Mollie's tears were flowing, and Sharon noticed Chris swipe a knuckle across his cheek. Agnes went to the buffet and brought a box of Kleenex to pass around. Without a word, Mollie wiped her eyes, then reached for Sharon, and the two embraced.

"I-I want to, Sharon, and I hope ... I hope ... I can. I don't like the way I feel—and I'm sure God doesn't either."

"I'm sorry, Mollie, I'm really, really sorry—including about the birthday party. Maybe you can tell me about it sometime." Mollie opened her mouth to speak, then closed it, straightened in her chair, and scrubbed her eyes again with the tissue.

Mrs. Baldwin came over and took the chair on the other side of Sharon. "I appreciate what you've done here, Sharon. I know it wasn't easy for you. Of course I forgive you."

"Thank ... thank you."

"Now, could I turn it around and ask you something? Have you asked God to forgive you?"

Sharon had half expected that question, but that didn't make it easy to answer. "I'm thinking about that, too. I'm still not sure how I feel about God. I feel like I've messed up my life, and that's one of the reasons I said no to Larry. I'm becoming more aware every day of ways I'm going to have to deal with the consequences. I–I remember that song you told me about ... something about God picking up scrambled threads or something."

"I'm glad you remember the song. It has a special message."

"Could you say the words for me again?"

"Of course. Mollie, the pie is all cut—could I ask you to serve it?" Chris began stacking the plates while Mrs. Baldwin drew her chair up closer to Sharon's.

"I'll write the words out for you, and I still hope to find the songbook with the other verses. But since we talked I've remembered the chorus, so I'll say the first verse for you again and then the chorus.

Dear Lord, take up the tangled strands
Where we have wrought in vain
That by the skill of Thy dear hands
Some beauty might remain.
 Transformed by grace divine,
 The glory shall be Thine.
 To Thy most holy will, O Lord,
 We now our all resign."

Tangled Strands

Mollie and Chris appeared with four slices of blueberry pie, which they set in front of each person's place. Mollie went back and reappeared with the percolator. No one spoke while she poured four cups of coffee and they passed cream and sugar.

"So what do you like about the song, Sharon?"

"I like that ... that it seems to give a bit of hope that things could get better."

"That's exactly what God can do for us. He is able to pick up the pieces of the difficult or sad things in our lives and make them into something that will weave some beauty for—"

"You mean like you do with the threads of your crocheting when you make a mistake?"

"Why, yes, Sharon. That's a good comparison."

"Maybe, but I still find it hard to accept that God let Mr. Baldwin die when you two still had many years you could have lived together, and why he let things turn out so badly with Tony. All I wanted was a little love and happiness."

33

"Ethan, why does God let bad things happen to us when he supposedly loves us?"

Sharon asked the question as she dipped a paint brush into a can of white paint and applied it carefully to the outside wall by Ethan's front door. He worked on a ladder several feet away painting under the eaves. A bright April sun warmed the air.

"Why do you ask, Sharon?"

"All my life, it seems, Mrs. Baldwin has been trying to convince me that God loves me, but it doesn't feel like it to me. I can imagine he loves *some* people—people like the Baldwins and the Thornes, but that doesn't convince me he loves *me*."

"Why do you think he wouldn't love you too?"

"Well, I've had too many things happen in my life that make me feel like God *doesn't* love me."

"You don't think bad things happen to everyone?"

Sharon was silent. What he said was true, and it made her comment sound feeble, but surely she'd had more than her share, hadn't she? Above everything else, if God loved her, wouldn't he have given her a mother who loved her, not one who would bail out on life with her?

"I know everyone experiences bad things," she finally said.

Ethan was silent so long that she wondered if he had heard her. Finally he cleared his throat and said, "Maybe someday I'll tell you about something God let happen in my life that was unbearably bad. For a while I wasn't sure I would survive it, but God brought a friend who knew what I needed to help me through it."

"Oh. I'm ... sorry—but glad about the friend." Of course it had to be about his wife dying, but she wasn't eager to talk about that, and she could tell he wasn't either.

At that moment, Jamie came galloping around the house, spurring his imaginary horse and shouting to his friend Joey right behind him. Sharon couldn't help smiling.

Ethan took a step higher on the ladder to reach one final section near the roof. "I've learned the hard way that sometimes God allows difficult—even terrible—things to come into our lives to get our attention and help us grow and mature—"

"But that doesn't sound fair!"

"I agree it isn't easy to understand." He backed down the ladder and moved it further along the wall. "I'm no theologian, but if we didn't believe God loved us, there wouldn't be much point to anything else we believe."

"You sound like Mrs. Baldwin." Sharon stood and stretched, then positioned herself to begin the other side of the door.

"I assume that would be a compliment?"

Sharon chuckled but said nothing, and they painted in silence until Jamie came roaring around the house again, Joey still at his heels. They came so close to tripping over the ladder that both Ethan and Sharon gasped.

"Hold it, cowboy! It's time to calm your horse and head him toward the barn. You, too, Joey. You may come back tomorrow. And Sharon, for a lady in your ... condition, I think you've had enough time around these paint fumes. Thanks for doing all that work around the door. I'm at a good stopping point, too, so it's time to think about those steaks I promised you in return for painting help. How are you at tossing a salad?"

In the kitchen, he set out salad ingredients for her while he waited for the oven grill to heat up. They worked companionably until the meal was ready. Since she had lived in Willow Valley since she was a child, she could tell him stories about the town that he hadn't heard. What would it be like if this were *her* kitchen and *her* family? She found that train of thought intriguing and not difficult to follow.

When the three sat down to the kitchen table, Ethan invited Jamie to thank God for their food. "Sank you, Jesus, for our supper, and sank you Saron is here, too. Amen."

While they ate, Ethan told of growing up in Buffalo and always wanting to get away from the city. "I find being a photographer in a small town much more to my liking, though I can't imagine doing it the rest of my life. Now, tell me about your family."

She gave him a crooked smile. "I was afraid you would get to that!"

"Why the face?"

"Well, there's not much to tell. My mother's been dead since I was little. My father drives a truck and is gone most of the time, and my grandmother got stuck raising me."

Ethan raised his eyebrows. "Do I detect a dissonant note?"

She made a face. "Oh, sort of. Gram and I don't appreciate each other very much." She stabbed at a reluctant cucumber morsel in her salad.

"What about your dad?"

"Oh, Pa's all right. I think he wanted to be a father, but he never quite figured out how."

Jamie slammed his empty glass on the table. "Daddy, I need some water!"

"That is *not* how you ask, Son!"

Jamie sighed heavily. "May I *please* have some more water?"

Sharon bit her lip to keep from smiling before she reached for the pitcher beside her plate. "Here, Jamie, I'll pour it for you."

"Sank you, Saron!" With a disarming smile like that, maybe children weren't terrifying after all. "I like you, Saron."

"And *I* thank you, Sharon," Ethan added, giving her an apologetic smile.

"I'm done, Daddy. Can I be 'scused?" Ethan smiled a different smile now, and Sharon didn't try to hide hers. With permission obtained, Jamie dashed off to play with his toy cars in the living room.

After they sat down to bowls of Jell-O with whipped cream, Ethan flashed her a grin that made her heart flutter for a moment. "Thank you for your help with the painting."

"You're welcome. I enjoyed doing it. I hope I did okay. I've never done any painting—nothing like that ever got done at our house."

"You did fine." He took another bite. "Uh, Sharon?"

She glanced up.

"Would you mind if I broached a more personal subject?"

"I–I guess not." Anyone else asking that question would set off alarm bells, but for some reason Ethan did not.

"Would you feel like telling me a bit about … about your baby's father?"

"I-I guess so. What do you want to know?"

"You met him here in Willow Valley?"

"Yes. Tony came to visit his cousins when he got bored working for his dad in Chicago. I was working for them, too, at Casanetti Auto. He used to hang around the show room, and then it turned out he was pretty good at selling cars."

"So you two hit it off?"

"Oh, yeah. He was so much fun! I guess he was what some people call a 'real ladies' man.' At first I enjoyed that and didn't see anything wrong with it—I suppose because I was the lady in his life at that moment."

"But you weren't forever?" His tone was gentle and those intense blue eyes held hers until she had to look away.

"Well, no, not exactly. After we were married, it took me a while to catch on that I wasn't the only lady in his life—" She pressed her fist to her lips. How could she have said that? It had been too painful to mention to anyone, even Mrs. Baldwin.

"I'm sorry if you didn't mean to say that." His grin this time radiated gentle sympathy. "I can forget I heard it ..." and he pressed his fingers to his ears.

She broke into a shaky laugh. "You're funny, Ethan."

"Well, I know that had to have been rough. You don't have to say any more. And you don't have to answer this if you would rather not, but I'm wondering how you feel about Tony now." He reached for her hand on the table between them and gave it a light squeeze. "I'm only trying to be a friend—and only *if* you want one."

Sharon returned his smile briefly. "Actually, it feels good to talk to someone about Tony since I don't want do it with the Baldwins."

He made another crooked face. "I can understand that."

She reached for her glass. "I guess I've had about every feeling in the book for the guy. I've been crazy about him, I've been super angry with him, I've even been afraid of him, and I just plain wanted to die when I couldn't change the way he felt about me in the end. When he died, at first I think there was a little sense of relief—" Now she clapped a hand to her mouth. What an awful thing to say. What would Ethan think of her now?

His eyes smiled, but his mouth remained sober. "Oh, I can understand why you would feel that way. And now? Do you grieve for him?"

Tangled Strands   171

"No, I don't think so, but that was a horrible thing to say."

"Don't be so hard on yourself. I think it was a natural thing."

"What I *am* starting to grieve for is what I did to Larry and how I ruined what he and I might have had together. If God loved me, why would he let me ..." She shook her head and scraped up the last of the Jell-O in her dish. Some things she still couldn't put into words.

"Not being God, I can't answer any 'why' questions for you, but I know that when God worked in my life, even with tragedy, I found in the end that I *could* trust Him to know what he was doing." He took her hand again, and this time he kept it until they got up to finish clearing the table.

Of the many things she didn't know, one she did know was that Ethan's hand felt good.

34

One night in early May, Agnes was drifting off to sleep when a muffled sound drew her back to consciousness. Was that sniffling? Weeping? She listened a moment longer and then followed the sound to where she knew it would take her—Sharon's closed door. She paused a long minute before knocking quietly. The night turned sharply silent.

"Sharon? May I come in?"

Still silence.

Agnes slowly turned the knob and eased the door open. The room was dark, but in the soft light from the doorway she made her way to Sharon's bed. The girl lay in an awkward sideways position necessitated by her pregnancy, her face in the pillow.

"Sharon? Did something go wrong at your appointment with Dr. Scott today?"

The girl shook her head against the pillow but said nothing.

"I thought things were going well with Dr. Scott. Or did I miss something?"

Sharon still said nothing.

"Sharon? Come on. I'm your friend! Surely by now you believe that, and you know you can talk to me about how you feel."

After a moment Sharon rocked up into a cross-legged sitting position, still hugging the pillow. When Agnes reached out and drew the pillow from her, Sharon relinquished it and abandoned herself to weeping on Agnes's shoulder. For several moments Agnes held her, stroking her hair and back and finally murmuring, "It's going to be okay, Sharon. I promise you it will."

The girl jerked away. "You can't promise that. You know you can't promise that, and neither can Dr. Scott."

"You're right. No one can promise you'll sail through the birth like a summer picnic. No matter what we do, it's still going to be childbirth. But I *can* promise you you're not going to go through this alone. I'll be there to hold your hand and cheer you on."

Sharon sniffed. "I'm glad about that, but … but Mrs. Baldwin, I'm so *scared!*"

"I know, Sharon, I know. I won't pretend that giving birth is easy." She paused. "Does it help at all to think about the millions of women who have gone through it from the dawn of history—and survived? I occasionally think about Eve who went through it without a clue of what was happening to her body."

Sharon let out a fraction of a laugh, then was quiet. "I suppose it should help, but the truth is, though I know you're trying to help, the more you and Dr. Scott talk about it, the more it becomes real to me, whereas before I tried not to think about it." She reached for a Kleenex and blew her nose.

"Is this why you declined to open the baby gift Mrs. Stauffer gave you at church yesterday?"

Sharon nodded. "That was bad of me, wasn't it?"

"It wasn't good since she offered for you to open it, but if you write her a nice thank-you note, I think she'll be fine. Can you focus on the fact that Dr. Scott and I are going to try and make this as easy for you as possible? So what do you think of Dr. Scott now that you've met him as an adult?"

"Since he's the only doctor I've been to *as an adult*, I don't have anything to compare with. But yeah, he's nice enough."

Agnes smiled in the dimness. "What do you say we get up in the attic tomorrow and bring down the bassinet Larry and Mollie slept in when they were born? We can make a new skirt for it, something to make it personal for *your* baby."

Sharon blew her nose again. "I'd rather not, if you don't mind. Everyone thinks doing things like that will make me feel better, but they only make me feel worse."

"Okay, then we won't—not yet. But, Sharon, please remember we're committed to helping you and you won't have to face it alone. You know Dr. Scott now, and he and I will both be there with you."

Sharon sniffed again, then put her arms around Agnes and murmured, "Thank you."

After a moment, Agnes drew back. "I haven't seen you working on the baby sweater recently. Have you had any problems?"

"I'm not sure. I'm getting used to the stitches so I don't have to think so hard about each one as much as I used to. But right now, I've come to something that doesn't look or feel right. I think I made a booboo."

"Don't you worry about it right now. You get to sleep, and tomorrow I'll look at it with you. The best key to fixing mistakes is if you find them and fix them before you go too far beyond them."

35

Agnes was dusting her grandmother's porcelain salt-and-pepper collection a few days later when the phone rang. She set a colorful parrot salt shaker down next to its mate. Why did the phone always ring at the most inconvenient times? When she heard her son's voice, she repented of her impatience.

"Hello, Mother? How's it going? Are your daffodils in bloom yet?"

"Yes, and the tulips are peeping through the ground."

"The daffodils were always my favorite anticipation of spring. Listen, Mother, I hate to do this, especially after not spending spring break at home." *Oh, no.* What was he going to say now?

"You know I never like to let you down. But I'm not going to be able to make it home for Mother's Day this year."

This had to be because of Sharon's presence in the house—didn't it? Now to find a way, once again, not to let her disappointment show. "Oh? Something's come up?"

"Well, yes. Our church is starting a Sunday school series on biblical and secular history. My friend Catherine and I are both eager to take it in."

"Catherine?"

"Catherine Harrison. Haven't I mentioned her? We were classmates, and now she works here at the college. We go to the same church."

"Oh. I don't think I've heard you mention her before. That sounds like an interesting study."

"Mother, you don't know how sorry I am, but it's important to get in on the beginning lesson of a series like this. Listen, I'll try to make it up to you later—when I'm out of school and before I start work on my thesis, okay? You be thinking of something special you'd like to do."

Agnes hung up the phone and returned to her dusting. A special outing with Larry? Now that had warm possibilities, but not seeing him any sooner? She found it hard to ignore that disappointment. She made a conscious effort to be content with the fact that her children were adults now and needed to live their own lives. But with Larry away for the last five years, she cherished the times she could expect to have him home.

She was closing the glass doors of the hutch Porter had built for her shakers collection when the phone rang again. This time it was her sister in Rochester.

"It's been close to a month since I've heard from her," Agnes told Mollie tearfully later that afternoon. "Last she wrote she was getting ready to take a trip to Niagara Falls with a

Tangled Strands

friend from church. Now all of a sudden—" her voice broke—"she's facing cancer surgery."

Mollie put her arms around her mother. "I'm so sorry, Mom. Since you're the only family Aunt Florence has, I think you should drop everything and go to her. There isn't any reason you can't, is there?"

"Well, I don't like the idea of being away with Sharon's pregnancy this far along—"

"But Sharon's baby isn't due for another six weeks. When's the surgery scheduled?"

"Next week—Wednesday after Mother's Day. I guess I would be back in time. But Dr. Scott's worried about Sharon. She's still uptight about delivering this baby. I hate to go off and leave her alone."

"Do you think she would come and stay with us while you're gone?"

"She might, but I'm afraid she might interpret that to suggest we don't think she can take care of herself."

Mollie's suggestion warmed Agnes's heart, and her hopes flared for a fuller reconciliation between the two friends. She had watched her daughter's resentment toward Sharon soften as Mollie became more aware of how vulnerable her friend was. The gentler spirit Sharon seemed to be developing helped, too.

"I told you, didn't I, that Dr. Scott has decided to do a home delivery for Sharon so I can be with her?"

"Yes, and I'm not surprised. I think that should work out well, don't you? But before that, you need to be with Aunt Florence for this surgery since she doesn't have any other

Tangled Strands

family. What kind of prognosis is the doctor offering her on the cancer?"

"Not too bad. He says they've caught it pretty early."

No matter the prognosis, helping her sister through the ordeal of surgery and the difficult emotional adjustments connected with it would mean so much to both of them.

Lord, do I dare take a chance on Sharon not going into labor early?

36

Sharon was lying on her bed one evening when she heard the phone ring and Mrs. Baldwin answer it. She grimaced at the sight of the round bump in her middle. The twinkle she'd caught in Chris's eye the other evening made her sure he was remembering the comment he used to make about ladies having swallowed a watermelon seed. Would she ever look the same again after this?

A few minutes later, Mrs. Baldwin stuck her head in the door. "That was Chris's mom on the phone. You remember her, don't you?"

"Yeah. The four of us played at Chris's house sometimes growing up, but not as much as we did here at yours. The Thorne house up there on the hill felt like a mansion to me."

"It's very close to a mansion, and Alec Thorne is a very successful business man, but the Thornes always act like ordinary people."

"What did she call about?"

"She wanted to invite you and me, along with Chris and Mollie of course, to have dinner at their house this Sunday. With this being the first Mothers' Day that Chris and Mollie are married, she said they should be with *both* their mothers. She suggests we make it a new family tradition."

"That's nice of her."

"Since Larry won't be here, there'll be just six of us. So it's okay with you that I said yes?"

"Sure."

Sharon watched the older woman leave the room, then rolled over on her bed and picked up her book again. Mrs. Baldwin must be disappointed not to have her son here, but personally Sharon was glad he wouldn't be. The thought of him seeing her in her present size and shape made her cringe. And what would it be like to see Mr. Thorne again? The thought of *him* seeing her as she was now was embarrassing enough.

When Sharon entered the Thorne house with Mrs. Baldwin on Sunday, her steps slowed. She remembered the house as big—but not this big, nor this … shiny. The foyer (was that what Mrs. Baldwin called it?) was as big as the whole downstairs of her pa's house, with shiny floors and dark paneled walls. The dining table was spread with china and goblets, and the silverware gleamed in the light of the chandelier. Were those fresh flowers in that huge bowl on the buffet?

Could it be that as a child she hadn't been aware of the chasm of difference between Chris's house and hers? But Chris had never seemed any different than the rest of them and just as much a brother to her as Larry—until Larry started being more than a brother after Mr. Baldwin's funeral. Her heart lurched at the memory.

Watching Chris and Mollie lavish hugs on both mothers, she allowed herself a fleeting moment to wonder what it would be like to have her own mother here today. No, it was impossible to picture it. A mother who did what her mother had done did not deserve to be called a mother.

When Mr. Thorne caught her eye across the room, he smiled and came toward her. She noticed that his eyes never once drifted from her face as he shook hands and asked her how she was doing. Now that was a real gentleman.

When they sat down at the table, conversations swirled around with little connection to her. Chris and his father talked business—some kind of problem they were having at Thorne Enterprises. The other ladies talked about some situation going on at church. The prime rib was delicious, as well as the delicate vegetables. Sharon was content to be unnoticed as she enjoyed herself in her own little cocoon.

When the crystal dessert dishes had been cleared away, Sharon became alert. Was this when the cards would be brought out? She touched the card under her skirt where she had surreptitiously placed it as she sat down. Mollie and Chris brought out wrapped packages for their mothers, matching gifts of a framed picture of each mother with the two of them on their wedding day. Sharon took a shaky breath. Did she really dare do what she planned? After Chris and Mollie had given each mother a card, Sharon shyly offered one to Mrs. Baldwin.

"Why, Sharon! How sweet of you, dear." Would she think the card too forward?

The room grew quiet. Finally Sharon glanced up and saw tears in the older woman's eyes. She held the card up and turned it toward the others. Mrs. Thorne was the only one close enough to read it, and she did. "To Someone Who's Been Like a Mother to Me."

When Sharon glanced around the table, she saw that Mrs. Baldwin's eyes weren't the only ones that were moist.

In the car on the way home in the late afternoon, Mrs. Baldwin reached across the seat and patted Sharon's hand. "I love my card. Thank you very much."

"I ... I had no idea what I was looking for when I went to the card shop, but when I saw that, I knew it was just right."

"That's very dear of you."

When they entered the house, the phone was ringing, and Mrs. Baldwin hurried to answer it. "Oh, hi, Ethan ... Sure, she's right here." She handed the phone to Sharon.

"Hello, Ethan."

"Sharon? I hope you've had a good day."

Why did his voice sound a bit strange and tight? She told him about dinner at the Thornes and the pictures Mollie and Chris had given their mothers.

A moment of silence dragged out. Then he said, "Would ... would you like to go with Jamie and me for some ice cream after church this evening—if you're going to church?"

She hadn't planned on going, but she knew Agnes would like her to. With this invitation from Ethan, why not? It would be nice to watch those crystal blue eyes again.

They left the church together in the balmy spring evening and walked to the only ice cream parlor in Willow Valley. Jamie was in a state of barely contained excitement, clutching a flat paper sack tightly against him.

As the waitress left with their orders, Jamie poked his father. "Now, Daddy? Now?"

Ethan nodded. With unfamiliar care and precision, Jamie drew from the sack a Sunday-school handwork project, colored somewhat unevenly. His eyes shining, he reached it across the table toward Sharon as far as his short arm would go. She took it from him with a "thank you" and a return smile that a moment later froze on her face.

It was a handmade Mother's Day card, signed in irregular but distinct blue crayon: "L-o-v-e, J-a-n-i-e."

Jamie bounced up and down on his seat. "Daddy says I forgot a hump on the 'm,' but I didn't want to change a thing," he declared proudly.

"I–I hope you don't ... mind," Ethan stammered. "Maybe I should have refused to let him give it to you. His ... his Sunday school teacher thought he was making it for Marietta. But he had his little mind made up and his heart quite set—"

Sharon took a deep breath to give herself another moment to gather her thoughts. Then she turned on Jamie a smile she hoped was as shining as his own. "Jamie, it's lovely! It's my first Mother's Day card, and I will put it on my dresser!"

She turned in her seat and opened her arms. "Come around here so I can give you a big hug." When she glanced at Ethan over Jamie's blond head, he was staring straight ahead, his face unreadable and his eyes glistening. Her heart tightened. What was going on here?

When Ethan dropped her off at home, Agnes met her with the news that her sister had fallen prey to a flu bug and the doctor had postponed her surgery until she fully recovered.

37

Larry was sketching a map on the board for his freshman ancient history class the last Friday in May when Catherine Harrison walked in.

He glanced over his shoulder. "Oh, hi, Catherine."

She extended a slip of paper. "There's a phone call for you, Larry. They said it was urgent."

Larry snatched the paper and glanced at the number. "It's my sister's number. Oh, no! I wonder if something's happened to my mother!"

As he laid the eraser on the ledge, he remembered his mother was not home. This was the day of his aunt's operation! Had something gone wrong with the surgery? He dashed out of the room and headed for the school office.

When Chris's voice came on the line, Larry burst in with questions. "Hey, what's the matter? Did something happen to Aunt—?"

"No, it's not your aunt, Lare," Chris interrupted. "But it's because your mom's gone to her and Mollie has the flu that we've got a problem—a gigantic one! Listen, is there any chance you could get away and come—like *right now?*"

"What in the world is going on, Chris?"

"Sharon's gone into labor early, and it looks like she's in for a rough time. She's at your mom's, like Doc Scott and your mom planned, but Doc—"

"Hold on, Chris! What's that got to do with me? Sharon made it clear—"

"I know, Lare, but you've got to forget about that. Doc and your mom have been worried about her—she's so uptight about this birthing thing. They had it all planned that your mom would be with her during the birth—in fact, your mom *promised* Sharon she wouldn't be alone—"

Chris stopped for breath, and Larry put in, "I remember Mother mentioning that to me. Are you sure Mollie can't do it?"

"Mollie's got a fever and can't go anywhere near Sharon! Listen, Lare, when Doc called me, I could hear Sharon moaning in the background. He said she's real shook up because the baby is coming while your mom is out of town."

"Ouch! I'm sorry, but I don't see what that has to do with me."

"Sharon needs somebody, somebody she knows and trusts. I'm telling you, man, she's scared silly, though she's trying to put up a brave front—"

"Isn't there anybody else, Chris? Anybody but *me!*"

"Like who would you suggest—me? Or Sharon's grandmother?"

Tangled Strands

"No, of course not! Her grandmother would only add to Sharon's trauma. But I know absolutely nothing about childbirth!"

"That's the doc's department, Lare. Sharon needs someone she knows and trusts simply to *be with her*, and you always had such a good way with her when she was upset. Anything you helped her with in the past is *nothing* compared to what she's facing now!"

Larry hesitated only another moment, then his resistance dissolved in a flood of panic and compassion for Sharon.

"Okay, Chris, I'll come! But I still have this class to teach, so it could be hours before I can get there. Who's going to be with her until then?"

"Nobody, I guess, unless Doc wants me to be. Can I tell her you're coming?"

"If you think it might help. Are you sure it isn't going to be all over by time I get there?"

"Don't I wish! Doc didn't sound like there was any chance of that."

When Larry rushed back into his classroom, the students had begun filing in. He was surprised to discover Catherine still there.

"I wondered what the problem was and if I could do anything to help."

Larry drew her to his desk and lowered his voice. He threw up his hands, and the words tumbled over each other. "Oh, you won't believe this one! Remember I told you about Sharon, the girl back home, the one who turned down my proposal?"

Catherine nodded.

"She's about to give birth. Everything was set for my mom to be with her because she's pretty scared, but my mom's in Rochester for her sister's surgery—"

"Oh, Larry! So what about your sister?"

"Mollie's down with the flu—and Chris thinks *I* need to go and be with her." Sounds around him told him restlessness was taking over his class. His gut tightened another notch.

"Listen! I think you should go." Catherine grabbed the textbook. "She needs you—"

"But I've got this class next hour!" Now that he had made the decision to go, frustration that he could not already be there made him want to bang his head against the chalkboard. He tugged at the book, but Catherine maintained her grip.

"What were you planning to teach this hour?"

"I was going to help them study for finals."

"Look, give me a minute to tell Angie where I'll be, and I'll stay with your class." She laid the textbook on the desk. "I'll be back in ten minutes--then you can get out of here! Look, here's my number." She grabbed a slip of paper and scribbled on it. "Call me if it turns out you can't get back for Monday."

The drive to Willow Valley had never seemed so long as Larry sped along the highway. True it was Friday afternoon, but why did so *many* cars have to be on the road, all seeming to move more slowly than the speed limit? His long-held convictions about breaking such limits crumbled a bit more with each mile. He would feel guilty later.

He couldn't believe he was doing this. Sharon had refused his proposal—so why was he going to her? He supposed because he cared. During those growing up years, she had been like a delicate bird with a broken wing, and they had all worked to help her deal with the distresses of her family life. Though they each had their special roles, he had been the most able to calm and settle Sharon when troubled emotions stalked her, like the night after his father's funeral.

A shiver raced down his arms at the memory of Sharon showing up at their door that night—wet, cold, and hysterical. All Mollie's and his mother's efforts to calm her had been to no avail. Finally, he pulled from the bookshelf the copy of *Heidi* that his father had often read to them, and without a word he took his place beside Sharon on the davenport. Imitating as much as possible his father's calm, steady voice, he read about Heidi's triumphant return to her grandfather on the mountain. Little by little Sharon's sobs subsided until she fell asleep with her head on his shoulder.

But she was thirteen then. Today was different. *This* was totally different.

Oh, God, what am I doing?

When he arrived at his mother's, he swerved into the driveway, slammed the car door, and sprinted for the front door, almost in one motion. He started to dash up the stairs, but panic froze him. What if Sharon were angry at him for showing up, for intruding into such a private event? He tiptoed his way up the rest of the stairs.

Sounds in Mollie's room drew him to the doorway, where he paused. Dr. Scott stood at the dresser with his back to the door doing something with a small bottle. Sharon's eyes were squeezed shut, her forehead creased in a frown, while a lady in a nurse's uniform checked Sharon's pulse. Chris sat in a chair beside the bed, reading aloud. Larry caught his breath. He was reading from the old, worn copy of *Heidi*.

"Psst!" Larry hissed softly from the doorway, and Chris glanced up. Instantly he was at Larry's side.

"How did you get here so fast? Never mind. I'm glad you're here!" He sobered. "It's getting rougher, and the doc says the worst is still ahead."

"Does she know I'm coming?"

"I told her once, but she didn't seem to believe me."

Just then Dr. Scott appeared beside them. He reached out to Larry, and they shook hands. The next moment a somber expression took command of his face. "Look at me, Larry. Do you realize how out of the ordinary this is? There's no way I could have gotten permission for this at the hospital. Do you have any idea what you are in for—or whether you are up to it?"

At a loss for how to respond, Larry dropped his eyes, but when he met the doctor's gaze again, his eyes were steady. "Frankly, Doctor, I have no idea if I am 'up to it,' but with my mother not available, I have to try. Promises have been made to Sharon, and it sounds like I'm the one available to try and keep them."

Steven Scott broke into a smile. "Now that's what I like to hear—a guy who is honest but determined. For Sharon's sake, I'm glad you're here. Knowing you, I think you may be okay, but anytime you're not, I want you out of the room—is that understood?"

Larry nodded, and the doctor turned his attention back to the bedside. Chris tapped Larry's shoulder and held out the copy of *Heidi* and a paperback songbook. Larry raised his eyebrows.

"Oh. Sharon asked me to get this from the coffee table, too—it has a song in it your mother has shared with her. Come on, what are we waiting for?"

Sharon's eyes were closed, the tight scowl on her brow deeper as she braced herself for the next onslaught of pain. At the sight of her, Larry's panic vanished. He picked up her hand and murmured her name. Her eyes opened, then widened and flooded with tears.

"Larry? Oh, *Larry!*"

His grip on her hand tightened, and he drew her fingers to his lips. "It's okay, Sharon, I'm here now."

The room dissolved around him. Nothing remained but the two of them. The past year, including Tony Casanetti, slipped quietly out of the room along with Chris.

Tangled Strands

38

Dawn was just breaking in the east when Larry pulled into Chris and Mollie's apartment complex. He was sorry to disturb them this early, and he imagined his mother was awake waiting for news, but his need for male company at the moment was so powerful it almost scared him.

Chris showed no surprise to find Larry at his door. "Come on in, pal." He paused. When Larry said nothing, Chris continued, "I assume it is over? I wanted to stay up and wait for you, but—"

Larry waved him to silence. "It's okay. Yes, it's over."

"*And—???*"

"The baby's a girl."

"Let me warm this coffee for you, and then you can tell me about it." After turning the burner on under the coffee, Chris pushed a plate of cold biscuits toward Larry, but he waved them away.

"Come on, Lare, it'll help if you eat something. Is Sharon okay?"

Larry nodded, then shook his head. "Chris, it's unreal! To think everyone of us is in this world because some woman went through an ordeal like that! How do they do it—and keep going back for more?"

"Was anyone else there besides Doc and the nurse?"

"Just the two of them. At first the nurse assumed I was the baby's father—" Larry slammed his fist on the table. "Blast it all, Chris, I *should* have been! I *could* have been if Sharon would have listened to me."

"Take it easy, Pal!" Chris laid a hand on his shoulder and squeezed hard. "The important thing is that someone personal was there to help Sharon get through it."

Larry sighed, and he felt his shoulders droop. "You're right. It would have been worse if she had been all by herself, especially after Mother's promise. Sometimes I felt the need to strap myself to the chair to keep from skipping out, and then I'd remember Sharon couldn't skip out, no matter how much she might want to."

"It was pretty rough, huh?" Chris poured steaming coffee in a cup. "One spoon of sugar like always?"

Larry nodded, and Chris set the cup in front of him.

"Plenty rough, Chris, though Doc Scott didn't act as if it was any different than usual. Sharon tried hard to be brave, but it just kept getting worse. Then ... then ..." Larry stared unseeingly across the kitchen.

"Then ...?"

"When the pain was at its worst, she started hollering at Tony about how angry she was at—."

"You're kidding!"

Tangled Strands　　　　　　　　　　　　　　　　　　　195

"No, I'm not. One time she even started crying and pleading for him to 'stop.' I could have torn the guy to shreds with my bare hands about then!"

"I'll bet you could have. Poor girl."

"Another time, she was real upset and couldn't stop crying. She kept saying she didn't dare be a mother—she might do what her own mother did. She kept moaning, 'I can't! I *can't!* Larry, tell them I can't!' I tell you, Chris, it tore me up in a million pieces!"

"I'm sure it would have been the same for me."

Larry pushed his chair back and wandered to the window. "It's weird because driving over here yesterday, I was thinking about how hysterical Sharon was the night of my father's funeral. I never saw her that way again—until tonight."

"I remember about that. By the way, your mom has found someone to stay with her sister so she can get back to Willow Valley today. Who is with Sharon now?"

"Dr. Scott said something about his wife coming to be with her." Larry sank back into his chair at the table.

Chris asked, "Does the baby have a name?"

"Yeah, she does. Sharon is naming her Elizabeth—that's my mother's middle name—Elizabeth Mollie. If it had been a boy, she would have been Daniel, for her brother Danny that died."

"*Hey!* What's going on?"

They both jumped and looked to see Mollie leaning against the doorjamb, hair disheveled and eyes squinting against the light.

Chris jumped up and went to her, feeling her forehead for fever. "Good news, Sweetheart! Sharon has a baby girl, and she has your name!"

"Oh? Good—hey! What's wrong with Larry?"

Larry started to speak, but Chris jumped in ahead of him. "I guess you could say our charming brother has a hangover," he chuckled. "He's been up all night with Sharon."

"Oh, that's right!" She approached Larry and peered into his face. "You mean you were actually *with* her while ... while the baby was being born?"

His lips pressed in a tight line, Larry nodded briefly.

"You're kidding, right?"

Chris put a hand on Mollie's shoulder. "No, Mollie, he's not. It was a rough night for both of them. But your mother promised—"

"I know, I know! But it should never have been *Larry* who had to do it, not after what Sharon—"

"Who would you have suggested, Mollie—*me?*"

Larry pushed his chair back. "Can you two save your bickering till I get out the door?"

Instantly Mollie was beside him. "Hey, Larry, I'm sorry! *Don't go!* It's just that it seems so—hey! Tell me about the baby!" But Larry continued toward the door, stopping only when his hand touched the knob.

"I can't tell you much," he said slowly, his back to them. "Her name is Elizabeth, and I don't know much more because ... because when the doctor was showing her to Sharon, I–I left."

"What do you mean, *left?*"

Tangled Strands

"I mean just that. I left. I walked out—without saying good-by. I'm not sure what came over me, but all of a sudden I couldn't handle it anymore."

Before Chris or Mollie could react, he closed the door firmly behind him.

39

Ethan McCrae glanced sideways at his son in the passenger seat beside him. He had seen Jamie excited in his four years, but never like this. They were on their way to see a new baby, and as Jamie kept reminding him, it wasn't just any baby. It was Sharon's baby. His son's love affair with Sharon would be comical if it weren't so touching.

Jamie's spirits had dampened when he heard the baby was a girl, but Ethan wasn't surprised that his curiosity and natural exuberance soon overcame his disappointment. Then he had badgered his father without letup.

"Let's go see Saron's baby, Daddy!" ... "Not today. It's too soon. Sharon needs to rest and get to know her baby herself." ... "*Today* can we go visit Saron?" ... "We can't go and visit without calling first." ... "Did you call Saron yet? She's going to think we don't like her baby since we're not going to see it!"

On the fourth day, Ethan relented and called to see if Sharon and Baby were ready for visitors.

During the drive to the Baldwins', Jamie sat primly beside his father. He kept smoothing his blue shirt and navy shorts, and twice he reached down and straightened his already perfectly aligned blue socks. When he caught his father eyeing him with amusement, he grinned sheepishly.

When the car stopped, Jamie was out of his side and had the door slammed before his father had turned off the engine. As Ethan knocked on the door, Jamie kept up a steady stutter step with his feet.

"Come on, Jamie, calm down."

His feet stilled, but a moment later they were in motion again. At last the door opened. If Ethan had not grabbed his shoulder, Jamie would have bolted right past Agnes Baldwin. The two adults chuckled, and Agnes stepped back so Ethan could enter. Jamie's eyes kept darting around the living room and the hallway beyond.

"Where is it? Where is it?"

Footsteps sounded on the stairs, and Jamie froze. Ethan felt his son's small hand slip into his. When Sharon appeared, dressed in a yellow jumper, a pink-wrapped bundle in her arms, Jamie's feet became anchored to the floor.

She walked to the davenport and sat down. After settling the bundle on her lap, she began loosening the pink wrapping. Ethan wasn't surprised that all eyes were on Jamie. His hand on Jamie's back, he nudged him in Sharon's direction, but not until she reached out and spoke his name did Jamie take a few cautious steps toward her.

When he was close enough to see the tiny, sleeping face, he clasped both hands behind his back and stood staring. Where did he learn a stance like that? Ethan guessed the two women were holding their breath for Jamie's response just as he was. They didn't have to wait long.

"Does it walk? Does it talk? Why doesn't it open its eyes?"

Ethan knelt beside him. "The baby is a person, Jamie, a real person—not an 'it.' Her name is Elizabeth and when you talk about her, you can say 'she.'"

"Well, then, if it—if *she* is a person, how come she just lays there and doesn't do nothing?"

"Well, Son, that's because she's so brand new. She hasn't had time to learn those things yet. That's how you were when you were first born, and even me, and everybody!"

He could see Jamie pondering that as Sharon uncovered one tiny fist and teased it open. Ethan read her intent and took his son's hand. "Look, Jamie! Put out your finger like this, and see? Elizabeth is holding on to it!"

The quiet in the room was deafening. For once his son had nothing to say.

The baby screwed up her face as if going to cry. Jamie's whole body trembled, and his feet began their stutter step again, but then the little face relaxed and the baby went on sleeping. Sharon took Jamie's hand and ever so lightly ran it over the dark, silky hair on her head.

Agnes reached out a hand to Jamie. "Jamie, why don't you come to the kitchen with me and let's get some drinks and cookies for everyone?"

He hesitated, looked at the baby, and then at his father as if concerned that the baby might disappear while he was gone. But when Sharon nodded to him with a smile, he skipped off after Agnes.

Silence enveloped Ethan and Sharon for several seconds before he eased himself down beside her on the davenport. "Motherhood becomes you, Sharon."

She pivoted to face him and a blush crept up her cheeks. He smiled and then they both laughed. "How are you feeling about all this now?"

Sharon drew the baby a little closer before meeting his eyes. Her words came slowly. "It's all quite awesome. I think I'm still somewhere in a dream. I have to pinch myself to believe she's real and that she is truly mine."

Ethan smiled again. "I know. I remember how I felt when Jamie was born. Listen, Sunday noon Jamie and I are taking a picnic lunch to the park. Would you and Elizabeth feel like coming along? Do you have a carriage or a stroller or any—"

Her grimace stopped him. "I–I think I would be too afraid to take her away from the house—at least not yet. I would be too nervous that something might come up that I wouldn't know how to handle." She glanced toward the kitchen.

How good that she had someone like Agnes at this time. Ethan reached for her hand and found her fingers icy. "I can understand that, Sharon. Of course you should wait until you feel at ease about taking her anywhere."

She flashed him a grateful smile.

"Here's another thought. How would you feel about leaving her with Agnes for an hour while you and I go to dinner?"

Before Sharon could answer, Agnes and Jamie returned with cookies and lemonade. Jamie held his head high as he offered each one a napkin. After Agnes sat down with glass and cookie in hand, Sharon spoke.

"Mrs. Baldwin? What would you think if I left Elizabeth with you some evening so—so I could go to dinner with Ethan?"

"Now that's a lovely idea! As long as you feed her just before you leave, we'll be fine." She turned to Ethan. "What about Jamie? Will he be going along?"

"No. I suppose I'll ask Aunt Marietta if she can come for the evening. I'm thinking of Saturday if that would be all right?"

"Saturday is fine, and I have an idea. Why don't you drop Jamie off here when you pick up Sharon, and he and I can look after Elizabeth together?"

40

Sharon studied herself in the mirror. What a treat to be in summer clothes again and to fit into something besides maternity clothes. She had lost everything she took to Chicago (thanks, Tony!), and though she had gone shopping last week, she didn't want to buy much until she had, as Mrs. Baldwin promised, her pre-baby shape back. This ruffled blouse and flowered skirt with an elastic waist were a wonderful find, and she loved getting back into bright colors. What would her hair look like pinned up on top her head? Would it give her a greater air of maturity to go with motherhood?

She was putting the finishing touches on the new hairdo when the doorbell rang. Six o'clock. Impressive that Ethan was right on time even with a child to get ready as well as himself. Would he be wearing a shirt that played up those blue eyes?

Ethan took her to the Chez Pierre, the simple French restaurant on Thorne Hill overlooking the town. Sharon had been there only once when Larry brought her on her birthday just before he went away to college. A burst of memories of her last birthday blindsided her with fresh waves of regret. She *must* drive them into the background and focus on Ethan.

He ordered *chateau briande*, complete with gourmet vegetables and the restaurant's signature feather-light rolls. While they waited, Ethan chatted about Jaime's latest escapades. Then they both grew quiet.

Finally, Ethan smiled as he said, "So you made it! You've delivered your baby and made a good start at being a mother. I'm happy for you!"

"Yeah, but it remains to be seen what kind of mother I'll be in the long run. If I didn't have Mrs. Baldwin, I wouldn't have the first idea what to do."

"Don't be so hard on yourself, Sharon. God can help you be a good mother. I promise."

"You think so?"

"I know so."

"But why should he help me? I mean, I've never paid much attention to him."

"It's never too late to start." The smile in his eyes made them even more intense.

Sharon let the subject lie. Something else was pressing more urgently on her mind. Did Ethan know about Larry's being with her during her baby's birth? What would he think if he knew? In the days since then, the fact that Larry had been there with her had torn her heart with frustration. If only she could talk to someone about it—someone besides Larry's mother or sister. She looked long and hard into Ethan's blue eyes and read only compassion.

"Could I talk to you about something ... personal?"

"Of course, if you want to."

"How much do you know about Elizabeth's birth?"

He took his time answering. "I'm not sure what you're driving at, Sharon, but I have been putting together some pieces of information. You told me Mrs. Baldwin had promised you wouldn't be alone, but I know from Aunt Marietta that she was out of town and Mollie was sick all week. I heard a rumor that Larry Baldwin was *in* town for a mysterious few hours last weekend." He held her gaze across the table. "Was Larry with you?"

She nodded mutely, and he hurried on. "Okay, I admit that's a bit unusual, but I think it's pretty wonderful that Larry's the kind of friend who would do that for you."

She toyed with her food and didn't look up, so he went on. "I wonder how you feel about that now. Would you like to talk about it?"

"Yes, I would. Are you sure you don't mind?" Silence wrapped them in a cocoon for another long moment. "I guess first of all, I'm grateful somebody was there. It would have been much harder if I had been alone. I mean, Dr. Scott and the nurse were kind and encouraging, but that's not the same as having someone who is like ... family ... ."

She lifted the goblet of water to her lips and took a sip before continuing. "So one side of my heart is glad, but as ... as far as Larry goes, I feel worse than bad. It was so unfair for him to have to endure an ordeal like that! It wasn't *right!*"

"Why do you say that?"

"Because ... because that's not what men *do*—"

Tangled Strands

"Not ordinarily, true, but I've heard chitchat that one of these years fathers are going to start being allowed in the delivery room with their wives—"

"Ya, but that's what you said—with their *wives.*"

"But I don't think anyone forced Larry to be there."

"The circumstances forced him!" She struck her fist on the table, rattling the tableware and making the water in their glasses tremble.

"Sharon, *I* believe God is in charge of all our circumstances." She scowled and was relieved when he changed direction. "What did Larry have to say about it?"

She looked away. When she heard Ethan start to retract the question, she jumped in to answer it. "Larry didn't say anything when it was over. He sort of disappeared ... "

"Disappeared?"

"He left ... without saying good-by or anything, like he couldn't wait to get out of there—but I don't blame him!" Her words rushed together. "I don't blame him at all. I would have made an exit long before if it had been me!"

Ethan laid his fork down and wiped his mouth. "And you haven't seen him since?"

"Of course not. I'm sure he got back to his school as fast as he could. Do you see what I mean when I say it was unfair to Larry—I mean he's supposed to be out of my life now, not getting called back to be involved in an emotional event like that!"

"What makes you so sure he's supposed to be out of your life? I realize you said no to his proposal a while ago, but are you sure that might not change?"

Tangled Strands

Sharon shook her head vigorously. "Oh, *no!* Whatever Larry and I had before has to be a dead issue now after the things that have happened."

"Why do you say that?"

"Well ... well ... because ..." She glanced at the napkin she was twisting in her nap, then back at Ethan. "Because I don't see any future for us, that's why. Too much has changed!"

41

They drove home in companionable silence, Ethan reflecting on their final conversation. How his heart went out to her, and he understood her concerns, but he decided not to say any more for now. She had seemed relieved when he changed the subject to the progress he had made on his house and yard. The picket fence was painted. With the spring rains, some fertilizer, and hours of uprooting stubborn weeds, his lawn was beginning to look respectable. Sharon promised to come and see it soon, but for now, he could tell she was restless about being away from her baby.

Outside the Baldwin front door, Ethan drew her into the shadows of the porch and turned her to face him. He laid his hand on one side of her face and caressed her cheek with his thumb.

"I'm happy for you, Sharon. I'm thrilled that you have Elizabeth now. There's not a doubt in my mind that you're going to be a good mother. You keep remembering that, okay?"

She nodded, wide-eyed in the darkness.

Not giving himself time to think about it, he bent and brushed her lips with his own. As he drew away, her hand came up to touch his cheek, and he could make out a smile on her face.

"Do you have your key?" he asked.

When he unlocked the door and they went in, they found Agnes in her rocking chair with Jamie sound asleep in her arms. The sight shot a physical pain through Ethan's gut. His son was missing so much without a mother! Guilt reached out its bony clutches to taunt him and intensify the pain.

He tried to get Jamie to the car without waking him, but at the closing of the driver's door, he came alive.

"Oh, hi, Daddy," he murmured sleepily. "Are we going home now? I helped Gramma B put 'Liz'peth to sleep. I did! You can ask her!"

"I'm sure you did, Son. But what's this 'Grandma B' business?"

"Oh, that's what we 'cided I should call her. Mrs. Bal ... Bald—whatever her name is, it's is too hard to remember!"

Ethan grinned in the darkness, but ten minutes later, melancholy gripped him again as he tucked his son into bed. The boy hugged his stuffed monkey and asked sleepily,

"Daddy, does 'Liz'peth not have a daddy like I don't have a mommy?"

"I–I guess so."

"Then couldn't you be her daddy and Sharon be my mommy?"

Ethan kissed his son's forehead and was grateful that, in his own hesitation, the boy dozed off again without waiting for an answer. In his own bedroom, he found the prospect of the empty bed mocking him more painfully than it had in a long time. Turning his back on it, he sat at his small desk, where his Bible still lay open from his quiet time that morning. Now he simply sat down and dropped his head onto his hands.

"Dear God," he began, "it's happening again. Satan is trying to clobber me with the guilt your Word tells me you have settled and buried. Lord, I have to believe that, but it's so hard when I see everything going on the same. Tonight again, the emptiness in my life feels like more than I can bear, and that doesn't even count what Jamie is missing! You've given me assurance that in your own perfect time you'll do what you know is right. But one thing, please, Lord? If you know that Sharon and Larry Baldwin should be together, then *please* don't let me fall in love with her!"

42

Agnes had finished wiping the counters and straightening the kitchen, but still no sound on the stairs of Sharon's coming down after putting Elizabeth to bed. Each evening she seemed to linger longer. Agnes smiled to herself. What a pleasant relief that Sharon was taking to motherhood as well as she was.

Finally, she wearied of waiting. Could Sharon have fallen asleep? The warmth of the bright summer evening could almost cast a spell. She glanced into Sharon's room and found her sitting in the rocker with Elizabeth nestled in her arms. Agnes chalked herself a plus for having had Chris bring the rocker upstairs and move the fan from Larry's room into Sharon's. Sharon glanced up and motioned her to come in.

"Is everything all right?" Agnes whispered.

"She's asleep, but I can't bear to put her down." Sharon paused. "I still can't get over the wonder of her. She's so … *precious*!" Her arms drew the baby closer.

Agnes's heart lurched, and she felt the sting of tears. She bent and gave the girl a one-sided hug. "I'm so glad, Sharon! She *is* precious, and I told you you'd love her, didn't I?"

Sharon motioned toward the bed. "Would you like to sit down? I want to talk to you about something, and I hope you won't be upset with me."

When Agnes had settled herself against the headboard and kicked off her shoes, Sharon went on. "Elizabeth is an elegant and beautiful name, but do you think it's a little overpowering for someone so small?"

"I can't argue with you about that!" Agnes chuckled. "Do you have something in mind?"

"I've been thinking I'd like to call her 'Betsey.' What do you think?"

"Oh, I think that's darling!"

"And you wouldn't be mad that I'm not using your name, as such, anymore?"

"Of course not! Officially, she still has my name, and I consider it a great honor. But this way, she can have her own version of it!"

"I like that. By the way, have you heard how your sister's doing?"

"Admirably well, bless her heart. She'll be starting her treatments in two weeks, and the doctors are optimistic. Now I want to hear more about your dad's visit this afternoon while I was out."

"Oh, that was unreal! He came over the minute he got back from his driving run to Tennessee and heard the news from Gram. He was all spiffed up and had gone out and

Tangled Strands

bought a gift. He was so cute! He reminded me of a shy kid on his first date." Sharon chuckled.

"You said he brought a pink shawl?"

"Yeah, it's over there on the dresser—if you can believe it! It's so out of character for him. I mean, he's never been any sort of elegant! When he left, he slipped me a twenty dollar bill to buy something for Eliz—for Betsey—and guess what!"

"I can't!"

"He's promised to buy her a crib when she outgrows the Baldwin bassinet! Elizabeth Mollie," she addressed the sleeping babe, touching a feathery kiss to her brow, "you don't know what a lucky baby you are!"

Agnes smiled, then sobered. She hated to bring up a discordant subject but felt she must. "Sharon? What about your grandmother? Do I gather she didn't come with your dad?" She braced herself for an acid response, but it didn't come. Instead, after a long moment, a sniff punctuated the silence. Agnes held her breath.

"Does she—does she hate me that much—" Sharon's voice trembled, "that she couldn't come and see my baby—her own flesh and blood?"

"Oh, Sharon, I'm sorry. I have to admit I don't understand your grandmother in this. Did your dad give any clue? Maybe she wasn't feeling well?"

"He didn't even mention her, and I felt too bad to ask. And then he was so delighted with E—with Betsey, I forgot about Gram."

"Sharon?" Agnes smoothed at some wrinkles in her housedress. "The thing that keeps pressing itself on my mind about your grandmother is that she's a tired and lonely old woman. She told me years ago something about practically having to raise her brothers and sisters after their mother died—that she wasn't even able to go to high school. Maybe what she needs most is someone to understand her and care about how *she* feels."

Sharon stood and stepped to the bassinet. As she laid the baby down, Betsey stirred and stretched but settled again in peaceful sleep. After watching a moment to be sure she was settled, Sharon adjusted the fan so it didn't blow directly on the baby. Then she joined Agnes on the bed, lying on her side with her head propped on one hand. The summer warmth was beginning to mellow as sunset neared.

"I wish I could say I love my grandmother ... but it wouldn't be true. I wish I did, but ...."

"God is the only one who can give us love for those we humanly don't feel love for." Agnes paused, then went on. "When we accept his love for us, despite our unworthiness, it makes it possible for us to love others even though they don't inspire love in us. Does that make sense to you?"

Sharon traced the design on the old quilt. "You mean, he makes us love people we don't even like?"

"Not 'makes us' in the sense of *forces* us, but if we allow him to, he can give us a love we don't naturally feel. Usually that starts when we choose to act in loving ways toward someone, whether we feel like it or not. Do you think it's possible your grandmother isn't sure how you feel about her

Tangled Strands

and whether she would be truly welcome? Have you thought of taking Betsey to her?"

"I would have been too scared before, but now that Pa is back, I suppose I could take her to see him. Then Gram would get included whether she wanted to be or not."

"I can't believe she doesn't want to be, Sharon. You know, speaking of grandparents, something else has occurred to me. Betsey seems so much like my own grandbaby, so I haven't thought about the other grandparents she has—" She paused as Sharon looked up sharply, "—ones who perhaps don't even know about her."

43

A tremor of alarm brought Sharon's eyebrows up. Who in the world? Mrs. Baldwin laid her hand on her arm. "I mean Tony's parents."

The words were a thunderclap on her heart. Tony's parents? How could she not have thought about their being grandparents to her baby?

"I think they have a right to know about her, don't you? A simple letter would do. I don't think you have to go into any details."

Sharon squeezed her eyes for a moment. "I suppose you're right. I guess I do owe it to them, though I don't know them at all. Tony only took me to see them once."

"Oh? What were they like?"

"Interesting because they didn't seem anything like Tony. His mom was real frail, like she wasn't in good health. His dad was, well, he was even more handsome than Tony, if that's possible, but very dignified. Their house reminded me of Chris's parents' house, it was so big and beautiful."

"I suppose that explains why Tony was used to living a lavish lifestyle. Could you tell anything about the relationship between them and Tony?"

"He was kind to his mother, but he and his dad argued a lot, mostly about how much money Tony was spending. Ha. Some joke that *didn't* turned out to be. But I guess you're right that I should write to them about ... their grandchild." What if they wanted to take her baby away from her? The tremor of alarm swelled to a whirlwind. She couldn't let that happen.

But no. Given Mrs. Casanetti's health, she doubted she needed to worry about that. Something else had her mind in a vice grip right now. She sat up and drew her legs under her, cross-legged. Dared she bring up the awful thing that kept sticking its ugly head up whenever she was with her baby? When she spoke, she could barely get the words out, and she saw Mrs. Baldwin lean closer to hear.

"There's something I can't get out of my mind." She took a deep breath. "It's about my mother." She paused another long moment, wondering how Mrs. Baldwin would respond. Now that she had introduced the topic, she could not change her mind.

"Now that I have a baby of my own, I can't—I don't ... I can't understand—" Suddenly the words burst out in a painful torrent before she buried her face in her hands. "How could she ever kill one of her children, let alone herself?"

She heard a small gasp from Mrs. Baldwin, and it was no wonder. Sharon couldn't remember ever voluntarily speaking of her mother. She simply couldn't bear to because it always brought back dark memories of the day she found out. and it renewed those awful feelings of abandonment. Any mother who loved her child could never do what hers had done.

Mrs. Baldwin reached out and caressed the top of her head. "That's a rough one, isn't it?" They were both silent for a few moments, then the older woman startled. "Sharon! I just thought of something, something your grandmother told me a long time ago that I'd forgotten about ... ."

Sharon leaned closer but not because of hope. What her mother did could not be changed, no matter what anyone remembered.

"Isn't it true your mother had another baby, one who died right before—before the tragedy happened?"

Sharon's eyes widened slowly. "*What?* Maybe. If I ever knew about that, it certainly didn't stay with me, but I think you may be right... ."

"I'm sure that's what your grandmother told me years ago. That suggests to me that it was because she was so upset about that—" She stopped, then started again. "If that's true, then what she did wasn't because she didn't love her children. I'm guessing it was because she did love the baby who died and was so upset when she lost it. Sharon, she had to have been incredibly upset to do what she did! Does that make sense?"

Sharon nodded slowly. "I wish I could remember more. I don't remember her at all, and there have never been any pictures around our house. I had forgotten about the baby, too." Her eyes widened. "You mean I had another brother or sister besides Danny?"

Tangled Strands

"I'm pretty sure about that, Sharon. You know, this might be a bridge you could try and build to your grandmother. Ask her at least about the baby who died, though it might not be good to ask her about your mother. I wonder if your dad wouldn't talk to you about her. It's certainly worth a try, don't you think?"

Sharon unfolded herself and bounced off the bed. "I've never wanted to do that, but I think I would like to now." She whirled around once. "Is there anything to eat in the kitchen?"

44

A little later, over a bowl of blueberries and milk, Agnes watched Sharon grow pensive again. What an unexpected evening this was turning out to be.

"Mrs. Baldwin? Do you ... do you think there was something ... wrong with my mother, something that made it so she couldn't deal with life, or at least not with bad things?"

So many times over the years Agnes had wondered that herself. Now to choose the right words in responding to Sharon ... .

"I doubt there was anything mentally wrong, if that's what you mean, though there's a strange kind of depression that some mothers suffer following the birth of a baby. It's possible she may have experienced some of that. Then if the baby died ... I can't even imagine the pain and trauma of that. Also, I believe when one doesn't know God and doesn't have an 'anchor' to hang onto when pain and sorrow are overwhelming—well, without that, it's easy to give up and go under."

"What do you mean by an anchor?"

"I mean faith, something to cling to when the bottom falls out. It's not only a matter of faith in the existence of God but in his sovereignty as well—in other words, the deep soul conviction that God is in control of everything and that he can work things out for good for his children, no matter how painful something is."

"You mean even the way you lost your husband?"

The question was sincere, not challenging, and it warmed Agnes's heart. "Oh, that was *hard*, extremely hard! But because of our trust in God's love and faithfulness, we could accept it as part of his all-wise plans for our lives. Although I grieved deeply and regret to this day that we didn't have more time together, I never experienced despair because I knew God would never leave me for a minute. I knew he would use what was happening to accomplish his purposes in my life."

"But how do you *know* that? How can you be so sure?"

How did one answer a question like that without resorting to platitudes?

"The answer isn't cut and dried, Sharon, but there are several ways. One is that the Bible teaches us it, and the Bible has been proven over and over to be trustworthy. There are some books in the living room bookcase you could read on that if you want to know more."

Gratified that Sharon was listening, Agnes continued. "Just as important to me is how many times I've seen God change people's lives completely when they gave their hearts to him. I've seen people hang on and survive with peace, and even be able to go on in the face of terrible tragedies. Of course, for me, it helped that I had Larry and Mollie, and I had to keep my focus on helping them to finish growing up."

Sharon met Agnes's eyes squarely. "I've been doing a lot of thinking, especially since Betsey was born. I guess I can't help but believe there has to be a God. I mean, anything as incredible as a newborn baby can't be an accident. And in spite of all my doubts over the years, the fact that he has given her to *me* makes me believe he must love me—like you keep saying he does."

Agnes's heart sang as she pulled a hankie from her apron pocket and wiped her tears.

Sharon grinned crookedly. "I know it isn't Christmas or anything, but sitting up there rocking Betsey at night, I keep thinking about Mary with her newborn baby in that stable. I know how awestruck I am with *my* baby. Mary must have been even more so—I mean, you really believe her baby was God's Son, don't you, and that God sent him to die for people's sins, or something?"

Agnes laid her hand on her heart. "I believe it with all my heart."

"But how could God love anybody enough to let his child die for them? I'm sure I couldn't! I can't even imagine it!"

"That's what grace is all about, Sharon, and why God's love is so amazing."

"But what about when we do bad things?"

"He still loves us, but sometimes he has to let difficult things come into our lives to turn us around to him again. This morning I read some verses that made me think about you."

She reached for her Bible on the kitchen desk behind her and flipped the pages. "Here they are in Lamentations 3. Listen. 'Though he brings grief, he will show compassion, so great is his unfailing love. For he does not willingly bring affliction'—or bring grief—'to the children of men.'"

"Does that mean he only brings 'affliction' when he has to straighten us up from our goofs?"

Agnes smiled. "I guess you could put it that way. God allows some things because they help us mature in our faith and trust in him more. Remember what I said about God weaving the threads of our lives together because he wants to make something beautiful of them, providing we let him?"

"You mean when we talked about your crocheting and the tangled-strands song?"

"Yes, and remember when I had to undo a whole section because I had made a mistake?"

"But I thought God wasn't supposed to make mistakes!"

"Of course you're right. God's not the one who makes the mistakes—*we are*. Remember how the song expressed it? 'Dear Lord, take up the tangled strands where we have wrought in vain.' *We* make the mistakes, or poor choices, in our lives—"

"You mean like I made with Tony?"

"If that's what you feel it was. That's when we need God to help us sort it all out—maybe even undo some things so he can make them right."

Sharon was silent, moving her spoon idly in the milk in the bottom of her bowl. Agnes found herself musing again on a thought that had been tugging at her. Now if she could find the right and careful way to say it ... .

"Sharon? Do you think what your mother did had any influence on your refusal to do ... to do what Tony wanted you to do to *your* baby?"

The girl gasped, and a look of horror crossed her face. "Oh! Oh, my! To think how close I might have come—and what he—he seriously wanted me to do!"

"But God protected you and prevented you, Sharon!" Agnes smiled and touched the girl's cheek. "I see this as a beautiful example of what we believe about God taking bad things that were never what he intended and turning them into his good purposes."

Sharon dabbed at her eyes. "I think I'm beginning to understand." She stared across the room for a moment. "Now with what you say about my mother not having an anchor—I guess you know I've always been terrified that what my mother did would rub off on me. Are you saying that if I let God into my life, I wouldn't have to worry about that anymore? Do you think he would want me—in spite of everything?"

Tears of joy blinded Agnes as she opened her arms and the two of them clung together across the corner of the kitchen table.

Tangled Strands

45

Later, after they had prayed together and cried together and Agnes had gone to bed, Sharon sat on the steps of the small back porch and gazed at the moon-bathed yard framed in shadowy evergreens. Her heart felt light and free, and her whole being seemed suffused in a quiet peace she had never known existed.

Eyes focused on the half moon, she spoke softly. "I don't fully understand what's happened, God, and I don't understand at all how it's going to unscramble the mess I've made of my life. But I want to thank you for my precious little Betsey. I know I don't deserve her, and I don't know how I'm going to raise her, but if you had the power to create her, then maybe you'll find a way to help me raise her, too."

She shifted her position, leaned against the post at the top of the steps, and hugged her knees. What would Ethan think when he heard about the step she had taken tonight? But she didn't need to wonder—she knew how glad he would be. As for Mollie and Chris, she could already feel a bear hug from

Chris, but Mollie ... would Mollie be just as glad? Yes, there was a good chance she might.

And what about Larry? All her efforts to keep him out of her mind had proven vain. Reflecting on her baby's birth many times a day was probably normal—the problem was that Larry was in all those memories. And whenever she thought of him, there was pain, pain because the visions that haunted her were of his presence with her during Betsey's birth.

It was so terrible that he had to be there!

And yet—the realization caught her unawares—she couldn't imagine the experience without him. But it wasn't supposed to be that way. And yet it had felt as if Larry *did* belong there. She remembered his wiping her face with cool cloths, murmuring her name and words of encouragement. She could still feel his hands, alternately gripping hers fiercely during a contraction and then gentle and comforting in between. She could see his eyes full of hurting and helplessness as he shared her suffering. And each time he quoted from a psalm something about "fret not" and "rest in the Lord" or read to her the words of the tangled-strands song, she had been able to reach deep within and lay hold of one more measure of strength and endurance.

Yes, having Larry share that experience with her had felt like the long-ago years when he had helped her in uncounted ways to come out of her shell and begin to put the discords of her life behind her.

Ah, but those warm feelings weren't all of it. She had other memories of Betsey's birth that were vague but disquieting. She could hear her own voice raised, shrill and

Tangled Strands

upset, but she could never be sure of the words. What had happened? What had she said or done that she could not remember? Did Larry know? She pressed her fist hard against her mouth.

No! *No*. Larry should not have been there. Or was Larry part of *God's* care, of his provision for her during the most difficult experience of her life? The thought startled her. Had God been looking out for her even when she had not yet granted him a place in her life?

There was one more memory, this one anything but shadowy. Every time it materialized in her memory, she experienced afresh the wave of emptiness that engulfed her when she turned from her first awestruck introduction to her baby and found Larry ... *gone*.

She had been too wrung out physically and emotionally to cover her reaction. Dr. Scott had caught it, and he had stayed there with the baby, showing Sharon how perfectly she was formed, how healthy she appeared, asking what her name would be, until Sharon recovered from her shock. When the doctor handed the baby to the waiting nurse, Sharon just closed her eyes and tried to shut out the world while they finished whatever else they wanted to do with her.

Now, on the Baldwins' back porch in the balmy summer moonlight, she bowed her head on her knees and braced herself for the familiar sense of bereavement that always accompanied those memories. But this time, instead of intensifying, she could feel it drift softly away from her spirit. In its place, she found an unexpected serenity.

And in the quietness of the night, her listening heart tuned in a distinct message. *It will be all right! I will take up the tangled strands and yet weave a worthy tapestry of your life.*

She had to believe it.

She sat quietly for a long time, savoring the beauty of the night and the new stillness in her soul. When she finally climbed the stairs, Betsey was beginning to stir. It was time for her late feeding. As Sharon sat in the rocker nursing her, a quiet conviction took shape in her heart. She must write to Larry. She must tell him how sorry she was that he had to be with her during childbirth. And she would ask his forgiveness for all the pain she had caused him.

Maybe then she could lay her feelings for him to rest. Maybe then he could finally and truly be out of her life.

And she must remember to give him back his class ring.

46

Larry took a deep breath before dialing the phone. This might not be easy, but he had to do it. Somehow he and Sharon had to clear the air between them.

His mother didn't answer until the fourth ring.

"Hi, did I catch you in the midst of something?"

"As a matter of fact you did. I was hovering nearby while Sharon bathes her baby."

Sharon and a baby—he still had difficulty wrapping his mind around that picture.

"I'm sorry to interrupt. Should I call back later? I want to talk to Sharon, but I need to talk to you first."

"This is okay. She's doing it at the kitchen sink, so I'll be nearby when she's ready for me. What can I do for you?"

"How old is the baby now?" He knew, but he wanted a stalling tactic.

"She'll be a month old on Monday. You should know that—you who remembers all those ancient history dates so well."

He chuckled. "Yes, I guess I do." And he did know that it was precisely three weeks and six days since that unreal experience with Sharon giving birth. It wasn't his favorite thing to think about. With no other ideas for stalling, he needed to get on with his purpose for calling.

"Sharon and I need to talk some things over, some serious things, and I think Fern Lake would be a great place to do it. Are you still friends with Phoebe Huntley? Do the Huntleys still have their cottage in the next clearing over from Fern Haven?"

"Last time I was up there, when I met Sharon in February, Phoebe and I waved at each other through trees. Why are you asking?"

"I thought you could ride along with us and have a visit with her."

"Now that has possibilities. Yes, I would like to. When are you thinking of doing this?"

"Since I'm in classes all week, the weekend is the only time. Any chance we could do it this Saturday?"

"I don't think we have anything planned, so that might be possible. It sounds like Sharon's done with the bath. You want to talk to her now?"

He heard his mother call to Sharon and tell her who was on the phone. He wished she hadn't, but it would have been awkward to ask her not to.

"It'll be a minute, Larry. I have to go take the wet baby from her."

Finally Sharon came on the line. "Hello?"

Tangled Strands

"Hi, Sharon. I–I got your letter. I was thinking, maybe we need to get together and talk? I have some things I want to say—actually, some apologies to make."

"Yes, we do. Do you have something in mind?"

"I've been thinking we could drive out to Fern Lake for the day. I've invited Mother to go along and visit her friend next door."

Sharon was quiet a long moment. Was she, as he was, remembering the summer evenings when the four of them sat on the dock envisioning the future when they would all be married and go to the lake with their children? At least Mollie and Sharon thought about things like that. He and Chris just listened with gentlemanly forbearance, casting an occasional surreptitious smile at each other behind the girls' heads. Or was she just trying to picture being at the lake with a baby?

Sharon's voice broke into his reverie. "I guess we could do that."

"I thought maybe, in addition to talking, we could ... enjoy a little fun. It *is* summer at Fern Lake, after all."

"Oh ... okay. You said your mom is going along?"

"She is. How about if I drive to Willow Valley Saturday morning early, and we can go on from there? You and Mother pack a lunch, okay? And take your swimsuit along."

He hung up the phone with a fresh knot in his midsection. What would it be like for Sharon and him to see each other again? How would it go with his mother along? Would they really be able to talk? He shook his head, hoping this didn't turn out to be a bad idea or even a disaster.

When Larry arrived on Saturday morning, he found things waiting on the front porch—picnic basket, thermoses, diaper bag bulging with who-knew-what necessities for a day, another bag with swimsuits and towels, and a strange contraption he recognized as some kind of bouncy seat for a baby.

He and Sharon greeted each other briefly. The fact that she barely met his eyes told him she was as ill at ease as he was. She pointed to the things on the porch. "Can you carry these out to the car while I get the baby?"

When she came out of the house again, Larry did a double take. In pink sun suit with ribbons and roses, even a matching bonnet, the bundle in Sharon's arms bore no resemblance to the slimy and screaming piece of humanity he had glimpsed in Dr. Scott's hands on that unforgettable day—was it already four weeks ago?

From inside the house they heard his mother's voice calling Sharon.

"Here, you hold her while I go see what your mother needs," and Sharon deposited the baby in Larry's astonished arms before turning and dashing up the steps, leaving him staring in panic and fascination at the tiny creature.

Her eyes were wide open, gazing at him. She blinked—once, twice, then screwed up her face and began to squirm. "Hey! Hey!" he cooed frantically, rocking his arms back and forth. "It's okay!" He pivoted to get the bright sun out of her eyes.

At the sound of his voice and relief from the sun, Betsey relaxed, and one corner of her mouth twitched as if she wanted

Tangled Strands

to smile. Larry became aware that Sharon had emerged from the house and was gazing at him from the top step of the porch. Their eyes met and held before she hurried down the steps and reached for the baby. He relinquished her with an unexpected flash of reluctance.

47

The drive to Fern Lake began as awkwardly as Larry had feared it might. Agnes insisted Sharon sit in front with the baby while she took her place in the back. What if they ended up with a squalling baby the whole way? And what kind of talking could he and Sharon do with his mother in the back seat?

He wiped the heel of his hand across his forehead. Sweat already? Despite its being July, he had left his window rolled up most of the way because of the baby. The morning had been cool, but now the heat was building. Did a baby in the car mean they had to suffocate all day? He rolled his window down to the halfway point.

"Will that be too much on the baby?"

"No," she said. She reached into the bag at her feet, pulled out a lightweight square of fabric, and laid it lightly over Betsey, who was now asleep. "We have to have some breeze, or we'll suffocate." She fingered the fabric. "Your mom gave this to me—said she used it with you and your sister."

"I guess that explains why it is blue?"

He turned on the radio, and they listened to a recounting of the day's news. President Eisenhower had breakfast with a senate group, and mention was made of the possibility of an interstate highway system. When they went to commercials with "See the USA in your Chevrolet," he turned it off.

After a few miles, Sharon broke the silence. "You know my job at the church finished when Betsey was born. Now I have a chance for another part-time job. Your mom says she's happy to keep Betsey during the hours I'm gone."

"Betsey?"

"Oh, that's what I've decided to call Elizabeth."

"Oh? I-I like it. So you're going to go to work."

She was quiet a moment. Then, "Have you heard about the debts Tony left?"

"Debts? No, I haven't. Are you saying *you* will have to pay them off?"

"Well, they're still settling up Tony's affairs, figuring out what assets he had as well as the debts. When we know how much I have to pay, then I may have to work more than just half days. I start on Monday."

"What will you be doing on your job?" If only Sharon hadn't taken the job at Casanetti Auto last year—but no! His thoughts must not go in that direction.

"The photography studio where Ethan McCrae works needs a receptionist. I know very little about photography, but I know office and filing procedures. That's what they're hiring me for."

Tangled Strands

"I haven't had a chance to get to know Ethan since he became choir director." Hopefully he could keep this sounding casual. "What can you tell me about him?" He glanced sideways at her, but her profile told him nothing.

"He's a nice guy." The off-hand tone of her voice suggested she too was working to sound casual. "His son Jamie is a bundle of energy, but in a fun kind of a way. He's completely smitten with Betsey, and I've been learning a lot about children. I don't know how Ethan keeps up with him! Last week at the carnival—"

"Carnival?" So now she was going out with this Ethan guy?

"Yeah, they had a carnival down near Painted Post. Jamie had never been to one, so Ethan wanted to take him." Fine, but did that mean *she* had to go along?

"Anyway, Jamie bounced from one thing to another so fast that both of us were worn out long before he was!"

He didn't want to hear any more about the carnival. "I've forgotten how Ethan lost his wife."

"In a car accident a couple of years ago."

"Does he talk about her?" His remarks were skirting the real question on his mind—what did Sharon think of this Ethan McCrae, but no way would he voice that aloud.

"I've only heard him mention her once, and it wasn't anything about her death."

That conversation died, and the awkward silence returned. He glanced in the rearview mirror and saw his mother with her head back and her eyes closed. Was she asleep, or feigning it?

Tangled Strands

Sharon spoke up softly. "Ever since you called, Larry, I've been trying to figure out how to tell you about something that's happened—something I've done."

He glanced at her sharply. Now what was she up to?

"Last week I decided to invite God into my life."

"You did? Hey, that's great! What did you—what led up to it, if you don't mind my asking?"

"Of course not. Actually, it was several things, and a lot of the credit goes to your mother. She's helped me understand so much, especially about God's love. And then I heard Ethan say some of the same things, and that helped, too."

Ethan again. How much time was she spending with this guy? It shouldn't matter to him, and he didn't like that it did. Sharon was still talking, so he tuned her back in.

"The biggest thing that helped me, though, was Betsey."

"In what way?"

"Well, despite all the ways your mom's tried over the years to convince me that God loves me, I couldn't bring myself to believe it until ... until I held this little one in my arms." She looked down at the babe asleep in her lap and drew her closer. "The fact that God has given her to *me* even though I haven't paid attention to him convinced me that he *must* love me."

He cast her a quick smile. "I can understand that. So how do you feel now, Sharon, about yourself and your life?" Now why did he have to go and ask that?

"Well, I've accepted the fact that God has forgiven me for the mistakes I've made. Your mom says that in spite of those things God is going to put my life together in a way that will please him."

She looked out the window, away from him for a moment, before continuing. "Another thing is that all my life I've been haunted by fears that I might do something terrible like ... like my mother did—"

Larry glanced at her sharply. "You were pretty torn up about that while your baby was being born, weren't you?"

She glanced back at him, startled. "So that's what it was! I knew something went on, but I've never been able to remember exactly what. Was that all?"

"You don't remember?"

"Not really."

"You were pretty upset with Tony, too."

"Oh?" Why did she keep gazing out the window? He wanted to be able to see her face when he talked to her about these things. Ah, there she was looking at him again. "Well, I'm not at all happy about Tony, but he did give me the most precious thing I've ever had—Betsey." Again she hugged the child closer and pressed a kiss on her dark head. "Your mom says I have to trust God to take care of my bad memories about him."

He said nothing, and a moment later she went on. "At least I'm going to try not to worry about my mother anymore. I know I have something now that she didn't have, and with God's help I hope I'm going to be able to do a better job of handling whatever comes in my life."

Larry took his eyes from the highway to gaze incredulously at the girl beside him. He couldn't believe what he was hearing.

Tangled Strands

Or seeing. He realized now there had been a glow about her in the awkward first moments as they prepared to leave, but it had registered only in his subconscious. Now he understood.

He reached across the space between them and ran the backs of his fingers over the baby's silky head, then pulled them away. "I'm very happy for you!"

The conversation drifted to other things, mostly Willow Valley acquaintances and Fern Haven memories, until Larry turned the car off the road and down the dirt drive to the cottage.

48

Sharon had dozed a few minutes when the motion of the car slowing and bumping along rough terrain brought her back to awareness.

"Everything looks just like you and I left it in February, Sharon," Mrs. Baldwin said. "That's always a good feeling."

Betsey had slept most of the way, but by the time they reached the cottage, she was restless and fussing. Once they were inside, Sharon announced, "She's hungry," and collecting baby and bag, she slipped into the bedroom she and Mollie had shared.

She could hear Larry coming and going through the front door, bringing the things from the car. She wouldn't be surprised if this excursion turned out to be a bad idea. How were they going to swim, presuming they could not leave the baby unattended? And a rowboat ride was out of the question. Sharon was fast learning about the changes that came into one's life with the advent of a child. Clearly it could be an awkward way to begin a marriage.

She could hear Mrs. Baldwin bustling about setting out the sandwiches they had brought. "Larry," Sharon heard her say, "could you get the bottle opener and pop the tops off these Royal Crown Cola bottles?"

When Betsey finished nursing, Sharon got into her swimsuit and pulled on a terry cloth tunic over it. With Betsey on her shoulder, she came out of the bedroom. Mrs. Baldwin walked over and tickled the baby's cheek, bringing a reaction to her whole face that would soon count as a genuine smile.

"Sharon, as soon as we finish eating, I'm going over to visit with Mrs. Huntley next door—do you remember her?"

Sharon nodded.

"What would you think, now that Betsey's fed, if I took her with me for a bit? She'll sleep for an hour or more now, won't she? I know Phoebe will want to meet Betsey, and this will give you and Larry a chance to swim or go for a boat ride if you want to."

A blessing on mothers for their intuition!

"Okay," she replied. "Thank you."

"Then let's sit down and eat."

Twenty minutes later, Mrs. Baldwin took the baby, picked up the diaper bag, and set off on the semblance of a path through the trees that led to the Huntley house.

After she left, Sharon did the simple lunch cleanup while Larry changed into his swimsuit. When he came out, she handed him a towel and they headed down to the dock. Sharon suggested they go for a boat ride first, and he agreed. The old Baldwin rowboat was another thing that stirred all kinds of memories—like the day she and Larry were out in it and it became clear to them both that what they felt for each other was no longer simply the friendship of childhood. But she could not afford to visit those memories now. She had the class ring in the bottom of Betsey's bag, and she hoped an appropriate opportunity would come up for it later.

Once they were out on the water, she hugged her knees in the warm sunshine and watched Larry as he rowed, hard and smooth, along the shore of the cove where the cottage stood. She took a deep breath as if to absorb into herself the quiet and peace of the setting. With it she became aware that the ache in her heart was almost a physical pain.

Why, oh, why had she messed up their world and destroyed the promising future they had anticipated? He could have been her husband sitting there, cutting a strong path through the smooth waters, and *their* baby gone with her proud grandma to charm a neighbor.

No! *No*. With fresh determination, she quenched those thoughts and concentrated on the beauty of the day, the midday sun blinding her as it danced on the water, and a family of ducks hovering contentedly in the shade near the shore. What was it about a lake that always held her spellbound?

They made the complete circle of the cove with not a word between them. Half of her wanted to know what was going on in Larry's mind; the other half shrank from it. When they glanced up at the same time and their eyes met, he smiled, and her nerves dissolved in a warm puddle inside her. Talking to Larry shouldn't be something to dread, especially now that she could ask God to guide their words.

Tangled Strands

"You ready to go back so we can catch a swim before Betsy comes back?" Larry asked.

She nodded. After he docked and secured the boat, he held out his hand and helped her step from the boat to the dock. She straightened and started to shed her tunic. Then she froze, turned her back, and headed toward shore. Self-conscious in front of Larry in a swimsuit! How could that be? He had seen her in swimwear since she was eight. Part of it might be that she hadn't fully regained her figure, but she knew that wasn't all. It was the suggestive motion of disrobing in front of him, something that had never entered her mind before.

With determination she again shook away her thoughts, slipped out of the tunic, dropped it on the grass, then ran the length of the dock and dived into the water.

How exhilarating to be in the lake again. She could feel the physical exertion unwinding the tension in her body as she swam out several yards from the dock. She rolled on her back in time to see Larry stretch for a moment and then dive in, too.

He surfaced just beyond her and continued with strong strokes, heading straight out towards the deep water. She watched him a minute, then took off to her right, swimming parallel to the shore in the direction where they had seen the ducks. A few minutes later, they had both turned around and were swimming back toward the dock.

They tread water for a bit, catching their breath, before Larry drifted in her direction. When he came close enough, she caught the suggestive twinkle in his eyes. Present time made a swift exit, and they were teenagers again. She knew what was coming, and she could only watch helplessly as he used the heel of his hand against the surface of the water and shot a hard stream of spray all over her.

"Oh, no, you don't, Larry Baldwin!" And she returned the shower with equal vigor.

When he had worked his way close to her, spraying incessantly, she instinctively turned her back and ducked. It was the wrong thing to do. Larry grabbed her from behind and dragged them both under. She flailed and struggled, then just as quickly he released her and allowed them to surface. They were gasping for breath and laughing so hard that it was a moment before they could regain their composure.

The next moment, they were silent, staring at each other, still breathing hard while embarrassment overtook them like an afternoon thundershower. Sharon turned and waded toward shore, while Larry hoisted himself on the dock. She brought towels and they stood drying off. Still without a word, they settled themselves on the warm dock, stretched their legs in front of them in the sun, and gazed at each other in awkward expectancy.

49

Larry brushed twigs from the weathered surface of the dock beside him. Finally, he spoke with difficulty. "Sharon, I–I feel terrible about the way I ducked out on you after Betsey was born. It was a rotten thing to do after all you had been throu—" but she motioned him to silence.

"No, Larry! I don't blame you for that. I just feel awful you ever had to be there in the first place. It wasn't fair or even ... right. Oh, don't misunderstand me!" She leaned forward, her face intent. "I'm so grateful I didn't have to go through it alone."

They gazed at each other a moment, then Larry grinned. "It *was* a rather unconventional way to spend a Friday night date, wasn't it?" Then he sobered and shook his head. "I still can't put into words what got into me to leave like I did, and I'm wretchedly sorry. Can you forgive me?"

He held his breath for her answer, but she sat in silence, running a finger over the worn boards of the dock.

"Sharon?"

She raised her eyes then, and he died a little at the anguish in them. Though he could tell tears were threatening, she met his eyes squarely as she spoke.

"Larry, I–I'm the one who needs to ask *your* forgiveness for–for the way I treated you last summer, for taking up with Tony without a word—"

He broke in then, his voice building in a crescendo of sudden emotion. "What *did* go wrong between us, Sharon? I've spent hours—days!—asking myself what I did, or didn't do. Whatever made it so easy for you to turn your back on all of us and just walk away like that?" He stopped, but not before he saw her wince at his words.

Now she looked away as she answered in a small voice, "I've asked myself that question a lot, Larry. I do know that even before Tony came on the scene, I was miffed at you ..."

"Miffed?"

"Yes, because ... because ..."

"Because *what*, Sharon? I know things were going downhill before that—but why?" He wished she would look at him.

"There were several things, but one I know—" She stopped again before going on. "When Chris asked Mollie to marry him, I thought you might ask me, but you didn't. I was disappointed and ... hurt ..."

"Ooooh." Larry's breath blew out in a long, drawn-out sigh that bordered on a whistle. "So that was it!" A fierce silence gripped them as he fought the urge to point out that changes in *her* were what had held him back.

"But there was more to it than that." She continued tracing the lines in the worn, gray wood. "God has been

Tangled Strands

helping me sort out some of it. I got more rebellious against ... spiritual things as I got older. Over the years I came to resent God for what happened to my mother and for me getting stuck with my grandmother to raise me." Her voice faltered.

"I can understand that."

"I thought God loved you and your family much more than he loved me because, well, because you had such a loving, complete family, and I didn't."

He reached for her hand, but she drew it away. Before he could think of a response, she went on, "As I got older, I think the conviction that God didn't love me ... and the hurt that my mother didn't love me enough to stick around and raise me—it all turned into anger at God for being ... unfair." She stopped then, and he knew she was not used to sharing her soul so openly. It humbled him that she was doing it with him.

"So do I take it something has changed your mind?"

A sheepish grin crept across her face. "As I said before, Betsey's arrival—speaking of which, here comes your mom with her now." She stood and waved as his mother approached through the trees.

"It looks like she's asleep," Sharon said. "Would you mind running to the cottage and getting her bouncy seat? If we put her here in the shade where we can keep an eye on her, she'll probably sleep a while longer."

A few minutes later, Larry watched as Sharon settled Betsey, still sound asleep, in her seat. His mother said, "Is it okay if Phoebe and I run to town? We used up all her eggs making macaroons, and Mr. Huntley is gone with their truck.

So could I borrow your car for a few minutes, Larry? It won't take us long."

"Sure, go ahead. My keys are in my pants pocket in the bathroom. You want me to get them for you?" But his mother was already halfway to the house.

In no time, she was back out, in the car, and had it started. Larry and Sharon watched her back it around and drive off through the trees before they settled back on the dock.

It took a few minutes for them to renew their conversation. Larry broke the silence without looking at her. "Do you think—way back then, that part of your anger was directed toward us, toward our family, and that maybe you wanted to strike back at us as well as at God?"

She looked at him then and shook her head as she said in a broken voice, "Oh, Larry, that is a horrible thought. If it's true, I promise you I wasn't aware of it." They gazed at each other, and she felt hot tears breaking through her efforts to resist them. "If it is true, how can you ever forgive me, for what I did to you and your family and for ruining our chances for ... whatever we might have had together?" She turned her face away then, rested her head on her knees, and wept soundlessly.

His first thought was to reach out and embrace her, but he caught himself, drew back, and sat frozen in his spot. How should he respond? How did he *want* to respond? He honestly didn't know.

Finally he asked quietly, "And how do you feel about those things now?"

Tangled Strands

She did not raise her head as she spoke through tears. "Of course I'm not angry anymore—at your family or at God. How could I be? All you've ever shown me is love and kindness. The only person I'm angry with now is myself."

"But, Sharon, so what if we lost a year? Does that have to be the end of everything? Couldn't we just—"

She looked up and shook her head, hard. "No, Larry! I told you, we can't pick up where we left off! Everything is different now."

Larry stared out over the lake a long time. Having his thoughts so jumbled was a strange feeling because he liked to keep everything in his world well ordered. Maybe now would be time to raise the question he had wanted to ask ever since she had refused his proposal in the spring.

"Sharon?" He waited until she looked at him again. "You say we can't pick up where we left off, and you may be right. But is there any reason we couldn't start over again now—forget about the past and begin at the beginning? I guess what I'm asking is if you would let me court you, if I may use an old-fashioned term. Could we date and do things together again, and then see what happens—how we feel about each other?"

This time she shook her head slowly. "I don't think so, Larry, because the problem isn't how I feel about you—"

He looked up surprised. "How *do* you feel about me?"

She hesitated. "I think a fairer question might be how *you* feel about *me*. After all, you're the one talking about courting and marriage, and you haven't really said."

He stared at her. This girl—no, this woman—expressing herself so boldly yet without anger—could she really be Sharon? After a long moment, he said quietly, "I thought I loved you, Sharon—for a long time I thought we loved each other. As far as I can figure it, I don't feel any differently now than I did before." He paused, then added with a mischievous twinkle, "Don't you think our time in the lake a while ago demonstrated that what we had together hasn't disappeared?"

She glanced at him, then looked away again before saying, "Or maybe that was just a fall-back to an old habit."

He did not answer. The last thing he wanted to do was get into a verbal battle with her. Being with her today was creating a response in him unlike anything he had experienced with her in the past. He could not believe the turmoil that just her nearness was causing him—nor how it had shaken him to see her in her swimsuit, confirming again how much she was a woman now, not simply an attractive young girl.

What was he to make of this new gentleness in her spirit? Despite the emotional content of their conversation, she had not said one harsh word. Was this a new Sharon he was seeing?

Betsey had begun to squirm and fuss on shore. Sharon rose and scurried toward her. Before reaching her, she stumbled, tripped, and went down with a sharp cry.

Tangled Strands

50

Larry sprang up and rushed to her side. She sat clutching her ankle, her face twisted in pain. "Oh, Sharon! What happened?"

She looked at the ground around her. "I guess I tripped on that washout between the dock and the shore."

"Is it real bad?"

She only grimaced.

"Do you think you can stand on it?"

"*I don't know.*" Her voice rose to a squeak and then broke off.

"Here, let me help you up."

She winced when she put weight on her foot, but with Larry's help she began hobbling toward the cottage. Behind them, Betsey's fussing built to a full-voiced protest. At the same time, the wind gusted across the yard and stirred up a whirlwind of leaves and dust.

"Larry! The baby! I can't just leave her—"

"Hey!" he said a bit shortly. "As soon as I get you inside, I'll come back for her!"

She grimaced again as he settled her on the davenport, then carefully stretched her leg out beside her.

"Is that okay?" he asked,

"Yes, but—" The sound of Betsey's distress had built to an alarming crescendo.

"I'm going, I'm *going!*"

Outside he discovered a dark bank of clouds across the lake. The wind had risen sharply. Scooping up the infant seat with the protesting Betsey, he hurried back into the cottage. He fumbled frantically with the straps to release the squalling infant so he could hand her to Sharon. Then he dashed around looking for the diaper bag his mother had brought back.

Now Sharon was crying, too. With her leg stretched beside her on the davenport and Betsey on her lap, she was trying to get to the baby's diaper, but the crying, squirming infant came dangerously close to throwing herself off.

"*Larry!* What am I going to do?"

"Here, just a minute!" He picked up the baby. "If you put your foot on the floor for now, I can lay Betsey beside you."

Finally, the diaper was changed, but by then Betsey's screams reverberated in the small room, and Sharon's sobs tore at his heart. She jostled the baby vigorously on her shoulder, but to no avail. Larry reached down, pried Betsey away from her, and—awe and apprehension forgotten—began pacing the room. She quieted only a moment, then resumed bawling. Finally, he stopped in front of Sharon and raised his voice above the baby's.

Tangled Strands

"Sharon, what can we *do?*"

"I don't *know!* I need your mom!"

He returned the baby to Sharon. "Here, take her, and I'll see if my car is back at the Wilders'."

Outside, he wasn't surprised to see no car beside the neighboring cottage. Walking back in, he shook his head and threw up his hands. "They're not back yet." The baby's distress had begun to intensify the tension in his own voice. "So what will it take to quiet her?"

"I don't *know!*" Sharon wailed. "Don't you see? This has never happened before, and I've always had your mother to tell me what to do!"

"Could she be hungry?"

"No! It's been less than three hours since I fed her, and everybody tells me babies should only be fed *every four hours*."

"Even if they're this upset? Here, let me have her again."

He resumed his pacing. When it brought him back to Sharon's side of the room again, she said, "Larry? Could you pray or something?"

Without hesitation, he replaced Betsey in her arms, sank to the davenport, and put his arms around both of them. Placing his lips close to Sharon's ear and pitching his voice above Betsey's distress, he prayed. "Dear God, we admit we're at a loss to know what to do, and there's no one here to help us. Please give us wisdom, and please help Betsey stop crying. Amen."

For a long moment, Larry did not move. Then he raised his head and looked into Sharon's eyes.

"Okay, so she shouldn't be hungry and 'everybody'—whoever that is—says babies should only be fed every four hours. But we're not everybody. If ... nursing her would comfort and quiet her right now, don't you think that that would be a good idea?"

Sharon hesitated, closed her eyes a moment, then opened them and nodded. He read the question on her face, released the two of them, and got to his feet. "Look, I'm going out to check the weather. It sounds like we're in for a thunderstorm."

The windows of the cottage had begun to rattle. As an afterthought, he rummaged in the baby's bag and pulled out a small blanket. Handing it to Sharon with a smile, he said, "Maybe this will help."

Before going out, he pulled on his shirt and jeans and brought Sharon an afghan from one of the bedrooms. Outside, a gust of wind tried to snatch the door from him. The surface of the lake churned with white caps, and the far shore looked like a gray, fogged-in morning. Rain was already falling there.

As the sounds of Betsey's crying subsided, Larry started back in, then decided to give Sharon more time. Drawing out his pocketknife, he trimmed spent blossoms from the rose bushes.

Just then, he saw his car pull up beside the cottage next door. Mrs. Huntley got out and dashed into her house as his mother backed the car around and drove away. A moment later, she drove into their clearing, parked in front of the cottage, and hurried out of the car and up the walk. Larry motioned her ahead of him into the cottage and followed close behind her.

Tangled Strands

Sharon had the blanket discreetly draped over her shoulder. Her face was tear streaked, and Betsey's diminishing sobs, mingled with suckling sounds beneath the blanket, punctuated the quiet in the room. He told his mother what happened.

"I admit that's what I would have done." She smoothed her wind-tossed hair with her fingers.

"How does your ankle feel?" Larry asked Sharon.

She moved her foot a bit and frowned. He sat beside her again and with a corner of the baby's blanket wiped the tears from her face. Outside, the storm broke, and driving rain began battering the windows.

"Was there anything left from lunch, Mother?"

"Not much. Just a couple apples and half a sandwich. Of course, there's always peanut butter and crackers in the cupboard."

"Good old peanut butter," Larry said. "Are you hungry, Sharon?" She shook her head. "As soon as this storm passes, we'll start back. Do you think your ankle will need a doctor?"

She shrugged and then shook her head again.

51

An hour later, the storm had settled into a hard, steady rain. Sharon had pulled on her tunic and slacks over her swimsuit, and Betsey slept peacefully beside her on the davenport. She was glad the wind had died down because wind always made her tense.

She was grateful they had done the things they had done before the storm. This was *not* what they had planned for their day, but they were making the best of it. Larry had drawn up a footstool and gotten out the old Monopoly game. Occasional soft snoring in the front bedroom told them Mrs. Baldwin was sneaking in a nap or two along with her reading.

The game gave her something to reflect on instead of the events of the day. But whenever Larry contemplated his move too long or was busy counting the money she had to pay him, her mind wandered to their conversation on the dock. Larry had talked about his feelings in the past, but even if he did say he loved her, it didn't change the way she had ruined what they had. It didn't make her worthy of him now.

When the rain finally let up, it was early evening. Mrs. Baldwin came out of the bedroom. "I think I'd like to walk down to the dock—for old times' sake." She picked up an umbrella from the corner by the front door. "The trees will still be dripping."

Larry watched her leave. "Being here always makes her think of my dad. He worked so hard to fix this place up after we bought it."

"I remember a little about that. Didn't we children hunt for stones for the path down to the water?"

"You and Mollie helped Mother do that while Chris and I worked with Dad to clear tons of underbrush around the place. You ready to try out your ankle?"

He helped her stand, and she tested her weight on her foot. "It's better." Her smile wavered a little. "But not great."

Suddenly she was keenly aware of his nearness, of his arm supporting her and the warmth of his body next to hers. Their eyes met and held, and the next thing she knew, both arms were folding around her and drawing her close.

"I'm sorry, Sharon," he murmured in her hair, "but I can't help it! I just want to hold you and love you and never let you go!"

She could not have resisted if she had wanted to, even without a bad ankle. His arms felt familiar and so good. What a relief to lean on him, to draw strength from him, just to have been with him all day. Her heart reveled in being this near him after so long.

Tangled Strands

But her mind began prodding her, reminding her without mercy that this was not right, that she had forfeited her chance to belong to Larry Baldwin. As she was gathering her resolve to push away, he drew back and smiled into her eyes. Her heart melted again. Before she realized what was happening, his lips came softly down on hers. The kiss lasted only a moment, but it sent her senses reeling. A moment later, he put her gently from him and began gathering up their things to get ready to go.

During the hour's drive home through the sodden, glistening twilight, they said little. Sharon insisted she would sit in the back with Betsy so Larry's mother could sit up front and visit with him. The day had taken several unexpected turns, and her thoughts and emotions were too fragile for dialogue. She suspected Larry's were, too. The events and conversations of the day had been too highly charged, but the soft music Larry found on the radio and the quiet exchanges between him and his mother seemed to enfold her in comforting arms.

When they arrived, Betsey was sound asleep. Agnes took her from Sharon's arms and headed in the house, leaving Larry to help Sharon. On the porch, he turned her to face him.

"We'll talk tomorrow, okay? You've had a big day. Can Mother help you with Betsey, and can you go right to bed? I think I'll drive over and see what Chris and Mollie are doing. Then tomorrow afternoon—well, I'll think of something special we can do so we can finish our talk."

She nodded, her eyes riveted to his face in the dimness. He bent to kiss her, but she laid her fingers on his lips. "Please, Larry—"

Tangled Strands

He settled for drawing her again into his arms and pressing her head onto his shoulder.

"It's going to be okay," he murmured. "It's going to be okay."

52

The storm of Saturday night had passed, and they awoke on Sunday to a fresh, rain-washed world. Sharon lay in bed listening for Betsey to awaken. She glanced at the clock and did a double take. The baby had slept more than six hours! Did yesterday's trauma wear her out? Or maybe, as Mrs. Baldwin promised, the middle-of-the-night feeding would soon be a thing of the past.

She closed her eyes and tried to gather her thoughts for the day. Today she and Larry were going to talk again—about their future. *No!* They had no future! She had to keep remembering that. But all she seemed able to remember was the feel of his arms around her and the closeness they had experienced the day before.

And his kiss. That puzzled her the most. Larry had kissed her before, and certainly Tony had kissed her—wild, passionate, demanding kisses that at the time she had taken as indications of his love. But never had there been anything like

Tangled Strands

the flame that sprang to life between her and Larry during that brief but tantalizing kiss last night.

She had been so sure she had forfeited her right to any future with Larry Baldwin. Yet what about the electricity they had felt with each other yesterday—the sense of oneness and companionship? *Could* she consider a future with Larry in spite of what she had done? She didn't think so. And did God have a divine opinion about that?

Dear God, I'm so new at this business of looking for what you want in my life!

One thing she knew for sure. She needed time to sort it all out and find out what God wanted to tell her now that she had set her heart to following his plan for her. But how? What could she say to Larry? And she hadn't given him back his class ring yesterday. She just hadn't found an appropriate moment.

Wait! Maybe there was a way, a way to gain time for them to determine what was right in God's eyes and best for both of them and Betsey.

A hesitant knock sounded on her door. "Come in," she called softly.

Larry pushed the door open for his mother, who entered carrying a breakfast tray. He spoke from the doorway. "Mother and I think you should take it easy on that ankle this morning, okay? How do you feel?"

"I slept fine, and Betsey hasn't been heard from since before one o'clock."

"Hey, that's great! I guess we wore her out yesterday, you think?" He grinned. "Well, have fun being lazy, and I'll see you after church."

Mrs. Baldwin set the tray in front of Sharon and arranged the pillows behind her back. "Larry went to the bakery this morning for fresh sweet rolls. His father used to do that for special occasions." She glanced at Sharon as if expecting some response, but Sharon just smiled.

Sounds from the bassinet told them Betsey was beginning to stir. Mrs. Baldwin went and bent over her.

"Listen, Sharon, you eat your breakfast, and when she gets fully awake, I'll come and diaper her before you feed her so you don't have to get out of bed. You still have clean diapers?"

"Yes, I think there are several left—enough to get us through until I can wash tomorrow morning. But you changed her so many times during the night when I first brought her home!"

"And I'll do it at least this once more. I'm serious. I'll be back in a few minutes. Now you just relax this morning and enjoy your baby. I've put the traditional Sunday roast in the oven, so dinner will be ready when we get home from church."

———◆◆◆———

When they returned shortly after noon, Larry watched his mother head for the kitchen before he went upstairs. What kind of mood would he find Sharon in now? He stopped in the doorway again. Betsey lay awake beside her mother on the bed.

"Hi. How's your ankle?"

Tangled Strands

"Pretty good. I got up and showered and dressed, and it wasn't too bad."

"Good. I thought we might drive up Thorne Hill this afternoon to the waterfall. How does that sound?"

"F-fine." Instead of looking at him, she caressed Betsey's tiny feet beside her.

"Have you thought about … what we're going to talk about?"

"I've hardly thought about anything else." She met his eyes then. "I've been praying about it, too," she added shyly. So things really had changed—and that had to be a change for the better, didn't it?

A strong knock sounded on the front door below.

His mother's voice carried up the stairs. "Can you get that, Larry? I'm in the middle of something in the kitchen."

Larry blew Sharon a kiss and bounded down the stairs. He opened the front door to find a bearded young man with a small boy. The man put out his hand.

"Hi. You must be Larry. I've seen you in church with your mom. I'm Ethan McCrae, a friend of Sharon's. Jamie and I missed her in church this morning, so we stopped by to see if she's all right."

"Uh…she's okay, but she twisted her ankle yesterday, and we thought she ought to stay off it this morning."

"Oh, I'm sorry to hear that."

"She says it's better."

Sharon's voice drifted down the stairs. "Do I hear Ethan down there? How about sending Jamie up? Betsey's awake."

Tangled Strands

Without further invitation, Jamie hustled for the stairs. Ethan and Larry studied each other. Finally, Larry said, "Oh! Would you like to come in? I hear your son is a great fan of Betsey's."

Ethan grinned as he stepped through the door. "He is, for sure. She's the first baby he's ever known personally."

His mother appeared from the kitchen, drying her hands as she came. "Ethan! How nice! Can you and Jamie join us— we have plenty of roast."

Larry looked at his mother askance, but she ignored him.

Ethan said, "No thanks, Mrs. Baldwin. The Sullivans are expecting us for lunch. But I was hoping to talk to Sharon and see if she's planning to come to church tonight for the special musical."

Sharon appeared at the head of the stairs. "Why, thanks, Ethan! I think I'll be able to make it by this evening."

"Good. Would you like me to pick you up, or will you come with—" he glanced from Larry to his mother.

Larry put in hastily, "Sharon and I are doing something this afternoon, and she might not be back in time."

"But, Larry," Sharon said, "don't you have to drive back to campus tonight? Ethan, if you would like to pick me up, that would be fine."

"Good. I'm also wondering, Sharon, if your dad wouldn't come with us if you invited him."

Sharon's face lit up. "That's a great idea, Ethan! He just might. I'll call him."

Tangled Strands

53

"It's cooler today, isn't it?" Sharon commented as they drove the asphalt road that climbed Thorne Hill. The air was mild in spite of the sunshine, the sky a cloudless blue above them. If only their talk would go well, but the knot inside her did not reflect hopefulness.

Larry drove into the parking lot of the overlook facing the fifty-foot waterfall. Two cars were parked, but no one was in sight.

"Guess the others must be hiking." He pointed to the stone bench. "Shall we get out and take in the view?"

Sharon nodded, and he came around to open her door. She let him take her arm and assist her, though by now she limped only a little. After they sat down on the nearest bench, he took her hands and words began bubbling out.

"Sharon, I don't know how you feel about yesterday, but I think it proves we *can* pick up where we left off—or at least start over again from where we are now."

She started to shake her head, but he cut her off. "No, listen to me! I'm ready to forget all about Tony Casanetti and any part he played in your life. I'd like to claim Betsey as my own child, including changing her name to Baldwin, and forget she ever had any other father—anything except to let you out of my life again. I survived that once, but I don't want to do it again! I think the way we used to feel about each is still there, and I won't believe you if you deny it!"

The picture he painted tried to find a home in her heart, but she locked the door tight against it. How could she make him understand that it was no longer an option? If only she could find the right words to express her thoughts, words that Larry would understand and accept.

"I won't deny it, Larry, because I know it would be a lie. But that isn't all there is to it! You *can't* forget about Tony— that's only hiding from the truth. I might like to forget about him sometimes, but I can't. I mustn't. He made a permanent mark on my life, and Betsey is only part of that."

She paused to catch her breath, and when he said nothing, she went on. "You can't just pretend he wasn't Betsey's father! Oh, I'm sure you would love her and treat her as your own. With time, you would be her father in the truest sense. But you can't just wish away Tony's being her father in a ... in a physical way. For instance, have you thought about the fact that she has grandparents in Chicago?"

The look on his face almost made her smile. "I thought not. At your mother's suggestion, I've written to them and sent them a picture, and they wrote back immediately."

"What did they say?"

Tangled Strands

"They sounded pitifully grateful I let them know about Betsey, and they said they want to have a part in her life. They want to be able to visit her and know her."

"So?" Larry shrugged. "I could live with that."

"I imagine you could. But Larry ... ." Now she bit her lip, pulled her hands from his, and looked away, out at the waterfall. She hated having to put this into words, but apparently Larry was set on ignoring it. "I'm not sure you've come to grips with the fact that I have been married—*married*, Larry! Have you faced up to all that means?"

If she waited for a response, she might lose the little courage she had, so she plunged ahead. If only she could keep her voice steady. "Larry, I've been another man's wife! I've slept in another man's bed, and I've had his child. I know that's not what you ever expected of your bride." She paused and pulled her eyes back to his. "I don't know what that does to you, but *I* can't live with it."

He got up then in silence and walked away from her to the stone wall. With his back to her, his hands in his pockets, he stared at the waterfall. She ached to go to him, to abandon herself into his arms and tell him that all she ever wanted was to belong to him forever.

But she did not move.

Without turning to face her, he said, "So what are you saying?"

"I have a suggestion. Remember a long time ago, when we were teenagers and I didn't want to mix with anyone but you and Mollie and Chris?" He nodded without turning. "You asked me to go along with your idea that we should date others. I didn't understand, and I wasn't happy about it, but you insisted because you said it was important."

Why wouldn't he say anything? What was going on in his mind? She had to keep going.

"Now I'm going to turn it around on you. I think we should both spend some time dating others again and see what happens. I think we need time to figure out how we really feel and what is best for all of us. I don't know how we find out what God wants, but maybe time will help with that, too."

He whirled on her. "Oh, I can see your little scheme! You would like to get something going with Ethan McCrae—is that it?"

Only with the greatest effort did she conceal how much his words stung. She took a deep breath.

"That comment is not worthy of you, Larry Baldwin!" Her voice trembled. "Ethan has been a good friend to me, and he doesn't deserve a crack like that. Jamie is my friend, too, amazing as that may seem. But all that is not the point, and I think you know it."

She stopped again, giving him a chance to say something, but again he turned his back.

"Larry, you've always been such a reasonable person, I can't believe you don't understand what I'm saying. I'm sure you have friends there at the college. Your mom mentioned someone ... Catherine? You could date her. Can't we please pray and ask God what he wants?"

His silence was louder than the sound of the waterfall.

Tangled Strands

"Please, Larry?" Desperation in her voice sounded sharp in her own ears.

He came and stood before her then. "I guess I understand what you're saying, Sharon," he began slowly. "I can see you've done a lot of thinking about this, about us. That encourages me, whether you mean for it to or not. But first, may I ask you a question, and will you answer me honestly?"

"I'll try."

"By saying things aren't right for us because ... because of what's happened, are you ruling out the possibility that there could *ever* be something for us?"

Would he misunderstand if she left the door open to that possibility? Would he take it to mean more than she intended? She had to take that chance. She had to be honest. Locking her eyes on his slate blue ones, she said without wavering, "I'm talking about now, Larry. I–I do not pretend to know about the future."

"But you're not ruling it out!" He seized her wrists and drew her to her feet, a slightly pompous victor's gleam in his eyes. Sharon tried to draw away, but his grip was firm.

"Okay. It's a deal, but only for a while. In the meantime, can I write you, or call you? Can I date *you*, too?" He grinned in youthful anticipation.

She shook her head. "No, Larry. That would only confuse things."

"I suppose you're right." He glanced down, disappointment in his voice. "In that case, Sharon Marie, I have one last request." He did not wait for a response. "I would like your permission to hold you once more and kiss you again. May I?"

She nodded ever so slightly, then watched, mesmerized, as he released one wrist, only to capture her fingers and bring the wrist to his lips, slowly, entrancingly, like a delicate ceremony. Then, just as slowly, with Sharon statue still, he did the same with the other wrist.

She willed herself to cover the tremor his lips set aglow on her flesh. Then, before she could recover from that, she felt his arms, strong, warm, and possessive, enfold her. His lips in her ear murmured her name. "Oh, Sharon, Sharon! There's been a gaping, pain-filled hole in my being for over a year, and you're the only one who can fill it."

Between words, his lips moved from her ear, to her cheeks, to her eyes, and finally—after another tantalizing second—they claimed possession of her lips as if they had always been rightfully his. A shiver washed over her, and then she felt herself lifted and carried away to a land of sunshine and wildflowers. Her arms went around him and completed the circle, and she found herself melting closer into his embrace and responding to him with her whole being.

No! a distant corner of her conscience screamed at her. *This should not be happening!* But she was helpless against the tide of emotion that engulfed her. Once again, it was Larry who broke the embrace. He took her wrists once more and put her gently from him, but not far. She could see on his face that he was as shaken as she was. No trace of the victor's smirk remained.

———◆◆◆———

Larry opened his mouth to speak, but no sound came. Instead, he brushed her lips once more with his, soft as a whisper, and then tried again. He took a deep breath in an effort to regain enough calm to express himself.

"I have a feeling we'll both have something to think about," he said, his voice unsteady. "You've made me realize, Sharon, how remiss I've been in asking God what *he* wants in this. I've just assumed he wanted what I wanted. But you're right; I need to do a lot of serious thinking—and praying. Do you think … ?" He fumbled for expression. "Could we maybe pray together, now?"

She nodded mutely. Her eyes had not left his face. He returned to the bench behind them. When he sat down and opened his arms, she came into them—as naturally as if she had done it all her life, and nestled against him.

For a moment, he just held her, savoring the joy of having her in his arms. When he opened his mouth to pray, he found himself so choked with emotion he could not get words to come out. While he struggled, his amazed ears heard Sharon's voice, barely audible but without a waiver.

"Dear God, you know I don't know much about relating to you yet, but I've come to accept that you love me, and I'm sure you love Larry and my little Betsey. Thank you for what a good friend Larry has been to me over the years—" At that, *her* voice broke, and she could not continue.

Larry's arms tightened and he tried to take up the petition. But he found himself unable to pray, "Dear God, Thy will be done." He had been determined not to take no for an answer from Sharon today, but now he knew that before he could do that, he had some soul searching and spiritual homework to do.

54

July descended on Willow Valley and wrapped the town in a cocoon of summer warmth. The winter's ice skaters emerged as boaters and swimmers at the river, and instead of building snowmen, children skated on sidewalks and climbed trees. Climbing roses adorned fences, and flowers splashed colors across the town.

Jamie McCrae learned to swim at Willow Park pool. Betsey Casanetti discovered her fists. Mollie Thorne found out she was pregnant. And Frank Champlin decided to delay his next trucking trip until he had a chance to know his granddaughter.

He was also getting to know his daughter. It amazed him the way he seemed more able to relate to her now—now that she was an adult and no longer that mysterious thing called a child. He found himself experiencing a piercing sense of loss over the years that had whisked past him while she grew up. After the deaths of his wife and his son, he had been so preoccupied with his own emotional upheaval that he had been unable to shoulder the role of a father to Sharon. For months, he had driven his truck in a stupor of horror and grief, trying to shake the gruesome moment when he had come home and found Belinda and Danny.

It had taken nearly a year before his pain succeeded in encasing itself in a protective and blessed numbness—numbness to the tragedy and almost to life itself. By the time he might have felt ready to take up the responsibilities of fatherhood again, the gulf of unfamiliarity between him and Sharon had widened alarmingly. And with being gone more than he was home, he had never found a way to bridge it.

Now he was eager to make up for lost time.

———♦♦♦———

Sharon's heart warmed when she answered the phone and found her father on the other end. This was the second time in a week he had called her. Such a surprise she wouldn't mind experiencing every day.

"You think Mrs. Baldwin would be upset if you and Betsey come for supper a couple times a week?"

"Of course not, Pa. In fact, I'm sure Mrs. Baldwin would be pleased about that. But what about Gram? She's not going to like cooking for an extra mouth."

"You let me worry about your Gram. I know how to take care of her." She grinned. Her father making jokes? This was new, but she liked it. She liked that it made them laugh together. "Do you think ...," he began again, "what would you think if I come to church with you on Sunday?"

Tangled Strands 275

"Oh, Pa, I'd love that."

The first time he went with them, they were surprised to hear him acknowledge that faith had played a real part in his life when he was young.

"But I got sidetracked and careless about taking care of my soul. I know I need to do somethin' 'bout that."

Sharon gave him a quick, somewhat awkward hug. Might she be ready to hear more about her mother than she had before? Might her pa be willing to talk to her along those lines? He surprised her without her having to ask.

"Belinda—your ma—was such a pertty little thing," he reminisced on the Champlin front porch one evening. "Some folks thought she was a bit moody, but it didn't never seem that way to me. I couldn't believe my luck when I found out she was gettin' sweet on *me*." He twirled a faded cap in gnarled brown hands, hands with fingers curled almost permanently from spending all their days wrapped around a steering wheel.

"How did you come to know each other?"

"Her family moved to town 'bout the time I was graduatin' from high school. I didn't get to know her, though, 'til I quit my railroad job. I started dating her near the end of her senior year. We was married in—I think it was October."

Sharon stared at her father in confused fascination. She had never wanted to hear about her mother, but now she found herself longing to hear more. Still sidestepping the term *mother*, she said, "How old was she when Danny was born?"

Tangled Strands

An unmistakable shadow crossed her father's face. "Oh, I dunno—nineteen or twenty. We was married a year or so when he was born, then a couple more before you were."

Sharon was silent. What would it have been like growing up with an older brother—like Mollie had! And life with a mother—NO! Exploring that idea still stirred too many painful emotions. She had made some emotional progress in the weeks since Betsey's birth, but apparently not that much.

She became aware that her father was speaking again.

"I wouldn't say you favor your ma much, though you're right pertty, too, just in a different way. You got her big eyes, but hers were more green than brown." He shook his head. "What color you reckon little Betsey's eyes is gonna be?"

"Well, mine are brown and so were Tony's, so I guess she doesn't have much choice." Sharon chuckled, relieved for a break from her reverie. She patted her sleeping daughter on a quilt beside her on the swing.

The screen door opened, and Gram made her cumbersome way onto the porch. She glanced at her granddaughter, then at her son.

"Frank, Sharon here's been askin' me about her baby sister what died right after she was born. I remember as how she died from some kind of breathin' problem, but I can't for the life of me tell Sharon what her name was."

Her father gazed out across the street. "We named her Bonnie Jean," he said softly. "Seemed the poor little mite never had a chance."

What must it have meant to her father to lose three members of his family in such short, tragic succession? For the first time it occurred to her that he might have been an entirely different father had it not been for those events.

But it was not too late! She could feel him reaching out to her, half apologetically, half fearfully, and she knew with all her heart she wanted to meet him half way.

His words broke in on her again. "Listen, daughter, how soon you reckon that bitty granddaughter's gonna be needin' that crib I promised? You know anything about buyin' cribs?"

She shook her head. "How would I? But I guess I can learn." Then, "You coming with us, Gram?"

Gram turned away. "Now why would I be wantin' to do that? I wouldn't do nothin' but get tired out and slow you down."

Sharon did not respond. Her efforts to reach out to her grandmother had met with mixed results. Gram had not been as openly hostile, but neither had she shown any warmth.

55

"I have to admit I haven't had much encouragement from her," Sharon reported to Ethan a week later when she returned a book she had borrowed. The summer sunshine warmed clear to her bones as she sat in the grass and watched him work on the flowerbeds around his front door. "I'm trying to change my actions with her to more like what would please God, but it's discouraging because I'm not sure I'm accomplishing anything."

Ethan sat back on his heels and looked up from his weeding.

"You have to remember, Sharon, that you're up against nearly a lifetime of difficult feelings between you and your grandmother. It's going to take more than just a few friendly words to build a new set of behavior patterns. That takes time."

Sharon dropped down cross-legged beside the flowerbed, picked up a trowel, and studied it absently. "I guess I should at least be thankful she's not cutting me down as much as she used to. By the way, did I report to you that they've decided Tony's death was accidental, not murder?"

"Oh, that's good. That gives Betsey a cleaner slate to grow up with, doesn't it?"

"Yes, I suppose it does. It feels better to me, too."

"Of course it does. Speaking of Betsey, what does your Gram think of her now?"

"Not much!" She struck the trowel on the concrete walk beside her. "Ethan, she hasn't had one nice thing to say. The only time she held her was when I practically forced her to—and then she just worried about Betsey spitting up on her!" She dropped the trowel and struck the fingers of both hands through her hair.

"I'm sorry, Sharon. I hope you won't give up. Keep depending on God to give you that love beyond yourself. It can't help but make a difference eventually."

Sharon sighed. "I'm trying, Ethan, I really am. For some reason, it's become important to me to win Gram over."

"And I'm sure God will honor that. Is your dad still here?"

"No, he left yesterday on another trip. This one will be ten days. I didn't like the sound of it, though. He's hauling a load of chemicals, something he hasn't often had to do."

Ethan reached for a different trowel. "Tell me about the new crib."

"Oh, it's lovely! It's dark wood and real shiny. Pa got all emotional over it. Said he wished he had been able to provide something that nice when his own kids were babies. I'm afraid it made him think some more about Danny and ... the baby girl. He even talked about how my mother used to sing her babies to sleep at night." She paused a moment, then went on. "It's helped me a whole lot to hear these things, to find out my mother wasn't some kind of monster."

A half hour later Sharon was up to her knuckles in black dirt helping Ethan thin out some zinnias on the side of the house. They did not notice Chris drive up. When they heard him call her name and stood up, the look on his face stopped Sharon cold.

Ethan stood transfixed, but Sharon moved toward Chris in an agonizing slow motion, fear choking her. "Chris—what?"

He put both arms around her and rested his head on the top of hers. "I'm so sorry, Sharon! It's—it's your dad," he managed brokenly. "There's been a terrible accident."

56

"I was just getting to know him!" Sharon stormed tearfully at Mollie's kitchen table three days after Frank Champlin's funeral. "After all these years, he was starting to talk to me and treat me like a person, not a piece of furniture." She reached for another tissue. "We were having a chance to make up for lost time."

Mollie turned off the flame under the soup and carried the coffee pot to the table. "I know, Sharon. I know. We all hurt so badly for you." She poured more coffee into their cups before sitting down. Her own eyes filled with tears. "Do you feel as bad as you look?"

"Probably. My head aches and my eyes feel twice their size from crying." She studied her friend. "You don't look too great yourself, Mollie. Are you still having trouble with morning sickness?"

Mollie made a face. "It's lessening, but only a little. I hope I'm over the worst of it. Where did you say you found that half-sheet of paper with your dad's final wishes?"

"In the drawer beside his bed. I'm glad Chris's dad knows how to turn it into something legal."

"Have you thought about what you're going to do with the house?"

Sharon shook her head. "I didn't even realize Pa owned the house we started out renting, but he must have bought it sometime ago since it's all paid for. Of course it's not worth a whole lot. I don't see anything to do but let Gram keep on living in it. I wondered why Pa didn't leave the house to her, and then I realized that of course he expected to outlive her."

"And your dad had a bank account number in the note?"

"That's what I'm most surprised about—the nest egg he left me."

"What did Chris's dad have to say about that?"

"Of course he says the first thing I have to do is pay off those debts of Tony's. I don't mind telling you it stirs up a whole new round of anger towards Tony that I have to spend some of my inheritance paying for *his* wayward living—not to mention having to pay for clothes I don't have anymore!" She squeezed her eyes shut in a deep frown.

"I'm sure it does. Is that going to eat up the whole thing?"

"Mr. Thorne doesn't think so. He says he can help me invest the rest so Betsey and I can have a bit of regular income. If it weren't for the debts, there might have been something for a down payment on a house one of these days."

"Do you think you'll need to keep working?"

Sharon nodded. "For the time being anyway. It will be a while before the probate is actually settled so I can get the

Tangled Strands

money—but the fact that he left everything so clear on that paper is a surprise in itself."

"I think there was a lot more to your dad than appeared on the surface."

"I was just discovering that. As far as the money goes, it will take more than what he left to support Betsey and me independently, and we can't live with your mom forever. However, a couple of days ago I got another letter from Tony's parents." She tossed her wadded tissue into a nearby wastebasket.

Mollie looked up. "Oh?"

"For starters, they sent me a generous check to cover the doctor and hospital costs for Betsey's birth, but of course I didn't use the hospital, so that gives me a little something extra to put towards the debts. They say they want to send a regular allowance for Betsey—to help raise her. So maybe with that along with what Pa left, we can get a place to live on our own before long."

Sounds from the bedroom told them Betsey was wakening. Sharon got up and went to her. When she returned, she was crying again.

"It's so unfair, Mollie! Pa was so happy and proud to have a grandchild! Why did God have to take him away when he was just beginning to enjoy her?" She blew her nose in another tissue and threw it away. "*Why*, Mollie? Is this how God rewards me for inviting him into my life?"

"God doesn't play games like that!" Mollie slammed her spoon on the saucer. "Don't forget, I lost my father, too—"

"*That* wasn't the same, Mollie—"

"Of course I know it wasn't! I know he was a warm and wonderful father, but God gave you some of that in the end, and you don't want to forget that."

"Of course I don't, but—"

"How do you think you might have felt about losing your dad if you hadn't had those good times with him recently?"

Sharon twirled her spoon in idle circles on the Formica surface. "I don't suppose I would be so upset."

"But would you trade the good things you shared in the end for not being so upset?"

"N–no. I suppose not. Are you saying that's part of what comes with loving—the more you love someone, the more it hurts to lose them? So what am I supposed to do—tell God it was a great idea?" Her voice cracked.

"Of course not! God understands how you feel. Remember, he watched his Son die just to save us undeserving human beings. I think it would help if you could focus on the good things he gave you with your dad before the end."

"I suppose you're right about that, Mollie." Sharon tickled her baby's cheek to make her smile. "I guess I *will* have some happy things to share with Betsey about her granddad when she gets old enough. But why couldn't God have just let him live, at least until Betsey was old enough to have memories of him? I still don't understand that!"

57

Mollie took a sip of her coffee. Her mother could answer questions like these better than she could. She certainly did not want to mess up this first heart-to-heart talk she and Sharon had had since her return.

"Sharon, if we understood everything God did, he wouldn't be any greater than we are. I've never forgotten something my parents said when they told Larry and me that Daddy was going to die. They said God hasn't promised we'll *understand* everything in life. He doesn't owe us explanations. He just promises he'll never leave us and that everything will work out for our best—according to *his* eternal perspective."

Sharon sighed. "There's so much I have to learn, Mollie. Do you think I'll ever know as much as you do about God and the Bible?"

"Please don't look to me as an example, Sharon! I did a rotten job of living like a Christian when you came back to Willow Valley. It took me a long time to come to terms with leaving God to work things out according to his plan, not mine. The Lord must have been terribly disappointed in me."

"I know it was hard for you to forgive me, Mollie."

"It has helped as you've let me know more about some of the things you dealt with before you moved here. But I still didn't act as I should have—"

"But you still know much more about what God wants than I do!"

"The important thing isn't how much you *know* but how much you live what you do know, and in that department you're doing well. But what would you think about the two of us getting together once a week to study the Bible—*if* you would like to."

"Would you do that with me, Mollie?"

"I would love to." Mollie met Sharon's eyes and smiled. "I have to keep learning and growing in my faith, too."

Sharon was silent. After a moment Mollie said, "You know what you remind me of, sitting here at my kitchen table? Larry sat in that same chair the morning after Betsey was born. He looked like he'd been through—well, exactly what he'd been through."

She said it with a chuckle in an effort to elicit a smile from Sharon, but it did not come. Instead, Sharon looked up and said, "And you know what you're saying that reminds *me* of? The look on Larry's face when he walked into the funeral home, after rushing down from Groverton when he heard about Pa, and he found me crying in Ethan's arms." Her face crumpled in distress and tears again.

"Oh, Sharon, I didn't mean to make you feel worse!" Mollie jumped up and walked to the stove. The pot did not need stirring, but she was suddenly awash with some of the old resentments towards Sharon on Larry's behalf. She too had caught the look on Larry's face that evening, and feelings had flared that she had worked to lay to rest.

From the stove she said carefully, "Don't worry about it, Sharon. You weren't doing anything wrong, and I would like to think Larry understood that."

"Even if he did, what about you, Mollie? I wouldn't blame you for being upset that Larry saw me in Ethan's arms. I know I've hurt you a whole lot, as well as Larry, with the way things have happened between him and me."

"Speaking of that," Mollie began warily, "do you mind if I ask you just how things *are* between you and Larry? We all thought after that day you and Larry spent at Fern Lake—"

Sharon cut her off. "There isn't anything to tell! Like I told your mom, Larry and I are giving it some time. And I don't have any more answers now than I did before."

"Well, what about Ethan? How does Ethan fit into the picture, if he does?"

"I don't know that either," Sharon said, not looking at her friend. "I don't know if I should say this to you or not, Mollie, but I've found myself wishing Ethan and I would fall in love. It could make at least some things simpler since he has been married before, too."

"But that shouldn't make any dif—"

The ringing of the phone startled them both. Mollie answered, then handed it to Sharon. "It's my mom. She sounds upset."

Sharon took the phone. As Mollie listened, a scowl knit her brow. What could be going on?

When Sharon hung up, her face was a study in contrasts. "Your mom just came from Gram's house. She says Gram's in a terrible state. She doesn't think she's eaten or changed out of her clothes since Pa died. She just sits in her chair and cries. She keeps wailing about being an old woman that nobody cares about. Your mom couldn't get through to her, and she wanted to know if I had any ideas." Suddenly Sharon's face lit up. "Mollie, could I leave Betsey with you for a while?"

Mollie raised her eyebrows but nodded.

"I'm going to see my grandmother!"

58

"No, Gram, it's all settled! Betsey and I are moving in here, and I'm going to take care of *you* for a change."

When her grandmother tried to protest, Sharon waved her to silence. "No, listen! You took care of me all those years, and now I have a chance to do something for you in return. Pa has left this house to me, but of course it's still your *home*. Betsey and I need to get established on our own, and there's no good reason we shouldn't all live here together."

This time Gram insisted on making herself heard. "Oh, no, you *don't*, Sharon Champ—whatever your name is now! All you wanna do is stick me with taking care of that kid of yours while you go gallivantin' off to some fancy, money-making job—and I won't have it!" Only running out of breath ended her tirade.

Sharon took a deep breath to steady herself against the painful words. *Dear God! If I ever needed you, it's now!* She drew up a low stool in front of her grandmother's chair and forced her to meet her eyes before she said firmly,

"I can understand why you might think that, Gram, but I'm going to prove to you that you are wrong! For now, you just have to take my word for it. Yes, I have a job, but I only work afternoons. And yes, Betsey needs someone to care for her while I work. But Agnes Baldwin has been doing that, and I imagine she might continue if I need—"

"Oh! So now it's you don't trust me with your kid! I suppose I, who brung you up by the sweat of my own brow, am not good enough for your high and mighty offspring—"

Sharon jumped to her feet and clapped her hands over her ears, turned her back and shook her head as if to drive away the angry, cutting words. Gram's voice finally trailed off, and the two remained frozen in a tense, silent tableau.

Sharon turned slowly and took another deep breath. "I don't have the time or energy to argue with you about it, Gram. I'll just have to prove to you that I'm doing this out of kindness and love—nothing else. Betsey and I are your own flesh and blood, and this house belongs to me. So we're moving in. You have your room downstairs, and I promise we won't interfere with that. Do you mind if Betsey and I make ourselves at home in the two upstairs rooms?"

The older woman glared at Sharon, then said sullenly, "Do whatever you've a mind to—you will anyway! Just don't you dare go near my room! And that kid o' yours better not keep me awake at night!"

As she drove back to Mollie's, Sharon's brain whirled. What had she gotten herself into? Yet as she explained it to Mollie, she came to the same conclusion. Her grandmother needed someone to look after her—*now*. Of course Sharon was

Tangled Strands 291

the logical solution. At the same time, moving into the house would provide her and Betsey with a place of their own, and most of all it would create for her a means of showing gratitude and God's love to her grandmother.

Thank you, Jesus, for helping me find you. Otherwise, I couldn't even think about doing this.

———◆◆◆———

Agnes was waiting for Sharon when she walked in the door. She took the sound-asleep Betsey from her and nestled her on the davenport with a cushion between her and the edge. The look on Sharon's face confirmed that what her daughter had just told her on the phone was true.

"Mollie called me like you asked her to. I'll admit I'm surprised, but I have to commend you, Sharon. Or did you chicken out of your decision on your way over here?" That Sharon had thought of this so quickly and taken action without hesitation thrilled Agnes's heart. Hopefully she wouldn't change her mind. "Come on. Supper's ready. Eating something should help."

They settled at the table, and Agnes asked a blessing. She watched Sharon serve herself macaroni and cheese and green peas—but why so little? Was she still concerned about getting her figure back, or was she that tense over her decision?

"I suppose I should have thought it through a bit longer," Sharon said now, "but as soon as the idea hit me, I knew it was the right thing to do. I'm just not at all sure I have what it takes to carry it through. I mean, if Gram keeps on being difficult, I'm not sure how long I can hang on. Am I crazy?"

Agnes finished serving her own plate. "I don't think so, but I can see why you might wonder that. This is a huge thing, and I'm proud of you for thinking of it and wanting to do it, dear. You're putting your faith into action."

The phone rang. Agnes got up and answered it, then handed it to Sharon. "It's Mollie."

Sharon listened, brushed a tear from her eye, said thank you a couple of times, then hung up. "Mollie says she and Chris are behind me all the way and will help me move any time I'm ready. Not that I have that much to move ... "

"I washed clothes today, so all your things and Betsey's are clean and ready to go in your suitcase. Don't forget the new crib," she added with a grin.

Sharon chewed on her thumbnail. "That beautiful crib is going to look totally out of place in that house. After not seeing the house for more than a year, I can't believe how dirty it is and how rundown it looks. I don't know what I think I'm doing taking my baby to a place like that."

"Then we'll have to give you a hand getting it cleaned up and fixed—"

"If we go in there and start cleaning, Gram will have a fit!"

"Hmmm. You're probably right. How about if we get together over dinner this Sunday and talk some strategies?"

A smile tugged at the corners of Sharon's mouth. "That sounds good. What would you think if I invited Ethan to come, too?"

Agnes studied the girl a moment. Ethan, huh? Interesting.

Tangled Strands

"Of course that would be ... fine."

Did that mean his four-year-old would be tagging along? She could picture that being either delight or disaster.

59

Sharon couldn't believe the warm support with which her friends rallied around her. Mrs. Baldwin promised to continue caring for Betsey when Sharon worked. Chris and Ethan moved Sharon's and Betsey's belongings, including the new crib, and Mollie plunged in to help her get settled. Sharon shed a few tears the first night she slept in her father's bed, but she deliberately turned her mind to thanking God for her blessings and soon fell asleep from exhaustion.

Looking at it from the inside, the condition of the house was especially shocking. It would take her weeks to get it into respectable condition.

The easy part of the strategy meeting was determining what needed to be done. Much more difficult was finding a way to convince Gram they didn't want to upset her—they just wanted to help and to be her friend. They decided they must start with one challenge only—that of befriending her, of trying to break through her angry exterior with kindness and friendliness.

"It's been far too many years since I visited your grandmother, Sharon," Mrs. Baldwin said. "If I start doing that again, hopefully it will begin to bring her out of this depression she's sunk into. And if I do it when I'm taking care of Betsey ..." She left the thought hanging.

"Do you think Gram has recipes, Sharon?" Mollie asked. "Old family recipes I could ask her for?"

"I don't know about anything 'old family' since her mother died when she was very young, but I know she had recipes on cards when I was growing up—nice idea, Mollie."

Sharon listened in amazement as one idea led to another. When she looked back two weeks later, the amazement had only grown. Her friends had found so many excuses to drop in on her, always making a point of speaking to Gram as well. She overheard Chris talking with her about money. He told Sharon later that Gram had a question about her small retirement income and no idea where to turn for an answer. He found it for her. Mollie heard her complaining about her arthritis and Sharon watched in disbelief as Mollie first secured Gram's permission and then redid the braid she wound around her head. Mrs. Baldwin came a couple times each week when she had Betsey.

Sharon kept looking for opportunities to speak positively to her grandmother, but her efforts showed little success. Even when she searched her memories for something positive in the past, it wasn't an easy task since she had appreciated so little while growing up. Had it been as bad as she thought, or had she just gotten into the habit of seeing everything through a negative lens?

Her most lingering disappointment was the way Gram still made no effort to take an interest in Betsey. As long as the baby did not cry too much, Gram made a show of ignoring her.

"Don't lose heart, Sharon," Mrs. Baldwin said. "I'm sure with time she will get used to having Betsey around. You watch."

"I hope so. We had the same argument about cooking that we had about Betsey that first day." She tilted her head and did a sing-song imitation of Gram. "I got no intentions of cookin' fer any extras 'sides me ... Oh, so my cookin' ain't good enough for you?" Sharon finished with an embarrassed laugh. Even though Mrs. Baldwin pressed her hand to her mouth, Sharon caught the hint of laughter in her eyes.

"I know it isn't funny, but ... So did you come to some kind of solution?"

"I decreed we'll take turns every other day until we figure out something better."

When Sharon got home from work one night, Gram said, "You ain't fergittin' it's your turn to fix supper, are you?"

"Gram! With Betsey in the house, you need to stop saying 'ain't'—" Oops. She had made a conscious decision to stop correcting her grandmother's grammar. How old was she—maybe as young as nine?—when she picked up the habit of doing that? True, she didn't want Betsey learning her speaking habits from Gram, but she shouldn't be worrying about that just now. She bent down to Gram's level by the armchair and

Tangled Strands 297

smiled at her. "I'm sorry. I shouldn't say things like that to you."

Gram snorted and looked away.

60

One afternoon in August when Sharon arrived at the Baldwin home to pick up Betsey, she found Mollie's car already there, so she parked hers on the street. A tightness tugged at her chest. She was grateful for how far she and Mollie had come since that awful day last winter when they shopped together, but it seemed they still had a ways to go before she felt only excitement, not apprehension, at the prospect of seeing her friend.

She followed the sound of voices to the kitchen. There she found Mollie and her mother at the kitchen table drinking tea. A third cup sat in the center of the table. So they expected her—that was nice. Mollie held Betsey and made friendly noises at her, to which Betsey responded with wide eyes and toothless grins. Mrs. Baldwin jumped up to get the kettle of boiling water for Sharon's tea.

When Mrs. Baldwin handed her the teacup, she met her eyes and said, "You have a special day coming up next week."

Ah.

The day she had avoided thinking about. Her birthday, yes, but also the anniversary of her taking off with Tony. What did one do with a day like that after the way things turned out?

"I know. I've been trying not to think about it."

Mrs. Baldwin took a sip of her tea. "It's a day that brings a mixture of emotions to all of us, isn't it?"

Sharon glanced at Mollie and said, "Your mom told me you made a party for me last year. I think I'd like to hear more about it—*if* you want to tell me."

Mollie nodded, but it was her mother who spoke. "It would have been a nice party, Sharon, with guests, balloons and streamers, and a cake with twenty candles."

Sharon grimaced. "I don't think I can ever tell you how sorry I am. May I ask how you found out I was gone?"

"When you didn't show up on time, Chris called your work, and they told him you didn't work there anymore. Of course we were shocked. I called your apartment, and your landlady said you'd moved out and left a lot of stuff behind, even clothes. That's when Chris and Larry went to your grandmother's house and found your note."

In the silence that followed, Sharon held her breath and felt the knot in her heart burrow deeper. Mrs. Baldwin's voice broke in softly. "I don't know if I should tell you this, but Mollie was so upset, she took off to Fern Haven in Larry's car without ever asking him or leaving a note."

"*You did?*"

Mollie looked sheepish. "I did."

"What did Larry do?"

"What could he do since there's no phone at the cottage? Fortunately, I came to my senses while I was still on the road, so I stopped at the pay phone on my way through Fernville." Mollie took a deep breath. "Larry told me to go ahead and stay a couple of days if I wanted to—he could use Mom's car."

"What did you do there?" Sharon asked.

"I mostly sat on the dock for hours and thought about the years we'd had together and all the things we'd done. I guess it's not surprising that the more I thought, the angrier I got. I finally realized that was only making things worse. So ..." She hesitated, looked at her mother, and then broke into a smile. "So I got back in the car, came home, and started planning my wedding to Chris! I managed to push my anger into the background, but as you know I never made peace with it."

"Oh, Mollie!" Sharon cried, her eyes filling with tears.

"Now, Sharon, this is not time for tears!" Mrs. Baldwin exclaimed. "All that is past now and you are back with us!"

She reached over and patted Sharon's arm. To her amazement, there was a gleam, almost a twinkle in her eyes.

A glance at Mollie showed a grin starting to appear on her face, too. Sharon raised her eyebrows.

"Would you like to hear how my mom dealt with *her* feelings?" Mollie asked. "She took those feelings out on poor, defenseless balloons!"

Mrs. Baldwin grinned sheepishly.

What was going on here? Were they really starting to smile over this memory that a moment ago had been painful? "How can you be smiling about all this?" she asked.

Tangled Strands   301

"Your coming back and all that has happened since then has taken most of the sting out of those memories and helped us see some humor in them instead. As for how I reacted ... "

Sharon raised her eyebrows.

"When I was dismantling the party things in the dining room and rolling up the streamers, the impact of what had happened hit me really hard. Suddenly I couldn't stand it, and I threw all the streamers into the air. Then I got my sharpest kitchen knife and made a little ceremony of popping the balloons, one by one, until they lay in pitiful scraps at my feet."

Now both Mrs. Baldwin and Mollie started laughing. Sharon almost felt like joining them, but she said, "I can't believe you're laughing!" She tried to sound accusing, but she knew the corners of her mouth weren't cooperating.

Mrs. Baldwin drained her cup. "Enough about that now. Now it's time to talk about celebrating—

"*How* can you want to celebrate something like—"

"Oh, no! We're not celebrating anything about last year. That is past and forgiven. We want to celebrate the *now*, that you are back with us and all the things God has done for you and for us *with* you since then."

"What ... what are you thinking?"

Mrs. Baldwin nodded to her daughter. "Go ahead, Mollie."

"Chris thought it might be nice to take you and Gram out to dinner, maybe to the steak house down in Painted Post—*if* you think you would like that."

———◆◆◆———

Before turning out her light on the night of her birthday, Sharon stood staring at the single yellow rose on her dresser. In the late afternoon, the florist had delivered it in a crystal vase. The card simply said, "Always, Larry."

What a birthday it had been. Though they had needed their strongest persuasion skills and digging deeper in her closet for a nicer dress, Gram had consented to go with them, and the dinner in Painted Post had been nice.

When they returned and stopped at Marietta Baker's to pick up Betsey, Ethan and Jamie were there. They presented Sharon with a devotional book and a leather-bound prayer journal.

"Jamie wasn't impressed with books as a birthday present." Ethan grinned crookedly. "He thought it ought to be toys or candy." The sound of their shared laughter unleashed some of Sharon's knots, and the sight of Jamie hiding in embarrassment behind his father's pant leg brought a fresh smile to her face.

Afterwards, they went to Chris and Mollie's for cake and ice cream and other presents. She loved the silky brown blouse Mrs. Baldwin gave her and the exquisite gold butterfly necklace from Chris and Mollie. The cologne from Gram surprised her—until Mrs. Baldwin winked at her from across the room. There must be birthday elves as well as Christmas ones.

That night sleep evaded her for a while as she savored with fresh awe the grateful realization that warm memories of her twenty-first birthday could now begin to replace the grim ones of her twentieth.

Tangled Strands 303

61

"So, Sharon, how do you think these first two weeks went?" Sharon felt like hugging Chris for taking the initiative to start this second strategy meeting, this time at his and Mollie's apartment. She wasn't surprised to see him quietly evolving into the leader of the group. Even during their childhood as a foursome, falling in step with Chris had come naturally.

"You've all amazed me with what you've done." She looked at each one—Mrs. Baldwin, Chris and Mollie, and Ethan—and smiled. "Gram is doing better. She's not sitting in her old chair moaning about things like she was before."

"Are things between you and her any better?" Mrs. Baldwin wanted to know.

"They are finally starting to improve a bit. If it weren't for all your encouragement and help, I probably would have sat down and cried a couple times every day. For a while it seemed like I began each day regretting the impulse that prompted me to move back into the house."

Mollie broke in. "Sharon said to me the other day that it was—and I quote—a decision born of valor, not of sense." They all chuckled, but their sympathetic smiles touched her most.

Chris rubbed his hands together and smiled at his wife. "How about you, Mollie? Anything you want to report?"

"She has let me do her braid twice now. I hope one of these days she'll let me wash her hair for her. That has to be a huge challenge, trying to bend over the sink at her age and her ... size. I'm sorry to say this, but I don't think it's been washed for months."

"I'm sure it hasn't—and for longer than that." Sharon cringed. Humiliation over other people observing her family's shortcomings had always been painful, but the love in this group softened it.

Chris said, "I've been helping Sharon get a handle on the household expenditures. Nothing has been done since ... since Sharon's dad died, and things were in a bit of a shambles, but we're sorting them out. How about you, Ethan? Did you get over to Sharon's in the last couple of weeks?"

Ethan hadn't said a word, but Sharon smiled at him now because she knew what was coming.

"As a matter of fact, I did. I picked up Sharon and Betsey for prayer meeting both Wednesdays, and I ... I noticed something." Sharon glanced away. "I suppose because I work in photography, I noticed there are no pictures around the place. Not a one. When I asked Sharon about it ..." he paused until she looked at him, and then he smiled, "she said she can't remember there ever being any pictures in the house. I had to

Tangled Strands 305

coax her a bit—" he winked at her, "but she finally gave me permission to talk to Gram about it."

Chris's brow shot up. "You didn't!"

"I did! I was very tactful and cautious, believe me, but eventually I asked specifically if there were any pictures of Sharon's mother and brother somewhere." All eyes were on him now. "Jamie," he called to the boy playing with his cars in the next room, "bring me that paper bag I brought with me."

Jamie did so, but Ethan made no move to open it. "Gram found a picture in an old trunk of a young woman with a small boy and a smaller girl. First she wouldn't talk about it, but when I charmed her a bit more, she grudgingly admitted it was the last picture taken before ... before the unthinkable happened."

Sharon put both hands to her mouth, then slowly held out one of them for the package, but Ethan grinned and moved it out of her reach.

"When did all this happen?" she asked. "I gave you permission to talk to her, but I don't know anything about *this*...." What on earth had Ethan been up to?

He grinned conspiratorially. "No, you don't know about this. I went back one day when I knew you would be at Mrs. Baldwin's."

Now he took his time opening the paper bag and drawing out something flat, wrapped in white tissue paper. He handed it to her. She accepted it with knit brows and began to unwrap it. As a picture frame emerged, one hand went slowly back to her mouth, and she looked at Ethan.

"You framed it?"

He smiled.

"Oh, Ethan!" She stared at the images a long time. "My ... my mother? ... and Danny?"

"*And you.*"

When she looked up to thank Ethan, her voice completely failed her.

62

Sharon breathed many prayers of gratitude as she and her friends continued to see fruit from their efforts with Gram. With people coming and going in the house, she watched Gram break out of her cocoon of grief and pick up the motions of life again. She began to change her dress every few days and tried to comb her hair herself. She spent time puttering in the kitchen, putting things to order. She put on a half-decent meal for Sharon on her nights to cook, and each time Sharon cooked, Gram found fault a little less. One day she even baked cookies when she heard Ethan and Jamie were coming by. Sharon breathed many sighs of relief in addition to prayers of thanksgiving.

When picking up Betsey after work one day, she called Mollie from Mrs. Baldwin's phone. "Gram made an effort to sweep the kitchen today, and later I found her trying to clean the bathroom mirror. Of course she mostly just smeared the grime around."

"You think she might be open to having some help?"

"I think we're getting close."

"Chris has come up with an idea. Labor Day is just two weeks away. What about a cleaning-and-fixing marathon that weekend?"

"Oh, I don't know how Gram would handle that."

"Yea, I suppose. But there's got to be a way. Any ideas?"

Sharon thought a moment. "You know, she has a sister about an hour from here. I wonder if your mom or I could talk her into going for a visit...."

It was no surprise that Mrs. Baldwin was the one who succeeded in convincing Gram to go and enjoy a visit with her sister, though she was still defensive and reluctant. Getting her permission to do some things on the house while she was gone was a greater challenge, but with repeated assurances that no one would touch *her* room in her absence, she relented.

Since the work would involve spending money, Sharon and Chris talked to his father and came away with solid help, encouragement, and a plan. Several things could be done, but others would have to wait.

It was time for another planning session. With undisguised relief and a great deal of enthusiasm, the group gathered again at the Baldwin house.

Sharon had settled herself in her father's room and Betsey in her old bedroom. Offering to do the work, Ethan and Chris urged her to replace the peeling wallpaper with paint in the two upstairs rooms. Mrs. Baldwin claimed the task of making curtains.

One evening Mollie called her. "Guess what!"

"What?"

Tangled Strands

"Larry's arriving tomorrow to help Chris and Ethan get started on the house. He has ten days before the new school term begins."

"Oh?"

"*And* he's recruited an extra hand—a lady friend from church who put herself through college cleaning houses. She insists she wants to help, so she'll get here on the weekend."

All Sharon could find to say was "That's good." So Larry had a "lady friend"? Well, wasn't that what she had suggested?

Working together that weekend, the three fellows stripped the old paper from both upstairs bedrooms. They painted Sharon's a soft green the last Saturday in August. During the following week before the holiday, Larry painted Betsey's room pink and replaced the chipped, stained sink in the bathroom. A new sink and counters for the kitchen would have to wait until there was more money.

All week, Sharon wrestled with conflicting emotions. *I'm not ready to see Larry yet!* At the same time, another part of her trembled at the prospect of being in the same room with him again, of their eyes meeting in that electric communication they had experienced in July. For the first time in two months, she allowed herself to acknowledge that she missed him. Nevertheless, nothing could change the fact that she had destroyed something valuable and had no right to try and get it back.

As it turned out, the entire week passed without their encountering one another. Was it consciously or unconsciously that Larry managed not to be at his mother's when she dropped Betsey off each day? And how did he also manage never to be working at her house when she arrived home?

In the weekend plans they laid, the fellows claimed the challenges of the heavier work—removing threadbare carpeting, stripping grime from floors and polishing them, laying the new rugs Sharon had bought for the living room and dining room, as well as repairing long neglected doors and windows. The girls would concentrate on cleaning cupboards and woodwork, on touching up battered furniture and scrubbing years of grime from the windows. Sharon never tired of trying to imagine what things would be like after all their efforts.

A delightful conclusion to the plans came when Mrs. Baldwin and Ethan's Aunt Marietta insisted on providing snacks and lunch sandwiches on the work days and chili for supper Saturday night. When Ethan wondered aloud about Jamie, Sharon came up with a suggestion. Couldn't he carry snacks and bottles of Coke to the workers and run some of the in-house errands? As for Betsey, Sharon loved that the group unanimously elected her mascot of the project.

They planned to work all day Saturday and Monday. Sunday after church and spaghetti dinner, they would make an outing to Fern Lake. How fun it would be to introduce Ethan and Jamie to that place, but the thought of being there again with Larry stirred up predictable knots.

Tangled Strands

63

They awoke Saturday to a leaden sky and muggy temperatures, but as Sharon welcomed the crew one by one, she could see the weather had not dampened anyone's zeal. Everyone came with arms full of cleaning equipment—now who had organized that?

Where was Larry? Just as she spotted his car up the street, Mollie called to her from the kitchen.

"Sharon, where do you want me to put the dishes and things while I clean the cupboards? You don't have much counter space."

"That's for sure." Sharon moved things around and removed some to the floor off a small table in the corner. "I guess you'll have to use this little space."

She turned to go through the narrow doorway to the dining room and collided with Larry.

"Oops!" He reached out to steady her. His hand still on her back, he turned to a petite woman behind him. "Sharon, this is Catherine Harrison, the registrar at Groverton. I already introduced her to the others."

Sharon moved away from Larry's hand on her back and put out both hands to Catherine. "It's so kind of you to come when you don't know any of us."

"Well, I've admired and appreciated Larry for a long time. I was in several classes with him and Chris before we graduated. I'm happy to meet *you*, Sharon. Larry's told me—"

"Okay, none of that, Catherine." Larry waved a finger in her face. "You've come to *work*, not to gossip—right, Sharon?"

Bless him for not letting the conversation go in that direction. She didn't want to know what Larry had told Catherine about her—or did she? What was she going to do if she kept running into Larry all day in this small house?

Later that morning, she took Betsey upstairs to change her diaper. Sometime this weekend she needed to get a batch of diapers washed. She hoped the old wringer washer didn't give her the problems she had the last time she used it.

She was just laying Betsey in her crib when Larry's voice from the doorway caused her to whirl around.

"Hey," he chuckled, closing the distance between them with quick steps, "don't look as if you've seen a phantom! I didn't get to ask you downstairs how you are." Now he was standing close with his hand reaching to caress her cheek.

She drew away.

He scowled. "Hey! Remember me? I'm a friend, not—"

"I'm sorry. I didn't mean it that way. Thanks for the work you've done here on the house this week. How are things at school?"

Tangled Strands

"Not bad. This thesis is a challenge, but I guess it is supposed to be if I'm to be worthy of an advanced degree." He glanced at Betsey. "I can see what this young lady's been doing—growing! She's about three months old now, isn't she?" He bent over, made friendly noises at the baby, and her face blossomed with delight.

Sharon felt Larry's arm across her shoulder and again she pulled away.

"What's wrong?"

"Please don't. You're just making it hard for me."

"Hard for *you!*" He drew back, his eyes narrowed. "What do you think it is for me when you keep pulling away?"

The tenor of his voice rose to an angry edge, something she'd seldom heard in Larry Baldwin. "I'm getting tired of playing games, Sharon—you know what I mean?"

"I said I'm sorry! It's just that I don't think I have any more answers now than … than the last time we talked."

"And what is it going to take, Sharon—to 'get answers'?"

She shook her head and refused to look at him. "I don't know, Larry. I do not know."

He turned on his heel and left the room without another word.

The rest of the day, Sharon avoided Larry and was glad he seemed to avoid her. She could tell Chris and Mollie noticed, and she sensed Ethan and Catherine pretending not to. She wished her eyes wouldn't zero in on every interaction between Larry and Catherine, and once she caught him staring when she was talking to Ethan.

Her heart felt like stone.

Thankfully, the group's enthusiasm for the task appeared unaffected, and they continued to work well into the evening. Watching them finish up and put their equipment out of the way for the night, her heart swelled with gratitude over what had been accomplished.

"Thank you for keeping Betsey tomorrow when we go to the lake," she said to Mrs. Baldwin as they said goodbye at the door.

"I'm happy to. I don't think she's ready for swimming lessons yet, do you?"

Sharon smiled.

"Sharon, would you like to ride with Jamie and me tomorrow?" Ethan offered.

"I'd love to."

"Okay then," Chris said. "Larry, you and Catherine can ride with Mollie and me." Dear Chris, jumping in that way to ease what could have been an awkward moment.

Moments later, Larry touched her elbow and drew her aside. "Can we call a truce? Let's not let what's going on between us spoil things for the others, okay?"

She nodded but could not manage a smile.

———♦♦♦———

Sunday afternoon at the lake passed pleasantly, with swimming, boating, and lazing in the sunshine. Jamie showed off his swimming prowess to anyone who would watch. Sharon had to keep squelching memories—of the day she and Larry

Tangled Strands

had spent there in July, not to mention long-ago times at Fern Lake, idyllic times she and Mollie, Chris and Larry had enjoyed as children and teenagers. Today she had to smile at the good-natured ribbing Chris took for his constant hovering over Mollie, worrying whether she was doing something an expectant mother shouldn't be doing. What would it be like to have someone care about you that way?

Hot dogs roasted on sticks over the old charcoal pit, followed by watermelon, completed the day. Catherine had never had s'mores, so of course someone had to show her how to put a roasted marshmallow and a slice of chocolate between two graham crackers—but did it have to be Larry?

On the way home, Jamie promptly fell asleep stretched out on the back seat of Ethan's car. Sharon leaned back in the front seat. Ethan took his eyes off the road to smile at her.

"You look rested and relaxed—do you *feel* that way?"

"I do." She and Larry had done something she wouldn't have thought possible. They had ignored each other all day. Seeing Larry rough-housing with Chris again had warmed her heart, but she forced herself to turn her attention elsewhere when he kept busy making sure Catherine had a good time.

She turned back to Ethan in the car. "How do you think the others feel?"

"Oh, I'm sure it's the same for them. I know I had a great time, and I enjoyed getting acquainted with this place that has such a history for you and the Baldwins." He stared at her a long moment, his lips parted as if he wanted to say something.

Please don't ask about Larry!

He returned his eyes to the road, then pointed to the sky ahead of them. "Have you ever seen such a magnificent kaleidoscope of molten gold as that in front of us now?"

Sharon's mouth dropped open. Magnificent kaleidoscope? Molten gold? Where did Ethan get such words?

"Did I say something wrong?" he asked.

She chuckled then and patted his hand on the steering wheel. "No, of course not." She grinned. "I like it when you use fancy words."

When they stopped at the Baldwin house where Larry and Catherine were staying and so that Sharon could pick up Betsey, Mrs. Baldwin and Marietta Baker brought out popcorn and punch.

"Betsey was fine all afternoon," Mrs. Baldwin reported, "though she didn't drink all of that last bottle and was a trifle fretful before I put her to bed. But she went right to sleep."

"Maybe there's been a little too much excitement this weekend," Catherine suggested. "She certainly has endeared herself to everyone!"

Sharon was in the kitchen helping Mollie wash up the popcorn bowls when Ethan appeared in the doorway.

"I don't want to alarm you, Sharon, but we can hear Betsey upstairs. It sounds like she ... has a problem."

In a flash, Sharon was on her way out of the kitchen. Mrs. Baldwin joined her by the time she reached the stairs. The sounds from her baby were definitely sounds of distress.

Oh, God! I leave her one afternoon and something happens to her!

64

Larry started to follow Sharon and then stopped and glanced around the living room. All conversation had ceased, and everyone looked at each other with concern. The next moment, Sharon's voice sliced through the suspense, screaming Larry's name.

At the sound, Larry bolted for the stairs. On the landing, he collided with his mother.

"She's burning up with fever! Tell Dr. Scott we're on our way to the emergency room!"

Larry started back down but stopped when he saw Chris dashing for the phone.

His mother disappeared upstairs again and a moment later reappeared with Sharon, her brown eyes wide with fright as she clung tightly to a squirming Betsey. As the three reached the foot of the stairs and headed for the front door, the baby's tight, congested breathing almost echoed in the silence that gripped the room. When his mother applied a wet cloth to her forehead, a scratchy protest escaped her throat.

Larry held the door open for them and then started to close it. Sharon's anguished voice stopped him. "Aren't you coming, too?"

Without a word, he stepped out onto the porch and again started to close the door. This time Chris's voice stopped him.

"Mrs. Scott's getting word to her husband."

The baby had started crying, and her fighting for breath increased as Sharon settled into the front seat of the car. Larry already had the engine started. Once the car began to move, Betsey quieted a little. Larry sped through the quiet streets as quickly as he dared. At the emergency entrance, he screeched to a halt, let the others out, and went to park the car.

When he dashed through the door into Emergency minutes later, Sharon ran to him, tears streaming down her face and a few dropping on Betsey in her arms.

"Larry! When is Dr. Scott going to get here?"

He gathered her in his arms, baby and all. "Take it easy, love," he murmured, rocking her back and forth with Betsey cradled between them.

The small emergency room was surprisingly busy for a Sunday evening in Willow Valley. Larry guessed there had been an accident. From one of the curtained cubicles, someone cried out in pain. A woman wept quietly in a corner while two teenagers tried to comfort her. His mother stood at the reception desk.

"Excuse me?" A nurse tapped Larry's shoulder. "I can take the baby now. We'll work on getting her fever down while we wait for Dr. Scott—please?" she added, as Sharon showed no sign of relinquishing her child.

Tangled Strands

As the nurse walked away with Betsey, Sharon turned back to Larry, her face crumpled in anguish. "Larry, it's happening just like it did to my mother! My baby's going to die!"

He took her shoulders and shook her gently. "No! Sharon, you don't know that! God is—"

"God wouldn't take my baby away, would he?" Her anguished cry tore at his heart.

"He loves her very much, Sharon! You *know* that. He's not going to leave you—or Betsey—for a minute! And it's not like your mother. Remember what you told me, that you're going to be able to handle things that happen better than your mother because you have an Anchor she didn't have—an anchor of faith. Remember?"

He continued talking to her, making his voice a soothing balm, and the panic in her eyes began to subside.

"Take a deep breath." He drew out his handkerchief and wiped her tears, then handed it to her to blow her nose.

The outer doors swung open, and Dr. Scott burst through them. He and Larry exchanged a quick handshake, and they pointed him in the direction the nurse had taken Betsey. Before entering the curtained area, he turned.

"You want to come, Sharon, or would you feel better waiting out here?"

Her eyes darted from him to Larry and back again. "Can Larry come, too?"

"Of course."

The three stepped inside. Ten minutes later Larry and Sharon emerged and joined his mother, who was pacing in front of the windows.

"He's pretty sure she has bronchitis," Larry reported. "They're giving her a dose of penicillin—"

"But how could her fever get so high so fast?" Sharon cried.

"Babies' fevers can shoot up a lot faster than older people's," his mother put in, "maybe because their little bodies are so small. I feel terrible. There must have been something I should have noticed earlier—"

Sharon put her arms around her. "Please don't blame yourself. I'm just glad—" her eyes widened— "I'm just glad we didn't take her to the lake with us!"

Larry left them talking in low voices while he went to find a pay phone to call those at the house. "As soon as you left," Chris told him, "the four of us stopped and prayed. We'll keep it up."

"Thanks. I have to go," Larry said. "Dr. Scott just came out."

The doctor gave Sharon a fatherly hug. "Your baby's going to be fine," he pronounced to audible sighs of relief. "These things have a way of creeping up on babies with almost no warning. You did just the right thing. But I would like to keep her here—"

"Keep her!"

"Probably just for tonight. We'll set her up with some oxygen—"

"Oxygen!"

Tangled Strands   321

Larry drew Sharon firmly back into the circle of his arm.

"She'll be more comfortable that way and get the air she needs without having to work so hard for it," the doctor explained. "Sharon, you're welcome to spend the night with her. The room has a cot, and I'm told they're not too bad."

Sharon looked from the doctor to Larry and his mother. "You mean all by myself? What if something happened?"

Instantly Larry said, "I'll stay if you want me to."

Dr. Scott broke in. "Nurses will be on duty, of course, and within easy call, Sharon. Besides, I think now that we've got her fever down, and with the oxygen and penicillin, Betsey should have a pretty good night."

He left them, and Larry turned to his mother. "Here are the keys to my car, Mother. You need to go home and get some rest in case Sharon needs you tomorrow. Ask Chris and Mollie to drop the car back here on their way home."

After his mother left, Larry drew Sharon to one of the waiting-room couches, sat down with his arm around her, and pressed her head into his shoulder.

"Now relax." He rubbed her temple with his free hand. "It's going to be all right."

After a long moment she sat up and looked at him. "Do you think—do you think I'll ever get to the point where I don't panic so badly? Where I can remember to ... to trust God from the beginning?"

"Sharon, trusting God doesn't mean we never experience anxiety. He understands that because he made us. But, yes, I

322 *Tangled Strands*

think with time and as your faith grows stronger, you'll be able to trust him better with the things that come along."

"You think I'll ever be able to be calm and collected in an emergency? I mean, tonight—"

"Now don't go laying guilt on yourself about tonight! Any mother whose baby is suddenly that ill would panic. Don't you think that's part of the maternal instinct God gave mothers?"

"But what if I had been all alone with Betsey? What if—"

"You *weren't* alone. God provided for that. But if you had been, he would have given you the presence of mind you needed to cope with it—I promise!" he added with a smile in response to her skeptical look.

An orderly appeared with a large steel crib and rolled it into the cubicle where Betsey was. In a flash Sharon was on her feet.

"Now take it easy!" said Larry, drawing her firmly to his side again. "They're just going to take her to a room for the night."

The orderly reappeared a few minutes later, a clear plastic tent now covering the crib. Betsey looked incredibly tiny and frail in the depths of it. Sharon clapped both hands to her mouth, and tears flowed afresh.

Dr. Scott approached them. "She's doing better already, Sharon. She'll be in Room 144. It's a three-baby room, and another mother will be staying, too, so you won't be alone." He motioned toward the departing crib. "You can follow them if you want, and I'll check in once more before I leave the hospital."

Tangled Strands

By the time everything was settled, it was nearly midnight. Larry led Sharon to the small waiting area at the end of the pediatrics ward, sat her down facing him, and took her hands.

"Tell me truthfully how you are feeling now. Do you want me to stay? I could snooze out here on this thing—" he motioned to the small couch where they were sitting.

"I think ... I think I'll be okay. I'd like to prove to myself that I can be. Betsey seems to be sleeping peacefully inside that oxygen tent, and since Dr. Scott thinks she's passed the worst, I think I'll be all right. But could we pray before you go?"

They remained facing each other and rested their heads each on the other's shoulders, fingers entwined between them. When Larry finished praying, he wiped a fresh tear from her cheek, then touched his lips lingeringly to her forehead.

"I want you to promise me," he said firmly, "that if you need me during the night—for *any*thing, even just because you're lonely—you'll call me, okay? You remember the number at the house?" He found a small pad of paper on the end table and scribbled a number on it. "Here. I'll sleep on the davenport downstairs where I can hear the phone."

She nodded soberly, then trailed her fingertips across his cheek. "Thank you for being here for me tonight."

"I'm glad I could be," he murmured. "I'm glad I wasn't at school."

65

When Sharon opened her eyes shortly before dawn, memories of the evening before flooded in. They had been drifting in and out of her dreams and wakeful moments all night. True, she did not know what she would have done without Larry, but ever since that spring morning in the park, she had known she was not worthy of a fine man like Larry Baldwin. Last night, in her panic and with Larry available and so willing, the most natural thing had been to turn to him for comfort and strength. With Betsey's crisis passed, however, she had to get hold of herself and not give him false hopes.

She slipped out bed, where she had slept fully dressed, and tiptoed to the door. In the waiting room across the hall, she recognized Larry's silhouetted form at the window, gazing out at the dissolving night. She crossed the hall and stopped at the door.

"Larry?" she whispered. Instantly he was at her side.

"How long have you been here?" she asked.

"Not long," he whispered. "I didn't sleep a whole lot, wondering how Betsey was—and you. I finally couldn't stand it anymore, so I just came. I hope you don't mind."

She wanted to say how nice it was to wake up and find him there, but she bit back the impulse. "It's fine."

"How was your night?" he asked as he led them to a couple of chairs. "Did you get any sleep?" He made a motion as if to embrace her, but she pretended not to notice and established a careful space between them.

"Some, but there was lots of coming and going. The other little guy just had surgery, so he was miserable, and his mom was up with him a lot. Betsey only woke up twice. The first time, the nurse brought her out of the oxygen so I could feed her. The other time I just patted her a couple minutes and she fell asleep again."

She paused and turned slightly away from him, not meeting his eyes. "I had trouble getting back to sleep remembering how scared I was for a while. But then I started thanking God for taking care of Betsey, and for doctors and medicines—and friends, and then I fell asleep okay."

"I'm glad. Would you sleep some more if I weren't here? I could go home now that I know you're okay."

She sensed his impatience with the distance she was maintaining between them. Part of her longed for him not to leave her, but she renewed her resolve and said, "Maybe that would be good. I might sleep a little more if Betsey doesn't wake up. What about today, Larry—the work we were going to do?"

"Oh, everyone is planning to pick up where they left off, but you are not to worry about it. Your only concern is Betsey. If Dr. Scott says she can go home, I'll come for you. But if you don't need me until then, I'll just work with the others. When is your grandmother coming back?"

"Tomorrow morning. Oh, I do hope she doesn't mind what we've done! But I'm afraid that would take a miracle! Larry, how can I possibly thank everyone or repay them for their kindness and hard work this weekend?"

"Don't you worry about it. It's been a pleasure for us. My mother always says the Lord will give you the opportunity someday to pass the favor along to someone else who needs it. Look, call me after you hear from the doctor, okay? If I'm not at your house, I'll be at Mother's."

He ran the backs of his fingers across her cheek, turned, and walked away.

———◆◆◆———

Larry arrived at the Champlin house with Sharon and Betsey just before noon on Monday. All morning he had been agonizing over Sharon's demeanor in the early hours. Driving to the hospital in the dark, he had dared to assume she would welcome his embrace as she had the night before. Instead, he encountered the barriers she had established between them weeks earlier at the waterfall. *Why?*

When he left her again and drove away into the sunrise, a flush of anger washed over him. Thankfully, a morning of hard work on the house gutters had let him channel the anger and frustration to good use. He hoped he could get to the bottom of things with Sharon before he and Catherine had to return to Groverton that night.

Now, as he cut the engine in front of the house, he turned to her. "I'm trying to figure out why the Sharon I left last night is not the Sharon I found this morning."

Clutching Betsey tightly, she did not look at him. "We can't get into that right now, Larry. I hope you don't mind."

He slapped the side of the steering wheel and faced straight forward. "Mind? I do mind! I'm getting tired of your playing games with me."

"I wish you could understand—"

"You're right—I *do not* understand!" He swung on her, patience evaporated. "How can you expect me to understand when you keep playing the chameleon on me? The feelings between us were very clear last night, as they were at Fern Lake, but now this morning you're pulling away again. What *is* it with you, Sharon?"

His voice had risen, and he made an attempt to lower it. "After last night, I envisioned our showing up today with a recovering Betsey, my arm around both of you, and you and me laughing together with a few kisses thrown in."

He saw her wince at his words before swinging to face out the window again. "That's just a daydream, Larry. I was upset last night. I wasn't myself. So, please, could you do as I ask?"

"I'll do it, but only because you asked." He paused. "Could I ask something in return?"

"Maybe."

"Could we have a few minutes alone before Catherine and I have to leave late this afternoon?"

She hesitated. "I suppose. Come up this afternoon when I'm upstairs with Betsey. By the way, have you seen that pizza place that just opened up in Willow Valley?"

"No, I don't think I have."

"It's right by the bank on Main Street. I suggested to your mother that I'd like to bring some in for everybody for supper—sort of finish out the work with a little celebration. It's the least I can do."

She gave him half a smile then, but instead of returning it, he opened his door and went grimly around to open hers. He saw her and Betsey to the door and then went back to work on the gutters without going in.

66

Sharon's heart felt like lead as she climbed the steps to the house. Inside, everyone gathered anxiously around Betsey. She opened her eyes and stared languidly at the hovering faces.

"I would say she looks better than she did last night," Mrs. Baldwin said.

"But she's not the sunny little mascot we enjoyed on Saturday," Mollie put in.

They backed off and urged Sharon to take her on up to the quiet of her bedroom. When she came back down, she found Jamie especially stricken.

"I guess I carefully understated how ill Betsey was," Ethan said, "but Jamie's sensitive antennae must have picked up more than I intended him to from our conversations this morning. It may take a few minutes to get him distracted and playing with his cars again."

Sharon wanted to try and comfort the child, but her own emotions were too splintered to be trusted. After watching him a few minutes, she went and found Mollie cleaning the dining room light fixture. "What can I do to help? Betsey went right back to sleep. I guess that's the best thing for her at the moment."

"Mother and Mrs. Baker are setting out sandwiches in the kitchen, but I think Catherine could use some help washing windows out front."

When she arrived on the porch, Catherine said, "Oh, hi, Sharon! I think this porch must have had a special charm once. Did you spend a lot of time out here when you were growing up?"

"No, not really, at least not when I was little, but a little bit since I came back from Chicago." With the loss of her father, the memories were bittersweet, and she didn't want to linger on them. Thankfully, Catherine didn't.

"Well, after hearing Larry talk about you, I'm glad for a chance to get to know you this weekend. And it's been a delight to meet that baby daughter of yours. She's a special treasure."

Sharon smiled. "Oh, I know. I can't imagine what my life was like without her. I'm so grateful to God."

They chatted several minutes while they worked. When the bell rang signaling lunch, Sharon started into the house, then felt Catherine's hand on her arm.

"Could you wait a minute? I know this is none of my business, but I think an awful lot of Larry, and…and my heart goes out to the two of you. I don't know what the problem seems to be, but I just want to say how much Larry cares about you, and I hope you'll be able to work things out between you.

I'm praying for you both because, frankly, I think God wants you together."

Sharon opened her mouth to protest, but the bell rang again, and they could see the group had begun to gather, so they turned and went inside.

The first person Sharon saw when she and Catherine entered the kitchen was Ethan, with Jamie in tow, sauntering in ahead of them.

"Ah, lunchtime! I don't mind telling you, these here bears is pow'rful hungry!"

They all laughed, and Chris and Larry joined them through the back door. Sharon took a deep breath to try and get her heart to stop racing.

Catherine said, "You make a good bear, Ethan McCrae, with that beard of yours."

Ethan bowed from the waist. "I take that as a compliment, Fair Damsel, and I thanks ye."

Where was this banter coming from? For a moment Sharon almost forgot her own concerns.

As they picked up sandwiches and chips, they discussed their progress on the work. Chris clanged his fork on a glass. Looking around at the group, he said, "Our emphasis for the rest of the day has to be finishing up things that are started. If you see something that needs to be done but hasn't been started, write it in that notebook on the table, and someone will get to it, sometime. But for the rest of today, focus on *finishing*."

Ethan said, "You know, with a little fixing up, this house is developing a decided charm." Putting on an exaggerated grin, he made a sweeping hand motion that included them all. "How about we all plan to work on *my* house the next time there's a holiday?"

Catherine laughed. "Are you suggesting, Sir Bear, that I come all the way from Groverton to work on *your* house? I would expect to find a bear like you living in a cave!"

"How can you say such a thing, Fair Damsel? My house is perfectly respectable—isn't it, Sharon?" he said over his shoulder as he headed for the dining room with two plates. A moment later he returned for a glass of tea.

"Respectable? Surely that would be stretching it from such a furry creature!" Catherine said.

He responded by turning on her, raising his arms, glass and all, and staging a mock bear attack, complete with sound effects. Jamie squealed with delight. When Catherine turned to flee, she bumped squarely into Larry, who reached out and steadied her, then drew her aside to speak in low tones. Again? Sharon looked away. What did the two have to talk about so much? Just because they were driving back to Groverton this evening ... At any rate, so much for bear fun.

It was all Sharon could do to keep her eyes from wandering to Larry and Catherine. She was angry at herself for feeling jealous and angry at herself for not being able to ignore Catherine's words. *Larry cares a great deal about you ... I think God wants you together...*

Well, maybe God had wanted them together, but she had gone and ruined it all.

"Hey, Sober-sides." Ethan's quiet voice in her ear startled her. "You had better rejoin the group, or someone's going to think you're not happy with our work."

She swung around to face him. His eyes, so full of teasing with Catherine a moment ago, now radiated compassion. She smiled an apology, murmured "Thanks," and crossed the room to speak to Mollie.

67

Sharon had to struggle with her concentration all afternoon. She had promised Larry some time alone, and her heart raced at the prospect, but she wasn't sure her resolve would hold if she were too much alone with him. With every breath of her being, she knew she did not want to hurt him, but nothing had changed in her perspective of their situation, except that every time they were together it seemed so comfortable and natural—and hopeless.

That proved nothing at all except how much she had lost when she went her own way last year. Maybe God would "take up the tangled strands" she had brought back with her and help her salvage something for her future and Betsey's. But it could not be with Larry. She felt too much shame at the thought of saddling him with "damaged goods" or the child of a guy like Tony. Yet no way could she tell *him* that.

And then she remembered. The class ring. She still hadn't given it back to him. This would be a perfect chance to do that, and surely doing it would bring a visible ending for both of them.

When she heard Betsey stirring and started upstairs, Sharon expected Larry to follow her, but he did not. *Does he realize I need to feed her first?* His thoughtfulness further unraveled her tumultuous state of mind.

She was burping Betsey when a gentle knock sounded on the half-closed door. Whoever it was waited until she said, "Come in."

"Hello." He stayed near the door. "Is now okay?"

She nodded, then stood up and carried Betsey to the dressing table. The afternoon was getting too warm for the sleeper she had worn all night, and Dr. Scott had warned against overdressing her during a fever.

"How's her temperature?" Larry came nearer.

"She still has a fever, but very little now."

She changed Betsey into a lighter outfit, then laid her down in the crib. Did Larry have to stand so close while he watched her?

"That's a beautiful crib. Did I hear your dad bought it for her?"

"Yes. It was one of the last things he did."

"She seems to be doing okay, doesn't she?" He reached down and smoothed the dark, silky hair on the baby's head, then took her tiny hand in his fingers.

Sharon stood beside him, statue still. The inches between them felt like a chasm. She was glad he made no effort to

Tangled Strands

touch her because she knew it would be the undoing of her resolve. Finally, he turned slowly, and they faced each other.

"After last night, Sharon, there is no longer any question in my mind about our belonging together."

She shook her head vehemently. "No, Larry! You don't understand! I admit that some of our old feelings still seem to be underneath. I guess they came out last night, but that doesn't mean we should allow them or encourage them."

He stared at her, eyes beginning to flash. "*Why* do you say that, Sharon? If this is how we feel about each other, then why wouldn't we—"

"No, Larry, we can't! I can't let you think we have a future together. "Here ..." She reached into the pocket of her dress and drew out his class ring. "I keep forgetting to give this to you."

He jumped back as if she held out a snake.

"You've got to be kidding!" His voice rose, and Betsey screwed up her face in alarm. Larry's hand went to his mouth, and he backed away a bit.

Sharon patted the baby and made soothing sounds. The moment Betsey quieted, Sharon straightened and held the ring out again, but Larry took another step back.

"This a the last straw, Sharon! I gave you that ring in good faith when I graduated from high school, and I have no intentions of taking it back now."

'You *have* to take it because for me to keep it would be a lie."

She held it out again, and she thought he was going to take it. Instead, he struck her hand from underneath and sent the

Tangled Strands 337

ring flying. It hit the wood floor hard. Betsey jumped and let out a cry of distress.

"Now see what you've done?" Sharon lifted Betsey to her shoulder, as much to comfort herself as to comfort her baby, and began pacing the small room. She paused in her pacing and turned toward Larry. "This is the way it has to be, Larry."

He threw up his hands. "I don't believe this! What's gotten into you?"

She saw the hard lines of his face and looked away. Anguish choked her and kept her silent. At least Betsey's head had relaxed on her shoulder.

"I thought we turned a corner last night." He slammed a fist into his other hand. "We should be picking up the pieces of what we lost and building from there." He glanced down at the ring. "Are you going to pick it up?"

"N-no."

He swung away from her, then turned back. "Okay, Sharon ...." His tight, painful tones scraped her nerves. "If this is what you want, then this is what you shall have." He stared at her while rubbing the hand he had hit. "I can't keep doing this, Sharon! I don't understand you, I don't *believe* you—I think you're lying to yourself, and it hurts too much to hear you keep saying these things."

He turned and started for the door.

"You're just ... you're just—*going?*" It was a stupid question, but she couldn't help blurting it out.

He stopped but did not turn. "I am. Right now I can't handle any more of your rejection. I've worked hard this summer to come to grips with the reality of Tony in your life, but it looks to me like you're still hanging on to him!"

"*Larry!*" she protested, stung, but he ignored her and stopped just before the door. "If you ever change your mind, you know where to look for me."

He went out and slammed the door.

Sharon flinched, the crack of the slammed door vibrating along her nerves. Her shoe encountered the ring, and she kicked it under the crib. Her head was beginning to ache from fighting off tears.

Aghast at the thought of having to go downstairs, she discovered she was trembling. Of course the others had heard their raised voices. Well, let Larry explain. She had to appear, but first she went into the bathroom and splashed water on her burning cheeks.

68

When they gathered around the pizza, the festive mood from lunch was nowhere to be found. Sharon stayed in the kitchen, but she could hear the others quietly comparing notes about what they had accomplished on the house—everyone except Larry. She hadn't heard so much as a word in his voice. After a few minutes, she took her pizza and drink and went back upstairs without having exchanged a word with anyone.

So much for a celebration of their accomplishments. So much for expressing her appreciation for their hard work.

Fifteen minutes later Mollie appeared in Betsy's doorway. "You better come." Her voice was grim. "They're getting ready to leave."

Sharon came down, bracing herself to be present and go through thank yous and farewells. Aside from Betsey's crisis, it had been a good weekend until a few minutes ago, and she was truly grateful for all that had been accomplished on the house. She had been looking forward to taking it all in and enjoying it once her world settled down again, but how could she do that after what had happened between her and Larry? She realized with a pang that her resolve not to hurt him had been unforgivably naïve.

Though she tried to be warm and enthusiastic in her gratitude, she wasn't surprised that the good-byes were stiff and awkward. Catherine gave Sharon a quick hug, but Sharon and Larry simply ignored each other as he and Catherine departed.

As soon as Chris closed the door behind the travelers, Sharon headed for the kitchen. Mollie's voice intercepted her.

"Sharon? Please stay a minute. We—we'd like to talk to you."

Sharon stared at the three who remained—Mollie, Chris, and Ethan. Why was Ethan still here? Clearly they were aware of what had happened upstairs, and her feelings ricocheted between resenting their intrusion and being grateful they cared. Apprehension quivered on her overwrought nerves as she walked to the worn chair in the corner and sat stiffly on the arm of it.

Beside Mollie on the davenport, Chris rested his elbows on his knees and cleared his throat. "Sharon, we're all your friends—"

"—and we love you," Mollie put in. Ethan lifted Jamie to his lap, hugged him close, and laid a warning finger to his lips.

"What we want to say," Chris began again, "is that, as your friends, we're all concerned about what's happening between you and Larry. It is clear to us that both of you have strong feelings, and we don't understand what ... what's keeping you apart," he finished in a rush.

Tangled Strands

Sharon stared at her hands. What had Larry said to them? Finally she said sadly, "I don't know what to say, Chris. All I know is that I hate myself for running off with Tony and spoiling any chances Larry and I—"

"But God has forgiven you for that, Sharon!" Chris and Mollie interrupted almost in unison.

"But that doesn't change the fact that nothing can ever be the same again!" Sharon's voice broke and tears threatened.

"Sharon," Ethan broke in, "would you be free to have dinner with me some night this week?"

They all gaped at him. What kind of question was that in the midst of the current discussion?

"Please?" Then, as if understanding their confusion, he looked at Sharon and added, "I have a story I need to tell you, something I think might help." He gave a half-hearted smile, but something unreadable in his eyes kept it from ringing true.

Throughout Betsey's ten-o'clock feeding, tears rolled down Sharon's face, some of them splashing on Betsey's plump cheeks before her mother noticed. As she settled Betsey in her crib, the phone rang. She picked it up, trying to steady her voice and gain command of her tears.

"You've been crying, haven't you?" Mollie declared immediately. "I don't blame you." She paused. "Chris tried to talk me out of calling. He's afraid I'm going to chew you out for giving Larry more grief."

Sharon smothered a sob and said nothing. Mollie went on. "Well, I'm not. I'm not even going to keep you long because I know it's bedtime. I just want to say one thing. I *am* your friend, Sharon. Chris and I love you and Larry so much, and it's killing us to see you struggling like this. Can you give us at least some idea of what's going on with you two?"

Sharon took a deep a deep breath and forced herself to speak calmly. "Larry is upset with me, Mollie, and I'm upset with myself. It's too complicated to explain—"

"What's complicated? If you love each other—and it looks like you do—"

"We–we aren't actually talking about love."

Mollie was silent a moment. "I'm speechless, Sharon. I don't know whether I believe you or not."

"Well, it's true, Mollie. All I can do is ask you and Chris to pray for us. As you probably guessed, Larry and I had a bit of a falling out. He has sort of ... lost patience with me."

Not since the night she fled from Tony had Sharon cried herself to sleep, but she did tonight.

69

Sharon awoke on Tuesday with a knot in the pit of her stomach. She couldn't be sure which was worse, pain over the night before or apprehension over the day ahead. It wasn't enough that once again she had hurt Larry and turned him away, but today Gram was coming home. How would she react to what they had done on the house? Would she take it as a personal affront, despite all their efforts to convince her otherwise? If she did, then she—Sharon—would be on the receiving end of all the displeasure and blame.

I can't take any more!

As she lay in bed nursing Betsey and trying to gather her thoughts for the day, she felt like burrowing under the blankets and letting the day get along without her.

Oh, dear Lord, help! Everyone talked about God giving strength and courage, as well as wisdom. She surely needed a generous helping of all of them if she was to get through this day! Could God really help her put Larry out of her mind so she could focus on Gram?

She was glad she worked afternoons so she would have the morning to pull herself together and make sure everything was in order around the house. She was also glad she would be there when Gram arrived. Why should she be glad about that? Wouldn't it be easier not to be there and thus not have to face any initial displeasure?

But she did want to be there! She wanted to be able to influence Gram as much as possible to be happy about the house and what had been done. She wanted to help her understand how much love had gone into all that work. And it wasn't just love for Sharon. How many times during the weekend had she heard her friends express concern about Gram's reactions and acceptance? They wanted to make Gram happy, too.

As she got up and dressed Betsey and then herself, she thought about calling Mrs. Baldwin. If she could come and stay with Betsey while Sharon fetched Gram from the bus station, then she would be there too when Gram arrived at the house. Everyone understood that Mrs. Baldwin was the one most able to communicate with Gram on an objective level, and almost every day Sharon recognized new ways hers and Gram's mutual history under this roof made her defensive with Gram.

She reached for the phone and then stopped. *No! I won't call her! I think she would come—and be glad to, but....* She needed to stop leaning on other people and learn to handle things herself. She supposed that included learning to trust God, to depend on his help instead of always turning to people.

The thought brought a smile of determination to her face. *Yes! I will face Gram, and face her with patience, and love, and compassion. After all, she's a tired and lonely old woman, and she hasn't had much happiness in her life. With God's help, maybe I can bring her some.*

Twenty minutes later, Mrs. Baldwin called. "Sharon? Did you say your grandmother's bus gets in at ten-thirty?'

"That's right."

"Well, I have a dentist appointment at eleven. I could pick her up and drop her by your house on my way. That way you wouldn't have to go after her. Would that help?"

"Yes, it sure would! I could get the wash going, and I wouldn't have to drag Betsey out."

"Well, that's what I thought. But the timing will be close. I may have to drop her off and keep going. Are you feeling the letdown today, or are you glad for the peace and quiet?"

"I guess a bit of both." What a relief that Mrs. Baldwin had already left the day before and hopefully hadn't heard what went on between her and Larry.

She was in the back yard hanging a load of wash when she heard the car pull up in front. Scooping up Betsey in her infant seat, she glanced at her watch. Ten-fifty. She came around the house in time to see Gram easing her bulk out of the car. Mrs. Baldwin waved and drove on.

Sharon walked directly up to her grandmother and hugged her with her free arm. "Hi, Gram! I'm glad you're back! Did you have a good time?"

Gram grunted an assent, but she was not looking at Sharon. Her eyes were on Betsey, still peaked from her bout with the high fever.

"What's a matter with the baby?" she demanded. "She looks terrible!"

"Oh, Gram, she's been sick! She had a high fever, and we had to rush her to the hospital, and she had to stay there all night—in an oxygen tent ...."

Her voice trailed off, partly from breathlessness but more in awe at the sight of two great tears swelling out of Gram's eyes onto her ample cheeks.

"Oh, no!" she muttered, her voice cracking slightly. "Oh, no," she said again, "not our baby!" Her hands reached toward Betsey and then jerked back.

"Would you ... would you like to hold her, Gram? She's a lot better. Come up on the porch, and I'll get her out of this seat." Holding her breath lest the spell be broken, Sharon led the way up the steps onto the porch.

"There. You sit on the swing and I'll give her to you," and she tenderly placed her baby in Gram's arms. Betsey looked up into her great-grandmother's eyes for the first time and gave her a wan smile.

That was all it took. More tears joined the others, and Gram's shoulders began to shake, though no sound came. In another moment Sharon joined her on the swing and wrapped her arms as far as they would go around the two. Her own tears dampened Gram's faded dress.

After a while, Sharon drew back, not knowing what she might read in the older woman's face once she had a chance to collect herself. Would she strike out now to cover her emotions?

Tangled Strands

In an effort to prevent that, Sharon lifted her head with a smile already shining through her tears. "What a couple of cry-babies we are!" She laughed shakily and shook a finger at Betsey. "And all because of you, young lady! Aren't you ashamed of yourself?" Betsey made a cooing sound and gave one languid kick in response.

"You think it's too cool out here for her?" Gram asked suddenly, feeling the baby's arms.

"Yeah, maybe we should take her inside. It was warmer out back in the sun where I was hanging clothes." Sharon picked up Betsey and waited for Gram to stand. "Would you like to carry her in?"

The older woman hesitated. "Better not try it," she concluded with no hint of malice. "I'm outa practice. I'll do my holdin' sittin' down till she gets a mite bigger."

"Fine," Sharon smiled. "You just let me know whenever you want to hold her, okay?" As she turned toward the door with Betsey, she remembered the house. *Here it comes!* She made one last-ditch effort to head off a negative response.

"Now you've got to come and see our house, Gram! Everybody worked *so* hard, and they so much want you to be happy about it!"

70

"I guess we'll never know how she would have reacted to the house if we hadn't first had the part about Betsey being sick," Sharon told Ethan at Chez Pierre's the next evening. "That softened her up a lot." She smiled at him across the candlelit table.

Ethan nodded briefly as he pushed his dinner around the plate with his fork. "That's good."

"I'm sorry we were so busy at work these last two afternoons that I didn't have a chance to tell you about it."

"That's okay."

"But I know it wasn't just chance that put it together. I know it was an answer to everyone's prayers, including mine." She smiled again. "Thanks for all you did."

"You're welcome. I hope it was a good example to Jamie, young as he is—the idea of helping others when an occasion arises."

"It was surprising how we were able to keep him busy, and it was a big help to have someone to run things back and forth without having to stop what we were doing or to come down from a ladder."

She stopped. Ethan was clearly preoccupied with something other than what she was saying. He had been all evening.

"What is it, Ethan? I know you said you wanted to talk to me about something, but I haven't a clue what it might be."

He still said nothing as he toyed slowly with the stem of his goblet. Had he changed his mind about what he wanted to say? She reached out her hand and laid it lightly on his.

"You don't have to talk about anything you don't want to, Ethan. You know that."

He shook his head and finally looked up at her. The blue of his eyes was strangely intensified by the emotions she could see him struggling with.

"No," he said slowly, "I have to go through with it, Sharon, for your sake—and Larry's."

The mention of Larry brought a tightening to her heart, and she drew away slightly. Ethan caught her reaction.

"Don't worry! I'm not going to give him competition. Not that I might not have liked to! I guess it's all right to tell you, Sharon, that it wouldn't have taken much for me to fall in love with you. There was a lot to recommend it, including how much Jamie loves you. But some instinct kept me cautious, and the more I learned about you and Larry and now that I have seen you together—well, I'm sure that's the way it has to be."

Her voice choked up somewhere between her lips and the turmoil in her heart, so she could not respond. She reached her hand back to his, and his fingers closed tightly over hers.

"What I wanted to talk to you about tonight, Sharon, was ... is ... well, forgiveness. Not God's forgiveness. I believe you've understood and accepted that. But did you know that sometimes we have to forgive ourselves?"

Her mind ran a quick flashback. "You mean what I said the other day about hating myself?"

"Yes, but not just that. I sensed that was at the root of the problem even before. So I have a story to tell you." A shadowy pain sharpened in his eyes, and she drew an involuntary breath. He glanced at her briefly as he asked, "Do you know how Ellen died?"

Sharon tensed. "In a car accident...that's all I know," she answered in a small voice.

Now his blue eyes looked steadily into hers as he said in a barely audible voice, "In a very real sense—I killed her."

Sharon sucked in her breath. "Oh, *no*, Ethan! You couldn't have!" That couldn't be true! Solid, gentle Ethan who had been so good to her?

"You and I have gotten to know each other fairly well, but not enough for you to discover that I have a temper—oh, yes, I do!" he added as she started to protest. "If you haven't seen it, it's because God and I have been working hard on it ever since ... ever since it cost me the dearest thing in my life." He looked away again, and her fingers tightened around his.

"Oh, no, Ethan," she whispered. "Are you sure you want to tell me about this?"

Tangled Strands

He nodded, and she could see him swallow as he worked to regain control of his voice. "Now that I've started, I have to finish. I thought I was beyond all this emotion," he apologized. "I really did—"

"It's okay! You've seen *me* emotional."

He gave her a crooked look and took a deep breath. "Ellen and I loved each other very much, but we fought an awful lot, too. I understand some of the reasons better now, but not all of them. On the one hand we were crazy about each other, but we clashed a lot about our differences. We were young and so intense—and, like many when young, we were pretty self-focused. I think if we had had enough time together, we could have outgrown it, or learned to appreciate our differences, but we didn't." He stopped.

"I'm listening."

"One night before going to choir practice, we got into it again. I made a negative comment about what she was planning to wear. That triggered an old discussion about 'helpful input' versus 'criticism.' We were still at it when we got in the car, only it had heated up more than usual. Three blocks from the house I was so busy ranting at her that—" His voice dropped, and Sharon had to lean toward him to hear. "I ran a stop sign ... and–and a pickup truck plowed into Ellen's side of the car—"

71

Ethan's voice broke, and he heard Sharon gasp as he stared out the window behind her at the lights of Willow Valley in the distance. Finally he forced his gaze back to her and said shakily, "Do you mind if we get out of here?"

She nodded, her eyes wide.

They had only half finished their dinners, but he could not face another bite. He motioned for the check, and they slipped quickly out into the September evening and walked in silence to his car. Without a word, he drove to the waterfall overlook half a mile beyond the restaurant, and parked the car. A misshapen, waning moon gave the night an eerie, seemingly inappropriate beauty, and the mild air was kissed with the fragrance of pine. Ethan ran his fingers through his hair and then rested his head on the steering wheel.

He did not speak, and after a moment Sharon asked softly, "Was she killed instantly?"

He shook his head without raising it. But the five heart-wrenching minutes he and Ellen had shared before she slipped away would be his alone until he died. He doubted he would ever share them even with Jamie. Finally, he lifted his head, took a deep breath, and turned to Sharon.

"No, but it was only a few minutes. She had been severely injured internally. The other driver had both legs broken. Of course I was to blame for the accident. I lost my insurance, and they took my driver's license away for a while."

He paused, studied his hands, then continued slowly. "I went into deep depression. I lost my job. Other people had to care for Jamie. I don't know what would have happened to Jamie and me if a retired pastor friend hadn't gotten a hold of me and laid some things on the line."

Sharon reached across the space between them and laid her hand on his arm. "I can't imagine how terrible you must have felt," she said, her voice barely above a whisper, "not only for taking Ellen's life, but also Jamie's moth—"

Ethan's sharp intake of breath halted Sharon in mid-sentence.

"That's not all, Sharon." His voice was ragged. "Ellen … Ellen was six months pregnant—"

"Oh! Ethan!"

In one swift motion she slid across the seat and reached out to him. The next moment they were weeping in each others' arms. He drew back and reached for his handkerchief.

"I think it's been nearly a year since I've shed actual tears over it," he said as he wiped the mingled tears from their faces. "But do you see why I had to tell you about it? Back then, I had to come to the point of not only accepting God's

354 *Tangled Strands*

forgiveness for my irresponsible behavior, but I had to forgive myself. Only then could I pick up the pieces and hope to salvage something from what remained of Jamie's and my world. Do you hear what I'm saying?"

"Yes, but—"

"No buts! As far as you and Larry are concerned, you have to forgive yourself for what you did, for spoiling what you had. You have to forgive yourself for the things that can never be as they would have been—things like, yes, you have been another man's wife, and yes, Betsey is another man's child, and yes—" he hesitated, "and yes, a wedding night won't be something new for you."

He stopped, hoping he had not offended her with his candor. She said nothing. "I guess what I most want to convince you about, Sharon, is that it can be done—forgiving yourself. Oh, it wasn't easy. I had to stop worrying about whether Ellen's family could ever forgive me, or whether Jamie will be able to when he's old enough to understand. I had to stop telling myself that I wasn't worthy to be his father because of what I had done."

He took a deep breath. "Maybe the turning point came when I realized that, despite my failure, God wasn't going to fire me from being Jamie's father. He just wanted me to give him a chance to patch up the mess I'd made and to heal my wounded heart and pain-filled memories."

——◆◆◆——

Sharon was silent a moment before responding. Then she said slowly, "I think God's done a marvelous job with you and Jamie. I knew you had sorrow in losing your wife, but I would never have guessed about the rest of it."

"And you know something, Sharon? You have a better chance of redeeming the damage than I did."

"What do you mean?"

"Ellen can never be brought back, but you and Larry can still put together a life and a marriage if you want to."

She shook her head vigorously. "It's not that simple, Ethan! I've thought and thought about it, but it just wouldn't be fair to Larry!"

He swung on her. "What do you mean by that?" The harsh edge on his voice was back.

"Larry is such a fine a person, and he deserves so much better—"

"Don't you think Larry should be the one to decide that? It looks to me like you two still have strong feelings for each other. Isn't that true?"

"I guess so, but—"

"What did I say about *buts*? Have you missed completely what I've been trying to tell you? If God has forgiven you, why should you refuse to forgive yourself? Are you a better judge than the Almighty about what is appropriate?"

The edge on his voice had intensified even more, and Sharon looked at him sharply. It was clear this effort on her behalf was costing him dearly. Humbled, she looked afresh into her heart while he stared unblinking into the night.

After a moment she broke the silence. "Of course I don't know better than God. It's just that it's a lifetime commitment, asking Larry to raise Tony's child, and I can't be sure that one day he might not regret the decision."

He faced her then, put his finger on her chin, and made her look at him. "I know what you mean. I had all kinds of concerns like that. But I've come to understand that when we follow God, *he* takes the responsibility for the consequences. No matter how hard we try, we can't guarantee the outcome of anything." He paused. "Can we, Sharon?"

"I ... I know you're right."

"And there's something else you'll have going for you. A marriage between you and Larry will be nothing at all like what you had with Tony. It will be a marriage of your hearts with a relationship with God at the center. And I am positive there will be the kind of soul commitment that Tony Casanetti never imagined. What do you think?"

As the implications of his words began to sink in, she felt a smile blossoming on her face. "You mean God could not only forgive me, but he might still allow Larry and me to be together?"

"Isn't that's what I've been trying to tell you, you little goose!"

"How can he ... do that?"

"If I were you, I wouldn't worry about the 'how.' I would just say a big 'Thank you, Lord!' and get on with claiming it as fast as I could!"

"Oh, Ethan! What an incredible friend you are! May I tell you something, since you did the same with me? I all but

Tangled Strands 357

prayed that I would be able to forget about Larry and fall in love with you because, well, it would have simplified things since you've been married before. But Ethan! What about you? I want *you* to find happiness and have someone to love again. How can I bear for you not to, especially after this?"

He lifted his hands and studied them a moment. Even in the dimness of the car she could detect a smile teasing the corners of his mouth.

"You can pray about that, okay? I think the Lord may have already started to do something about it."

She stared at him. "What do you mean?"

"Well, think a minute. What's happened to this old bear in the last week ... ?"

"You mean ... you mean the Fair Damsel?" Sharon clapped her hand to her mouth. "Oh, Ethan!" Then she gave him a quick hug and a resounding kiss on the cheek before sliding swiftly back to her side of the car and folding her hands primly in her lap.

Their shared laughter drifted out into the night and mingled with the hum of the waterfall.

72

Sharon awoke on Thursday with a song in her heart, though she had to think for a moment to remember what had put it there. Oh, yes. That incredible evening with Ethan and his assurance that it might yet be possible—and in God's will—for her and Larry to make a life together.

Could they? Had Larry meant his last words—that his feelings wouldn't change and if she every changed her mind, she would know where to find him? She snuggled into the comfort of her bed and luxuriated in the thought, then reached for her Bible on the bedside table. She pulled from the back a paper on which Agnes had written the words of the tangled strands song. Now she noticed the second verse more than she had before.

Take every failure, each mistake
Of our poor human ways
That, Savior, for Thine own dear sake,
They may show forth Thy praise.

She pressed the paper to her chest, closed her eyes, and breathed another prayer of thanksgiving. The idea of a life with Larry was so replete with possibilities and joy that she hardly knew where to start dreaming. One thing she knew with certainty. She would gladly spend every breath of the rest of her life making it up to Larry for what she had done and for the time they had lost. What would it be like to love him freely, openly, every day?

But no! This would never do. If she started thinking along those lines, she would never get anything done, and she still had a baby, and a job, and a grandmother with whom she was making tenuous progress at an improved relationship.

She smiled. Gram had been so cute since she got back from her sister's. Outwardly she was still grim and aloof, but it seemed every time Sharon's back was turned, Gram stopped to coo at the baby. Once Sharon caught her tickling Betsey to make her giggle.

And Betsey was coming into such a winning age, now that she was getting back to her healthy self. She loved smiling and kicking and waving her little arms. Twice Sharon had caught her trying to turn over, so leaving her unattended for even a moment would soon be out of the question. Having Gram around to keep an eye on her would be a real help.

But Gram was still Gram. She had not cared for the color of the new rugs, and she was sure she was going to break her neck on the clean, polished floors. Her complaints, however, were not laced with acid as they had been in the past. She was just being Gram, Sharon reminded herself, and she had to keep remembering that. The day before, when Gram settled in her armchair, she asked Sharon to bring Betsey for her to hold. Dressed now and with her bed made, Sharon began brushing her hair. Her mind returned to the evening before and Ethan's encouragement to forgive herself for what she had done. He had been so serious, so sure he had an answer for her heartache over Larry.

Forgive oneself. But *how?* Was it a complex, theological thing? What did forgiving yourself look like in real actions? Surely she and Larry couldn't just plunge ahead and pretend her going off with Tony hadn't happened, though she remembered Larry's wanting to do that. Suddenly the urge for answers overwhelmed her, and she hurried downstairs to the telephone in the living room.

When Mollie answered, her voice sounded groggy.

"Oh, Mollie, I woke you up, didn't I? I'm sorry."

"Don't worry about it. It's time for me to wake up anyway. I've never had such a hard time waking up in the mornings as I'm having with pregnancy."

What would Mollie think about her evening with Ethan? The only way to find out was to start telling. Her friend listened quietly. Telling about Ellen was the easy part. More awkward was relaying Ethan's conviction that Sharon and Larry might still have a future together.

"What does he mean, Mollie, that I have to forgive myself?"

Mollie was quiet. "I have to admit I've never thought about it, Sharon. Maybe we should start with what any

Tangled Strands 361

forgiveness means. Let's think about what it means that God has forgiven you."

Sharon was thoughtful. "It means God isn't holding my sins against me anymore."

"That's a start, yes. Anything else?"

"Doesn't it mean God isn't going to punish me for my sins anymore?"

"That too." Mollie paused. "Do you think that might have something to do with your forgiving yourself? Do you think you are trying to punish yourself for what you did?"

"Wow," Sharon said softly. "I suppose I am." She was silent a long moment, processing what had been said.

"And, Sharon, it occurs to me that by continuing to punish yourself, you are punishing Larry, too."

Sharon gasped. "Oh, Mollie! I never thought about it that way." After another silence, she asked in a small voice, "So, Mollie, what do I do now?"

"What do you think you should do? What do you *want* to do?"

"I think ... I think I need to talk to Larry to tell him some of this. But, Mollie, fall classes started this week at Groverton, and I have no idea when Larry might be coming here again."

"You have a phone—"

"Oh, I couldn't talk to him about this by phone."

"So what's stopping you from going there?"

"You mean to Groverton? By myself?"

"You found your way all the way back from Chicago by yourself. Do you think you could do it if you had directions?"

362 *Tangled Strands*

"Maybe. But I have to consider Betsey and her feeding schedule. Let me think about it."

73

Sharon found Gram in the kitchen, already dressed, and her hair, if not combed, at least smoothed down.

"Felt like havin' me a egg this mornin', and thought maybe you would, too."

Sharon didn't feel like an egg, but when she saw Gram already had three in the skillet, she accepted the peaceful gesture with grace. At mid-morning when she was worming Betsey's arms into a jacket for a grocery-shopping trip, Gram spoke up.

"You think it might be easier on the little mite to stay here instead of draggin' her out? I s'ppose I wouldn't mind watchin' her."

Sharon held her breath. "Well, that would for sure be easier for her, and it would help me, too, not having to carry her. Shall I leave her here in her seat? Are you sure you don't mind, Gram?"

"If I minded, I wouldn't o' offered," she snapped, "unless you're thinkin' you wouldn't trust me with her."

Sharon started to retort but caught herself. "No, Gram, that would be fine." She settled Betsey back in her seat, grabbed her purse, and slipped away before things tensed up anymore.

When she returned, Betsey was asleep face down on Gram's shoulder in the old armchair—which meant Gram had picked her up and carried her there.

"Your friend Mollie called," Gram told her. "I said as how you'd call back. But would you mind takin' this baby off o' me first? She's gettin' me hot."

Sharon smiled to herself and collected her daughter, who stretched and squirmed but continued sleeping. After laying her down, she dialed Mollie.

"I've been thinking," Mollie began without preamble. "Maybe Catherine could help you pull this off. She might be able to tell you where and when you can find Larry so you wouldn't waste time tracking him down or waiting for him to get out of class."

"Maybe...."

"Don't you think you could leave Betsey with my mom for several hours and go and come back in one day? Talk to Catherine, and when you know when you might want to do it, call my mom."

"But I don't have a phone number for Catherine."

"I'll get it for you. I'll call Larry and ask for it as if *I* want to talk to her. And then I *will* talk to her—sometime."

When Sharon hung up, her heart pounded. Could she make a trip to Groverton to talk to Larry? How would he react? Should she call him in advance, or surprise him? And

Tangled Strands

what would she say to him? How could she communicate to him that God was doing something special in her heart, that she wanted no more throwing up walls between them? How did one go about breaking such news? Her heart still pounding, she headed upstairs to get dressed for work.

She parked her car in front of the photography studio and got out. What would it be like to see Ethan this afternoon? Would it be awkward after last night? She quickly found out. When he passed her desk moments later, he nodded in her direction but did not speak or meet her eyes. Determined to put the relationship at ease again, she intercepted him on his return trip.

"Hey! Now who's being sober?"

In response to her smile, his face relaxed and he grinned. At five o'clock he walked her to her car.

"So how has today treated you?" he asked, leaning on the driver's window.

"Pretty good. I'm more concerned about you. Last evening was not the kind of thing sweet dreams are made of. Are you okay?"

He shrugged. "I'll be all right. I've made it through before, and I'll do it again. I think I'll take Jamie to the park this evening. Have you thought about the things I said, about you and Larry?"

"Y-yes."

"Have you talked to Larry?"

"Oh, no, I'm not ready for that yet. But I am thinking about going to Groverton to see him."

"Good for you, and I would say the sooner the better."

"Well, whatever happiness may come my way from this day forth, I'm going to owe to you, Ethan McCrae."

"Oh, no, you don't! You give your Heavenly Father every ounce of the credit. If he managed to use me as his instrument, well, that's just another one of his amazing ways of bringing good out of my tragedy. But if you don't lay fast claim to that guy who's in love with you, I just might turn you over my fatherly knee and teach you a stronger lesson!"

"Yikes!" She started her engine. "I had better get out of here!"

He grinned and stood back as she put the car into reverse. When she glanced back, she sighed. How forlorn he looked, standing in the spot where her car had been. But by the time she was out on the street, her mind was already on what it would be like to make a trip to Groverton—to see Larry.

When Sharon reached home, Gram had started supper, though it was Sharon's turn.

"How nice, Gram!" she said, establishing Betsey in her infant seat on a counter so she could watch the proceedings.

"Well, I figured as how I was here, I might as well. Besides, supper gets too late for me when I hafta wait'll you get home to make it."

Later, while Sharon was washing the dishes, Mollie called. "So did you talk to Catherine yet?"

"Yes, on my coffee break."

"What did she say?"

Tangled Strands   367

"She said she would think of a way to get Larry over to her house Saturday morning—something about her stove needing fixing. Then she'll leave us and go do her grocery shopping."

"Hmm. It might work. So are you going to tell him you're coming?"

"I–I don't think so, Mollie. I can't picture myself talking to him except face to face."

"Have you talked to my mom?"

"Yes. She said I could drop Betsey off as early as seven in the morning. Betsey did okay the couple of times I've tried her with a bottle, so I figure I can miss one feeding. Even that, though, will give me no more than two hours in Groverton."

"So you'll have to make the most of your time. Have you figured out what you're going to say to Larry?"

"Oh, how I wish! I've been thinking and thinking and praying God will show me—at least how to get started."

"Oh, he will. I'm sure of that. Now for my last question. What are you going to wear?"

"I hadn't even thought about that." How could she not have? "As you know, almost all my things got left in Chicago. I've had to buy things to wear to work, but I still don't have much to choose from."

"I've noticed that. So you and I are going shopping tomorrow morning, at least for a new sweater. Maybe we can even find a matching outfit." Mollie paused, and Sharon heard her draw a long breath. "Sharon, whatever happens between you and Larry is your business, of course. But you and Larry mean the world to Chris and me, and we would be ecstatic if things worked out for you two. Of course we'll be praying."

"Thanks, Mollie," Sharon said quietly. Her heart swelled with gratitude for how far she and Mollie had come since her return to Willow Valley. "And I would love to have you help me shop for something new to wear."

74

Friday morning Sharon slipped downstairs to the kitchen and turned on the oven. She got out Gram's old recipe file and rummaged till she found one for muffins. She smiled as she slid the pan into the oven a few minutes later. Hopefully Gram would be pleased as well as surprised with a change of menu for breakfast. After setting the timer, Sharon slipped back upstairs before Gram came out of her room.

When she returned with Betsey, Gram had the coffee brewing and was setting plates on the table. "Makes a nice smell," she said.

Sharon glanced at her sharply. *Gram saying something complimentary?*

"Thank you, Gram! How are you this morning?" She approached and with her free arm gave her grandmother a brief hug before settling Betsey in her bouncer seat.

"Can't complain." She busied herself pouring her coffee. "Gotta question for ya. I got a mind to do some sortin' and straightenin' on the stuff in my drawers. Ya think I could take the bitty one to my room in this here seat while I do that?"

"I think that's a lovely idea!"

Sharon pulled the muffins from the oven and took them from their pan. When she and Gram were both seated, she paused. She had been saying a silent blessing before her meals, but now she caught Gram's eye on her expectantly.

"Go ahead," the older woman said. "Say it out loud if you've a mind to."

My, this was a milestone morning!

She was starting on her second muffin when Gram spoke again. "Could I ask ya a question?"

"Sure, Gram."

"That son of Agnes's—what's his name?"

Sharon froze. "Larry. Why?"

"Him and you was sweet on each once, weren't ya?"

"Y-yah."

"You think ... now as you're not married to that ... that other guy, you think you and Larry might get together again?"

Sharon busied herself screwing the lid back on the jelly. "Wh-why do you ask, Gram?" Then, as an afterthought, "Would you like that?"

"Well, I never knowed him real well, but he was always nice to me—and he has a mighty fine ma."

This was the most conversation to come out of Gram since Pa's death. *Hurry and answer so she doesn't retreat into her shell again.* "Larry is a special person," she found herself saying. "And he has been a good friend to me. I guess it is possible ...

Tangled Strands

something might develop between us again," she finished in a rush. *Oh, Gram, if only you knew!*

Later that morning Sharon and Mollie agreed on a soft yellow sweater that could be dressed up with accessories. For this occasion, she chose a flowered scarf, which she knotted at her shoulder, then anchored with scatter pins.

It had been a gift from Larry on her eighteenth birthday.

75

All week Larry Baldwin had found himself distracted. Now as he drove to Catherine Harrison's house, he tried to concentrate on what might be wrong with her stove. Not only had she been vague about the problem, but mostly his mind kept wandering to Sharon. He had done little all week but think about her. Except for giving diligent attention to the classes he taught, focusing had been an uphill battle in every aspect of his life, including work on his thesis.

He had done more praying than ever in his life. It took a special effort to make his prayers for Sharon not so much that she would come to see things his way but that she would find whatever peace seemed to be eluding her. For himself, he prayed he would be able to make peace with whatever God wanted for Sharon and him. Above all, he prayed that God's will would be clear to them both, whatever it was.

As he rang Catherine's doorbell, he corralled his thoughts once again to the task at hand. He wished he knew more about stoves.

And then he walked through the door and found Sharon rising from Catherine's davenport. Her face was pale, her eyes wide, and her apprehensive expression reminded him of her on the day of his father's funeral.

"Sh-Sharon?" He took two steps towards her, then stopped.

"Larry," she said softly, and the caress in the tone of his name on her lips was like a fresh breeze on a summer evening.

He turned to Catherine, and the twinkle in her eyes answered the question on his lips. "You–*you* are behind this!"

"I am," she admitted smugly.

"What's going on?"

"You and Sharon need to talk—"

"You mean you lied about your stove?"

"No, Larry, I don't lie. I *have* had trouble with my stove, and I did ask if you could come over this morning. I just neglected to mention that the problem with the stove was two weeks ago." She grinned for a second, then sobered. "Look. There's coffee in the kitchen and a coffeecake fresh from the oven. I need to do my Saturday morning grocery run, so please, you two make yourselves at home. I should be gone about an hour."

Catherine hugged Sharon and gave Larry's shoulder a friendly pat, then picked up a jacket from the chair. "I'll be praying for you," she said as she went out the door.

The two stared at each other. Larry couldn't remember ever being tongue-tied in Sharon's presence. His mind scrambled for something to say. Motioning for her to precede him into the kitchen and choosing to take refuge in something impersonal, he asked, "What did your grandmother think of the house?"

They found everything as Catherine had promised and more. Two handsome cups with saucers and matching plates awaited them on the table beside a fragrant coffeecake, with a percolator hot on the counter nearby. While Larry poured the coffee and Sharon served the cake, she reported the promising interactions she had had with Gram that week.

"She even asked me about you," she ventured shyly as she sat down in the chair Larry pulled out for her.

"She did? What did she say?"

Sharon took a bite of cake and took her time savoring it. "She wanted to know if, now that I'm not married to 'that other guy,' if I thought … if I thought you and I might get together again." She traced the pattern on the placemat with a finger and did not raise her eyes.

He paused with his fork half way to his mouth. "May I ask how you answered her?"

"I said … you have always been a good friend to me and I guessed it was possible something might develop between us."

Larry let out a burst of laughter that died as quickly as it was born. Another long pause followed as they busied themselves with eating in grim silence and did not look at each other. His plate empty, Larry pushed it away. "And what's that supposed to mean, Sharon? Has something changed since I saw you Monday?"

"Y–yes."

More silence.

Tangled Strands

"And are you planning on telling me about it?" He heard the tinge of sarcasm in his voice but made no effort to dispel it.

"Yes. But it's not that easy—"

"Oh, here we go again! And I suppose you're going to say it's still complex and hard to explain!" He could see by the glance she cast him that his words had stung. Now why did he go and say that? "I'm sorry, Sharon. That was uncalled for. But—"

"Never mind. I deserved it. But it *is* complicated because it involves ... it involves my date with Ethan the other night."

"You can't be serious! You've come all the way to Groverton to tell me about your date with Ethan?" No regrets for the sarcasm now.

She set her cup down, straightened in her chair, and looked him in the eyes. "As a matter of fact, I did. So do you want to hear about it, or not?" Now her glance did not waver, and now it was his turn to feel stung.

"I ... I suppose."

While her coffee turned cold, she told him about Ellen and about Ethan's despair and guilt after her death. Larry could see her choosing her words carefully. *An interesting story—but what did it have to do with him?* Nevertheless, he admired the courage he had seen come to her rescue, courage that allowed her to hold his gaze unflinchingly.

Suddenly he saw it fade, and her eyes dropped. With a tinge of impatience, he said, "And—?"

"And ... " she pushed her chair back and walked to the sink, her back to him. "And he says I have to forgive myself for running off with Tony."

So it did have something to do with them. He rose and came to stand behind her, close but not touching her. "Do you think that's what you need to do—forgive yourself?"

"Oh, there's no doubt about that, but, Larry, it isn't easy!"

Silence reigned several more seconds as Larry's heart processed what he was hearing. He ached to touch her but hesitated. Would she pull away again? When he heard her draw a deep breath and start to turn toward him, he tensed.

"I've come today because ... because I need to admit to you, Larry, that I ... I do love you."

Wings of hope and cobwebs of fear tumbled together in his heart. This was what she came to tell him? Did she really mean it?

"Is this a new discovery?" He held his breath.

She shook her head. He thought she was going to say more, but she didn't. Now courage, laced with joy, swelled in his heart. He lifted her chin and made her look at him. "Would you say that again please?"

A light sparked in her eyes and made his heart tremble. Slowly, with a voice that did not waver, she said, "I love you, Larry Baldwin. I think I always have, and I know I always will."

76

While Larry freshened the coffee in her cup and poured himself another one, Sharon wandered back to the living room. She stood at the window gazing out at the changing trees and waiting for her heartbeat to quiet. Two frisking squirrels reminded her poignantly of the one she had encountered in the park in the spring. So much had happened since that day. How much she had learned—about herself and about trusting a Heavenly Father for her soul and her very life.

Her heart was bursting as she relived the embrace she and Larry had just shared in the kitchen. Never as long as she lived would she forget the look on his face when she said she loved him. His arms had closed around her, and she found herself held so tightly she could scarcely breathe. When she drew back, she was amazed to find tears in his eyes. A moment later his lips touched hers in a kiss that was more a sacred seal of hope than a token of passion. Passion, she had a feeling, would have its day—in time.

"Sharon?"

She turned to find Larry on the couch, their cups on the coffee table. With one arm he motioned for her to join him, and she settled into its circle with a rush of joy she wasn't sure she could contain. The kiss they now shared tasted of a delicious fire.

He drew back, but only enough to see her face. "So tell me more about all this. How does one go about forgiving ... oneself?"

She pulled away, reached for her cup, and took a sip while she sorted out her thoughts. "I don't understand it all, by any means, but Mollie and I think one thing it means is I have to stop punishing myself for what I did last year."

"Is that what you've been doing?"

"I think that's part of it. Mollie suggests that in punishing myself, I've been punishing you."

"Interesting. So what do you have to do to stop?"

She gazed at him over the rim of her cup. "Well, I hope coming here today is a start."

He smiled, then sobered. "Could I ask you more about Ethan's part in this?"

"Sure. What would you like to know?"

She had to make sure Ethan didn't become a source of tension between her and Larry. Larry must not misunderstand this friendship that had come to mean so much to her.

After a moment he said, "And why was Ethan telling you about this?"

"Because he felt our problem—what was coming between us—was much like what held him back for a long time."

"And he wants to see us get together?"

Tangled Strands 379

"He said the more he learned about us and then seeing us last weekend ..." she hesitated. "He said he felt in his heart we belong together."

"So you're sure neither of you is harboring a secret crush on the other?"

A twinkle flashed, then disappeared and she met his eyes squarely. "I promise you we aren't. We're just good friends."

Larry studied her. "So ... does this mean you would marry me?"

A light came on in her heart that she could feel spreading across her face. "If you think you still want me."

He kissed her nose. "I can't imagine anything I could ever want more in my entire life. *Will* you marry me, Sharon Marie?"

She traced the dear, familiar lines of his face with her finger. "It would be the greatest privilege of my life."

At that moment, she remembered the time. *"Oh!" Where was a clock?* "What time is it?"

Larry glanced at his watch. "Eleven-twenty-five."

"Oh. Oh, good. I have a few more minutes." She let out her breath and hurried on. "I was supposed to tell you when you first got here that I could only stay a little while...."

"And I've meant to ask you where Betsey is."

"She's with your mother, and I need to be back by mid-afternoon because your mom has a hair appointment." She looked uncertainly at Larry. To her relief, he took charge.

"What time do you need to leave?"

"Soon after noon"

"Well, that doesn't give us much time. I know we just ate, but we should probably get you some lunch before you start back. There's a deli down the street. What do we need to talk about before you go?"

"Oh, Larry, I feel like we've just gotten started!"

"Oh, we have. Listen, are you doing anything this evening? Any dates with Ethan?" She looked at him sharply, but when she saw his eyebrows raised and a twinkle in his eyes, she grinned and shook her head.

"Then, look. I have a one-o'clock meeting to talk about some snags in my thesis. I hope it won't take long, and then I can head for Willow Valley—"

"You would drive all the way back there on such short notice?"

"I would drive to the *moon* to be with you at this point, lady of my heart. I want to see some things anchored down before I find you floating away out of my life again!"

She threw her arms around his neck and whispered, "Not a chance! Me thinks you may be stuck with me."

"I am absolutely counting on it." He stood up and helped her to her feet.

A few minutes later, too keyed up to focus on eating, Sharon watched Larry nibbling on a salami sandwich.

"Look," he said, "I should be in Willow Valley by 5 or 5:30. Can someone watch Betsey again for a couple hours this evening so we can go to dinner?"

"I'll talk to your mom when I pick her up."

"How much does my mother know about … the events of this week?"

Tangled Strands

"She didn't at first, but lately, between Mollie and me, I think she has gotten a complete picture."

They ate without speaking for a few minutes, staring at each other and suppressing smiles. Finally he broke the silence. "So ... are we ... do we need to talk about a wedding?" he finished in a rush.

"I guess we'll have to talk about that tonight," she said. "I should be going."

"Listen, just for the record and your thinking in the meantime, it looks like I will finish my thesis on schedule in December, but I've signed a contract to teach here until the end of the school term in May. Is that going to be a problem?"

77

On the way back to Willow Valley, Sharon's heart alternated between turning cartwheels and skidding into a panic button. Mostly the cartwheels won out.

As she turned down Lazy River Road, she breathed a prayer of gratitude. Such a sweet prayer Mrs. Baldwin had voiced that morning when Sharon dropped Betsey off. She had not demanded anything of God nor told the Almighty how to handle things. She had simply petitioned angels to protect Sharon as she made the trip and asked that Sharon and Larry might feel God's presence surrounding them as they talked. Sharon smiled. God had answered on every score.

Mrs. Baldwin met her at the door. She looked at Sharon, her face one big question, and then opened her arms. Sharon fell into them—and burst into tears.

"Hey! What's the matter? Are you okay?"

Sharon wiped her eyes on her sleeve and worked to get control. "Oh, I'm okay," she said, half laughing, half crying. "It's just … it's just been an emotional day."

Mrs. Baldwin raised her eyebrows. Sharon drew a deep breath. "God answered our prayers. Larry and I had an amazing time together."

"Oh?"

"I–I told him I love him and–and he asked me to marry him."

With an exclamation of joy, Mrs. Baldwin threw her arms around Sharon again. "And you said …?"

Her throat too choked up for words, Sharon could only nod vigorously.

"So is there going to be a wedding? Hey! Where did that smile go?"

"Someday, I guess. I don't know when. We didn't have time to talk about it except Larry says he has to teach until May. He's driving here this afternoon so we can talk some more."

Before Sharon gathered up the sleeping Betsey and headed for home, a plan was born. Mrs. Baldwin would reschedule her hair appointment. She insisted she would make dinner for Larry and Sharon at her house ("It will be easier for you to talk about serious things"), and she would go to Sharon's to visit Gram and look after Betsey.

She found her grandmother sitting in the kitchen stirring a steaming cup.

"What are you drinking, Gram?"

"Hot cocoa—want me to make you some?"

"Oh, that would be lovely—thanks. Let me take Betsey upstairs so she can hopefully sleep a little longer."

When Sharon sat down to her cocoa a few minutes later, Gram studied her expectantly but said nothing. Sharon couldn't help grinning. "Well? Would you like to hear about my day?"

"You went to see *him*, right?"

"Right. Remember what you said about us maybe getting together again?"

Gram grunted.

"Well, it looks like maybe it's going to happen."

"You mean you're gonna marry him."

"It looks that way—but it may not be very soon because he has to teach there at the school until May."

Gram studied her. "So couldn't you go and live with him there?" A touch of the old belligerence sparked in her eyes. "Or would you be thinkin' I couldn't get along here by myself?" Then just as quickly her face fell. "Oh. I forgot. This is your house now."

"Oh, Gram!" Sharon telegraphed a frantic prayer for help. "Don't say things like that! Remember I told you this may be my *house* but it is still your *home!* You have to believe me about that." She laid her hand on Gram's arm. "And as far as your living by yourself, that would be up to you."

"Humph!" said Gram, sounding unconvinced.

"I'm serious, Gram. Look, Larry and I will have a chance to talk about all this tonight. I couldn't stay too long today because of Betsey, so Larry is coming to Willow Valley this evening. We're going to eat together at Mrs. Baldwin's." Thankfully the belligerence on Gram's face had softened.

"Ya won't be eaten' here?"

Tangled Strands

"No, Gram, but your friend Agnes wants to come over and see you. Do you feel like fixing something for the two of you to eat? There's some leftover spaghetti from the other night. You could heat it up if you like, and there's stuff to make a salad. Then she said she would love to go with you to take Betsey for a walk in her new carriage."

Hearing Betsey beginning to whimper upstairs, Sharon headed up to get her.

At six-forty-five Sharon stood at the mirror putting on pearl earrings and thinking about the evening ahead. Her heart raced at the prospect of seeing Larry again—but would they feel awkward with each other after the events of the morning? What if he'd had second thoughts about asking her to marry him?

That thought produced a flash of panic that found nowhere to take root and promptly withered in the sunshine of what she knew to be truth. She brushed the crown of her hair back and fastened it in bobby pins and then a yellow bow. The dark brown, silky blouse Agnes had given her for her birthday looked good with her beige skirt. Dare she ask Gram to borrow Great-grandmother Magdalena's cameo pin? Certainly she would never have dared ask in the past.

Betsey was fed and bathed and in a bright yellow sleeper. Gram had the new carriage, a gift from Chris and Mollie and the Thornes, on the porch ready for the walk.

Back in her room with a smile after borrowing the pin, Sharon fastened it on her blouse and peered into the mirror for final approval. She couldn't see any need to add rouge to her cheeks—they had more color than usual without any help.

A knock on the door downstairs brought her heart to her throat. He was here!

As she arrived at the foot of the stairs, Mrs. Baldwin reached for Betsey, and Sharon relinquished her without conscious thought. Her eyes were on Larry, two steps behind his mother. At the sight of him standing there, looking so dear and familiar and stirring such a delicious chaos inside her, all her questions vanished. She simply walked into his arms, and he closed them around her.

"I missed you!" he whispered.

"Me too." His kiss, chaste and proper as it was because of their audience, still lit a spark.

He released her and went directly to Gram, where he took her hand in both of his and said how nice it was to see her again. While speaking briefly with Mrs. Baldwin about Betsey, Sharon could not miss the happiness in the older woman's eyes. *Am I going to be able to call her mother now?* As Larry headed for the door, Sharon gave Betsey a kiss and Gram and his mother each a hug and whispered a quick "I love you."

Tangled Strands

78

Minutes later at his mother's house, Larry stepped back so Sharon could go ahead of him up the walk. Before he could locate his key, she pulled one out. How did she—?

"I've lived here more recently than you have," she reminded him with a grin.

Inside they found the dining table set for two on each side of a corner, with lace cloth and candles, cloth napkins, and the Baldwins' best dishes and gold-rimmed glasses.

"My, but your mother went to a lot of work!"

"I can assure you she enjoyed every minute of it." He found matches lying beside a candle, and a moment later a velvety glow enfolded them. "Dinner is in the kitchen ready to eat. Don't you just love Mother for realizing we would rather not spend this evening in a public place?"

They worked together in the kitchen to fill their plates with ham, glazed carrots, creamy potatoes, and fluffy biscuits.

Sharon said, "As soon as I came to live with your mom, she remembered how I loved her glazed carrots."

Ah, memories. "It was the only way she could get you to eat a vegetable when you were a kid!"

After they were seated, Larry smiled and reached for her hand before bowing his head. "Heavenly Father, I thank you for this food and for Mother's loving preparation of it. Thank you for your hand on Sharon's and my lives up to this moment, and thank you that *you* know what lies ahead for us. Thank you for the love you've given us for each other, and I ask your blessing on everything we say and do this evening. In Jesus' name, Amen."

He did not release her hand. "So how are you feeling now? Any regrets about the morning?"

She shook her head and smiled. "None on my part—how about you?"

"Not even a sliver!"

"I had some special conversations with your mom and Gram when I got back, and I brought Mollie up to date by phone."

"I assume she and Chris approve?"

"Oh, she hasn't told Chris about my going to Groverton. She thought he would like to hear about it from you." Chris didn't know? Surprising him was something to look forward to. Larry grinned at the prospect.

"Interesting. So what happened with your grandmother?"

Sharon took a sip of water. "Like I told you, this past week with Gram has been most interesting. I'm beginning to see some of her icy exterior melt—or at least thaw."

"Oh?"

Tangled Strands   389

She repeated the conversation for him, pausing after Gram's crack about the house.

"Did that upset you?"

"Not as much as it would have in the past. The Lord is helping me."

His heart swelled at this new Sharon. "So do you think she would be willing to live alone again—that she wouldn't feel you had abandoned her?"

"I think it's possible, but we'd want to watch to make sure she didn't fall back into depression. I think God is working in her heart too, even if she isn't asking him to."

"My mother wondered if we could get married over Christmas."

Sharon looked up. "Really? You think we could?"

"I think it's worth talking about, but the more I think about it, now that the walls between you and me have come down, Christmas seems a *long* way off!"

They stared at each other in the candlelight, and Larry could see in Sharon's eyes the same anticipation he felt. Could he and Sharon, after all these years, suddenly be talking about getting married?

"What about Thanksgiving?" she asked.

"I don't have much time off then." He laid his fork on his empty plate. "Are we finished here?"

She nodded and waited for him to pull out her chair.

79

In the living room they settled together on the davenport. Sharon took a deep breath as Larry leaned back and drew her head to his shoulder, both arms enfolding her. For several long moments they just held each other.

"Can you believe we're doing this?" he whispered in her hair.

She shook her head against his shoulder, then drew back, laid her hand on his cheek, and ran her thumb over his lips.

"I need you to kiss me again," she murmured, "to help me decide if this is real or if I'm just dreaming." *What a bad girl she was!* But not an ounce of guilt rose up to tarnish the thrill.

After complying with her request, Larry tweaked her nose and said, "It will be my pleasure to refresh your memory any time. So now, Sharon *Casanetti*, let's get back to the subject of when we can get married."

She was so taken back by his emphatic use of Tony's name that she almost missed what followed. Before she could express her surprise, he went on.

"I called you that on purpose to demonstrate to you—to both of us—that I have dealt with the reality of Tony in your life and I don't need to hide from it anymore. Yes, you were enchanted with him once, enough to run out on what you and I had together. Yes, you married him, and yes, he fathered Betsey—but *I'm* the one who is going to be her father for the rest of her life."

He paused to catch his breath, and she stared at him. Did he really mean what he was saying?

"And now you're going to marry *me*. Your name is going to be Sharon Baldwin, as I've long pictured it being, and it can't be too soon for me! All that's important now is the beautiful wedding you and I are going to have."

She pulled away from him and stood up, her back to him. Here it was again, nearly as distressing as ever. How could she plan a wedding to Larry after the travesty of a wedding—and a marriage—she had been through with Tony?

"Sharon? What is it?"

"I–I don't deserve a beautiful wedding after … after … ."

He rose and pulled her back into his arms, then drew back and looked into her eyes. "Stop me if I'm wrong, but isn't this what your friend Ethan was talking about? It's time to put your wedding to Tony *behind* you. Now you're going to have a proper and memorable one! You're going to hold your head high, your eyes are going to shine, and you're going to walk down that church aisle to me in a white dress—"

"You mean a wedding dress?"

"Of course a wedding dress! You're getting married—remember?"

"But...but people who have been married before aren't supposed to wear white dresses, remember? I should probably just wear a suit or something. ..."

"Did you wear a real wedding dress, with lace and a veil and all, when you married Tony?"

She cringed. "You know I didn't."

"That's my point. You haven't had the wedding every girl deserves, and I want yours to me to be something that will send memories of that other one fleeing with their tails between their legs, never to show their faces again."

The image made her smile. Her mind went back to Ethan's comment about God overruling his feeling unworthy to be Jamie's father. Did God want to do that for her? Was it another part of that forgiveness stuff? She drew a deep breath. "I see what you mean, and I love you for it." And she felt the sunshine creep back into her heart and onto her face.

Before they sat down again, Larry extinguished one lamp and dimmed the other. Sharon lit the candle on the coffee table and savored the warm glow. Candles had not been part of her home growing up, but she knew they would be in her future home.

Larry drew her close again. "Seriously, Sharon, taking Betsey and your grandmother and my school schedule into account, can we get back to a wedding date?"

If she had not loved him before, his concern for those who were now her responsibility would have won her. But his thoughtfulness solved nothing. How could she even *think* of going anywhere now that Gram seemed to need her and their relationship was beginning to heal? And Betsey! How was one supposed to talk about a wedding, let alone a honeymoon, with a baby in the picture? Guilt again pummeled her heart, and she turned away.

"Sharon? Now what is it?"

She did not look at him. "I have to think about Betsey."

"Oh, I'm not forgetting about Betsey! I don't know how long you were planning to … to nurse her, and as much as I long to make you my wife, I don't want our marriage to interfere with that. Do you think—?"

But Sharon shook her head. "Larry, are you sure you don't resent having to take a baby into account when talking about your wedding? And if you don't, *why don't you?*"

80

The room had grown chilly. Sharon felt herself shiver, and she wasn't surprised that Larry noticed. He got up and put a match to the wood and kindling already arranged on the hearth. She watched him, a knot of suspense in her heart, yet at the same time a feeling of anticipation and joy she could not escape. Was God really working things out? If so, she must believe and keep trusting him with the details.

Larry came back and settled in beside her. "You are right that I don't resent Betsey in our lives." His gaze was steady. "And there's a simple reason I don't. I love *you*, Sharon, and I already love her. She is precious. I can't wait to get to know her better and to make her mine—legally and in every way. Can you understand what I'm saying?"

She shook her head. "No, I can't say I understand, but—I believe you."

She could see Larry struggling to compose himself before speaking again. When he did, he was noticeably subdued.

"Sharon? There is something else I need to say about Betsey. I'm going to love her and care for her as if she were my own flesh, but I realize there is one dimension where we'll have to acknowledge she isn't."

She glanced at him sharply, the knot in her heart tightening again.

"This was where I had my hardest battle during the summer," he admitted, toying with her hand in his. "It was difficult coming to grips with the fact that as Betsey grows up she will have to know that I am not her ... her father ... biologically. And I think she will have a right to know positive things about Tony and your ... your relationship to him."

Sharon caught a flash of frustration in his eyes, and her heart ached all over again—for him, for herself, even for Betsey. She drew her hand away and knew she had to voice her feelings.

"I know, Larry, and I'm wretchedly sorry. Betsey *should* have been your child—"

He laid his fingers on her lips. "Hush, love. It means a lot to hear you say that. However, I'm sure that after tonight that thought should never again be voiced between us. We've both been learning from God about accepting what is past and not cultivating futile wishes about things we can't change. So I need you to make me a promise."

"Yes?"

He sat up straight and waited for her to meet his eyes. "If a time ever comes when I seem to be forgetting what I've said here tonight, please remind me and help me give it back to the Lord, okay?"

He smiled then, and she could see peace once more taking command in his heart. Seeing it, she was able to claim it for herself as well and return his smile.

———◆◆◆———

"Now," Larry said firmly a few moments later, "if I didn't know better, I would think we were trying to avoid discussing that wedding date. It seems to me the last suggestion on the table was Thanksgiving, but Sharon—" he ran his fingers through his hair. "I–I don't want to wait even *that* long for us to be married!"

"I know," she said softly, "me neither."

"Is there any chance that six weeks would be long enough for you gals to put together a wedding—if you decide it is okay with your Gram? Maybe we could get married late in October and just take a weekend at Fern Haven—if by then you could leave Betsey with Mother that long. Then we could take a little more time over one of the holidays, maybe *with* Betsey."

She was thoughtful. "It has possibilities—that is, if I can bear being separated from you at all anymore!" She turned suddenly in his arms, and the next moment they were kissing with a fresh urgency born of too many endless days when they had been bereft of each other. When they reluctantly drew apart, he took her by the arms and placed a careful distance between them.

A grin crept across her face. "Guess what I was just thinking. You know my son, Daniel Porter—the one Betsey didn't turn out to be? Well, he will now be born a Baldwin—"

"You mean you're ready to talk about having other children after—after—"

"After my experience delivering Betsey?" She laughed and ruffled his hair. "Of course I want other children—your children. You see, now that I have Betsey, I know I would go through every minute of it again for her, and besides—" now she grew serious, "—it could never be like the last time because now it will be *our* baby, and we will truly be in it together. Can you understand that?"

"I understand the last part about its being *our* baby, but I'm still amazed you're ready to do it again."

"Oh, not right now today!" she exclaimed, and they laughed together. He started to kiss her again, then thought better of it. He still was not used to the freedom to hold and kiss her whenever he wanted, and it made him feel like a giddy child on Christmas morning. But he knew that too many sweets and treats could get one into trouble.

Suddenly he released her and jumped to his feet. He pulled her up and into his arms and began whirling round and round with her.

"Larry!" she squealed, "what's got into you?"

He did not stop whirling as he exalted, "I'm so happy I can't stand it!"

81

When he finally set her down, they were both breathless, she from sheer amazement over what she had just witnessed in the usually so reserved and dignified Larry Baldwin. The next moment, in a pantomime she had often seen Chris do, he wiped the radiance from his face with a motion of his hand and stood at sober attention.

"Woman! What have you done to me? I shall never be the same again!"

They laughed. She couldn't remember when she had ever enjoyed laughing like this. Perhaps Larry hadn't either? She could feel some of the tensions of the past year unwinding. Maybe it could heal a few scars as well. Still laughing, she seized his hand and dragged him into the kitchen.

"How about a cold drink?"

Standing with glasses of iced tea in hand, they were still giggling. She said, "We want Chris and Mollie for our attendants, don't we?"

"You better believe it!"

Suddenly she turned away.

"Sharon?" He put his hand on her shoulder and turned her back. "Tears! What did I—?"

She shook her head. "It's not you, Larry," she said, her voice threatening to break. "It just hit me that Pa won't be here to walk down the aisle with me!"

He drew her close again and whispered, "I'm sorry, love, I'm so sorry! I know your father would have been proud." He paused, then drew back and smiled. "But I know someone else whom I'm sure would be more than pleased to do it ...."

She stared at him, her brows drawn.

"Did you ever hear that Chris's parents lost a little girl when she was quite young? I'm sure his dad would be honored to walk you down the aisle."

"And he's been so good and helpful to me!"

The calendar on the wall behind Sharon caught Larry's eye.

"Here, let's check out this calendar," he said, taking it from the wall. "Ah, October has a holiday, remember? Columbus Day, which falls on Tuesday this year—and look! That's the night of the full moon!"

"Oh, Larry, really?"

He paused, knitting his brows a little. "I'm pretty sure I could get someone to cover my class on Monday, and we won't have any on Tuesday. That would give us a long weekend ...." He left the sentence hanging, watching for her reaction.

"Really?" she whispered. "Oh, Larry!"

"I think it could work. I could get here for a rehearsal Friday evening, then we could get married sometime Saturday and head for Fern Lake."

He watched her face as it blossomed with joy and possibilities. "We'd have Sunday, Monday, and part of Tuesday," he continued, "and I could get back to Groverton by Tuesday evening."

She grinned sheepishly "I have to admit that when we were teenagers, I dreamed about a honeymoon at Fern Lake …"

"Well, Chris and Mollie did it, even though it was December. Good for a whole lot of snuggling, I imagine."

"And fires in the fireplace."

"Of course." He grinned as he backed her against the counter, arms on either side braced against the cupboards, and smiled into her eyes. "You know something, Sharon Marie Champlin Casanetti about-to-be-Baldwin? I'm loving you more every minute! I imagine we need to check with Pastor Hawkins about his schedule before we set anything in concrete."

"*And* your mother and Mollie. So can we start breaking the news?"

"Just one more thing first." An impish smile lit his face. "We have an appointment next Saturday with old Mr. Curtis."

"Saturday? Mr. Curtis?" Then the light dawned. "You mean—the jeweler?"

"Of course the jeweler! You're to go in and browse this week when you have a chance."

"You already talked to him?"

Tangled Strands

"I did when I got in at 5:00. I should be able to get back here next weekend. If tomorrow weren't Sunday, we would go see him then." He picked up her left hand, kissed her ring finger, and studied his grandmother's ring.

"Do you remember it?" Sharon asked.

"I do. And I think we should put this away for Betsey someday, don't you?"

She smiled and nodded, her eyes misting over.

82

"So we pulled a good one on you, did we, Chris?" Larry asked over a cup of steaming hot cocoa at the Thornes' kitchen table as the four listened to the clock chime midnight.

Chris shook his head. "I can't believe I didn't suspect something when I couldn't get Mollie to talk about you two this week. Every time I said something about you, she changed the subject. I started wondering if she was in denial about your ... situation."

"So were you asleep when you heard the knock on the door?" Sharon wanted to know.

"I had just dozed off—after spending most of the evening worrying about you two and praying for you while Mollie was at a bridal shower. Several times I told God frankly that it just seemed like there *had* to be answers for you two if you really loved each other—and it surely looked to the rest of us like you did."

"It sounded as if you were tearing the door down while we waited for you to open it!" Larry took another sip of cocoa.

Tangled Strands

"After I heard your voice, my head was spinning because I knew you were in Groverton, but it sounded like you. I was all thumbs trying to get the lock undone."

"From the bedroom," Mollie broke in, "I couldn't figure out what all the noise was. Your hollering at me, Chris, was scrambled up with other voices—it sounded like an invasion."

Sharon laid a hand on Mollie's arm. "I see you're still shaking your head, Mollie."

"I can't believe you want to try and pull off a wedding in a month! I can't believe Mother okayed the idea."

"Oh, she had the same reaction as you at first—until we made it clear that we want a *small* wedding." Sharon stroked Mollie's arm on the table. "Can you understand why Larry and I don't want to wait long—after all the years this relationship has simmered?"

Mollie broke into a grin. "Oh, I can understand all right! And I'm so happy for you, I can hardly take it all in."

When Sharon finally got to bed, it was the wee hours of Sunday morning, and she had a hard time falling asleep. Reliving the joys of the day alternated with plans and concerns for the future. One moment she was smiling over the shock on Chris's face when she and Larry showed up at the door; the next she was trying to anticipate Gram's reaction to their news. One moment she was luxuriating in memories of kisses they had shared; the next she was wondering what it would be like to be away from Betsey for a couple of days. Another moment she remembered Larry's bewilderment when he found her at

Catherine's; the next she was trying to picture shopping for a wedding dress. She glanced at the clock by her bed. It was Sunday now, and she could anticipate the surprise on people's faces when she and Larry showed up in church together.

At last, exhausted, she slept. The cries of a hungry Betsey awoke her. A glance at the clock sent her bolting out of bed. Larry was coming to breakfast, and they were going to talk to Gram before church at 10:30.

83

Despite its frantic start, the rest of day unfolded as a proper and memorable Sunday ought to. Sitting in the swing on her front porch that evening after seeing Gram and Betsey to bed, she watched a red sky fade to dusky rose. Larry was spending a last few minutes with his sister and Chris before heading back to school. Wouldn't she love to be a bug on the ceiling listening to what they were saying!

She pulled her shawl more tightly against the evening chill and hugged herself in gratitude and wonder as she relived her favorite parts of the day just past. Though old habits had made Gram fume and mutter about a *man* coming to breakfast without warning, in the end fragile new patterns allowed her to congratulate Sharon—and even Larry. She'd seemed to believe them when they said they'd be happy to have her come to Groverton with them—or stay in Willow Valley. She told them she would have to "study on it." When they invited her to go to church with them, she said perhaps another time—after she had a chance to figure out if she had anything fittin' to wear.

Sharon's favorite part had been when she and Larry were leaving and Larry asked Gram if he could give her a hug like Sharon had. Sharon would long cherish Gram's blush and murmured permission.

Their reception at church had warmed their hearts. Mr. and Mrs. Thorne were beyond words with pleasure. School friends of Larry's pounded his back with elation to find him back with Sharon, and Sharon got feminine squeals and hugs from both old friends and new. Pastor Hawkins said he would go out of his way to find a mutually satisfactory wedding date, and he urged them to carve out time to get together with him at least once to talk about Christian marriage. What might that be like?

The warmest memory of the day was when Ethan, sitting on the platform where he would lead the singing and the choir, caught sight of them coming in the back door together. It was comical to watch his efforts not to burst into a grin. That had to wait until on the front steps after the service. Sharon controlled her urge to throw her arms around Ethan, which of course would not be appropriate now.

Larry reached to shake Ethan's hand. "There's no way I can ever thank you, man, for what you've done for Sharon and me. May God reign his blessings on you in a million ways."

Ethan's face had taken on a deep emotional look—not tears, but what Sharon suspected might have been tears on a woman. He swallowed hard before he spoke.

"I'm just happy it helped. This is just an example of how God can work with something broken and use it for something good."

After church the family had gathered at the Baldwins' for what Sharon assumed would be a traditional Sunday dinner, but Mrs. Baldwin, Mollie, and Chris turned it into a delightful celebration of the engagement. They invited Gram and, with reassurances from Larry's mother, she had agreed to join them. Undoubtedly Mollie was responsible for the balloons and streamers and Chris for the elegant dinner music coming from the record player.

When Sharon and baby arrived with Gram before dinner, Betsey had become the instant center of attention. Sharon watched as Larry stood and approached cautiously.

"Do you think she would come to me?" he asked. "I wanted to do this at breakfast, but we were busy talking. I mean, how do you suggest I get acquainted with my daughter?"

The group went silent. Fascinated, they watched as Larry spoke softly to the baby. He did a couple of peek-a-boos until she gave him a tentative grin. Then he reached out in slow motion, ready to back off at any moment, but Betsey raised no protest. The next moment he was holding her, like a man might handle a fragile china cup. Betsey gazed at him curiously, assessing him, and finally broke into the hint of a smile.

One last memory was after church when she had approached Ethan about singing at the wedding.

"I'd be honored. Do you have anything in mind?"

"Maybe the tangled strands song, but I'd also like something about God's love and his faithfulness."

In the cool evening, Sharon hugged herself and smiled, wondering what second song Ethan would choose.

84

In the deepening dusk now, Sharon spotted Larry's car turning onto her street, and her pulse quickened. After parking, he almost skipped up the short walk to the house. When he reached the top of the steps, she walked into his arms for a hug and a kiss before he drew away and peered around the porch.

"Betsey in bed?"

"Her and Gram. It was a big day for both of them."

"And how about the mother and granddaughter?"

It took Sharon a second to figure out he meant her. "The mother and granddaughter is floating somewhere on Cloud 199, unable to absorb all that has happened in the last—what is it? Thirty-six hours?"

"That's a good way to express how *I* feel, too." He sat down on the swing and pulled her down beside him. Looking into her eyes, he murmured, "If I start kissing you now, I might not make it back for classes tomorrow morning, so I think I'll save that until I'm on my feet and ready to say good-bye."

A tremor ran through her, and she caught her breath. "I'm still having trouble believing this is happening," she whispered, then straightened and pulled her shawl up a little further. "I love this time of day, don't you? The night sounds remind me of Fern Lake."

"They do, don't they?" He paused. "Mother said she and Mollie would get out to the cottage sometime to make sure everything is ready for a honeymoon. But we'd better not start talking about *that* tonight either. Did you ladies get some planning done this afternoon?"

"We got a start. We're going dress shopping Thursday morning, and I'd like to take them with me when I go to look at rings. That will be so much fun."

"Sounds good," Larry said. "Did I tell you I'm dipping into some of the money my dad left me? Mr. Curtis knows my price range."

"You've thought of everything, haven't you?" She snuggled her head a little deeper into his shoulder. "We decided that even though we are keeping it small, we should send out proper invitations, so we gals will stop by the printer's and see how one goes about ordering them. Meanwhile, we need to anchor down that guest list. Mollie says we can wait till the following week to shop for her dress."

They were quiet a moment as they watched the half moon sink and then disappear below the line of trees at the end of the street. Larry spoke in a muted voice. "Mother and I had a melancholy conversation while waiting for all of you to arrive for dinner...."

"I'm guessing it was about your dad?"

He picked up her hand and kissed her fingers. "You're right. Mother mentioned him first, and I realized I hadn't allowed myself to think about him yet. I remember thinking when he died how hard it would be not to have him around when I got married ... or had my first child—things like that."

"I was too upset at that time to think this far ahead, but I sure feel his absence now."

"We all do." Then Larry chuckled softly. "Can you picture how much he would adore Betsey?"

"Oh, he would, wouldn't he?" After a moment, she started giggling.

"What?"

"I overheard you asking Chris if his dad's lawyers could start proceedings for you to adopt Betsey."

"Oh, did you? And did you hear his response?"

"Oh, yes!" She giggled again. "He said—and I quote—they might be able to start on some paper work, but he was sure they would want you married to the mother before they let you adopt the daughter."

Larry poked her playfully. "That's our Chris, always fast with a clever response. But he has another side, too, doesn't he? What did you think of the blessing he prayed at dinner?"

"It almost made me cry. I loved that he asked us to hold hands around the table while he prayed. Did you notice Gram? I'm sure she's never done that in her life, and it took her a minute, but I was so glad when she let your mom and Mollie take her hands on either side."

"By the way, in case you haven't figured it out, I do plan to take Chris's advice."

"Advice?"

"On marrying Betsey's mother before I adopt her. I can't wait to come home to the two of you every evening."

"Where do you work on your thesis?"

"Mostly in the library, but my typewriter is at home, so when I've finished researching and am ready to type it up, I'll have to do it at home." He glanced at his watch, then stood up and stretched. "Speaking of which, I don't imagine Groverton is getting any closer on the map right now."

She didn't rise with him. How could she bear for this day to be over? How could she bear for him to leave her?

And then she remembered.

This wasn't an ending. It was a beginning. The sun would rise again tomorrow, and the moon—a little larger—would set again. Larry would still love her, and she would still be free to acknowledge her love for him. It might take a while to unravel all the tangled strands of the past, but they had a lifetime ahead of them. And they now shared a common trust in the God who loved them beyond anything she had ever imagined.

She lifted her hand to him, and he drew her to her feet. Instead of taking her in his arms as she expected, he framed her face in his hands, kissed her thoroughly once, then gently, then with a feathery touch.

"I'll call you every night, and I'll be back next weekend."

She watched him drive away, then breathed deeply of the night air before turning back into the house and locking the door behind her. As she walked by Gram's closed door, she

Tangled Strands

brushed her fingertips across it and whispered a thank-you heavenward.

Up in Betsy's room, the streetlight through the trees cast a soft glow on her sleeping child. She drew a deep and trembling breath and gripped the side of the crib while tears of joy slipped down her cheeks. She found herself toying with the ring on her left hand, imagining what it would be like to wear Larry's diamond there instead. Yes, this one should be put away for Betsey. Slipping it off, she dropped it into the top drawer of the nearby dresser.

At that moment she remembered the class ring Larry had refused to take back. It must still be under the crib where she had kicked it. She bent down and peered into the dimness. That tiny dark spot must be it. Reaching under, she drew it out. After studying it a moment, she pressed it to her lips, then with a rush of joy slipped it on her ring finger. It would do nicely there until Larry replaced it with something else!

The End

Transformed

Dear Lord, take up the tangled strands
Where we have wrought in vain
That by the skill of Thy dear hands
Some beauty might remain.

> Transformed by grace divine,
> The glory shall by Thine.
> To Thy most holy will, oh Lord,
> We now our all resign.

Take every failure, each mistake
Of our poor human ways,
That, Savior, for Thine own dear sake,
Some beauty might remain.

Touch Thou the sad, discordant keys
Of every troubled breast
And change to peaceful harmonies
The sighings of unrest.

Where broken vows in fragments lie—
The toil of wasted years—
Do Thou make whole again, we cry,
And give a song for tears.

Music available at
http://www.hymnary.org/text/dear_lord_take_up_our_tangled_strands

Tangled Strands

Made in the USA
Lexington, KY
28 September 2018